Praise for Karen Whiddon

"A nice backstory and exciting plot make this a must-read."
—*RT Book Reviews* on *The Wolf Siren* (4.5 stars)

"*The Lost Wolf's Destiny* is action-packed with a lot of twists and turns that lead the reader on an amazing ride."
—*Fresh Fiction*

Praise for Jane Kindred

"This gothic-inspired modern romance is built on a supernatural base that drips with intrigue, mystery and some deliciously dark humor."
—*RT Book Reviews* on *The Lost Coast*

"This complex and wickedly decadent dark fantasy bombards the reader with its sensuality and heartbreaking reveals while building to an explosive ending."
—*RT Book Reviews* on *Master of the Game*

Karen Whiddon started weaving fanciful tales for her younger brothers at the age of eleven. Amid the gorgeous Catskill Mountains, then the majestic Rocky Mountains, she fueled her imagination with the natural beauty surrounding her. Karen now lives in north Texas, writes full-time and volunteers for a boxer dog rescue. She shares her life with her hero of a husband and four to five dogs, depending on if she is fostering. You can email Karen at kwhiddon1@aol.com. Fans can also check out her website, karenwhiddon.com.

Books by Karen Whiddon

Harlequin Nocturne

The Pack Series

Wolf Whisperer
The Wolf Princess
The Wolf Prince
Lone Wolf
The Lost Wolf's Destiny
The Wolf Siren
Shades of the Wolf
Billionaire Wolf
A Hunter Under the Mistletoe (with Addison Fox)
Her Guardian Shifter

Visit the Author Profile page
at Harlequin.com for more titles.

THE TEXAS SHIFTER'S MATE & THE DRAGON'S HUNT

KAREN WHIDDON
AND
JANE KINDRED

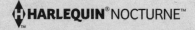

Recycling programs
for this product may
not exist in your area.

ISBN-13: 978-0-373-20870-8

The Texas Shifter's Mate & The Dragon's Hunt

Copyright © 2018 by Harlequin Books S.A.

The publisher acknowledges the copyright holders
of the individual works as follows:

The Texas Shifter's Mate
Copyright © 2018 by Karen Whiddon

The Dragon's Hunt
Copyright © 2017 by Jane Kindred

This edition published by arrangement with Harlequin Books S.A.

For questions and comments about the quality of this book,
please contact us at CustomerService@Harlequin.com.

® and TM are trademarks of the publisher. Trademarks indicated with
® are registered in the United States Patent and Trademark Office, the
Canadian Intellectual Property Office and in other countries.

HARLEQUIN®
www.Harlequin.com

Printed in U.S.A.

CONTENTS

THE TEXAS SHIFTER'S MATE

Karen Whiddon

Dedicated to animal rescuers everywhere.
Those who work in the trenches, saving lives,
fostering, transporting, evaluating, doing home
visits for potential adopters and showing animals
love so they can find their forever homes.
I salute you!

Chapter 1

The heavy oak door, scarred and weathered, looked like it had been salvaged from an ancient medieval castle. Above, a simple sign. No words, just a rusted iron bar from which hung two chain links, each half of what had once been whole. There were no lanterns, not even a streetlight to illuminate the shadows. The entrance sat near the end of a dead-end alley, innocuous enough that no soul, human or otherwise, would give it a second glance. Unless of course, one knew what lay inside. No humans ever would.

Shayla Dover had learned of Broken Chains, the bar behind the battered door, from her friend Maddie Kinslow, who happened to be a Shape-shifter. They'd met at a spin class. Maddie had known right away that Shayla wasn't human, and hadn't batted even an eyelash when Shayla had revealed her true nature. Of course, during her first visit with Maddie to Broken Chains, Shayla had learned being a Mermaid in human form wasn't even the most uncommon of the numerous paranormal beings frequenting the bar.

Broken Chains accepted everyone. The only criteria—no human could ever enter. Vampires, Shape-shifters of all types, as well as Mermaids, Spirits and Wraiths mingled free of judgments, vendettas or complaints. A live band played most nights, rotating groups with enough different genres of music to suit all tastes. The small dance floor stayed crowded, and snagging a table became a matter of luck and skill.

Alcohol was sold, as well as specialty beverages that suited each particular kind of clientele. One sign boasted that Broken Chains carried twenty-seven varieties of blood, especially popular among the Vampire crowd.

Shayla loved the place. For the first time since making the choice to live on land, she felt she had found a spot where she belonged as much as she did under the sea.

While she'd known Houston and areas south of there had to be teeming with non-humans, she hadn't given much thought to the sheer variety of species. In Broken Chains, she'd met numerous Shape-shifters, Vampires and even a Merfolk or two. From Maddie, Shayla had learned how many different kinds of Shape-shifters there actually were. The Wolves, along with their governing body, the Pack, were the most numerous. But there were Lions and Leopards and Bears, even Dragons! Of course, some considered the Merfolk a kind of Shape-shifter, since they could change their beautiful, shimmering fish tail into human legs. None of that mattered once inside Broken Chains. Everyone was welcome.

Tonight, Shayla and Maddie were meeting for drinks

after Maddie got off work. Maddie worked as a police dispatcher for Galveston PD and hated her job.

Shayla was self-employed, doing well running an internet business she'd founded specializing in rare artifacts found under the sea. Though she occasionally loved to scour the ocean floor, her family also gladly kept her supplied with inventory. The market for collectors, until now untapped, seemed limitless. Due to the priceless nature of her inventory, she only needed one or two big sales per quarter to be prosperous. Most times she did much better than that. She loved being an entrepreneur, loved the treasure-hunting aspect of her work and enjoyed the income her job provided.

Still, despite her success, she found herself often at loose ends. She'd begun thinking about what other type of business she might start. Maybe something that Maddie could help out with, something that would get her friend away from her stressful dispatcher job.

Shayla arrived a few minutes early, rapping three times on the door and waiting, before repeating the sequence with two extra beats tagged on to the end.

The door opened, just as it always did, and Shayla sauntered inside. Instantly, she felt a sense of peace. Funny thing to consider a bar her home away from home, but she did.

The band tonight—one of Shayla's favorites—played a slow bluesy song, a melody that made Shayla want to twirl and sway. Maybe later, she'd dance. Glancing around the already crowded bar, she grinned to see Maddie had snagged a table. Maddie stood, waving to get her attention. Waving back, Shayla hurried over, happy she'd spent the time to turn her long black hair into a thick braid.

"Glad you made it early," Maddie said, grinning. Her curly red hair hung loose around her shoulders. "I've been here an hour, circling like a hawk on a hunt, until I got this table."

"I can't believe it's already so crowded." Shayla glanced around as she pulled out a chair to sit. "It's a Tuesday night. Look at all the tourists in their beach-wear. I feel overdressed."

"Pffft." Maddie snorted. "You live to wear those cute little dresses and your heels. Heck, if I had a figure like you, I'd wear them, too."

"A figure like mine?" Shayla eyed her friend's lush curves. "I'm a toothpick. You're the one with the figure. I can barely fill out my B cup."

"I'd rather be skinny." Maddie shrugged. "But isn't that the way of things? We always want what we don't have."

"Maybe." Shayla didn't believe in wasting time pining for things she couldn't have. And truth be told, she considered herself lucky. Just like her mom, she could eat whatever she wanted and never gain weight. She'd also learned long ago never ever to say that to another woman.

"The place is full of Vampires," Maddie grumbled. "Who knew they enjoyed vacationing at the coast?"

Shayla had to grin at the Shifter's disgruntled tone. While they generally got along, Vamps and Shifters had a natural reserve with each other. This despite the fact that Maddie and her were also best friends with Carmen, who happened to be a Vampire. Shayla enjoyed pointing out to each of them that they were the poster children for each giving the other species a fair chance.

"Speaking of Vamps…" Shayla glanced at her watch. "Where's Carmen? She should have been here by now."

"I know." Maddie glanced around. "She's lucky we saved her a chair. It'll be completely full in another hour. This place is becoming more and more popular. Used to be I knew everyone in here. Now, it's about half and half."

"More strangers, more potential new friends. It's all good." Shayla signaled at Johnny, her favorite bartender. He nodded and a minute later brought her a glass of white wine, a nice chardonnay, her usual. Maddie already had her beer, a dark one this time.

The band announced they were taking a break and left the stage. While she'd enjoyed the music, Shayla was glad since this would give her and Maddie an opportunity to talk without having to shout.

"How's things at the job?" Shayla asked. Maddie always had great stories about the drama going on both inside her emergency communication call center and in the outside world. Shayla loved hearing these, since her own work was so solitary.

"I don't know how much longer I can take it there." Maddie's usually ready smile vanished. "With the tourism season upon us, crimes are skyrocketing. They're demanding we work more hours to cover the personnel shortages. All of us are exhausted and miserable and crabby. I almost didn't get off work in time to make it here. One of my coworkers had to cover the last hour for me."

"That sounds rough," Shayla commiserated, even though she had no real frame of reference.

"Oh, it's only just starting. First, we have spring break, which is next week. And then, you know how things are once summer arrives. The island is packed." Shaking her head, Maddie took a slug of beer. "They know I take night classes at Texas A&M Galveston. I can't miss those, but my supervisor told me the job has to come first. I don't think they can force me to work mandatory overtime, but who knows." She sighed. "I've already paid for this semester, so if I don't attend class, I forfeit the fees. I'm working on redoing my resume so I can see what other employment might be available."

This was the first time her friend had mentioned leaving her job. "I could maybe give you some part-time work," Shayla offered. "But it wouldn't pay as much. And it'd be extremely part-time. I don't have a lot extra that I can't do myself. In fact, I was thinking of finding something else to help occupy my time."

Maddie tilted her head, smiling once again. "You're so sweet for offering. Actually, I might take you up on it if they drive me insane enough. Who knows, maybe I can cobble together several part-time jobs and make it work."

"Maybe we can start our own business," Shayla mused. "If you could do anything, what kind of work would you like to do?"

"Private detective work." Maddie didn't even hesitate. "You know my father owned a PI agency. I worked there from the moment I could walk. I hated that Mom sold it after Dad died."

At that moment, Derek, the bass guitarist, and Rory, the lead singer, came over to chat. Their band played Broken Chains several times a month, and the two men continually asked Shayla and Maddie out, alternating which man asked whom. Both women found them amusing, but had no desire to mess up the fun dynamic they currently enjoyed with the band.

The drummer, Waylan, wandered over, reminding the others it was nearly time to get back onstage. Shayla and Maddie shared amused looks as Rory and Derek took their leave, promising to stop back before the evening ended.

"Hey," Maddie said, motioning to Shayla that she should lean in closer. "Don't look now, but the man right behind you has been eating you up with his eyes. Messy, dark blond hair, silver-blue eyes and a body to die for." She sighed. "He's drop-dead gorgeous, so you'd better hope he comes over."

Feigning interest, Shayla nodded, though she didn't turn around. Instead, she took a sip of wine and focused on the band, who were now getting ready to play another song.

The two women sitting at the table right behind his bar stool were both stunning. When he swiveled around to face the band, they were right there in his line of vision, their beauty a welcome diversion from his dark thoughts. Zach couldn't keep from staring despite his preoccupation with finding Nantha. One of the women's auras revealed her to be Shifter, and he'd bet the other, the slender gorgeous dark-eyed one with long, jet-black hair, was Mermaid. He'd spent enough time with his younger stepsister, Nantha, and her pretty Mermaid friends to recognize that certain glow in their aura.

Pretty didn't even begin to describe this woman. Heart-shaped face, high cheekbones and lithe, graceful movements combined to make her breathtakingly gorgeous. Her long-lashed, emerald eyes spoke of Asian heritage, and the curve of her lush lips revealed her sensuality.

There wasn't a single man in the bar who hadn't noticed her or her redheaded friend. They were both stunning and sexy, in opposite ways.

Any other time, Zach might have approached the table with a flirtatious smile, offering to buy her a drink in exchange for a dance. However, now that he'd agreed to an engagement arranged by his stepfather, his flirting days were over. He could only fervently pray that his fiancée, a Mermaid he hadn't yet met, resembled this one.

Right now though, he had more urgent and pressing business on his mind. Nantha had gone missing and he needed to find her. He'd come to Broken Chains with the intention of asking every Merfolk in the place if they'd seen her.

Might as well start now. He turned, locking gazes with the raven-haired Mermaid. Hounds, he felt the impact of her beauty like a punch in the gut. Even by Mermaid standards, she was gorgeous. Her eyes were the deep green of a stormy sea, framed in long, jet-black lashes. The pout of her lush lips had him longing to claim them with his. Damn. Summoning up all his willpower, he pushed the jolt of attraction aside and stood. Both women eyed him as he took the couple of steps necessary to bring him to their table.

Of course right at that moment, the band started playing again.

"Excuse me," he said loudly, wishing the music could have held off a few more minutes. "Have either of you seen this woman?" He passed the redhead a picture of Nantha, one of his favorite ones of his younger stepsister. He well remembered the day that snapshot had been taken. Nantha had been about to return home after a visit. She'd stood in knee-deep water, filled with the joy the touch of the sea seemed to give its people. The full moon reflected on the calm night sea colored everything with a silver tranquility. She looked young, carefree and happy.

The red-haired Shifter shook her head, handing the photo to her friend.

The Mermaid's long-lashed eyes widened as she accepted the photograph. She inhaled sharply, her gaze rushing from Nantha's image to his. Of course, she immediately recognized that Nantha was Mer. "She's lovely," she finally said, raising her voice to be heard over the music. She passed it back. "But I'm sorry, I haven't seen her. When was she in here last?"

"She hasn't been here. She's too young." He swallowed, trying to contain his disappointment. Of course it wouldn't be that easy. It never was. "Her name is Nantha. She's my sister, and she's missing."

The two women exchanged glances. The red-haired Shifter looked Zach up and down. "What happened to her?" she asked. "How do you know she's missing? She might just be taking a long swim or something."

The Mermaid nodded. "We have been known to disappear under the sea for extended periods of time. I'm guessing, though, that you have more reasons that make you think something has happened to her?"

"I do." He didn't elaborate. Instead, he dragged his gaze away from the attractive pair and began scanning the bar for other Merfolk he could ask.

"I'm Maddie," the Shifter woman said. "And this is my friend Shayla. We'll do our best to help, but I need more information. Such as where and when? What exactly happened to give you reason to be concerned? I work as a police dispatcher, and details are always helpful."

"She has a point," Shayla agreed, noting his hesitation. "I get that you'd planned on walking around asking everyone in here if they'd seen her, but if you really want help finding your sister, we'll need a few details."

Briefly, he considered. She was right, about giving out more information. "She's actually my stepsister," he said. "My mother married her father, Ion. They come on land for weekend visits." Which wasn't at all unusual. Lots of Merfolk enjoyed experiencing life out of the water for short periods of time. Of course, Shayla already would know that.

"So she disappeared here, on Galveston Island?"

"Yes. She and her father were about to return home to the sea, and she went out for a walk. She always loves to walk the edge of Stewart Beach. The far end, near the rocks. Right around sunset, when the crowds thin out." He swallowed hard. "She had a habit of doing this every time before she and Ion went back under the sea. But this time, she didn't come back."

Shayla nodded. "I see. That area is particularly beautiful."

"And dangerous," the redhead interjected. "Especially when the tide comes in."

"Not for a Mermaid." Both Zach and Shayla spoke at the same time. He caught himself exchanging a quick look of recognition with her. He might be Pack, but he'd spent enough time around his sister and stepfather to know more than usual about the Merfolk.

"Zach Cantrell," he said, introducing himself. "Nice to meet you, Shayla and Maddie. Now, if you'll excuse me, I've got to show her picture around and see if anyone might have seen her. It's a long shot, but right now it's all I have."

"Wait, hold on." Maddie pinned him with a fierce

stare. "You still haven't given us any usable information."

"Like what?"

"Like, did she have any enemies? Anyone you can think of who might have wanted to do her harm?"

Shayla made a groan of protest.

"Sorry," Maddie said, sounding anything but. "This is necessary. Most people are abducted by someone they know." Waving her hand, she included Zach in her gesture. "This could really help. We need to get all the facts."

To his amazement, he realized she'd taken out a pad of paper and a pen and had begun jotting down notes.

Shayla saw him looking at her friend's paper and shrugged. "She works as a police dispatcher. She's good. If you really want her to help find your sister, give her as much information as you can."

Shifting his weight from foot to foot, he cleared his throat. While he really hadn't planned on having extended conversations with anyone, he figured this actually might be helpful.

"Pull up a chair," Maddie ordered without looking up. "Start at the beginning."

Not sure whether to allow himself to feel hopeful, he gave in and sat. Some of his dejection must have shown, because to his shock, Shayla reached out and placed her small hand over his.

This simple act of comfort made his throat tighten, even though he had to restrain himself from jerking his hand away. The gesture seemed too intimate somehow, though no doubt this feeling was extremely one-sided, due to the depth of his attraction to her.

When she finally moved, he could breathe again.

Aware he couldn't show his relief, he looked anywhere but at her. Despite that, he couldn't help but be far too conscious of her every movement, the way she shifted slightly in her chair, her graceful movement as she reached for her wineglass and took a small sip.

He cleared his throat. "There's not a lot to tell. Nothing unusual happened that weekend. Nantha and her father Ion came ashore Friday afternoon for a weekend visit. As usual, they came ashore on the private beach near my mother's house. I met them at our meeting place, a rocky cove that's roped off and marked as dangerous to humans."

"Which kept it mostly free from both locals and tourists alike," Shayla added. "Most humans are pretty good about obeying the signs."

He nodded. Though it had only been two days, that evening would forever be impressed in his memory. Like always, Ion and Nantha had swum up to the rocks with the sea caressing them. They'd poked their heads up out of the choppy waves, waiting for Zach to give them the all-clear signal before they climbed up on the rocks and changed their form. Sparking lights surrounded them as they did, reflecting on the water like a thousand fireflies. Though the light show was identical to what happened when Zach shape-shifted into Wolf, the combination of water and lights never failed to mesmerize him.

Fifteen years ago, when Zach's mother had announced she was marrying a Merman with a young Mermaid daughter, Zach had been skeptical. But even at ten years old, Zach had seen his mother's grief over his father's passing become a kind of stoic acceptance. She'd been lonely and sad, and she'd directed all her energy into raising her young son. Then she'd met Ion, and her entire world changed.

Zach had recognized the happiness that made her glow when she'd gone someplace with Ion. The fact that she'd actually introduced him to Zach told him the relationship had grown serious. When Ion had wanted to ask her to marry him, he'd asked Zach's permission first. In all the years since, they'd all become a tight-knit, loving family.

Which had now been ripped apart. He swallowed.

"Are you okay?" Shayla asked, making him realize he'd gone silent.

"Sorry. I'm worried about my sister. This isn't at all like her."

"How did a Shifter like you come to have a Mermaid for a sister?" Maddie asked, clearly recognizing his aura.

"My mother, who's also a Shifter, married her father. He's Mer. Nantha was very young."

"What happened to her mother?" This from Shayla.

He forced himself to meet her gaze. When he did, again the flare of attraction zinged through him. "She died shortly after Nantha was born."

"When exactly did your sister vanish?" Maddie asked, pen poised. "How long has she been missing?"

"Sunday. Two days ago."

"She'll be needing to get back to the water soon," Shayla added. "Especially if she spent the weekend on land. One week is about as long as we can go. But I imagine you already know that, right?"

He nodded. "That's one of our main concerns. Though Ion says it's ten days."

Lips pursed, which somehow made her look even sexier, Shayla considered. Finally, she shrugged. "That's pushing it, but he's right. I've made it that long. It wasn't pretty—I got sick. But once I was back in the water, I was fine."

"What have you done so far attempting to locate her?" Maddie asked. "Did you check with the Pack Protectors? I think they might help in a case like this, since she's related by marriage."

Momentarily startled, he stared. Even though he knew she could tell by his aura that he was a Shifter, he hadn't told her what kind of animal he became. While he was Wolf, and definitely part of the Pack, he could just as well have been another species entirely.

However, if this helped with finding his sister, he saw no problem with breaking a few rules. "Yes, I've already enlisted the help of the Pack Protectors. They promised to let me know if they heard anything about a missing Mermaid." He grimaced. "I have to say, they didn't seem really concerned."

"They've probably got more pressing Pack business," Maddie said, her tone commiserating. "But at least you got the word out with them."

"True. I really wish there was some sort of investigative agency where supernatural beings could turn to for help, besides the Pack Protectors." He took a deep breath, willing himself to sound calm rather than desperate. "I've done all I could think of on land. And since I'm not a Merman, I have to believe my stepfather is conducting a thorough search under the water. I'm trying really hard not to think about the horrible things that might have happened to a naïve and sweet young woman like my sister. I just wish I could hire someone to look for her. Someone who could travel under the sea."

Shayla went very still. She and Maddie exchanged a glance.

The two women exchanged another glance.

"That might be possible," Shayla began, her voice low and serious.

"It just might," Maddie agreed, looking at him. "But Shayla and I were just talking about starting up our own private investigative agency. It's been a lifelong dream of mine." When she paused, Shayla took over.

"Maddie's family used to run one. She got her feet wet, so to speak, working for her father. Maybe you could be our first customer." She grimaced. "I guess it depends how desperate you are. While she knows her way around the business, I have zero experience. But I'm Mer, and can search underwater."

Looking into her emerald green eyes, he didn't even hesitate. "Yes. I'm in. Find my sister."

Shayla shook her head. "Don't you even want to know what we charge?"

Though he wanted to say he didn't care what it cost, as long as they were successful, he knew better. "I'm sure it will be reasonable. Just get me the details as soon as possible. Of course, I'll also pay any expenses incurred in the search." He couldn't believe his luck. Having another Mermaid hunt for his sister beneath the sea, and a Shifter who could help with the on-land search, was more than he'd hoped for. He glanced at his watch, jiggling his leg in impatience. "The sooner you can get started on finding her, the better."

"We'll need you to sign a contract," Shayla said smoothly. "We'll need to get that document drawn up. Can you meet us back here tomorrow night around eight?"

"Definitely." He pushed to his feet. "Finally, I feel like I'm doing something constructive. I'll see you ladies tomorrow." Bracing himself, he looked at Shayla first and held out his hand.

When she took it, an electric shock rushed from his fingers up his arm. Her eyes widened, letting him know she likely felt it, too. The way she jerked her hand free confirmed it. So it wasn't just one-sided. Interesting.

Curious to see what would happen, he turned to Maddie; they also shook. Nothing happened. Absolutely nothing. He wasn't sure whether to be relieved or worried.

"Until we have the paperwork signed, please consider this a handshake agreement," he said. "That way, you can get to work immediately."

"We will," Shayla replied. "We'll do our best to find her."

"Thank you." He felt like a bit of the weight had been lifted from his shoulders. Even if they were totally inexperienced, having a Mermaid assisting was huge. At least he was no longer searching alone. "I appreciate your help more than you know."

"Do you mind leaving the photo with us?" Shayla asked. "We can show it around. I assume you have another copy?"

"I can print one." He handed it over. "I'll see you tomorrow night." He left the bar, feeling more hopeful than he had since Sunday night.

Chapter 2

Shayla watched him go, her fingers and arm still tingling. Damned if there wasn't something about that man. "Now we've done it," she told Maddie. "We've got to make this work. That man is pinning his last hope on us."

"And rightly so." Maddie's confidence made Shayla smile. "I'm a damn good police dispatcher, though I'm ready to do something else. A paranormal private investigation agency would be perfect, especially since I grew up with one, even though my family dealt with humans. I know the ins and outs of human law enforcement in this city. Plus, I have contacts. All of that's got to count for something, right?"

Shayla nodded. "It's interesting that I just said I wouldn't mind finding something else to occupy my time. I'll need to do some research. I know next to nothing about private investigators. We need to look into rates so we know what to charge. Do we need to get licensed?"

"Only if we plan on working with humans." Maddie grinned. "Since we don't, I think we'll be okay without one."

"True." Shayla grinned back. "We're also going to need a name. Something catchy."

"I've got that covered. I already know what we'll call ourselves," Maddie said. "Perfect for a paranormal private investigation firm." She gave a dramatic pause.

Crossing her arms, Shayla waited her out.

Finally, Maddie made her pronouncement. "We'll call ourselves the Shadow Agency. Since so many of us operate in the Shadows."

"I like that," a sultry voice said. Carmen Vargas had come up to their table unnoticed. It was one of the more unnerving skills Vampires had. She pulled out a seat and smiled at them. "Especially since Shadows are a huge part of my life. Even more so than yours." With her blond, spiky short hair and bright blue eyes, Carmen looked like anything but the Vampire she was. "So what exactly are you two up to now?"

Maddie told her. "And we already have our first client."

"I want in." Carmen leaned forward, her long silver earrings catching and reflecting the dim light. "Who better to work in the Shadows than a Vamp?"

Shayla considered her. "What about your job?" Carmen worked nights as a government researcher and scientist.

"It won't be a problem. I set my own hours. I'd love to help you two get this business off the ground."

Maddie nodded. "We just came up with the idea a

few minutes ago. But if Shayla agrees, I think the three of us would make great partners."

"Yes." Shayla's answer came immediately. "Let's talk specifics."

Over the next several hours, with Maddie taking notes, they hammered out all the details they could think of for their new business, the Shadow Agency. Since they wouldn't be dealing with humans at all, they decided not to incorporate or worry about insurance. Shifters, Merfolk and Vampires weren't the type to sue if something went wrong—they'd just get even.

"We need to decide on rates," Maddie said next. "Since we'll be splitting the payment three ways."

"Not necessarily," Shayla said. "I think the initial fee should go to the company. Each of us will be paid by the company depending on how much work we put in to each case. For example, this missing Mermaid. If I do a lot of underwater investigating, then I would bill the Shadow Agency for my time. Ditto on any time either of you devote to it. All of our payments come from the company rather than the client."

"That makes sense." Carmen flashed her white teeth in a smile. "I think this calls for another round of drinks." She signaled Johnny, who dipped his head in acknowledgment.

"I think we need to get busy," Maddie started to protest. "Time matters when someone has been abducted."

"True," Carmen agreed. "But Shayla can't exactly jump into the ocean right now, so it's going to have to wait until morning."

Maddie looked from one to the other. "One more drink," she finally agreed. "And then I want to go home and get started on the computer at least. I'll start calling my contacts in the morning."

"What are you drinking?" Shayla asked. Broken Chains kept a wide variety of exotic blood for its Vampire clientele, along with usual bar beverages, both alcoholic and non.

"This is European Farmer," Carmen said, draining her wineglass. "First time I've tried it. Pretty good, too."

Shayla shuddered. "I'll just stick with my wine," she told her friends.

"Me, too." Maddie raised her nearly empty glass. "Beer is better than blood, at least for me."

"I beg to differ." When she took another sip, Carmen deliberately flashed her fangs. As she'd known it would, this made the other two laugh.

Though Maddie had to be at work the next morning, the three of them ended up staying until last call. Shayla had switched from alcohol to seawater, though Maddie had continued to drink beer. She claimed her Shifter metabolism gave her a higher tolerance. This seemed true, since in all the time Shayla had known her, she'd never seen Maddie even tipsy.

Carmen stood, drawing several men's eyes. Tall and slender, her vivid good looks matched her personality. No one, upon first meeting her, ever suspected her to be a Vampire. She delighted in this and exploited it whenever she could.

"I'll walk you two out," Carmen said, showing her teeth. Due to the obscure location of Broken Chains, they had to walk through some sketchy areas of Galveston before they could even catch sight of a cab. And Shayla refused to set foot on the bus. Something about going around the island driven by a complete stranger while packed into a bus with other total strangers made her entire body feel out of tune. Plus, the buses stopped running at eleven thirty. Since tourist season had started, there would be tons of cabs the closer they got to Broadway.

Shayla and Maddie nodded. Carmen knew how much they appreciated her help. More than once they'd been accosted by a human male with bad intent. Though Shayla had taken to carrying a pistol with her, using it would draw more attention than she wanted to deal with. Ditto with Maddie shape-shifting into a Wolf.

Carmen, on the other hand, had no objection to getting a little fresh blood if she had to. Self-defense, she called it. She never took enough to mortally wound anyone, just to weaken them. She'd explained to her friends that not everyone bitten by her would automatically become a Vampire. She had to consciously choose that path, releasing an enzyme when she bit. So far, she'd never made another Vampire. She claimed she wasn't sure if she ever would.

Which explained why there weren't a lot more Vampires running around Houston and areas south of there.

Of the three of them, naturally Carmen felt most at home with the dark alleys and empty warehouses. She glided through the shadows, making Shayla realize her friend was a perfect fit for the Shadow Agency. They each had their own set of skills to bring to the table.

Maddie strode along confidently, too. Only Shayla felt off. Not exactly in the moment, somehow. She was conscious of the distant pull of the harbor and the need to soon slip into the water. Land was fun, but it never would be her true home.

Despite the late hour, the other two women were still

energized with excitement. Maddie wanted to get started searching immediately and Shayla agreed with her. Carmen, on the other hand, seemed more focused on getting their business up and running. There were, after all, a hundred things that needed to be done. Flyers and business cards made and printed. A mission statement written. Rates and fees for various services agreed upon. She and Maddie chatted back and forth, assigned each other numerous tasks, though Maddie clearly was itching to leave and get busy. Shayla listened, still feeling a bit detached. She wanted to focus on the case at hand first, even though, of the three of them, she had more spare time. Carmen and Maddie, each with their jobs and other activities, would have to parcel out slots of time for this new venture. Maddie also let them know she'd decided to wait before quitting her job, at least until she could be certain her salary would be enough. She had bills to pay.

Since both Shayla and Carmen could set their own hours, neither would be impacted as severely as Maddie if the Shadow Agency failed.

"But it won't," Carmen declared, her sultry voice ringing with certainty. "Because we've found a niche with a need. As long as we provide good customer service and fulfill that need, we're a shoo-in for success."

Shayla nodded, still lost in her thoughts. Maddie noticed.

"You're awfully quiet." She elbowed Shayla in the side. "What's wrong?"

"I can't stop thinking about that poor missing Mermaid," Shayla admitted. "Nantha. She's young. The young ones are often overconfident and reckless. I have a feeling that there's a lot more to this story than Zach realizes."

"Or maybe more than he's letting on," Maddie interjected.

"No, that wouldn't make sense," Shayla argued. "His number one priority is finding his sister. Why would he hide anything, especially if it might be helpful?"

"True," Carmen said thoughtfully. "I admire the way you're so focused on this case."

"She's also pretty focused on him," Maddie pointed out.

Carmen's brows rose. "Really?" she drawled. "I'm guessing he must be easy on the eyes then. So tell me, Shayla. Was he sexy?"

Maddie laughed. Shayla blushed. "Maybe," she allowed. "He's Shifter. I'd definitely call him hot. Tall, dark blond hair cut short in one of those deliberately messy styles and light gray eyes. Rugged features, which match his muscles." She stopped when she realized both her friends were staring at her.

"What?" she asked, her face heating. "You asked if he was sexy. I was just describing him for you."

The other two women broke out laughing.

"If *you* think he's sexy, then he must be to die for," Carmen teased. "You hardly even notice when I try to put some really gorgeous Vampire men in front of you."

"Same here," Maddie interjected. "I've made it a habit to have a few of my unattached Shifter friends stop by our table over the last few months, and you didn't react to any of them."

Shayla's blush had become an outright burn. "Well, maybe that's because this one is different," she said, flustered.

"Is he now?" In true Carmen fashion, the Vamp

wasn't going to let this go. "Interesting. Very interesting indeed."

"I agree." Maddie and Carmen exchanged looks. "Sounds like that's settled then," Maddie said. She seemed so satisfied. If she'd been a feline Shifter she would have purred.

Confused, Shayla glanced from one to the other. Her two best friends appeared to find this massively amusing, whatever *this* might be. Finally, she just had to ask.

"What's settled?"

"You called dibs!" Both Maddie and Carmen spoke at once, grinning from ear to ear. "Finally. We're so happy for you. It's about time." They high-fived.

Shayla opened her mouth to protest and then closed it. She could tell the more she spoke, the deeper a hole she'd dig. Let them think what they wanted. Zach Cantrell was attractive. She was female, so of course she'd noticed. End of story. Her friends knew better than anyone that she had no intentions of getting involved with a man right now. Not for a long, long time, if ever. Her fiancé had died and she never wanted to feel that kind of pain again.

Later that night, once she'd let herself into her house, she went out on the back deck, the side that overlooked the water. The sounds of the waves lapping up against the shore always comforted her and tonight was no exception.

When she'd first made the impulsive, heartbroken decision to abandon the sea for land, she'd gone upstate, to a small town between Houston and Dallas. The town sat near a large, freshwater lake. She hadn't realized lakes wouldn't work the same as the sea, and it had taken her becoming seriously ill for her to understand she'd need to live close to the ocean. So she'd moved to Galveston

Island. She'd rented for six months, just long enough to see if she liked it. She did.

Her business procuring and selling rare artifacts found on the ocean floor made more than enough money for her to purchase a single-family home right on the water—a steal at less than a million dollars. From her house, she could not only see the water, but swim in it from her own small, private beach. This brought her peace and no shortage of happiness. And since the house came with a small boat slip, whenever she needed to go under the sea, she simply took the boat out and anchored it before letting her tail grow back.

Perfect solution. She'd truly come to love Galveston Island, even though in the spring and summer it became crowded with tourists. For her, it was the perfect compromise between her new life on land and her old one under the sea.

Maddie lived on the island too, though farther inland, close to The Strand. She shared a small apartment with another woman, also a Shifter. As for Carmen, when anyone asked where she resided, she simply answered in a warning tone that they didn't really want to know. Shayla assumed that meant a cemetery crypt, but who knew? These days, the Vamps had gotten away from their traditional dwellings. It could be entirely possible that Carmen might have a luxury house or condo near the bay. She had that well-groomed look that money brought.

The next morning, after her breakfast of kippers and eggs, Shayla went out in her boat. Her body had already begun to let her know she'd stayed away from her natural habitat too long, and, even though Zach Cantrell hadn't signed a contract yet, she planned to do some investigating while she was under the water. While she didn't know Ion or his missing daughter, Nantha—just like on land, the Merfolk had numerous cities with thousands of residents—she could still ask around. The news that a Mermaid had gone missing would travel like a tidal wave among her people. For all she knew, it might already have.

The weather couldn't have been more perfect. Overcast and slightly chilly, the steady mist that fell ensured she'd have privacy on her swim. She motored past Stewart Park, the beach where most of the tourists swam in the late spring and early summer. Since it was late March, a few weeks after spring break, she knew the beach would be mostly deserted, and it was.

She moored her boat about two hundred yards out, in the area where she'd once seen someone conducting a scuba diving class. Dropping her anchor, she slipped out of her raincoat and shirt, leaving only her bikini top. Brightly colored swimsuit tops had become popular among Mermaids, especially since so many of them enjoyed spending time appearing human. With the sea calling her, she slipped over the edge of the boat, beginning the change from legs to tail as soon as her skin hit the icy water.

The first shock of the cold had her sucking in her breath, but then as she slipped under the waves, her Mermaid nature took over, joyfully reuniting with her still-beloved sea. In her grief after losing her fiancé Richard, she'd had to forgive the very nature of the thing that was part of her essence. The marriage had been arranged, true, but the two of them had hit it off immediately, minutes into their first meeting. Sometimes, she'd thought, you meet someone and you just *know*. They'd both felt that way.

The wedding would unite two separate kingdoms. The celebrations had started immediately. Though they'd met several times in the weeks that followed, they hadn't yet gotten around to discussing where they would live. Even though she'd known she'd have to move to his kingdom where he would someday rule, she'd been so blinded by love that it hadn't mattered.

The wedding plans had gone into full gear. It would be an elaborate ceremony with dignitaries attending from seas all over the world. Her dress had been chosen and fitted, the sea anemones ordered and the invitations mailed out.

And then everything had changed in the flip of a fin. Richard had been out celebrating with his friends. He'd been drinking, and was clearly inebriated when he'd run into the massive great white shark in an isolated area.

Shayla often hoped the substantial amount of alcohol meant he hadn't suffered as much pain.

The shark had later been hunted down and killed, far too late.

The kingdoms had also been stunned. His family went into mourning. Her family did, as well. As for Shayla, her grief turned into rage. She'd gone crazy, acting out, hurting the ones who'd only sought to comfort her. At least as long as she filled herself with fury, she had no room for the pain.

But once this had burned through her, she felt hollow and empty. She became a shadow of her former self, taking comfort in the gray numbness, glad she couldn't seem to remember how to think, how to feel.

She'd sworn off the sea and tried to turn her back

on the ocean. Coming ashore on South Padre Island, she'd headed north, inland, hoping to put as much distance between herself and the water as she could. She'd even managed to convince herself the tales of a Mermaid needing to be around water were old wives' tales without a single kernel of truth in them.

Now she knew better. She needed the sea as much as she needed air to breathe when she was in her human form.

For its part, the ocean recognized her, too. Just like the land, the sea was a living, breathing organism, and as such, the instant she touched its surface, Shayla became an integral part of it. Joy flooded through her, joy and wonder and a tiny bit of aching grief that she pushed away.

Time to swim. She dove under. As usual, a few minutes passed before her eyes adjusted to the murky depths, but as she swam away from land, gradually going deeper, the entire seascape changed.

Use of sonar by humans to discover shipwrecks had made life more difficult for the Merfolk to keep their cities hidden. But in the deeper parts of the ocean, there were mountains and valleys, just as there were on land, and it was in those valleys where their civilizations had grown. In all of the history of humans, there had only been a few documented instances of them being able to travel so deep, though they'd started using unmanned probes, which Merfolk had taken to destroying if one came too close.

Shayla would have to swim for at least an hour to reach her former home. She'd have to assume that Ion and Nantha had come from the same city, as it was closest to the Gulf coastline of the southern United States and Mexico. Though there were several other possibilities, most farther south, though she knew of at least one settlement northeast near Florida.

In her search for the missing Mermaid, her family's home seemed like the perfect place to start.

During the long swim, several sea creatures came to say hello. Fish of all kinds, small schools of striped bass, winter flounders, shad and drums, and so many others she stopped trying to identify them. Dolphins, a huge eel and then some sharks, including one ancient great white shark that she carefully avoided. Most times the sharks left Merfolk alone, as they recognized them as fish too large to be taken without a fight. In Richard's instance, he'd cut himself on some coral. Drunk, disoriented and bleeding, he'd been easy prey for a huge shark.

Pain knifed through her. No. She wouldn't think of this. Not today. Again, she focused on her surroundings and kinder, gentler creatures. A small group of lined seahorses swam up and gently kissed her before swimming away in search of food. Several species of whale that usually swam just a bit farther south of here surrounded her, vocalizing in the deep peaceful tones of their kind. The sound resonated, echoing off the ocean itself, filling Shayla with peace, easing the last lingering remnants of her grief.

This would always be her true home. On land, she occasionally managed to forget how much she loved the underwater world. Once here, she wondered how she ever stayed away.

Finally, she reached the outskirts of her home, a city known among her people as Coral. She swam under a natural rock archway, and as usual, the first glimpse of Coral had her heart skipping a beat.

The city glowed softly, appearing as if it had been constructed from the most precious essence of oysters, the pearl. Muted white, intermingled with bright flashes of color from the live coral gardens, from a distance her home had a mysterious, ancient air. She could only imagine what the humans would make of it if they happened to send an undetected probe close enough to photograph it.

The nearer she drew, the more the place vibrated with life. Fish as bright as the deep-water coral swam up to greet her, escorting her around the protective shield and into one of several unmarked entrances.

Inside, the city teemed with life. Merfolk, as graceful as the fish, swam in the streets, going about their daily lives. Noticing her, several greeted her and waved, others shouted hello, the sound traveling as waves through the water, tickling her skin. This made her smile. These days, sometimes she could come home and forget about her past pain.

She went directly to her parents' house, a large free-form structure made of cobalt glass and green coral, shot through with swirling silver accents. Like all of the buildings here in Coral, the shape and color complemented the sea that surrounded them. Her family's home was larger than the others, due to their royal status. Only the palace, where her brother now resided as king, was bigger and more ornate.

Shayla swam to the door, opening it and going inside without even knocking. Now that her parents were retired from ruling, they occupied their time with various other activities, sometimes together, more often separate. It was fifty-fifty whether she'd even find them at home.

Inside, she headed directly for the kitchen. When her

mother saw her, she cried out and swam to give Shayla a hug. "You just barely caught me," she said. "I was about to leave for afternoon class."

On alternate days, her mother, Blythe, taught young Merfolk the art of preparing fish. Chef Blythe, the kids called her. After acting as a wise queen for several decades, Blythe had been glad to rid herself of her crown and scepter. Most days, she preferred a more casual style, unless she was teaching a cooking class. She wore her long, inky hair up in a tightly wound bun these days.

"Will you be here later today?" Blythe asked, releasing her.

Though Shayla knew her mom would be disappointed, she told her she couldn't stay too long. "I'm actually working," she said.

"On finding artifacts?" Blythe waved her hand in the general direction of the study. "I'm pretty sure your father has several in there waiting for you to pick up."

"I'll grab them before I head back," Shayla said. "I'm actually looking for a missing Mermaid."

"What?" For a second, Queen Blythe returned. Her mother straightened, lifting her chin and fixing Shayla with a no-nonsense stare. "Explain."

As succinctly as possible, Shayla did. When she'd finished, Blythe frowned. "And you say her father's name is Ion? The name sounds familiar, though I can't place it."

"If you do, or if you hear any information about Nantha, will you give me a call?" Shayla asked.

"I sure will." Blythe returned her attention to what she'd been doing when Shayla arrived—packing cooking supplies into a tote. "Right now, though, I've got to run."

"Where's Dad?" Shayla asked. "Please tell me he's not up at the castle pestering Merc again."

"He's not. Your brother banned him." Blythe smiled, since they both knew such a ban wasn't really possible. A sitting king couldn't forbid a former ruler from visiting the castle. Nor would he really want to. "Since your father had so much difficulty with retirement, he's gone back to fishing a lot. I tried to get him to volunteer at guppy school, but he refused. Whatever. At least he seems happy."

"As long as he continues to look for inventory for me, that's awesome," Shayla said, even though no one had asked her permission. "He finds the best stuff."

"You know he and your brother are in a competition to see who can find the most valuable artifact, don't you?"

Intrigued, Shayla sat on one of the bar stools. Made of coral and glass, they perfectly complemented the stone countertop. "That's actually pretty awesome," she said.

"It's good for you, isn't it?" Blythe hefted her tote and squared her shoulders. "Who knew humans would pay so dearly for such things?" She smiled, hugging Shayla once more, quickly this time. "I'm sorry I can't stay and visit, but you're welcome to come with me and watch the class."

"I would," Shayla said. "But I'd planned on going around and seeing if anyone near here has ever heard of Nantha. I wish I'd thought to ask where her family lived. I figure they're probably from this city, but I have no idea which part." And since there were thousands of Merfolk living in Coral, she'd need to narrow it down quite a bit."

"Nantha is an uncommon name," Blythe mused thoughtfully. "I'll ask around, too, and let you know if I hear anything."

"That'd be great."

"When will you be back?" Blythe asked as she swam

toward the front door with Shayla right behind her. Despite being a retired queen, and underwater renowned chef, she'd kept her slender figure. Sometimes when she and Shayla went out together, they were mistaken for sisters. Not a hint of gray touched Blythe's dark hair, and her face still appeared free of lines or wrinkles. Shayla hoped she'd be as fortunate when she became her mother's age.

"I'm not sure," Shayla admitted. "But since I plan to aggressively work this case, I imagine it will be sooner rather than later."

Blythe cocked her head, studying her daughter. "You look happy," she mused. "Happier than you've been in a long time. I think this new business venture might be agreeing with you."

Immediatcly, Shayla thought of Zach. Her entire body heated. Glad her mother couldn't see, she nodded. "I think so, too."

With a wave, Blythe swam off. Shayla wandered around the house for a moment, peeking into the study to see what her father had found, before she left to go canvass the part of town closest to her parents' home. She figured it couldn't hurt, though she knew she'd do better once she learned where exactly in Coral Ion and his daughter lived.

Chapter 3

For the next two hours, Shayla traveled up and down the busy streets, wearing her long, dark hair up in a tight bun in hopes of disguising herself. She hoped no one would stop her, wanting to talk about Richard's death or asking her where she'd been. The harder she made it to recognize her, the better her ability to move about freely.

She wasn't sure, but maybe so much time had passed that people didn't recognize her. No one even gave her a second look as she made her rounds, stopping into cafés and bakeries, shops and drugstores, asking everyone she met if they'd heard anything about a missing Mermaid called Nantha. If anyone who recognized her was surprised to see Princess Shayla, back home in Coral, they didn't show it. She was greeted with enthusiasm from everyone, and by now it seemed they felt enough time had passed that they no longer offered her their condolences. Maybe they believed the reminder would only make her sad. Since she tried not to think about Richard or the void he'd left in her life, she felt relieved.

As for Nantha, no one had heard anything, nor did the name sound familiar. Which meant Zach's stepsister hadn't been connected in any way to the royal family, close or extended. That left three other quadrants of the city yet to be explored. This search could take several days, as Coral was a good size.

Shayla made a mental note to use the photo of the girl she'd gotten from Zach and make up some laminated posters to place around town. That and prepare a list of questions to ask him once he'd signed the contract, starting with exactly where the missing Mermaid had lived and where she'd gone to school, and if she'd had a job. Shayla needed to speak with her friends, find out if Nantha had a serious boyfriend or if she'd had any man or girlfriend trouble.

Though she wanted to speak to her father before heading back to Galveston, she had no way of knowing where exactly in the vast ocean he'd decided to go fishing. Briefly, she entertained the idea of visiting the castle and saying hello to her brother, but with all the court protocol, she decided to skip it this time.

Which meant this trip had accomplished nothing. Mentally chastising herself, Shayla got ready for the long swim home. She stopped by her parents' house once more to pick up the three artifacts her father had found. Bundling them into her backpack, she swam away. Though she hadn't had any success, she'd been operating on very little information. At least now, she felt better prepared for the meeting tonight at Broken Chains. Once Zach had signed the contract and answered her questions, she'd be better able to spring into action and help find his stepsister.

All the way home, she kept an eye out for great white sharks. Luckily, she didn't encounter any. Though usually the vivid sea life relaxed her, she felt uneasy. Uncomfortable in her own skin, especially her Mermaid tail. The relative quietness of her swim home did little to distract her from thinking about Zach. Though she'd never admit it to her friends—heck, she could barely admit it to herself—something about him drew her. Mostly his raw sexual appeal. After all, it had been years since she'd opened her body to a man.

When she finally reached her boat again, Shayla pushed off her exhaustion, and she swam close. Reaching up, she grabbed hold of the back step and pulled only her upper body out of the water. Shoulders and neck, nothing more. A quick look around to ensure there weren't any witnesses, and she initiated the change from fish tail to human legs keeping that part of herself hidden beneath the waves. Sometimes this could be painful, especially after a long swim like she'd had today.

At least the exercise helped her nerves. Though her legs were weak, she wobbled up her pier after securing her boat, glad her neighbors paid little attention to her.

Once she got inside her house, she took a hot shower and prepared herself a meal. Though normally she relished the quietness of living alone, tonight she felt restless, even lonely. She didn't like that. She hadn't felt that way in a long time.

To keep herself busy, she decided to clean up the things her father had found for her so she could list them on her website for sale. They were really great artifacts. One of them, a remarkably intact little treasure chest most likely from a sunken ship, contained ancient gold coins and an assortment of brightly colored gemstones. She'd most likely sell them separately, though she might offer them up together and see if she had any takers.

This alone would fetch a pretty penny. The other two things—excellent finds on their own—would also sell quickly. Good, because she had a hunch she'd have to finance the Shadow Agency until it got up and running. Which might actually be a while. Though Zach, as her first client, would help pay some of the expenses, his bill wouldn't be enough to support them for too long.

Zach. She thought of his tall, powerful body. Muscular and rugged, everything about him seemed the opposite of Mermen, who were, as a general rule, trim and slender. Zach wore his masculinity like a cloak, and his confidence beckoned to her. Zach! There he was again, intruding into her peaceful afternoon. This first case felt more like helping a friend than a job, despite the fact that she'd never met Zach before. Except tonight they'd be signing a contract and money would change hands. How much, Shayla had no idea. Maddie would be handling the amount of their fee, promising it would be reasonable and in keeping with what other people charged.

Since no one knew, Maddie had promised to research what kind of rates private investigation firms charged and type up a handy guide for each of them. Carmen had said something about finding them office space, which could become really interesting since no one even knew where Carmen lived or how her taste ran in buildings. Shayla had to wonder what kind of space the Vampire would consider normal for a business such as theirs.

Of the three, only Shayla had begun the physical investigative part of things. Maddie had scoured the internet and reached out to her contacts, while Carmen had asked questions down near the waterfront. Of course, Shayla was the only one able to explore under the sea. Once the contract had been signed, she'd also go to the Neptune Pod, which was the Merfolk equivalent of the Shifter Pack Protectors. She had no doubt Nantha's father would have already started the process of beginning an investigation, but it couldn't hurt to let them know someone else was actively searching, as well. Especially a royal princess.

Though worry still made his chest tight, at least now Zach felt a renewed sense of hope. Running into the two women at Broken Chains had been the luckiest thing to happen to him in years. As one day turned into two without word from his sister, desperation had set in. Now, just because he'd made an impulsive decision to stop in the bar for a drink, he'd have help. He definitely didn't mind paying for assistance, because with Ion gone under the sea and his mother an emotional wreck, he'd never felt so alone and powerless.

Especially since he couldn't shake the feeling of guilt. He'd promised Nantha he'd look after her while she was on land. And somehow, he'd let her down. He had no idea what might have happened to her.

A thousand scenarios, each more horrible than the last, drifted through his head at night when he closed his eyes and attempted to sleep. Truthfully, he watched way too many crime dramas on TV. The story lines filled his head with dark and disastrous possibilities, things that wouldn't even have occurred to him if he hadn't seen the programs and realized what awful acts humans were capable of. He hoped nothing like that had happened to his sister.

Instead, he kept busy searching. The Monday after she'd disappeared, he'd called in sick to work. Tuesday, the same thing. Wednesday, he showed up, if only to put in to take the rest of the week off as personal vacation days. At the last moment, he'd changed that to taking a two-week long vacation. No one could argue since Zach hadn't taken any actual time off in close to three years.

Because sleeping brought nightmares, he fueled himself with caffeine and tried to stay awake as much as possible. He'd even done a quick shape-shift into his Wolf self in order to search the area around his mother's house by scent. Despite the incredible ability of his Wolf nose, he'd turned up nothing.

Every waking moment since Sunday night, he'd spent searching or thinking about where Nantha could be. He longed for a clue, a hint, anyone catching a glimpse of a tall, willowy blonde with bright blue eyes. He'd done a thorough search of the western area of Galveston Island, close to where she'd disappeared. After that, he'd haunted all the touristy areas, including the beaches, before moving on to other residential neighborhoods.

Despite this, he'd turned up nothing. Absolutely, freaking, nothing. He wished he could have taken the extra step of filing a missing person report with the human police, but Merfolk didn't have human identity. He'd spoken with the Pack Protectors instead, even though they worked with Shifters rather than Mermaids. They'd treated him kindly, if dismissively, but at least they knew to be looking for her. It hadn't helped his state of mind when the Protector taking the report had suggested slyly that maybe his sister had run off with her boyfriend, needing to escape her overprotective brother.

Zach had tamped down his rage at the smirking man. The man didn't know his sister. If he did, he'd never have made such a comment. Nantha might be mischievous, but she adored her family. She'd never do something so irresponsible. If she'd had a boyfriend she'd wanted to run off with, she would have told them all before she waved goodbye. Clearly, her life was in danger, no matter what the Protector believed.

After the sting of that encounter, Zach still didn't regret reaching out to the Pack Protectors. This wasn't about him. He couldn't let injured pride come between him and a chance to rescue Nantha. He'd simply asked to speak to someone else. However, something the second Pack Protector said when taking Zach's information worried him. "Another one?" he'd asked, before appearing to catch himself. After that, despite Zach's repeated attempts to get him to elaborate, he'd refused.

Another one. Had other Mermaids recently gone missing? If so, why? These were the kind of questions that kept him up at night. Maybe Shayla would know. He'd ask her later that evening when they signed the contract.

The Shadow Agency. He liked the name. And even though he knew only one of the woman had any experience whatsoever with private investigation, he knew they'd all give the search everything they had. And he couldn't ask for more than that.

So now he had help, which eased his panic somewhat. He wanted to let his mother know too, hoping it would help her, as well. But it would have seemed odd to tell her that he'd enlisted the assistance of two women he'd met in a bar, so he didn't. Not yet. His shape-shifting mom, June, had gone out hunting as Wolf every night since Nantha had disappeared, hoping to catch a hint of her scent. That was all she knew to do; that and stay close to home in case Nantha returned of her own volition.

Despite how ridiculous it might sound, Zach allowed himself to feel the first bit of hope he'd had since Sunday night. The knowledge that he'd hired a Mermaid and another Shifter to help him search for Nantha made him feel more proactive. He definitely could use another pair of eyes and ears under the sea, because he had no way to know what was going on there unless Ion told him. And truthfully, Nantha's father seemed too devastated by his daughter's disappearance to be of much use. Since Zach loved his stepfather as deeply as if he were biological, the older man's pain had become Zach's, as well.

It was a giant cluster of worry and fear. He didn't see things improving until Nantha was found, which had better be soon.

In the middle of all this, he couldn't stop thinking about Shayla. Even worried about his stepsister, the image of the gorgeous Mermaid haunted him.

Zach would never forget how Ion had reacted when Nantha had vanished. At first, the older Merman had clearly thought she was playing a joke on him. Nantha had a mischievous streak and frequently liked to tease both her father and Zach. She'd gone for her usual walk, just as she always did before returning to the sea.

But as the search turned into hours and the daylight disappeared, they'd all begun to realize that something was very wrong. They'd driven to Stewart Beach, leaving June at home in case Nantha showed up. Zach and Ion had walked the sand, asking anyone they encountered if they'd seen a woman alone. No one had.

Finally, as the sun dipped below the horizon, Zach quietly had to admit defeat. He'd suggested they return home, just in case Nantha showed up there. Of course, they both knew she hadn't as June hadn't called.

Though he'd agreed, Ion had stumbled on the walk back to the car. When he got inside, Zach saw the older man had gone ashen. When they pulled up to the house, Zach had gone around to help Ion out. Again, Ion swayed and nearly fell.

Watching from the front door, June had rushed over to support and reassure her husband. Zach stepped back, glad she at least had a distraction. Soon enough, she'd realize what both he and Ion already had.

Nantha was missing. Something, somewhere, somehow, had gone very wrong. Despite that they'd turned up nothing—no sign of a struggle, no blood, no witnesses—she'd disappeared. Zach's best guess was that she'd been taken. The one thing that gave him solace was the fact that none of Nantha's personal belongings had floated up to the surface.

Later, when none of them wanted to make eye contact with the others and silence made the air feel heavy enough to choke on since no one knew what to say, each grappled internally with their own panic. While no one had the slightest idea what might have happened, they all knew their beloved Nantha was in danger. But where? And how? This not knowing, not having a clue, made it all worse somehow.

Finally, Ion had said goodbye. He'd gone home, diving into the ocean, determined to find his daughter if she was there. June had taken to her bed, her earlier hysterics becoming a sort of dry-eyed grief. She could barely function. Despite this Zach had to leave her alone. He couldn't stay and reassure her while there remained a very real chance he could still find his little sister.

When he'd left them, Ion had promised to report back if he discovered any news. As of today, they still hadn't heard anything at all from him. June had managed to get herself together, but Zach could tell she was a nervous wreck. She'd already phoned him three times since eight o'clock that morning asking if he'd heard anything, anything at all. Finally, he'd gently told her that she'd be the first to know if he did. He planned to call her later in the day even if he had not.

His small apartment in Texas City felt cramped, so he didn't stay there long. He drove south to Galveston, figuring he could grab a meal and take yet another walk along the seawall and Stewart Beach. This time of the year, with the exception of spring break, was his favorite next to autumn. The thousands of tourists hadn't yet descended on the island, and while the Houstonians came down on the weekends, the pleasant weather and lack of crowds made everything nice.

Abruptly he realized nothing would be nice again until Nantha came home. He headed down to the pier and Joe's Crab Shack, where he could grab a shrimp po'boy and a beer.

Even then, he showed Nantha's photo to everyone who walked by his table, just in case one of them might have seen her. No one had. He refused to let this dampen his spirits. After all, he still had time until darkness. After his meal, he'd do another circle of the seawall.

He'd simply keep searching until he met Shayla and Maddie at Broken Chains, signed the contract and handed over his retainer fee. Then and only then would he truly feel as if he wasn't simply spinning his wheels.

While he looked, he'd ask every business to put up a poster. Earlier, he'd had the foresight to print up some missing person posters. He'd left some with his mother, asking her to go around her neighborhood and get them up. For himself, he stuck close to the businesses, restaurants and shops. After traveling all around Broadway, The Strand, the seawall and the pier asking store owners to put them up, he realized he'd need to print more. He stopped back into the same print shop where he'd had the first batch done and ordered again. They ran them off while he waited, declined to charge him anything. He thanked them, the kindness of the small gesture warming his heart. He also noted they already had one posted to their window.

Making a second round to hit all the places he hadn't the first time, as the sun began to set, he ended up with a few hundred of the posters left. Exhausted, he decided to go home and shower, maybe grab a sandwich before heading to Broken Chains to meet Shayla and Maddie.

As full darkness fell, he drove back toward Harborside Drive. Across from the cruise ship terminals, there were various parking lots as well as commercial businesses and warehouses. Some of the older buildings hadn't been repaired since Hurricane Ike tore through and were still boarded up. Broken Chains was hidden down an alley between two such buildings. Most humans viewed the area as dangerous and stayed away. The bar's Vampire and Shifter employees made sure to clear the alley before opening for business each night.

As he made his way toward the alley, he glanced around before making that last right turn. There, the sign with no letters, swinging in the night breeze. If any human chanced upon it, they'd definitely believe it a remnant from the time before the hurricane.

Zach stopped, inhaling deeply, waiting before he actually tapped the code out on the door. He'd always loved the moment before entering. The atmospheric setup—the dead-end alley, towering medieval door. The precise number of knocks in a certain cadence, and the vetting before one was allowed in. He wondered what happened if a human accidentally made it this far and tapped on the door. He wasn't sure, though he knew for certain they would not be allowed inside. Broken Chains was for paranormal entities only. Among the entire world owned by humans, this place was theirs alone. A safe haven.

Once he'd made it in, he stood still and scanned the premises, a peace settling over his weary body. The muted lighting, the clinking of glasses and dishes, the sound of the band tuning their instruments and the hum of quiet conversation. For whatever reason, the bar was even more crowded on this Wednesday night than it had been the evening before. Mid-week point, perhaps? The pleasant buzz of noise made him feel welcome, at home.

Once again, as Zach made his way through the crowd, he was glad the bar didn't allow smoking. Shifters had sensitive noses, and a room full of cigarette smoke made most of them feel nauseous. The last time Zach had visited a human bar, the smoke had been so thick he hadn't even ordered a drink before turning around and walking right back out. These days, the humans had become health conscious, and more and more establishments banned smoking.

Shayla and Maddie had said they'd meet him here at eight. He'd arrived half an hour early, and judging from the lack of places to sit, he hoped they'd gotten here even earlier. If not, they'd all be standing and circling the room like hawks until someone actually got up and vacated their table.

The band continued to warm up. There were five of them. A different group from the night before. Broken Chains constantly rotated their musical act. Zach had heard everyone wanted to play there, and competition was so tight that they were booked months in advance. He liked the fact they changed up the music. Something for everyone that way. From the sound of their warm-up, this band sounded like they played eighties music. He shrugged, continuing to wade through elbow-to-elbow people in search of the two women.

He reached the back edge of the bar and turned to go down the other side. Nothing, though every single table was full. A few other Shifters whom he'd spoken with previously waved. He waved back, though he didn't stop to talk.

Once he'd made a complete circuit of the packed room, he climbed the narrow staircase to check the second floor.

There weren't as many people up here. He felt like he could breathe. There they were. They'd taken a table near the back, as far away from the balcony railing to below as possible. He approved of their choice, where it would be quieter.

Shayla and Maddie spotted him. Shayla waved. As he made his way toward them, dodging a waiter with a tray of drinks, he realized a third woman had joined them. A blonde with short, spiky hair and too-perfect alabaster skin. He stopped in his tracks. Something about her… Then he knew. The hair on his arms rose, and he pushed back the urge to growl. *Vampire.* His entire family had been blessed—or cursed—with the ability to instantly recognize a Vampire, even one who blended well with the human population. Though Shifters and Vamps had long ago forged a truce and these days the two got along, he couldn't help his initial visceral reaction. Hopefully he'd been far enough away that no one at the table would have noticed.

Resuming his progress, he inclined his head toward the newcomer before pulling out the remaining empty chair. From the cold way the Vampire regarded him, he guessed she felt the same way he did. Inherent enemies couldn't help their initial reaction. It was in their DNA.

Still standing, he kept one hand on the back of the chair. He really wanted to know what she was doing here. This was to have been a private meeting between him and the Shadow Agency.

"Evening," he said as a greeting, including all three of them in his glance, though he slid his gaze away from the Vampire as quickly as possible without appearing rude.

"Hey there, Zach." Shayla's wide smile made him catch his breath. Tonight she wore her silky black hair pulled back in her trademark complicated braid. The hairstyle showed off her high cheekbones, sensual lips and striking eyes. She was, he thought, absolutely stunning. Even his inner Wolf sat up and took notice.

She gestured gracefully toward the Vampire. "This is Carmen Vargas. I'm sorry you haven't had a chance to meet her before now. She's the third partner in the Shadow Agency."

Third partner? This was new. Privately, he wondered how wise that decision might be, but as an about-to-be client, he figured the Vampire could go places neither he nor the others could. Beggars couldn't be choosers.

Right now, he could use all the help he could get locating his sister. If a Vamp could help find Nantha, he'd let her.

He finally lowered himself into the chair, directly across from the now-glowering Vampire. Shayla glanced from him to Carmen and back again. "What?" she asked, spreading her hands, showing off her bright blue nail polish. "I'm picking up a strange vibe. Do you two know each other?"

"No," Zach answered. He forced himself to relax, aware the other Shifter, Maddie, had gone into full alert. Seemed his inner Wolf wasn't the only one paying attention. "We don't."

"It's okay," Carmen interjected, finally taking her gaze off him. "Sometimes age-old instinct trumps common sense."

In the interest of getting along, he let that comment go. After a second of startled consideration, Maddie laughed. "Don't worry, Zach. The same thing happened to me the first time I met her."

Of course it had. Despite Zach's dislike, Carmen had a point. Age-old instinct could be difficult to overcome. Still, it would help if he tried to make a start. He forced himself to meet the Vampire's gaze. "You're right, I'm wrong. My apologies." He took a deep breath and continued. "I know lots of Vamps, and this hasn't happened to me in a long time. I'm not sure why I let myself get caught up in it this time."

For whatever reason, his remark made Carmen laugh.

Shayla touched his arm. "I think it might be because Carmen is the most emphatic Vampire I know. Though most can't see past her beauty, once you get to know her, you'll wonder how you didn't notice. She's very, very Vampiric."

Shaking her head, Carmen only laughed harder. "Thank you," she finally managed. "I guess."

"You're welcome." Shayla pulled a manila folder from her bag, fixing each of them with a stern look. "Now shall we get down to business?"

Zach nodded, glad to have Shayla to distract him from his lingering animosity. "Definitely."

"Um, drinks first?" Carmen protested, arching one perfectly shaped brow. "We waited for you," she told Zach. "And I'm thirsty. I need some refreshment before we discuss business."

"Sounds good to me," Maddie agreed, lifting her hand to signal a waitress. Instantly, a short woman with purple-and-pink hair appeared at their table. Shayla ordered white wine, Maddie, a wheat beer, and Carmen asked for a glass of an Argentinian weaver's blood, straight up. For himself, he went with dark beer, earning an approving look from Maddie.

Shayla slid a manila folder across the table. "Our contract," she said. "Take your time reading it."

Tuning out the noise from the bar downstairs, he read over the contract. It seemed straightforward, so he went ahead and signed. Since he'd had no idea what kind of retainer they might ask for, he'd made sure to bring a thousand dollars in cash, ten one-hundred-dollar bills neatly folded inside his wallet. If that wasn't enough, he'd negotiate, or find an ATM.

Turned out, one thousand dollars was exactly what they asked him to put down. The contract had also spelled out other fees, but to his surprise the document said if they weren't able to accomplish their goal for whatever reason, they'd refund his money. All of it.

In other words, they guaranteed success or their services were free.

Chapter 4

"I like your confidence," he said, palming the money and handing it over so that no one else could see. Shayla took similar care, closing her hand over it and lowering it into her purse. He was glad she hadn't decided to make a production out of counting it on top of the table. The bar might be full of other Shifter, Vamps and Merfolk, but that much cash might prove too big a temptation for some.

Underscoring everything, he felt the buzz of his attraction to Shayla, making him hyperaware of her.

Their drinks arrived and Shayla asked them all to do a toast. He felt a little uncomfortable clinking glasses with a female Vampire holding a glass full of blood, but he managed to keep his revulsion hidden, he thought.

Once they'd all taken sips from their assorted drinks,

he leaned in. "Now tell me your plan. I want to know what steps you're going to take to find my stepsister."

Shayla nodded. She reached into her purse and pulled out several sheets of paper and a pen. "I need you to fill out this questionnaire. Once I know more about Nantha—where she lived, went to school, worked and who her friends are, I can go back under and start asking questions."

"Why all the focus underwater when Nantha disappeared on land?" Maddie wanted to know.

"Good point," he agreed. "I'm thinking that's what her father is doing also."

"Maybe, but how many young people are going to reveal any secrets Nantha might have had to her father?" Shayla smiled gently. "You know how that is. I feel much more confident they'd be willing to talk to me. And the more we can learn about her life undersea, the more we can look for clues as to who might gave grabbed her and why."

She had a point. Sort of. "Unless her abductor is human."

"And that's where I come in," Maddie interjected smoothly. "Carmen is assisting me. We're exploring the human possibilities, among others."

He nodded and began writing down the answer to the questions. Luckily, Nantha had confided in him. Otherwise, he wouldn't have had a clue.

As he wrote, Shayla leaned over, trying to decipher his handwriting upside down. "Good," she commented. "I'm glad to see she's from Coral. That's my hometown, and I know it like the back of my hand."

Carmen watched silently, continuing to sip on her drink. Maddie checked her phone. "My brother just texted me. He's a Pack Protector. I filled him in on all this. He says there's already an investigation open."

Relieved, he nodded. "I contacted them, and they said they'd look into it. They didn't seem really concerned."

"Yeah." Maddie looked down, clearly not sure if she should finish speaking. When she raised her head and met his gaze, he saw determination in the set of her chin. "He says since you didn't get a ransom note and there's no indication whatsoever that Nantha is in danger, we have to consider the possibility that she might simply have run off on her own."

"No." Zach focused his attention back on the questions. "The human police said something similar when I reported her missing. But Nantha's not like that. She'd never do anything to worry her family. If she wanted some time away, she would have at the very least left us a note."

Maddie nodded. Shayla simply watched him, the compassion in her lovely eyes making his throat close up.

"Are you sure?" Carmen asked. "Because just about everyone has secrets they don't want their family to know."

His instinctive response—to snarl at her—he pushed back down. Instead, he mentally counted to five, taking slow and steady breaths before answering. "I'm sure. Nantha is one of my best friends."

"I'm sorry, I have to ask this." Color high, Shayla cleared her throat, though she didn't look away. "Were you and Nantha romantically involved?"

"What?" He couldn't believe her question. The supposition made him feel nauseous. "Of course not. She's my sister, for hound's sake."

"Stepsister," Carmen drawled. "Correct me if I'm

wrong, but there's no blood relation there at all. And from what I can tell, this Nantha is one hot babe."

"She's pretty." Brotherly pride mixed with revulsion made him swallow hard. "And, yes, I do have to beat back human suitors when she's visiting on land. But all Merfolk are blessed with good looks." He jerked his head toward Shayla. "You all know that."

"I'm sorry." Shayla sounded genuinely regretful. And, he thought, a tiny bit relieved. "But it's something we had to ask."

Not *we*. *She*. Did she really think so low of him to even consider the possibility that he and his baby sister were having an illicit love affair?

"I can see from the look on your face that the idea repulses you." Carmen again, detached and observant. "So we'll put that possibility to rest. Please, go ahead and fill out the rest of the questionnaire. We're especially interested in knowing about any boyfriends Nantha might have or have had. Past ones would be of special interest."

Boyfriends. Question sixteen. He paused, taking a moment to think. Nantha always had a crush on someone, but it seemed to change every couple of weeks. He knew she dated, but she'd never mentioned anything serious.

All three women nodded when he passed this information on. "I'll look into it when I go back to Coral," Shayla said. The low thrum of her voice reached deep inside of him, sparking arousal. To hide this, he swallowed hard and focused on the questionnaire.

Once he'd answered all the questions to the best of his ability, he slid the paper across the table. Shayla took it and began reading. She asked for clarification on one of two things—he'd listed a few odd jobs where Nantha had worked, but only a couple of places where he thought she might hang out. As for hobbies, the only one that came to mind was reading.

"Surely there must be more," Shayla pressed. "What about exercise, working out? Or fishing? Does she like any sports?"

"No. She's actually pretty quiet." He thought for a moment, then sat up straighter. "Music. She loves to sing and dance."

Nodding, Shayla scribbled that down on the form. "Most Mermaids do," she commented. Picking up her glass, she drained her wine. He realized both Carmen and Maddie had already finished their drinks, as well.

Eyeing his still mostly full beer, he took a sip. Briefly, he considered slugging it all down, but decided against it, especially since Shayla didn't seem nearly as affected by him as he was by her.

He slid his own folder across the table. "I had some fliers printed up. I spent the day going around the island having them put up. They're laminated, so they should do well under water. Feel free to take them with you if you think they might help."

"Perfect!" Shayla beamed at him, which made his heart skip a beat. "I can definitely use them. I think they'll really help."

"I hope someone who knows where she is sees them," he said, his chest suddenly tight.

Shayla slapped some money on the table. "Drinks are on me," she said. "I don't know about ya'll, but I need to go. It's been a long day for me."

The other women stood, as well. Relieved he didn't feel obligated to sit and make small talk with the others, he pushed back his chair and did the same.

Below, the band played a steady stream of eighties hits. He knew once they got downstairs, it would be damn near impossible to hear anything.

Apparently, Shayla realized this, too.

"We'll get to work immediately," she said, holding out her hand. He reached out, and again, the instant their fingers connected he felt a jolt straight to his core. From the way her eyes widened, he had to think she felt it, too.

"You've got my cell number."

"Yes." After she released him, he shook hands with the other two women, keeping his face expressionless when he touched the Vampire. He knew his feelings were irrational, and while he didn't completely understand them—after all, he even had a couple of Vampire friends—he didn't have time to indulge in self-analysis. Getting his sister back was all that mattered.

Leaving his unfinished beer on the table, he followed the women downstairs and out of the bar. Once they reached the end of the alley, the three women went in the opposite direction. At a slight loss, he stood and watched until they disappeared from sight.

Now what? He could get in his car and head home to his place in Texas City, but he knew his mother would still be awake and frantic. Keeping her company would be the best thing to do. Plus, he needed to fill her in on what he'd accomplished today with the fliers, as well as tell her about hiring the Shadow Agency. He also needed to know if his mom had heard anything from Ion.

When Zach arrived back at his mother's house, she met him at the door. "Don't you ever check your messages?" she asked, her voice shaking. "I sent texts, too."

This was so unusual it worried him. Eyeing her, he realized she looked unusually pale. Her blue eyes were red and puffy, as if she'd been crying. And more than her voice shook. Tiny tremors rocked her slender frame.

"I'm sorry," he said, pulling her close for a quick hug. "I didn't hear my phone. It's been a crazy kind of day." He pulled his cell from his pocket and checked. Four missed calls, an equal number of messages and texts from his mother saying simply, "Call me immediately."

Dammit. When he raised his gaze to meet his mother's, he saw tears now streamed down her cheeks.

Dread momentarily paralyzed him. "Nantha?" he asked, hardly able to force the words out past the lump in his throat. "Do you have news? Is she…" He swallowed hard, unable to finish the sentence.

"Oh, no. Not that." His mom gave him a quick, fierce hug. "It's okay, honey. She's still alive," June said. "Sorry, I should have realized you'd think the worst. Come with me." And she turned and went toward the kitchen, knowing he'd follow.

Which he did, right on her heels. Oddly enough, his horrified assumption of the worst appeared to have calmed her. Hand steady, she reached for a folded piece of white paper on the counter, and handed it to him. "Take a look. This is crazy."

"What is this?" he asked, accepting it. "Who's it from?"

"Read it," she managed, before turning away. Despite that, he could see that she covered her mouth with one hand in order to muffle her sobs.

Dread coiling low in his gut, he opened the single sheet of paper, noting the way it had been precisely folded into three exact, equal sections. He also noted the high-quality paper; not your ordinary, run-of-the-mill copier paper. Interesting. And then he began to read.

TO THE FAMILY OF THE MERMAID KNOWN AS NANTHA, it began. Typed, not handwritten. All in caps. Swallowing hard, he forced himself to continue reading.

SHE IS ALIVE, the missive continued. AND OF NO USE TO US. IF YOU WANT HER BACK, YOU WILL DO WHAT WE SAY. WE ARE WILLING TO EXCHANGE HER FOR TWO OTHER MERMAIDS. BUT THEY MUST BE VIRGINS. MORE INSTRUCTIONS WILL FOLLOW.

And that was all. No way to contact the letter writer, no instructions, other than asking for two virgin Mermaids.

"What the hell?" He read it again to be sure he'd gotten it right. "Is this someone's idea of a joke?"

But now his mother was crying so hard she couldn't answer. He hugged her, wondering what kind of son of a bitch would even think of writing such a thing. "Have you told Ion?" he asked gently.

"I've asked him to come immediately," she managed. Communicating with those under the sea could be touch-and-go. Apparently, she'd actually managed to make contact.

A knock on the patio door made him freeze. Zach spun around, ready to do battle. When he realized who it was, relief flooded him. "It's Ion," he said, releasing his mother so he could unlock and open the door. "He must have gotten your message."

"Zach." Though he only had eyes for his weeping wife, Ion jerked his chin in a quick nod at Zach as he rushed to pull June into his arms. "What is this?" he asked, kissing her forehead. "Speak to me, darling. You said it was urgent. Tell me, what's happened?"

His questions only made her cry harder. Ion glanced over her shoulder at Zach, one brow raised in question. "Do you know?" he mouthed.

"Yes. She—we got a letter," Zach responded, unable to keep from reading it one more time. "About Nantha. It's crazy. It doesn't even make sense."

Ion gently steered June to a chair. "Sit, love," he ordered. "Let me take a look at this."

Zach handed it over, watching as the Merman silently read it. And then reread it.

"What do you make of it?" Zach asked when Ion raised his gaze from the paper to meet his. "Do you think it's genuine?"

"Unfortunately, yes. It doesn't read like a prank. The letter writer is definitely serious." He read it once more, exhaling sharply when he got to the end. "This isn't good at all. But, on the plus side, this means my daughter is still alive."

Zach nodded. "If they're telling the truth, yes."

At his words, his mother shot him a teary-eyed glare. "Think positive," she admonished him. "Nantha *is* alive. She has to be."

"Of course she is," Zach replied, keeping his voice gentle. "I have no doubt about that."

Reading the missive once more, Ion frowned. "The request for virgin Mermaids has me stymied, I must admit. It sounds like something from ancient legends."

Zach nodded, aware of what the older man meant, and didn't dare say out loud within his mother's hearing. Sacrificial virgins, meant to appease either some mythical god or monster.

Insanity, right? But clearly, the letter writer believed what he or she had written.

"Well?" June demanded, wiping at her eyes with the back of her hand. She stood, looking from her husband to her son and back again. "What are you going to do about this?"

Again, the two men exchanged silent looks. Zach knew they'd talk later, in private.

"I've hired a paranormal private investigation firm to help search," Zach said. He went on to tell them about the three women, one Mermaid, one Shifter and a Vampire.

His mother recoiled at the last, but didn't comment.

"I want to meet with them," Ion declared. "Especially the Mermaid. It would help me tremendously to have someone else helping me under the sea."

"I want to meet them, too," June put in, her voice fierce and determined. "Since one of them is a Shifter, she may be able to find a way for me to help."

"Fine." Zach didn't see the harm in setting up a gathering. In fact, it might actually help to have the others see who else was involved. "I'll see if they're available to meet tomorrow night at Broken Chains."

Both Ion and June nodded. Like everyone else in the paranormal community, they'd visited the bar more than once. While there were several others up north in Houston, Broken Chains was the oldest and most well-known.

"I've also involved the Pack Protectors," Zach continued. "They've promised to keep an eye out."

Though June nodded, Ion scowled. "I don't see how they could help. They can't search under the sea."

"We don't know that's where she is," Zach said.

"You'd better hope she's under the ocean," Ion shot back. "She's got to have seawater or she'll die."

June's eyes welled up again at his words, making Ion curse. He gathered his wife close, murmuring soothing words to her. Zach took that opportunity to leave the room.

Stepping out onto the patio, he stared into the darkness. Nantha was somewhere out there, scared and worried, held captive by some fools with insane ideas about sacrificial virgins. He wondered if she knew that one thing had apparently been what saved her—that she wasn't a virgin.

Shaking his head, he dug his phone out again and punched in Shayla's number. She answered on the second ring and listened intently while he told her about the letter. "It's true, what your stepfather said," she told him. "Centuries ago, virgin sacrifices were a thing. Or so the legends go. The humans claimed it was to appease a dragon or, even earlier, various gods and goddesses. Under the sea, the dragon usually was a giant squid. Once in a while, in really ancient times, I've read about an angry sea god, Poseidon or one of his demigods."

"But those were all ancient tales. Some of them might have even been myths," she continued. "I'm not sure why someone would be trying to resurrect those stories in today's world. Poseidon has a temper, but even he's moved beyond asking for virgin sacrifices."

Poseidon? He decided not to ask.

"Maybe someone is trying to start a new religion, or a cult?" he asked. "Have you heard anything about something like that?"

"No. But not only will I let the Pods know, I'll definitely ask around when I go visit again. Which will be soon. I plan to put up those missing person posters you gave me and visit the neighborhoods where she went to school and worked."

"Good." He told her about Ion's request for a meeting with the Shadow Agency.

"That's fine," she immediately said. "As long as you're okay with it. You are the client, after all, so what you say goes."

"Tomorrow night?" he asked. "Say around eight, at Broken Chains?"

"Let me get with the others, but I'm sure that'll be fine. I'm going to call and see if I can reserve a private room for a few hours. It'll be easier to talk that way."

Once he agreed, she ended the call, promising to let him know if anything changed.

He wandered back inside, noting his mother and Ion had disappeared to their bedroom. He knew he should head back home to Texas City, but it had been a long day, and his mother kept the guest bedroom bed made up for situations like this. He grabbed a bottle of water and went to bed early.

When he woke the next morning and wandered out into the kitchen to grab some coffee, his mother had started frying up some bacon. The smell made his mouth water.

"Good morning," she said, smiling, her posture relaxed. "I'm glad you decided to spend the night. I know it's a lot farther for you to go into work, so I figured a good breakfast would help."

She seemed so pleased with herself and so much happier than she'd been the previous night, that he didn't have the heart to tell her he'd taken two weeks' vacation. Plus, if he told her that, she'd want him to hang around the house most of the day. He needed to get back to the heart of the island as well as make a few phone calls. He hadn't yet informed the Pack Protectors about the note, and he knew they'd definitely want to know.

Dutifully, he took a seat at the table, happy to eat his mother's cooking. It revived his spirits to see her looking so much better.

"Where's Ion?" he asked, once he'd cleaned his plate and pushed it away.

She smiled. "He headed out at first light to talk to his contacts in his underwater city. He'll be back by afternoon. He also wanted me to tell you he's sorry, but considering what's happened, he's going to have to postpone your meeting with Teredia."

Teredia. He blanked for a second before remembering she was the Mermaid Ion had wanted Zach to marry. Though Zach hadn't met her yet, Ion had claimed the alliance would help Nantha tremendously, by virtue of family connections. In the photo he'd shown Zach, Teredia was stunning.

When Zach had asked why someone who looked like that would need an arranged marriage, Ion had laughed. "It's complicated," he'd said. "I'll let her tell you, if you'll agree to do this for your sister."

Zach had given his tentative agreement, with the caveat that he could back out if Teredia and he weren't a match. He didn't have much of a social life—engineers weren't known for their scintillating conversational skills—so he'd told himself it wouldn't hurt to try and be open to new experiences. Then he'd promptly put it to the back of his mind. Clearly Ion hadn't.

"That's fine." He waved his hand dismissively. "I can't even think about that right now. But I'm glad Ion's going to be back tonight." He told her about the meeting at

Broken Chains that night at eight. "Can you make sure and let him know?"

"Of course." She carried his plate and hers to the sink. "I'm looking forward to meeting your friends. I just wish it was under better circumstances."

He started to point out that they weren't exactly friends, but decided against it. Whatever she needed to believe to make herself feel better was okay with him.

"Thanks for breakfast, Mom." He kissed her cheek. "I've got to go. I'll see you at Broken Chains, tonight."

The sadness in her gaze echoed how he felt in his heart. He sighed and left. He knew the drive back to Texas City would feel twice as long as usual, but he wanted to go home and change before making those phone calls.

On the way there, his cell phone rang. Caller ID showed Unknown Caller. His heart skipped a beat. While it was possible someone was calling who'd seen his poster and had information about his sister, he had a gut feeling this was something else.

"Did you get the note?" a low voice growled. Masculine, he thought, though the voice-garbling software made it difficult to tell.

"I did." He kept his tone even, stifling the rage that filled him. Somehow, he managed to keep it contained. "How did you get this number?"

"Never mind that," the anonymous person said. "Have you considered my offer?"

Though there were many ways Zach could have responded to that, he knew he didn't have time to waste. "Consider it? I have no idea where I'd find virgins, never mind virgin Mermaids."

"Really?" The caller sounded unconcerned. "If you

don't, then my little captive's father should know. Ask him. Otherwise, tell him his daughter is going to die. You have one week. No longer." And then, with a click, the person ended the call.

Stunned, Zach stared at his phone. He punched Redial, but only got a recording stating that the call could not be completed as dialed.

Clearly, this meant the letter writer had been serious. While he could infer from this that Nantha was still alive and they might be able to save her, he knew beyond a shadow of a doubt he couldn't be part of some sort of sacrifice. Two innocent lives for his sister's? No.

But would Ion feel the same way? For the first time ever, Zach wasn't certain his stepfather would do the right thing.

While this was something else he'd discuss with the Shadow Agency, he decided he wouldn't tell June just yet. Due to the letter's implications, he could only imagine her reaction. No, when and if he decided to fill Ion in, he'd need to catch the Merman alone before he went back to the ocean.

For the first time, he wondered why the captors had chosen to reach out to him rather than Nantha's father, especially since they wanted virgin Mermaids.

Chapter 5

Shayla got to Broken Chains early, before the place had even begun to fill up. The band hadn't even arrived yet. Johnny, the bartender, looked up when she entered, his expression surprised. "You're really early," he commented.

"I rented a private room," she told him, smiling. "Can I get a ginger ale?" The soft drink had become a favorite. And it was far too early in the day to drink.

"Of course," he said, pouring the beverage into a glass without ice, just the way she liked it. He checked a clipboard. "You've got room three. I'll start a tab."

"Thank you." Carrying her drink with her, she headed toward the back of the bar, where bright red double doors separated the main area from the private rooms. Rumor had it that all kinds of deals were conducted in those four windowless spaces. Shayla didn't know for certain, as she'd never rented one before.

Lately, every time she set foot in Broken Chains she marveled at how this place—a bar, for shark's sake— felt so much like home. But here was truly the first place she'd ever been where no one was judged for any reason. Talk about diversity—Shifters and Vampires and Merfolk, and who knew what else, all coexisted in harmony. The knowledge, as well as the experience of finally feeling as if she belonged somewhere, made Broken Chains her home away from home.

Once she stepped through the double doors, she stood in a short hallway that ended with a full-length mirror decorating the wall and reflecting her image back at her. There were two doors on each side, numbered. Number three was the last door on the right.

She went to it, grasping the knob. Giddy with anticipation, she opened the door and stepped inside.

The perfectly square room looked like a conference room. Beige walls, boring artwork framed in walnut, dark hardwood floors and a large round mahogany conference table with six upholstered chairs.

At first disappointed, she shook her head and laughed. What had she expected really? Red upholstered couches and gilt coated lamps? This wasn't a whorehouse, after all.

For whatever reason, she thought of Zach. It had been a long time since she'd battled such a fierce attraction to a man. Of course, since he was her client, this was not only inappropriate, but dangerous. She needed to keep her full attention on the investigation.

Setting her tote bag down on the table, she pulled out her laptop and powered it up. Might as well check the internet connection before the meeting. Maddie had also promised to be there early so they could get everything set up. Carmen, too, though, like Maddie she'd had to work so would have to come straight from her job. As long as they were here before Zach and his family.

Shayla opened a thick manila folder. She'd printed out all of the research she'd done on virgin sacrifices, both in human history and Merfolk. She'd been tempted to ask her father to speak to Poseidon, but she knew all kinds of trouble came from getting the Sea God involved.

She slipped off her high heels, rubbing her aching feet together before taking a seat. While she loved the way the red-soled, spike-heeled shoes looked, she still hadn't gotten used to walking in them. That hadn't stopped her from buying several pairs. She figured she might as well build up her collection.

Now to deal with the business at hand. Time to make notes and see if she—along with Maddie and Carmen— could come up with any sort of plausible theory as to who might be holding Nantha. All before meeting with the young Mermaid's parents and Zach at eight.

Maddie arrived thirty minutes later, when Shayla had just gotten into the research. Distracted, Shayla looked up when the door opened, slightly disoriented.

"Hey," Maddie said, by way of greeting. "You seem really lost in thought."

Shayla indicated the papers scattered all around her on the table. "Research." She glanced at her watch, surprised to see thirty minutes had already passed. She'd also just about drained her ginger ale.

"Great." Maddie pulled out a chair. "Fill me in."

Shayla told her what she knew about the note and the follow-up phone call that Zach had received.

"Virgins?" Maddie asked, her tone incredulous. "So are we to infer from this that young Nantha is not?"

"Apparently." Shayla shrugged. "She's seventeen, after all." And her people were known to have a very casual attitude toward pleasures of the flesh.

Maddie grinned. "I know what you mean." She indicated the stack of articles. "What have you found out?"

"I don't have anything but folklore."

"Ah. The old virgin sacrifice trope?"

Shayla nodded. "Yes. For all I know, that could be nonsense inserted just to cause a smoke screen and throw off searchers. I just hope whoever has this young Mermaid understands how badly she has to be in water every so often."

Maddie nodded, her gaze troubled. "We've got to find her," she said. "It's not only our first case, but I can't help but think of my own little sister. I can't imagine how I'd feel if something like this happened to her."

"Agreed." Shayla thought of Zach, of the way his hard features softened when he spoke of his stepsister. Seeing a man like him, so strong and rugged, at such a loss, made her feel as if she'd do anything to wipe that look of pain from his face.

"Since we don't know if the demand for virgins thing is real or a smoke screen, we've got to find out if there are any other missing Mermaids," Shayla continued. "I've already left word with the Pod—our Mer-council. Surely they'll have records if anything like that has happened."

"Right. And both you and Zach have contacted the Pack Protectors. So there's that."

Shayla nodded, struggling not to show her frustration. "You know in human disappearance cases, the first twenty-four hours are the most important. They say the chances of the victim being found alive diminishes exponentially for every hour after that. We're at day four now."

"That can't be good." Maddie sighed. "This is the part where I wish we had more experience as private investigators."

"I agree, but I'm not sure how even experience would help in this instance," Shayla said. "We have no witnesses, no evidence, nothing except this weird sort-of-ransom note. According to Zach there's not even a way to contact them."

"Yet," Maddie said darkly. "I'm sure that's next."

The door opened, and Carmen glided into the room. Quickly, since Zach and his family would be there soon, Shayla and Maddie filled her in.

"Missing Mermaids," Carmen mused. "If there are, we've got to find the reason. That's what will lead us to the perps. Revenge? Lust? Love? Or is it something else?"

No one spoke, because no one had an answer. Shayla divided up the research, and they all began reading.

As before, time seemed to fly. A waiter appeared, bringing a pitcher of ice water and a tray of glasses. Carmen ordered a bottle of blood. Both Shayla and Maddie decided to stick with water.

Finally, Zach and his parents arrived. The instant Shayla caught sight of him, all the air seemed to leave the room. He ushered them inside, fussing over his mother, a tiny female Shifter with delicate features and neatly braided hair. Shayla's gaze drifted past her to the stepfather, a tall, angular Merman whose mouth fell open in shock when he met her gaze. Crud. She should have thought of this. For whatever reason, she hadn't considered the possibility that he'd recognize her.

"You're..." Clearly stunned, he couldn't finish.

"I'm Shayla," she said firmly, holding out her hand. "One of the owners of the Shadow Agency."

"Sorry," Zach said, turning. "Shayla, this is Ion, and my mother, June. And this is Maddie and Carmen. They're the other two partners." He took a deep breath. "They're all helping search for Nantha."

June nodded, her gaze slipping past Carmen to return to light on her son. Meanwhile, Ion continued to stand, apparently frozen in shock. He didn't take Shayla's hand, though he did perform an awkward sort of bow in her general direction.

Of course, Zach noticed. "Ion, what's wrong?"

Slowly, the tall Merman swiveled his silver head to meet Zach's gaze. "Is this some kind of joke?"

"What?" Clearly puzzled, Zach frowned. "I'm not sure what you mean."

"Princess Shayla." Ion turned to face her, bowing again. "I am honored by your presence, though I admit to being confused. What ruse is this?"

Great. Now her secret was out in the open. Shayla sighed. She'd really hoped Zach's stepfather would have the sense to keep her underwater status to himself. She hadn't told anyone, not even her closest friends. Glancing at them, she swallowed hard. Even Maddie and Carmen stared, their expressions both stunned and confused. Of course, she couldn't blame them. They'd had no idea she was anything other than an ordinary Mermaid.

Meanwhile, Zach looked from her to his stepfather and back again. "Princess?" he asked, his tone incredulous. "What the hell are you talking about?"

Stomach churning, Shayla readied herself to explain. She dreaded the moment when the easy acceptance vanished from her friends' sweet faces, replaced with either misplaced envy or awe or something even worse. She hated the way people treated her when they realized she was royalty. This had been one of the reasons she'd chosen to live on land.

The steady thump of a bass guitar managed to penetrate even this small room. The music had started. She actually wished they were out in the main bar, so there'd be a distraction.

"Your friend is a royal princess," Ion informed Zach, his tone icy.

Zach eyed her, a question plain on his face. Slowly, she nodded. "True."

He didn't respond. Would his opinion of her change? Would he consider her an entitled, spoiled royal dabbling in playing at becoming a private investigator?

Would they all look differently at her now?

"I live on land now," she said, directing her comment to Ion. Aware of the avid curiosity in her friends' faces, she knew she'd have to give more information than she wanted to. "I might be royalty under the sea, but here I'm just an ordinary Mermaid."

Carmen, bless her heart, laughed. "That's priceless," she said.

Neither Maddie nor Zach cracked a smile.

"Look, ya'll," Shayla said, spreading her hands in a gesture of supplication. "Please, don't be weird. I'm just me. Nothing has changed."

Slowly, Maddie nodded. "Okay," she said. "I guess."

Though Zach nodded, too, the tightness in his jaw didn't relax. Shayla wished she had the right to touch him, to press her lips against the pulse beating at the base of his throat and reassure him that nothing had changed.

"Your Highness," Ion began.

"Please," she interrupted. "Call me Shayla."

"You were engaged." Ion crossed his arms and leaned back in the chair. "I remember the hoopla, because you were supposed to marry Prince Richard from Gill. When he died, instead of choosing another, you decided to come live on land."

Inwardly wincing at the accusation in his tone, she glanced from him to his wife. "Just like you chose a Shifter," she gently pointed out. "You can't truly hold that against me, now can you?" But many did. In the great underwater cities, the royal line of succession was considered inviolate. The fact that she'd chosen to abandon her heritage once and for all was something some people considered inexcusable.

But in spite of that, her parents had been her strongest supporters. After all, her brother had succeeded to the throne. When he married and had children, the line of succession would bypass her completely.

She considered restating this fact to the other Merman, but not only did he probably already know, she owed him no explanations.

Fury and disappointment blazed from his silver eyes. She'd been looked at like that a lot after her heart had broken when Richard had died. Some people thought she'd lost her mind. None of this mattered to her, especially since she'd removed herself from all of the underwater world.

She sighed. If Ion didn't want her handling his daughter's case, that was his problem. Zach had hired her and until he fired her, she'd continue investigating.

Zach stood. "Look, I'm not sure what's going on, but whatever it is has nothing to do with the search for Nantha."

"That's right," June said, putting her hand on her husband's arm. "Please don't let politics interfere with the search."

At first, Ion didn't respond. Shayla's heart sank. Luckily, right then the door opened, and a waiter came in to see if anyone wanted a drink.

While everyone placed their drink orders, Shayla rolled her shoulders, trying to ease some of the stiffness. She looked up to find Zach watching her, which made her heart skip a beat. As their gazes locked, he smiled. "It's okay," he mouthed.

Though his smile made warmth blossom inside her, just like that, the pressure in her chest eased. Hoping her desire for him didn't show, she ordered her usual white wine, aware that once the waiter left, she'd need to regain control of the meeting, as well as herself.

As soon as the door closed behind him, she cleared her throat. "Ion, I'm sorry that you apparently have objections to working with me, but your son has employed our agency to find your daughter. In light of that, I won't be offended if you want to leave. Otherwise, I'm going to have to ask you to keep your feelings to yourself."

As the elder Merman peered down his nose at her, she braced herself for a possible explosive reaction.

Instead, to her relief, he nodded. "You're right," he said. "My apologies."

"None needed." Exhaling, she pulled out her questionnaire and slid one across the table to him. "I've already had Zach fill this out, but I'd like to get your input, too.

I know you'd be more familiar with your daughter's activities at home in Coral."

Accepting the form and a pen, he lowered his head and began to write.

"Ahem." Carmen, tilting her head. "While he's doing that, I think you owe us an explanation."

Her heart squeezed. "Do I?" Maybe if she kept things light, nothing would change.

"Yes," Maddie interjected. "You do. *Princess.*"

Ion glanced up at that, his mouth tightening. He didn't comment, returning his attention to filling out the questionnaire.

Though he didn't speak, even Zach watched her with a look of expectation.

"Fine." Shayla shrugged. "I'm a Mermaid princess. One of many. My brother took over the kingship once my father retired. Once he's married and has children, I won't be anywhere near close to being in line for the throne." Chin up, she took a deep breath. "My fiancé died a few years ago. And I've chosen to live on land rather than under the sea. That sums it up nicely."

To her surprise, both Maddie and Carmen simply nodded. Zach reached across the table and squeezed the back of Shayla's hand. "I'm so sorry. How long ago did this happen?"

Surprised, she could only gape at him. Finally, she found her voice. "Two years now."

"How…"

"The initial report said he was eaten by a shark," Ion interjected, without looking up. "A freak accident. Mermen simply don't die this way. We can outswim everything." He shrugged. "It was believed he was drunk, but the coroner's report revealed he'd been poisoned. No one knows by whom. The general consensus was that it was some chemical in the alcohol he drank."

Again, the grief. And the guilt. As if she somehow could have stopped it, as though if she'd been there, she could have saved him. She bowed her head, taking the time to get herself together before speaking.

Maddie and Carmen had her back. "That's terrible," Maddie said, the hard edge to her tone a warning. "And I don't understand why you feel the need to rehash it all right now."

"Exactly," Carmen interjected. "Unless you, Ion, had some part in his death."

June gasped. Ion whipped his head up, fury flashing in his silver eyes.

The situation had just deteriorated rapidly.

"Enough." Shayla pushed to her feet, so hard her chair crashed to the floor. "This meeting is not about me. Or you, Ion. It's about finding Nantha. And unless you can stay on topic, I'm afraid I'm going to have to ask you to leave."

Instead of apologizing or changing the subject, Ion glared at her. She realized that this Merman apparently believed the crazy rumors that had floated around about her.

His next words confirmed that. "The sea claimed him. A Merman who had no reason to die, but did. So tell me, Princess Shayla. You fled the sea after his death. Are you happier now that you're free of him?"

Shayla gasped.

"Ion!" Both Zach and June spoke at the same time. "That's enough."

"Sorry," he said, sounding anything but. "Her marriage to Prince Richard of Gill would have forged a huge bond between two cities. The economic repercussions were enormous. He suffered greatly before he died. And people say she's always wanted to live on land. Now that she's single, she can."

Shayla lifted her chin, shaking. "You don't know me, and I can bet you never knew Richard. You have no idea how I felt when I lost him, no clue how his death broke me. How dare you? Excuse me," she said to her friends, Zach and his mother before stalking from the room. Either Ion didn't realize or else he didn't care, but she could have him hauled into court for speaking to her like that.

Though she wouldn't. Because that would start all the gossip and finger-pointing up again, and she sure wasn't up for dealing with it.

Once out in the pulsing noise of the bar, her anger slowly bled out of her. She took a deep breath. Royalty had enemies, though she usually managed to steer clear of them. Crazy reactions like Ion's were one of the downsides to being a princess.

A hand on her shoulder had her whirling around, fists upraised.

"Hey." Zach. He leaned in close to her ear, so she could hear him. The warmth of his breath on her skin made her shiver. "I'm sorry about my stepdad."

"It's not your fault. I should be used to that crazy kind of drama, but I'm not. I don't know if I ever will be." She had to put her mouth almost on his ear, tempted to use her tongue, though she didn't. "It's one of the reasons I left home. The gossip and craziness made my grief even worse."

He nodded, taking her arm and steering her toward the back of the bar, where the band wasn't as loud. She

fought the urge to lean into him. "It must be hard, losing someone you love like that."

"Yeah." She tried a laugh, but it fell short. "That he
drowned seemed like kind of a bitter irony. Your stepdad wasn't the only one who felt like the sea settled the
score. I mean Merfolk and sharks usually coexist. If
they don't, we outrun them or kill them. There had to
be something else. And there was. He was poisoned. To
this day, they haven't found out who did it."

"Yikes." He winced. "Again, I'm sorry. That must
have been really hard on you."

The kindness in his eyes made her swallow. She eyed
him, wondering how she could be talking to Zach about
her ex-fiancé whom she'd truly grieved while simultaneously aching to touch him. The masculine confidence
he exuded made her feel a way she'd never felt nor expected to feel. Protected. Safe. Cared for.

Dangerous territory. Blinking, she forced herself to
concentrate on the topic at hand.

"It was," she allowed. "I confess there were a lot of
nights when I wondered. I tried to live inland, in the
rolling hills of central Texas, near a big lake. It seemed
reasonable. I'd be as far as possible from the sea, but
near water."

"I take it that didn't work?"

"No. I got sick and nearly died, so I had to come back
here. Mermaids need the ocean, salt water, to survive."

He still leaned in, close enough for her to see the way
the hair on his arms stood up. Why? Could it be he felt
as attracted to her as she did him? Her entire body went
warm at the thought.

"At least you learned to cope with it." He tilted his

head, studying her. "You seem well-adjusted and confident."

She liked the way he tried to encourage her, to find the positive. "Now, yes. But not then. Once I returned to live close to the ocean, I wanted vengeance. I was sick with it. I swam the seas, sang to every ship I saw. There were nearly several shipwrecks before my father and brothers tracked me down and dragged me back to home. I took my pain and anger out on the wrong people." She shook her head. "Luckily, no one was hurt or died."

"Luckily." He shifted his weight from one foot to the next. His broad shoulders, rugged features and overall general hotness earned him constant coveting glances from other females, though he didn't appear to notice.

When he took her arm, Shayla had to grin. "I'm over it now," she said. "The revenge part, that is. As for the grief, it comes and goes in waves. Mostly, I guess I'd say I'm at peace."

"I'm glad." His deep voice rumbled in her ear. "And now you're smiling again. I was worried for a moment there that you and Ion were going to do battle."

Refusing to let bitterness spoil her mood, she shook her head. "I've found it's better to try and rise above people who make comments like that."

"I agree." And then he placed a quick, soft kiss at her temple.

She froze. Just that simple press of his lips on her skin had her craving more. Every fiber of her being ached to lean into him and put her arms around him and pull him close. For a better kiss. A *real* kiss. The kind that would make her toes curl in her shoes.

Dang. What had gotten into her? She wanted him. She might as well admit the truth, if only to herself.

Hell, whenever they were within ten feet of each other, all she could think of was how it might feel to slide her hand over his muscular arm, splay her fingers across his chest, tug his face down to hers for a kiss. Because she hadn't felt this way since she'd lost Richard, the strength of her desire stunned her. More than that—a small shiver of foreboding skittered up her spine. It had her worried.

The Shadow Agency had just gotten started. If she wanted the business to be a success, she couldn't afford to lose her focus, even for a distraction as tempting as the sexy Shifter. And as for him, she knew he'd never forgive either her or himself if they didn't recover his sister.

Neither could let physical attraction get in the way of that.

The problem was, she could tell he felt the same. The way he looked at her when he thought she wasn't watching—as if he'd like to do all the same things to her she ached to do to him. Plus more. Her body tingled down low at the thought.

It had been a long time since she'd welcomed a man into her body. For Merfolk, this could only happen when in their human shape, of course.

Shaking her head to clear her thoughts, Shayla brought her attention back to Zach. He watched her, his gaze dark and knowing, as if he knew the spiral her thoughts had taken.

"Are you ready to go back?" he asked. "Or would you prefer I ask Ion to leave?"

She considered. "I can be professional, as long as he can. I have to tell you, though. One more outburst like that, and I won't be held responsible for my actions."

He eyed her. "Maybe I should get him to go first then.

He's beside himself over Nantha's disappearance. I have no idea what he might say or do."

"I was kidding." Though only partly, which she kept to herself. "Let's go back and see what happens."

"Are you sure?"

"Of course." She lifted her chin and turned to make her way back to the private room. "Hopefully Ion will have finished filling out the questionnaire. Once I have both of your answers, I'll have a better starting place of where to go and search."

"Wait." He tugged her back, up close to him, sending a shiver up her spine. "There's more. Neither of my parents know about the follow-up phone call or the fact that whoever has Nantha has now given me one week to come up with the payment they requested."

Shocked, she stared. "You haven't told them?"

"No." Expression grim, he grimaced. "My mother's going to freak out when she learns we have one week or my sister will be dead."

"We've got to tell them," she informed him immediately. "Maybe it will help once they learn Maddie's brother is a Pack Protector. It's possible he can trace the call next time they phone you."

"I hope so. And I know you're right. But fair warning. I think my mother's going to get hysterical."

"Come on." Now she grabbed his arm, pulling him back the way they'd come. "She'll have to settle down. Everyone needs to focus one hundred percent on getting Nantha back. One week is actually more time than I expected."

Chapter 6

When they opened the door to the private room, everyone instantly went silent. Zach figured they were all discussing Shayla's newly discovered royal status. He really didn't care about that. All he wanted was to find his sister. Then and only then would he let himself think about anything else, like the strength of his attraction to her and vice versa.

Ion stood and, avoiding looking at Shayla, jerked his head toward the door. "Zach, I need a word in private," he said. Which turned out to be perfect. That way, Zach could tell him about the phone call without his mother listening in.

"Sure. Let's go out into the hall."

But once they stepped out of the room and closed the door behind them, Ion grimaced. "This isn't far enough." He pointed to the closed door. "I can't take a chance of being overheard. Do you mind if we step outside for a few minutes?"

Curious, Zach agreed. They made their way through the packed bar to the exit. Once in the alleyway, they went a few feet away from the entrance. The cooler night air felt good on his overheated skin.

"Listen," he began. "There's something I—"

"Wait," Ion interrupted, looking from left to right as if he thought they might have been followed. "I need to tell you about that Mer-Princess you hired. Shayla. Her fiancé drowned, and she hasn't been right since."

Zach nodded. "I know about that. It's got to be difficult for her to lose someone she loved to the sea."

"Exactly." Ion seemed to pounce on the word. "In fact, it was rumored at one time she blamed other Mermaids. Claimed someone poisoned him. And when she thought humans did it, she went off and started singing to their ships. Luckily, the king intervened and put a stop to that."

Again Zach nodded, not sure what his stepfather was getting at.

"You need to be careful around her," Ion proclaimed. "Many in my circles consider her mentally unhinged."

Despite the fact that Ion hadn't detailed exactly what circles these were, Zach kept quiet. He didn't see the point in fanning the flames.

"And now," Ion continued. "You've hired someone to look for Nantha who might actually be behind your sister's disappearance."

"What?" Zach blinked. "You can't be serious."

"I am. If she's not directly behind this, there's a strong possibility that she knows who is."

Zach wasn't sure how to respond. On the one hand, he didn't want to flat out accuse Ion of talking crazy.

On the other, Nantha had nothing to do with Shayla's fiancé's death. This was crazy talk and he suspected Ion knew it. The older man's grief had completely clouded his judgment.

Ion sighed, correctly interpreting Zach's silence. "At least consider it," Ion demanded. "I know to you it might sound far-fetched, but so does a demand for two virgin Mermaids."

"I will. As a matter of fact, I'm going to bring it up with Shayla in private." Which he would, if only to let her know the craziness apparently had never gone away. "When I see how she reacts, I'll have a better handle on the possibility of it being true."

"Don't. Don't mention it to her. Just keep an eye on her and see if she does anything that might lead us to Nantha."

"Ion, she's going to be searching for Nantha under the sea. I really hope she's successful. And if you really believe it's possible she's somehow involved, it makes sense for me to discuss it with her."

At that, Ion looked down. "You can't. She's a member of the royal family. I live there. The consequences of accusing her of a crime like this—especially if it turns out to be false—would mean my imprisonment. Maybe even my death."

As Zach watched his stepfather, he realized the older man was serious. "I'll be careful."

"No." Ion sounded panicked now. "I shouldn't have said anything. Forget I mentioned it."

As if he could. "Finding Nantha before something bad happens to her supersedes everything else. Even that."

After a moment, Ion sighed. "You're right. But if you can, please don't mention my name."

"Of course."

"Now what were you wanting to say?" Ion asked.

Zach told him about the phone call.

"One week?" Terror edged the older man's voice. "Did you ask to speak to her?"

Proof of life. Damn. He wished he'd thought of that. "I did not," Zach answered regretfully. "I was so stunned by the call that I couldn't think."

"Well, if you hear from them again, demand to speak with her. And let them know that you're working on fulfilling their demands."

"What?"

"To buy time," Ion clarified. "We need all the help we can get."

Whew. For half a second, Zach had thought Ion was seriously considering coming up with a few virgin Mermaids.

"Let's go back in. We've got to fill in Mom."

Ion winced. "How about you wait until your mother and I leave. She's been hysterical due to how long it's been since Nantha disappeared. If she finds out her supposed captors are only giving us a week, she'll lose her mind."

Zach nodded. "How are you holding up?" he asked quietly. "I know this has been weighing heavy on all of us, but you…"

For an instant, Ion's patrician features crumbled. He swallowed hard, and visibly got himself under control. Until he opened his mouth to speak and all that would come out were a few disjointed syllables that sounded as if he was gasping for air.

He cleared his throat and tried again. "I'm doing the best I can," he managed. "I want my baby girl back."

"We all do." Zach squeezed the older man's shoulder. "Now let's return to the meeting. Will you please be civil?"

Ion slowly nodded.

As they turned and walked toward the door, Ion's words replayed over and over in Zach's mind. *Proof of life.* Not once had he ever allowed himself to consider the possibility that Nantha might be dead. Not once.

And now, he had to. Hell hounds, he hoped that caller phoned again. Because he knew he wouldn't sleep well until he spoke to Nantha and knew she still lived.

As soon as they reentered the room, Ion refused to look at anyone but his wife as he informed the others that he and June had to go. He waited by the door for June to collect her things, his gaze averted so he wouldn't accidentally meet anyone's gaze. The air felt heavy in the small room, and no one seemed to know what to do with themselves. Shayla, Maddie and Carmen occasionally glanced at each other, but they mostly watched as June fumbled with her tote bag while Ion made no effort to help her. Finally, Zach went over and quietly helped her rearrange everything. "It'll turn out all right, Mom," he murmured, kissing her cheek. "I promise to stay in touch. If I hear anything, anything at all, I'll let you know."

She nodded, her mouth working soundlessly as she gazed at him with tears in her eyes. Finally, she walked to the door, taking her husband's arm as she murmured a quick goodbye.

The tension that had vibrated in the room went with them. Shayla exhaled. "Whew," commented Maddie. Even Carmen, still silently sipping her blood drink, appeared relieved.

Exchanging a quick look with Zach, Shayla asked Maddie if her brother could trace the call.

"Let me see your phone," Maddie demanded. Once he'd handed it over, she used her own cell to make a call. They all listened silently as she repeated what Zach had just told them to whoever was on the other end. "Sure, I've got the number," she said, looking up. "Zach, what's your cell phone number?"

Once he'd given it to her, she passed it on. "Okay," she said. "Let me know what you find out."

After ending the call, she slid his phone across the table to him. "That was my brother Tanner, the Pack Protector. He's going to see if he can trace the call."

"That'd be fantastic," Shayla said, her green eyes glowing with excitement. Even Carmen's usually stone-faced expression changed.

Dragging his gaze away from Shayla, he forced himself to consider what his stepfather had said about her. He had to ask her about it, but he wouldn't do it right now, in front of her friends.

A few minutes later, Maddie's phone rang. Immediately all chatter ceased. Everyone went silent, watching as she answered.

"Yes," she said. "I see. Well, thank you for trying."

Attempting to contain his disappointment, Zach eyed her, pretty confident he knew exactly what she would say.

"He couldn't trace the number to a person," she said, exactly as he'd feared. "But, he was able to tell the call came from land rather than under the sea."

"On land?" Shayla spoke, the surprise in her voice echoing his own. "That's interesting."

"Is it?" Carmen interjected. "All this means is if Nantha's captors are Merfolk, they came up on land to make the call. Much more difficult to trace that way, so that makes sense."

"Even more specific," Maddie continued. "He says the call originated in Houston. Not any of the towns in between there and Galveston, but Houston. That's a huge city."

"That could mean anything." Zach dragged his hand through his hair in frustration. "Merman on land, human working with a Merman, hell, it could even be a Shifter."

"Or a Vampire," Carmen said grimly. "Though kidnapping people isn't really our thing." She pushed to her feet. "I need to go hunt. I think I'll go explore the area down by the pier and see what I can find out."

Maddie stood as well. "I've got to leave, as well. My brother has promised to see if he can narrow the call's origination down even farther—North Houston or South. He wanted me to bring him a later dinner, so I'm going to do that."

Zach and Shayla said their goodbyes. Once the others had gone, Shayla sighed. "Can I see the note?" she asked. "I'd like to take a look at the writing style and syntax."

"Sure." Pulling his wallet out, he removed the slip of paper and unfolded it before passing it across to her. He waited in silence while she read it, trying to figure out the best way to approach bringing up what Ion had told him. It was awful, pretty terrible, and he couldn't come up with a way to ask her without sounding accusatory.

"Do you mind if a take a picture of it?" she asked, pulling out her cell.

"Of course not."

She snapped several photos. "Thank you," she finally said, handing it back to him. He took it, folding it neatly and putting it back in his wallet. Still he couldn't seem to figure out the right opening statement.

Apparently, Shayla noticed. She touched his arm, the light contact making him ache for more.

"Zach, are you all right? I know all of this has been tough on you. You seem a little off tonight."

He started to nod, and then didn't. "I'm struggling to figure out the best way to ask you something," he admitted.

Raising her head, she met his gaze. "Just go ahead and ask." Her candid look told him she felt she had nothing to hide.

There were several different ways he could phrase the question. He mentally reviewed each one and simultaneously discarded it.

"Just ask," she urged. "It's about my reaction after my fiancé drowned, isn't it? I'm guessing Ion said something."

Relieved, he nodded. "You knew."

"I saw your stepfather's reaction when he looked at me. Once he got past the initial shock of who I am, all he could think about was how I was after Richard drowned. I'm not proud of it, but it's pretty common knowledge where I come from."

Richard. A good, steady-sounding name. It sounded more human than Merfolk, actually.

"I went crazy for a little bit," she admitted. "I said some things I shouldn't have. My grief got tangled up with rage and regret and…" She swallowed hard, momentarily looking away. "I hated the thing that I was. I no longer wanted to be a Mermaid. The irony of knowing that I could swim in the same sea that took Richard's life… It felt like too much to bear."

He watched as she took a deep breath, and then squared her shoulders and lifted her chin. "I'm better now. But I admit, sometimes I still wonder how such an awful thing was possible. Poison? Who would do such a thing?"

"I take it they never caught his killer?"

"No." The simple word conveyed all her frustration, sorrow and anger. Yet she managed to still stand tall, her bearing regal.

Hell hounds, the urge to touch her had him clenching his hands into fists to keep from reaching out to her, despite everything.

"Every royal has enemies," she continued, her expression grim. "Mine used my breakdown against me. I take it your stepfather is one of them."

"I don't think he considers you an enemy," he said, aware he had to be careful for Ion's sake. "But he says he's heard rumors. You know he's worried sick about his daughter. We all are."

"I know." To his shock, she leaned in and impulsively bumped her shoulder to his. Even this, the slightest of friendly movements, had his body tightening with desire.

"We'll find her, Zach. I promise you. No matter what it takes." She began gathering up the papers both he and Zach had filled out, placing them back in her manila folder. "Now at least I have a place to start. If I can talk to her friends, I might be able to find out who took her."

Though his mouth had gone dry, he managed to speak. "Hopefully. But what if this isn't personal?"

"Ninety-five percent of child abductions are by someone the child knew," she pointed out. "And while technically, I know none of you think of Nantha as a child, she's still pretty young. A teenager."

He nodded. "By human standards, she's still a child at seventeen."

"Here's what I'm going to do. I'm going back home to talk to her friends and coworkers, see where she hung out and find out if she had any male beaus. I'll also put up the rest of the posters you gave me."

Her brisk, no-nonsense tone made him feel slightly better. More settled. "When?" he asked.

"Tomorrow morning, right after dawn. If there's anything down there that might help us locate her, I'll find it." She flashed him a smile, confident and sexy. Again, he felt that twinge of connection. "Maddie's brother said he'll continue trying to trace that phone number. And Carmen is excellent at skulking around the waterfront at night, talking to the drunks and other denizens of the underworld, to see if she can learn anything."

He had to grin at her choice of words. "Skulking?"

She smiled back, which of course had him wanting to kiss her. "That's what she calls it. She takes pride in being the most Vampire-like Vamp she can be."

Even he disliked those Vampires who tried to come off as hipster humans who happened to be immortal and believed they were cool because they liked to prowl the night searching for blood. He had to appreciate Carmen's approach, even if she made him a bit uncomfortable.

"I'm thinking I need to head home," he said, as exhaustion washed over him. "But please, call me as soon as you get back from under the ocean tomorrow."

"I will." She scribbled something on a piece of paper and held it out to him. "As for you, here's all three of our numbers. If those people call you again, let Maddie know so she can have her brother try and trace it."

He took the paper, glancing at it before folding it to

put in his wallet near the ransom note. "And I'll make sure to ask to speak to Nantha."

"Proof of life," she agreed. "Always a good thing."

Though he'd never hated a phrase more, he nodded. Nantha had to be alive. He didn't know what he'd do if she wasn't.

Early the next morning, as Shayla prepared to go back to her home under the sea, those three words haunted her. Proof of life. As she dove under the waters and began the long swim, with each stroke of her arms and flip of her tail, the phrase repeated over and over in her mind like a mantra.

None of what had happened made the slightest bit of sense. She'd done some research into abductions, and most of them were done by someone the victim knew— a family member in most cases. If there was a ransom demand, it was usually for money. Not some weird request for virgins.

That's why she suspected this wasn't about a ransom. If it was, if the abductor was truly serious about wanting an exchange with virgin Mermaids, she'd have to guess he or she was a human who'd somehow stumbled onto learning about the existence of Merfolk. Only a human would have such a crazy idea as demanding virgin Mermaids, as if such beings would have some sort of magical powers.

But then what? What did the captor plan to do with virgins once he had them? Surely they wouldn't be used as a sacrifice.

For the first time, Shayla allowed herself to wonder if Nantha had truly been abducted at all. Though Zach refused to even consider the possibility, maybe the teenager had run away. Which would make the odd ransom request a smoke screen. While she didn't know Zach's stepsister, she could picture a seventeen-year-old giggling over the request.

Maybe that was one possibility she could consider. At least, add it to her list. It would fit too, except for the fact that they'd been given a deadline. One week. And then what? Did they mean to kill Nantha?

Hopefully, today she could find something out. Some hint, some clue, that might give her insight into what exactly had happened.

The farther out she swam, the deeper the ocean and the cooler the actual temperature of the water. She stayed down about one hundred feet, keeping her eyes open for sharks, giant squid or other natural enemies to her kind. So far, so good. Nothing but the occasional school of fish, most of them preoccupied with finding food.

She continued to swim, determination fueling her, overriding her exhaustion. Though she really craved a nap when she got home. Nothing too long, just an hour or so, enough to rejuvenate her. But, no, there was too much to do and not enough time. The nap would have to wait. She'd stick to her plan, and see if she could learn anything new.

When she reached her parents' house, she swam inside. The kitchen—her mom's usual hangout—was empty.

But this time her dad sat in his recliner in the den, arms crossed, as if he'd been impatiently waiting for her.

"Dad?" Surprised to see her father, Shayla rushed over for a hug. "What are you doing home?"

Though he got up from his chair and hugged her back, he didn't crack a smile. "I came to wait for you," he said, confirming her suspicion. "Your mother told me you were coming today."

The gravity in his voice had her worried.

She tried teasing him. "Well, you sure don't look happy to see me."

"I…" He shook his head, a reluctant smile curving the corner of his mouth. "I came to speak to you, before your brother summons you before the court."

"Summons? I don't understand. Why would he do that?"

"There have been rumors swirling around court, though no formal complaint has been made against you. Apparently the family of one missing Mermaid named Nantha believes you might have had something to do with her disappearance."

"What?" Stunned, she didn't bother to hide her shock and dismay. Ion. "That's crazy." She showed him the flyers she'd laminated. "I've been hired by her stepbrother to find her. And her father, Ion, knows this. I met with him last night. He wasn't very nice—in fact, he spouted off similar accusations, but I never would have believed he'd go this far."

Her words didn't appear to reassure her father. If anything, her statement deepened her dad's frown. "Then why would he make such an accusation? He's saying you were involved with the abduction of one of your own people, Shayla. This is very serious."

He had a point. Why would Ion do such a thing? What did he hope to gain by this?

"I don't know." She hesitated. "Though I have my suspicions. Ion didn't say anything to me, but he spoke to his stepson, Zach. Apparently, he's one of those who still believe I'm out to avenge Richard's death."

Instantly, her father's expression cleared. "I see. Now this at least makes a modicum of sense. I've never heard of this Ion, though your mother did tell me you were searching for a missing Mermaid. Let me call your brother and let him know." Picking up the red phone that went directly into the palace, he paused. "Are you free for lunch later? That is, if Merc agrees you don't have to come in just yet?"

Since Merc liked to play practical jokes on her and had since they'd been guppies, she wouldn't put it past him to insist she spend several hours answering questions at the palace.

"Dad, lunch sounds great, but do you mind if I head out before you talk to Merc? You know how he is. And I have a lot of places to cover before I have to return to land."

He nodded. "You have a point. As long as you don't get too busy and forget about me."

"I won't." Studying her notes, she reaffirmed her planned schedule out loud. "I should be over near Seaweeds at lunchtime," she said. "Do you want to meet me there?"

"Sure. But, Shayla, tell me again why you're searching for this missing girl here. As I understand it, she disappeared while on land."

"We don't know that for certain." She sighed. "She and her father, Ion, were visiting his wife on land. They were about to return to the sea when she vanished. Apparently, she had a mischievous streak, and at first they thought she might be playing a joke on them." She told him about the ransom note, and then the phone call Zach had received.

"Virgins?" The former king appeared dumbfounded.

"To be honest, that part right there sounds like a joke. From someone who is either not very bright or hasn't kept up with their mythology." He shook his head. "Virgins. Honestly. What they're asking is inconceivable. As if we'd go out and round up a couple of innocents and demand they be willing to let themselves be handed over like chattel."

"I know." His outrage ignited her own. She'd been so intent on the weirdness and reason for the request that she hadn't stopped to think of the other aspect of it. "Right now, I'm focusing on who might have had some sort of grudge against her. I plan to speak to her friends, visit places where she worked and find out if she had a boyfriend. Meanwhile, if they contact Zach again, he's going to ask for proof of life."

Her father winced. "That's realistic. I have to say, none of this makes sense. I fail to see what the abductor would hope to gain. Surely he or she must be aware no one would try to trade other Mermaids—virgin ones, no less—for her. Sadly, the only conclusion I can come to is that the person making the request is mentally unhinged."

"I agree that's a possibility. That's why it's imperative we find her as quickly as we can. I've talked to the Pod—as has Ion—and her stepbrother has brought in the Shifter Pack Protectors. There are a lot of people looking for her, but right now we don't have a single clue where she is."

And Ion gunning for her to be questioned and possibly arrested had her wondering how badly he actually wanted his daughter to be found.

"What do you think of all this?" her father asked. "Do

you have any theories? I'm interested to know. And of course, I'll help you in any way I can."

She sighed and then told him everything, every single possibility that had occurred to her, including her new questions about Ion and his motives. The former king listened in silence, and when she'd finished, he quietly pondered her words.

"Have you looked into the mythological significance of virgins, specifically virgin Mermaids?"

"I tried." She shrugged. "I did see some studies indicating that originally we were believed to be half bird, half woman, then later half snake." Her smile felt more like a grimace. "I'm not sure how I feel about that. But I also read that later, the image of a half woman, half fish came into play. And I know all of the stuff about virgins, specifically sacrificial, but I can't tie the two together. A virgin Mermaid? Why?"

"Why indeed." He took a deep breath. "Maybe we should ask Poseidon. He knows everything."

"Poseidon?" Shayla froze. The ancient god of the sea terrified her, even though she'd only met him once. "You can't be serious."

"I am. Why not? You know he and I are good friends."

"The great Poseidon has better things to do than worry about one lost Mermaid." The second the words left her mouth, she winced. "Though of course, I'd welcome his help if he were so inclined to give it." Unfortunately, as everyone knew, Poseidon's help always came with a cost. She reminded her dad of this.

"That's only if he finds the request boring or stupid. He'd find this interesting, believe me." Her father spoke with assurance. "He loves a good mystery. And if anyone would know about the whole virgin mythology, he would."

She took a deep breath. "But I'm not sure we could afford the price. Despite what you say, you know he'd demand some sort of payment."

"That's possible," he agreed. "Though sometimes he's willing to wager on the outcome. Let me talk to him and see what he thinks."

"Just don't promise something you can't deliver." Mermaid lore was full of stories of Merfolk who'd thought they could outsmart the God of the Sea. It never ended well.

"Gotcha." He leaned in and kissed her cheek. "Though since it's a long journey to Poseidon's court, I'm going to have to take a pass on lunch. We'll do it next time. When will you be back?"

Staring at him, she battled mixed emotions. "Are you sure you want to involve him? Couldn't you wait a few days and then see if we still need help?"

"You said the caller gave you one week. I don't see how the situation could be any more urgent."

Again, he had a point.

"Fine," she conceded. "But I'm really disappointed you're standing me up for lunch."

He chucked her under the chin. "Something tells me you'll survive until the next time you visit."

"You're probably right. I do plan to check in pretty regularly. It shouldn't be more than a few days, if that."

"Good." With a jaunty wave, he left. On his way to seek out a cantankerous old god. The thought made her shudder.

Because she had a lot to do, Shayla tried not to worry about him. Aware she needed to get busy as well, she took off to begin her planned journey.

Chapter 7

Swimming back toward Galveston, instead of scouring the ocean floor for artifacts like she usually did, Shayla used the time to think. This entire scenario with Nantha missing, the request for virgins, and with Ion going to her brother and insinuating Shayla might have had something to do with it had her wondering what exactly everyone might be trying so hard to hide. Because her gut instinct told her all of this weird, extraneous stuff, was a smoke shield hiding the actual truth.

But why? Why go through so much trouble? If Nantha had run off, why wouldn't she just contact her family and let them know, so they wouldn't worry? If someone had actually abducted her—for whatever reason—why ask for something as improbable and impossible as virgin Mermaids in exchange? Surely, the abductor would know no one would trade one innocent life for another.

As she pushed her body through the sensual heaviness of the deep ocean, she considered alternatives. Out of respect for Zach—and belief in his opinion of his step-sister—she'd disregard for now the option that Nantha had vanished of her own free will.

Which would mean she'd truly been abducted. But for what purpose? None of Nantha's friends claimed to know anything about a boyfriend or stalker. Shayla had also talked to people she'd worked with and her teachers in school. Again, no red flags had surfaced.

Her thoughts kept returning to Ion. He'd deliberately tried to implicate her in his daughter's disappearance. What she didn't understand was why.

Maybe her father's idea had more merit than she'd first thought. If anyone could cut through the murky water, Poseidon could.

The instant she stepped onto dry land and retrieved her things, she looked at her cell phone. Two missed calls, one message and a text. Her mother had texted, her father had called, and the second call had come from an unknown number. She punched the button to listen to the message, astonished when she realized someone from the Pod had contacted her. Of course, she'd filed a report with them as soon as she'd taken on Nantha's case.

Of course she called them back first. Her parents could wait.

But she got voice mail. Disappointed, she left a message with her name and number. Her mother had texted a simple please call me when you get this, so that's what Shayla did next.

"Is Dad okay?" she asked the instant her mother answered.

"Yes. He's on his way back. He didn't have to visit Poseidon after all."

"Good." Then, realizing this meant something had happened, she asked, "What's going on?"

"Have you spoken to your brother?" Blythe asked, excitement making her voice high-pitched. Without waiting for an answer, she continued. "The Pod has contacted him. Apparently, they've learned of a trio of young Mermaids who were attempting to lure fishermen."

Which was against the law. The Pod and king, who at the time had been Shayla's father, had made such acts illegal and criminal. In these days where everyone had a cell phone that could take videos, the danger to the underwater kingdoms was too great.

Still, from time to time, a few wild and unruly teenagers became so full of themselves and their Mer-beauty that they couldn't resist trying out their songs on unwary fishermen. One time back in the 1970s, a couple of idiotic sixteen-year-olds had even caused a foreign tanker ship to sink. The Pod had worked hard to cover that up.

The last thing any Merfolk wanted was for humans to learn of their existence. Just like all the other paranormal beings, they'd enacted laws to keep that from happening.

"Interesting," Shayla commented. "I wonder if that's why someone from the Pod left me a message."

"Probably." Blythe's voice rose even higher. "Because there's more. They told your brother that one of the young Mermaids was Nantha Deangelo."

"What?" Though Shayla had been walking back up to her house, she stopped in her tracks. "Are you sure?"

"Yes. The two who were arrested confirmed it."

"Two?" A chill snaked up Shayla's spine, only partly

because she remembered her own imprisonment for the same crime. "Mom, what happened to Nantha?"

"That's just it." Her mother took a deep breath. "The girls were hysterical. They say she was captured. The very men they were trying to lure to their deaths grabbed Nantha and fled."

When Shayla phoned and asked him to come over to her house as fast as he could, Zach broke speed records. He was lucky he didn't get a ticket.

He rushed up the sidewalk. She opened the door before he even reached it.

"What is it?" he asked. "What's happened?"

"I've received some news about your sister. Come inside. Have a seat. You'd best be sitting down when I tell you."

Sitting down? Zach's gut twisted as he followed her into the kitchen. "So help me, if she's dead, just spit it out."

"She's not dead. At least, not that I know of. Sit." She pointed to the kitchen table as she went to the fridge and retrieved two bottles of beer. And then she proceeded to tell him what her mother had said.

"She what?" Staring at the beautiful Mermaid sitting opposite from him, Zach struggled to process the news. "I can't…"

She slid a beer across the table. "Here. I have a feeling you're going to need this."

Grateful, he took a deep drink. Once he'd carefully set the bottle down, he met her gaze again, ignoring the usual jolt of attraction. "You're saying my baby sister disappeared on purpose, at first."

"Right."

"And then she was getting her kicks trying to drown human fishermen when she was actually captured."

Shayla nodded. Without taking her eyes off him, she sipped her glass of wine. "And the humans who grabbed her know she's a Mermaid. This could spell disaster for not only our kind, but every paranormal species. The Pod is meeting with your Pack Protector and your council. They've invited the Vampire Council and all the others."

He swore. While what had happened carried a huge potential for disaster, he couldn't yet get past the shock of the betrayal. Nantha—sweet, always laughing, the baby girl Zach had carried around on his shoulder. His stepsister, Nantha, had let her entire adoring family think her dead or in danger. She hadn't given a single thought to how much pain her disappearance might have caused them.

And then she'd ended up getting captured after all. "I don't know whether to be furious or worried," he mused out loud.

"Hopefully if the other two Mermaids got a good look at the fishermen and their boat, we might have a chance of locating them. They're being interrogated by the Pod right now."

Dragging his hand through his hair, he nodded. "That would be helpful."

"Yes." She smiled at him over her wineglass. "It would."

He felt the pull of that smile, like a lure drawing him to her. For one crazy instant, he wondered how she'd react if he climbed up over the table and kissed her.

Instead, he forced himself to focus on her bewildering news. "Despite the gut-wrenching knowledge that my baby sister lied to us, the end result is the same. She's being held captive."

Her smile faded. "True."

"So if her captors are a couple of fishermen, what's with this demand for virgin Mermaids in exchange?" he asked, somehow keeping his voice level. Despite that, the warmth in Shayla's long-lashed emerald eyes told him she understood the emotions raging through him. "What's that all about?"

"The Pod is working to determine if that's real or if someone else who knows that happened is trying to cash in on your sister's capture," she said. "Consensus right now is that whoever has Nantha is most likely who sent the note. And called you. No one understands the virgin Mermaid request, though. That part is still unexplained." She swallowed. "And of course, we still need proof she's alive."

He winced. "About that. I didn't get a chance to tell you with all this going on, but they called again." Despite his attempt to sound unaffected, his voice broke. Dammit. "I asked to speak with her, for proof of life. As soon as I did, the caller hung up."

She went silent, no doubt reaching the same awful, stomach-turning conclusion he had. "Maybe," she ventured, summoning up a smile that had to be just for his benefit, "he didn't have access to her right then. He'll probably call back."

God, he hoped so. Right now, that was the only possibility he was prepared to face. "They'd better. I appreciate your effort to be positive." Restless, he got up, wishing he could get his hands on something to punch.

His inner Wolf, awakened by the turmoil inside him, grew restless. Zach realized right then what just might help release some tension. He needed to change and hunt. Let his Wolf out to run.

He decided that he would, after he finished this meeting with Shayla. His favorite place was north of Galveston Island, near his home in Texas City. Since he knew he'd need to deliver this news personally to his mother, he'd invite her to shape-shift and hunt with him that night after he told her.

"Does Ion know?" he asked. "I can only imagine how hard he'll take this news."

"I'm not sure." Shayla's mouth tightened. "But I'm thinking he would have been notified." She looked down before raising her head and meeting his gaze. "There's something I need to tell you. Ion went to my brother, the king, and filed a formal complaint against me. He claimed I had something to do with Nantha's disappearance."

Zach struggled to make sense of her words. "Why would he do that? I don't understand."

"Neither do I. If he's so worried about his daughter, why would he let his feelings against me take precedence over that? He must realize how much I intend to help search for her."

"I'm concerned about Ion." Zach took a swig of beer. "He's been acting odd ever since Nantha went missing. At first, I put it down to his concern over her disappearance. But he's been treating my mother weird, shutting both of us out. And now this."

Realizing he'd picked up his beer again, he took another gulp and then set it back on the table. "I'd better go," he said, his throat aching and his eyes stinging. "My mother's going to be devastated when she hears this."

The kindness in her expression nearly undid him. "I

understand. I'll call you if I receive any new information."

Later, when he pulled up to his mother's house, he killed the car engine and sat in the car instead of immediately going in. While he'd rehearsed numerous different ways to give her the news, in the end he understood the delivery didn't really matter. The end result remained the same. Nantha had done the inconceivable. And her blithe disregard for everyone else had resulted in her placing her own life in danger.

Finally, he got out of the car and headed up the sidewalk. There was a slight possibility that Ion, who'd surely been informed by now, had immediately traveled here to commiserate with his spouse. But judging by the way Ion had taken to remaining under the sea except for the occasional weekend, Zach doubted it.

Sure enough, when he walked into the house, he found his mom sitting in her recliner, reading.

"Zach!" She smiled and jumped up, giving him a quick hug. "Such a pleasant surprise."

"I wish it was." Gently he steered her back to her chair. "I think you should sit down."

His words wiped the smile from her face. She dropped back into her chair, hand to her chest. "It's Nantha, isn't it?" she asked. "Please don't tell me she's been killed."

"It's not that," he reassured her. "But I do have bad news of another kind."

She listened intently as he told her the information Shayla's Pod had passed on. June's expression changed as she realized the truth. "You're saying Nantha did this on her own? Let us believe she'd gone missing and worry ourselves sick?"

Slowly he nodded. "And because of that, she's gotten herself in real trouble."

June grimaced. "Does Ion know?" Then, before Zach could answer, she answered her own question. "Of course he does. The Pod would have notified her father first."

If she wondered why her husband hadn't come to her with the news, she didn't say it out loud.

"This is incredibly frustrating," she said, pushing herself up out of her chair, her jerky movements revealing her inner struggle. "I feel like I should do something, but I don't know what. These fishermen who grabbed her—do they mean her any harm?"

"That I don't know." He reminded her of the ransom note and call. When he told her of the most recent conversation and how he'd asked for proof of life only to have the call abruptly end, she blanched.

Inside, his Wolf had grown more and more agitated, likely in response to Zach's riotous emotions. "I thought I'd go hunt tonight," he said. "It's been a while, and my inner Wolf is restless. Do you want to join me?"

Immediately she nodded. "That might be the only way I can release some of this tension." She checked her watch. "Let's go now. It's certainly dark enough."

"Sounds great." He jingled his car keys.

"Oh, wait." The eagerness vanished from her expression. "Maybe I should stay here in case Ion shows up."

He managed to bite back the first thing that popped into his head. Casting aspersions against his stepfather would only make his mother feel worse. Instead, he managed to shrug. "That's up to you. But don't you think it's more likely Ion will arrive in the morning?"

Though she still hesitated, she finally nodded. "You're probably right. He hasn't come after dark since the early days of our marriage." The regret in her voice made him sad.

"Well then, come on." He needed to get her into the car before she changed her mind. "It's time for a little mother/son hunt."

"Yes, it is." Though her attempt at a smile was wobbly, it was a start.

He felt a little bit of the grimness inside lighten. "It's been way too long."

Once they reached the park, he noted there were two other cars in the lot. "I wonder if those people are still out on the trails," he mused. "Most times, humans won't go hiking after dark."

"That's true." She shrugged. "I'm not concerned. For all we know those cars could belong to other Shifters who came out here to hunt just like we did."

She had a point. "Are you ready?" he asked, his inner Wolf already half-giddy with anticipation of knowing he would soon be set free. "Meet you back here when we're finished?"

Instead of answering, she jumped out of the car and ran toward the woods. Feeling better than he had since Nantha vanished, he laughed and ran after her.

Once she entered the forest, she veered from the hiking trail, pushing through underbrush. He followed, knowing she wouldn't stop until they were sufficiently remote from all things human.

The smells here were different. Damp and musky, the earth seemed raw and primitive. The thicker undergrowth gave way to smaller paths, natural ones made by animals. Here, a Wolf could feel at home. Here, the hunting would be abundant.

"Does this look good?" June asked, dropping to all

fours without waiting for his confirmation. She already knew, because they'd come here to shape-shift before.

With a nod, he moved on past her, wanting to give her a little privacy while shifted.

For a second, he knew a sharp instant's regret that he could never share a hunt with Shayla. If she had been Shifter, he knew she'd make a beautiful Wolf. But she wasn't and would never be, so it was foolish to even think about. He tried to picture her in her natural shape, with a vibrant, shimmering tail, but couldn't. All he could think about was how she'd look naked, in his arms.

Pushing the thoughts away, he focused on his Wolf, eager to break free. Finally, he judged he'd gone far enough and began removing his own clothing, folding it neatly and placing it inside the backpack he used for exactly this purpose. And then he cleared his mind of everything but the moment at hand and dropped to the ground and began the change.

The sparkling lights, like fireflies, surrounded him. They seemed brighter this time, somehow. His Wolf, eager to burst free, tried to rush things, which always, without exception, meant pain. Zach forced his beast to wait, giving his human body time to make the adjustments to take him from man to beast.

His bones lengthened and changed shape. With excruciating clarity, he felt his pelt begin to grow, his skull become more angular. A flash of pain, here and there, quickly gone. Finally, filled with savage joy, he stood as Wolf, breathing in the moist scent of the damp earth and forest. In this form, his body felt compact, more muscular and much more in tune with nature. Wild and free, the burdens of his human existence fell.

When Wolf, he used his sense of smell first and his

vision second. Scenting the breeze with his nose, he determined his mother had already taken off and was heading north. Low to the ground and moving fast, he went after her.

He picked up the scent of others hunting in the woods this night, and by tacit agreement he avoided them and they him. Every once in a while, someone would organize a group hunt and several of the local Shifters would hunt as a pack, but with the popularity of drones these days, and the danger of exposure, those had become few and far between.

This, though, was different. A much-needed run through the forest, crashing through the underbrush at breakneck speed, uncaring if the smaller creatures heard him coming and fled. He'd hunt later. For now, he'd enjoy being a Wolf.

His mother must have felt the same way. At one point, she zipped past him, a lupine grin on her face, tail high in a jaunty wave. They ran circles around each other, and when they reached the meadow, he tackled her the way he'd used to when he'd been a younger pup. She rolled, and he went with her, joyous camaraderie filling his heart. This moment, his worries and cares as a human were nonexistent, as he lived completely in the moment.

They passed several hours in this fashion. Because of their dual nature, part human, part Wolf, shape-shifting regularly kept them healthy and vital. When they changed back to human, their focus would feel sharper, their senses keener. All due to the experience of becoming their other self. This was how life as a Shape-shifter had always been, each side taking something from the other and giving back a different set of rewards.

Most times after the play ended came the hunt. And

tonight would be no exception. He caught a careless rabbit and feasted, aware his mother most likely was doing the same somewhere else in the forest.

When he'd finished, he knew the time as Wolf had come to an end. Since time passed differently while in his Wolf form, he had no idea of the exact hour, but the sky had begun to lighten. That meant it would soon be dawn. Time to change back to human and go home.

When he arrived at the car, he saw his mother had gotten there before him. She waited in the passenger seat and waved at him.

"I feel much, much better," she said, once he'd gotten in and started the engine.

"Me, too." Though worry about Nantha had already started creeping back in, he pushed it away. His mother must have been doing the same thing, because neither of them spoke as he drove back to her house.

Once there, she invited him inside. "It's so late—or early, as the case may be."

He checked the clock, not surprised to see it was past four.

"You might as well see if you can grab a few hours of sleep before you head back to the city." She underscored her point with a yawn.

"You're right," he replied, not bothering to keep his weariness from showing in his voice.

Once inside, he saw how eagerly she glanced around the house, unable to keep from hoping Ion had shown up. Zach went to her and put his arm around her slender shoulders. "He'll be here tomorrow, I'm sure."

"I know." But her smile seemed sad anyway. "I'm going to go lie down. If you're still here when I get up, I can fix you eggs and bacon."

Though he hadn't planned to hang around that long, how could he abandon her when her husband apparently already had? He'd need to stay until Ion showed up, which better be first thing in the morning. Like in a few hours. This morning.

"Sounds great," he said, releasing her. "I've got to head back before noon, but I'll try to catch a few hours shut-eye first." And he wondered when Nantha's captors were going to call him again.

As it turned out, Zach didn't have to wait long for a second phone call. Again, Caller ID showed Unknown Number. And again, the caller used some sort of voice distortion software, making it impossible to tell if the voice belonged to a male or a female.

"Well?" the person demanded. "The clock is ticking. Have you got me what I want?"

"I'm not getting you anything until I know my sister is alive," Zach said, his voice flat and hard. "I need to speak to her."

Silence. His demand must have shocked the abductor.

So he repeated it. "I want to talk to my sister. Now."

The caller swore and ended the call.

Furious, Zach punched Redial. As before, he got the same recording. The call could not be completed as dialed. What did the refusal to let him speak with Nantha mean? His gut twisted. His baby sister had to be alive. The alternative wasn't acceptable.

The next night, Shayla called a meeting at Broken Chains. Maddie showed up before Carmen, so Shayla filled her friend in on the news.

"Wow." Maddie indicated the beer bottle. "I'm guessing Zach didn't take it well."

"No. But then, who would?" Shayla sighed and took a sip of her wine, waiting while Maddie caught the waiter's attention and ordered a drink.

"Are you okay?" Maddie asked, once she'd asked for her usual beer. "You look exhausted and stressed."

"Thanks." Grimacing, Shayla shook her head. "This case is weighing on me more than I thought it would. I can't stop thinking about Zach."

Tilting her head, Maddie studied her. "Are you... interested in him?"

Shayla sighed. "I'm not sure. Probably. Yes." She briefly covered her face with her hands. "I have feelings. I haven't allowed myself to explore, and I'm not at all sure he feels the same way."

"I thought so!" Maddie exclaimed, leaning forward. "I'm glad. It's about time."

The waiter delivered her beer just then, also bringing Shayla a second glass of wine, even though she hadn't finished her first.

"I have no expectations," Shayla confessed, after the waiter moved away. "He and I have never discussed it. The awareness is just there, simmering under the surface. At least on my part. Right now, it's a business relationship, you know that."

"Pffff." Maddie almost spit out her beer. "Why can't it be both?"

Shayla considered. "It's our first case. You know as well as I do that it can make or break the Shadow Agency. I want this venture to be a success. I can't jeopardize that simply because I'm attracted to him."

"I do, too. But he's a Shifter, and I strongly suspect he's Pack, like me. We're very physical beings. And I can see the electricity sparking between the two of you."

Intrigued, Shayla eyed her friend. "Can you really? Because it all felt one-sided to me. Maybe once his sister is found, we can pursue it and see where it goes."

Again Maddie made a rude sound. "Why wait? Throw the guy a bone. I'll bet he could use a little 'comfort' right about now." She winked.

Despite herself, Shayla felt her face heat. "I can't be the one to make the first move."

"Come on, now. You're a freakin' Mermaid! Isn't that what you people do, entice men?" Maddie leaned forward, taking Shayla's hand. "I know you were devastated over losing Richard, but it's been two years. In all the time I've known you, this is the first time I've seen you show interest in a man."

Chapter 8

Shayla didn't respond. She didn't have to. Her friend was right. And Maddie knew it, judging from the look on her face as she took a long drink of her beer.

"Promise me you'll at least try," Maddie pressed. "Even if it's just a little release-the-tension sex. I don't know a single male Shifter, or male anything for that matter, who wouldn't be up for that."

"Up being an appropriate term," Carmen drawled. She'd glided up to the table without anyone noticing. Though her sudden appearance startled Shayla, and Maddie too, since she'd jumped, they'd come to realize that was just her way. "Sorry," she told Shayla, sounding anything but. "I couldn't help but overhear most of that. Maddie's right. You've got to grab your chance for fun, for happiness, when you can. You know as well as anyone how quickly things can change."

Like what had happened with Richard. The familiar pang of grief came, though the sharpness of it had lessened over time. "You know what?" Shayla said, smiling at both of her friends. "You may be right. I'll never know until I try."

"That's the spirit," Maddie crowed. Carmen nodded, pulling out her chair and signaling the waiter, who immediately brought her a glass of her favorite blood.

"Such service," Carmen purred, looking the young waiter up and down with her long-lashed eyes. "Thank you very much."

He colored and dipped his head in acknowledgment. When he noticed the way Carmen's gaze fixed on the pulse beating at the base of his throat, he shook his head in bemusement and hurried off.

"Tasty treat, that one." Carmen smiled as she took a sip of her drink. "Mmmm. So where are we on the case?"

Shayla filled her in quickly, not leaving anything out. When she finished, Carmen sat in silence for a moment, digesting the words.

"Karma's a bitch, ain't it," she finally drawled. "You know, Shayla, if that girl made those fishermen fall in love with her, that's likely why they grabbed her. If that's the case, she's probably safe." She frowned. "The only thing that doesn't make sense is the request for virgins in exchange. That makes me think more of sacrificial rather than adored captive."

"Exactly." Shayla finished her first glass of wine. "My father even mentioned talking to Poseidon."

Both women stared. "The God of the Sea?" Carmen asked. "Seriously?"

Maddie closed her mouth. "Poseidon's a real…person?"

"Being," Shayla corrected. "He's kind of like the ultimate King of the Ocean. Immortal, powerful, et cetera, et cetera."

"All-knowing, all-seeing?" Carmen didn't bother to hide her skepticism. "If that's true, he could solve this case for us. I hope your father asks him. And soon."

"The only problem is Poseidon always demands a high price. More than money or things. Sometimes, the end doesn't justify the means. Now that we know more of the story, I don't think my dad will bother Poseidon."

"Unless you ask him to."

"Which I won't," Shayla said, her voice firm. She and Carmen had a stare-down for a few seconds. The Vampire had a bossy streak and knew it. The only way to deal with that was to be just as forthright.

Finally Carmen dipped her chin and conceded. "Fine. But think about how the client would feel if he knew there was such a simple solution."

"Contacting Poseidon isn't ever simple. And there's no guarantee he'd even help. He's been known to be quite capricious." Which was putting it mildly.

At least Carmen didn't try to argue with her this time. She simply took another sip of her drink, eyeing Shayla. "Then what else do you have planned to help solve this case?"

"I'm not sure. The captor has given us a short timeline. But until Zach is allowed to speak with his sister, we don't even know for sure she's alive."

"I've got my brother trying to trace the calls," Maddie said. "And both the Pack Protectors and the Pod are involved."

"Now that we know she did this deliberately and got snared in her own trap, our focus has shifted," Shayla pointed out. "The Pod are interviewing the other two Mermaids to pin down location and time. Once we have that, we can find out which fishing boats were in the area."

"Assuming whoever nabbed her is a commercial fisherman," Carmen pointed out. "If it was just a couple of guys out in a private boat, you might have a bit more trouble."

"True." Shayla smiled. "But we can talk to the marinas in the area and ask to see their surveillance cameras. Those will show anyone who went out fishing that day."

Carmen nodded. "You sound like you're pretty confident."

"I am. This additional information will help us find the kidnapper much more quickly."

"Before the week deadline is up," Maddie added, her voice hopeful.

"Do you have any idea if the fisherman was near Galveston?" Carmen asked. "Or farther down the coast, by Corpus or South Padre?"

"No. Mermaids sometimes swim great distances. Nantha and her friends could have been anywhere in the gulf. Louisiana, Mississippi, Alabama, even Florida. Though I'm hoping they were close to Texas. It'll make this guy much easier for us to locate."

"I'll chat up the local fishermen," Maddie said. "Though I don't think any of them will readily admit to seeing a Mermaid, once they have a few drinks they might mention someone they'd heard of who has."

"I'll go with you." Carmen shifted her weight in her chair. "And if there's anything else either of you can think of that I can do to help, let me know."

Shayla nodded. The band was about to start, which

meant they'd soon have to shout in order to be heard. In actuality, she wanted to take a break from talking about this case. And about Zach. Right now, more than anything, she needed to relax and recharge. Listen to music and hang out with her friends. Maybe even dance.

"What's this about Zach?" Carmen asked. "That's who you two were discussing when I walked up, right?"

Maddie grinned and answered. "That's right. I'm trying to convince Shayla to loosen up and have a fling."

"Please." Shayla fixed both her friends with a mock stern look. "I really don't want to talk about him anymore. Can't we just have a few drinks, enjoy the music and each other's company?"

Both Maddie and Carmen laughed.

"That's a cop-out," Carmen said. "I never figured you for being one who'd back down from a challenge."

"I'm not backing down. I just want to give it a rest for one night. Can't we do that? Please?" She took a long, deliberately slow drink of her wine to keep herself from saying anything even remotely combative. They definitely didn't need to start arguing among themselves. They'd been friends first, long before they'd formed the Shadow Agency and before a sexy Shifter named Zach had strolled into the bar.

Carmen, however, loved nothing more than a good fight. "I think you're afraid," she began, leaning forward. The lazily amused smile she flashed made Shayla clench her teeth. That, too, was unusual. Most times she found Carmen's machinations entertaining.

Looking from one to the other, Maddie laughed. It sounded forced, as if she, too, sensed the underlying tension. "Come on, you two. The workday is over. Can we just hang out and relax? The case will still be there tomorrow. So will Zach."

"Agreed," Shayla said instantly, greatly relieved. Though Carmen was a bit slower to respond, finally she nodded.

The music started, cutting off further conversation.

Tonight's band played upbeat dance music. Several couples got out on the small dance floor. This started a steady stream of single men approaching the table, asking one or the other of the three women to dance. Which was fun and perfect for Shayla's state of mind. While out there shaking and moving, she didn't have to think.

She danced until her feet hurt and she couldn't catch her breath. Back at the table alone, she begged off accepting another dance invitation, claiming she needed to take a break. She didn't invite the man—who appeared to be a Shifter—to sit down, even though he waited, clearly hoping she would. Finally, he got the hint and walked away.

Shayla motioned for a drink refill, and the waiter brought it, telling her someone at the bar had bought it for her. She shot a bland smile in that general direction, careful not to make eye contact. Though on any other night she might have welcomed masculine company, all she could think about was Zach. She wished he hadn't left, wished even more that she could have experienced being held in his arms while moving around the dance floor to a slow ballad.

Because if she'd had that opportunity, she'd find out if he wanted her. One of the things Merfolk excelled at while in human form was the art of seductive dance. She usually took great care to rein it in, like tonight. But with Zach, all gloves were off. She wanted him with the same intensity that she craved water. She wanted him as if she needed him to exist.

Stunned, she took a large slug of her wine. How had something this intense managed to slip by her? She'd known she found him attractive—hell, what woman wouldn't? But this longing, this desire, it went deeper than that.

She couldn't stop thinking about him. And not just because of the case.

When her phone rang and Caller ID revealed Zach's number, Shayla's heart skipped a beat. Though she wondered if she'd be able to hear over the music, she answered, cupping her hand around the phone at her ear to help.

"Are you still at Broken Chains?" he asked, sounding surprised. "I can hear the band."

"Yes." Again the longing. "We're hanging out, doing a little drinking, some dancing. I'm thinking we might close the place down." Especially since both Maddie and Carmen were still on the dance floor. They'd only been back for a minute or two here and there before someone else appeared to drag them back out. Since Shayla had perfected the art of cold disinterest, she'd reached the point now where men were leaving her alone. If she wanted to dance she simply picked one, got up and asked him. As of yet, no one had turned her down.

"Wow." Zach went silent, which was a good thing as she wouldn't have been able to hear him over the guitar solo.

As soon as that song ended, the band announced their last song and launched into a slow one. The bartender yelled out "Last call," and the waiter appeared to ask if she needed one more drink. Though Shayla shook her head, Maddie and Carmen rushed up, both asking for another. Maddie looked flushed and out of breath, but happy. Even Carmen appeared tons more relaxed. Their dance partners had followed them back to the table, but both women waved them away.

"What time does the bar close?" Zach finally asked.

Shayla half turned away so she could continue the conversation. "In an hour. It's nearly five a.m.," she said. Out of respect to their Vampire clientele, Broken Chains closed at 6:00 a.m. "What's wrong? I have to think the only reason you would call me this late is because something happened."

He sighed. "I couldn't sleep and I just wanted to hear your voice."

Her heart stuttered, and she nearly choked. Catching both Maddie and Carmen eyeing her, she got herself back under control. There were several ways she could respond to that, none of them anything she wanted her friends to hear. She wasn't even sure she'd have the courage to say them out loud. Especially not in front of an audience. The music helped, but both Shifters and Vamps had really good hearing.

"Are you okay?" she asked, her voice softening as the last notes of the song played. The band thanked the room, people drifted back to their tables and many of the other customers began to leave. The band began packing their instruments. At least she could hear much clearer. But then everyone else could also hear her.

"I'm trying to be." His candor shocked her. "But there are times when it's not working. My mom and I hunted tonight. We got back about an hour ago. She didn't take the news well and both of us needed to blow off some steam. I hope that enabled her to get some rest."

Clearly, it hadn't helped him. Yet the knowledge he'd been thinking of her while lying awake in his bed made her feel tingly inside. She fell silent while she tried to think up something to say.

"I'm sorry." His tone changed, becoming clipped. "I can tell you're busy. Tell Maddie and Carmen hello for me. I'll talk to you tomorrow." Abruptly, he hung up.

Shayla stared at her phone, wondering if she should call him back and ask him what had just happened.

"Earth to Shayla." Maddie nudged her. "What's going on? Who was that? You're acting strange."

"Even weirder than normal," Carmen interjected. "What gives?"

"It was Zach," Shayla admitted. "He's having trouble sleeping. That's all."

Her two friends exchanged a look. "Really?" Carmen drawled. "That's interesting. Does he want you to come over?"

"No. It wasn't a booty call or anything like that. He's worried about his sister."

"Uh-huh." Maddie shook her head. "So he called you at five a.m.? Nope. I think it was definitely a booty call."

This time, the good-natured teasing just made Shayla smile. Because inside she wished it had been a booty call. Who knew, maybe she could have helped steer the conversation that way. Maybe the fact that she'd been in a bar instead of at home in bed had given Zach second thoughts. "Are you guys ready to go?" she asked.

"Sure." After downing the last of their drinks, Maddie and Carmen gathered their things. They made it a rule to stay together for safety's sake, especially this late at night, or early in the morning. This rule was generally to protect Shayla, since both Carmen and Maddie could easily protect themselves.

Along with several other patrons, they filed from the bar and into the long, narrow alley. Once they reached the street, they turned right, still moving along with a few others. The group thinned as they left the warehouse area, many melting away to return to their own homes or haunts.

Shayla couldn't wait to get home and climb into her bed. She knew once she closed her eyes, she'd dream of Zach.

Dammit. Staring at his cell phone after hastily ending the call, Zach cursed whatever urge had compelled him to give in to the need to hear Shayla's voice. What if she'd been sleeping instead of hanging out at the bar? How would she have reacted to having a client wake her?

He needed to remember that's exactly what he was to her. A client. No more, no less. These aching longings to see her, touch her, hear her, were aberrations he should put aside. At least until Nantha was found. After that, maybe Shayla would be amendable to exploring a different kind of relationship. Hopefully, one that involved nakedness and limbs tangling in the bedsheets.

He burned at the carnal images as he imagined Shayla, her perfect skin gleaming, under him in his bed. The stab of desire made him groan. Already aroused, he almost rushed to take a cold shower to cool himself off.

But he didn't. Instead, he handled his arousal with the same methodical precision he applied to daily problems at work. Not by giving himself release, oh, no. He wanted that to be with Shayla. He'd let the need continue to build, the better to savor the rush and the eventual explosion when they came together.

So instead, he forced himself to think of other things. Like where the hell was Ion when his wife needed him?

Somehow, he must have dozed off. When he next opened his eyes, the sun had fully risen, and he could smell bacon frying. Which meant June was already up and making breakfast. Perfect. He'd grab a bite to eat while waiting for Ion. And then once his stepfather had showed, Zach would head back to his own home before planning the rest of his day.

Hopefully, Ion would have some more information about Nantha. He'd think his stepfather would have talked to the Pod or something. Because right now, Zach felt as if they'd reached an impasse. Aside from somehow rustling up a couple of virgin Mermaids who were willing to become sacrifices, Zach had no idea what to do. Other than talk to Shayla and the rest of the Shadow Agency and see if they could come up with any other ideas. The caller had given them one week. With each passing day, they were running out of time.

"Good morning!" Smiling at him, June appeared chipper and in an excellent mood. Only the dark circles under her red-rimmed eyes and the downward slant to her mouth told a different story. Like always, when she was upset, she liked to keep busy. She cooked and cleaned, often baked. Like now. It appeared she'd actually been up a while. Three cakes, several dozen cookies and a batch of muffins were testament to how badly Nantha's disappearance—and her husband's conspicuous absence—had affected her.

"Mornin'," he said, managing to smile back.

"I hope you're hungry."

"I am." His stomach rumbled, as if to prove a point.

"Good. Because I made enough to feed both you, me, Ion and a small army."

Her rueful smile tugged at his heart. He could feel the twinges of a headache coming on. "Mom, I'm sure Ion will be here soon."

"He'd better be." Filling a plate with scrambled eggs, bacon, toast and several strawberries, she carried it over to him. "In the meantime, eat as much as you want."

"It looks delicious." And smelled like heaven, too. "Have you already eaten?" he asked as she poured him a mug of coffee, setting it in front of him before she retreated to stand over by the stove, where she had a clear view out the window of the ocean.

"I'm not hungry." Grimly, she drank from her coffee cup, still staring.

"Come on, Mom," he coaxed. "Please come and sit and have breakfast with me. I won't feel right eating unless you do."

The loudness of her sigh told him she knew exactly what he was doing. Still, it worked. She put a little food on a plate and sat down across from him.

Now he could dig in. His mother even took a few bites, though mostly she just watched him eat.

"Ion's not answering his phone," she finally said, her inner pain coming through clear in her voice. "I'm not sure why."

"Maybe he went too deep," Zach reassured her. The Merfolk had developed phones that worked underwater, but only to a certain depth. If they traveled beyond that, the phone stopped working, until they came back up.

"Maybe," she allowed. But she didn't sound convinced. Still, she took a couple more bites of scrambled egg, nibbled on a piece of bacon, and some of the tension seemed to dissipate from her posture. "This has really affected him, Zach. And now knowing she did it deliberately? I just don't understand why Nantha would do something like this. I mean, she likes a good joke and can be mischievous, but nothing like this. It's not like her at all."

A few days ago, he would have said the exact same thing. Now, he had to wonder if he'd truly ever known his baby sister at all. Because the Nantha he'd believed he knew would never have hurt her family like this. Not for anything or anyone. There had to be more to the story. Or, being a teenager, she hadn't really thought things through.

And Ion's rapid personality change made Zach wonder if there was something the Merman knew, some secret he kept hidden from his wife and stepson.

After Zach had eaten his fill, he helped his mother bag up the leftovers and stow them in the fridge. He tried to shoo her out so he could do the dishes, but she refused. "You know I have to stay busy," she told him. "If I don't have something to occupy myself, I think too much."

He understood. Instead, he poured himself another cup of coffee and carried it out to his mother's huge back porch. From there, one could see not only the ocean, but all up and down the beach. He even had a clear view of the rocky outcropping that the Merman used when he came ashore.

Aside from a few humans sunbathing, the beach appeared deserted. As for the sea, while Zach could make out the silhouette of a tanker way out in the bay, he saw no signs of any larger sea creature breaking the surface of the water.

Noon came and went and still no sign of Ion. Though he knew his mother no doubt kept trying to reach her husband, Zach stepped outside and dialed his stepfather's number. The call went straight to voice mail.

Damn. He glanced at his watch. He really needed to get back home.

Impulsively, he placed a call to Shayla. She answered on the first ring, sounding surprisingly chipper for someone who'd closed down a bar a few hours earlier.

"Any news?" he asked. "My stepfather hasn't come to fill my mother in and he's not answering his phone. She's getting pretty worried about him."

"Nothing," she replied, the warmth in her voice instantly making him want her. "But I'll be sure to let you know if anything changes."

"Same here." He ended the call, turning to go back inside when his phone rang. Thinking Shayla must have thought of something else she wanted to say, he answered. "What'd you forget?"

"Zach?" Not Shayla. The unknown caller. "I understand you wanted to speak to your sister."

Instantly every nerve went on alert. "That's correct."

"Here she is." Silence, then someone moaned.

"Talk to your brother." This time, the caller forgot to digitally alter his voice. Clearly a man.

"Zach?" Nantha. Sounding weak, but still Nantha. Alive. "It's me. I'm… I'm sorry." She sounded as if she was about to cry.

Nantha's tears were one thing Zach had always been powerless against. Now, though, his relief was so great he couldn't allow them to bother him. "Are you all right?" he asked.

"I'm alive. They don't hurt me. And now that they

know I have to be in the seawater, I feel much better. I almost died, I think—"

"Enough." The abductor came back on the line. This time, he'd gone back to disguising his voice. Though tempted to tell him not to bother since he'd already heard him, Zach kept his mouth shut.

"Now, you have your proof of life. What about my demands? Are you ready to make the exchange?"

"Virgin Mermaids are kind of hard to come by," Zach said. "Surely there must be something else you want. Money, maybe?" He held his breath, hoping the caller didn't demand some outrageous amount like ten million dollars. Coming up with that would be as impossible as finding two virgin Mermaids willing to be sacrificed.

"Five days," the caller snarled. "And then she dies." He ended the call.

Zach swore. And swore again. He went back inside the house to find his mother cooking something else. This time, she appeared to be mixing batter with a grim sort of determined concentration.

"I talked to Nantha," he said.

Her expression lit up, just like that. "She's alive?"

"Yes. I didn't get to talk to her long, but it was definitely her."

June cried out. She gave him a fierce hug. "Thank goodness." Grabbing her phone off the kitchen counter, she smiled through her happy tears. "I need to tell Ion."

But as she listened, her smile slipped a notch. "No answer," she finally said, ending the call. "I don't understand what's going on with him. I know he's heartbroken and I understand he's searching under the sea, but he doesn't answer the phone at all anymore, never mind return my calls when I leave a message."

She lifted her chin, trying for bravery, though hurt shone from her eyes. "It's like once Nantha disappeared, he did, too."

"I'm sorry, Mom." He didn't know what else to say. "Hopefully once everything gets back to normal, he will, too."

"I hope so." Sniffing, she returned her attention back to her baking. "I'm making an angel food cake. Your favorite."

"I've got to go," he told her, dropping a careful kiss on her cheek. "Are you going to be okay here alone?"

"Yep." Her instant response came too quickly. "And I'll keep the cake refrigerated so you can have some the next time you're here."

"Sounds good." As he turned to go, she caught at his arm.

"Zach, please find your sister. I know she's done wrong, and she might be in a heap of trouble down there under the sea, but she's still my girl. I love her." Her voice wobbled, and her eyes filled with tears.

"Of course we're going to find her." He took her hand. "Don't you ever doubt that."

"I don't." Her immediate answer made him smile. "Promise you'll call me if you learn anything?"

"I promise." As he let himself out the door, he cursed Ion. While he understood his stepfather's pain, his mother needed her husband, too. They should have been able to lean on each other for support during this trying time. Instead, Ion had pulled away, retreating into his own world.

Chapter 9

As he got into his car, Zach found himself thinking of Shayla. Wondering where she was, what she might be doing. He even got his phone out with the intention of calling her. Instead, he stopped himself.

Shayla had become a distraction of epic proportions. And right now, he couldn't allow himself to be distracted. Once Nantha was found and returned home safely, then and only then could he afford to explore the connection between them.

Mind made up, he dropped his phone into the cup holder and started the car to head home. He'd just gotten to the seawall where he planned once again to look for any sign of Nantha, when his phone rang.

Shayla's name popped up on the screen. His heart skipped a beat. "What's up?" he asked.

"I have a plan," she said, sounding upbeat and well rested.

"Great. What is it?"

"I've got some work to do before I can talk about it, since it's so urgent. Once I know more, I'd prefer to discuss it with you in person, along with Maddie and Carmen. Can you meet us at Broken Chains tonight? I'm thinking early, before the band shows up. How's six sound?"

"I'll be there." Deliberately he kept his tone business-like. If she noticed, she didn't comment. He had to admit he was interested to hear her plan.

Shayla felt energized. The idea for saving Nantha had come to her while showering. She couldn't believe she hadn't thought of it before.

It would work. It had to. The time had come to be proactive rather than reactive.

She practically inhaled an early dinner before heading to Broken Chains. When she arrived, shortly after five thirty, to her surprise, there were still quite a few other customers there.

"Happy Hour," the waitress told her when she asked. "We have a special one for Saturdays. People come after shopping. They usually leave before the second crowd arrives." She smiled. "The late-night customers, the ones who come to hear the band and drink and dance."

"So there's not really any time the bar is less crowded?" Shayla asked.

"Between six a.m. and noon, but we're closed then."

They both laughed. Shayla went ahead and ordered her wine. She hoped everyone arrived right about the same time. She didn't want to reveal any details of her plan until they were all present. And she knew her friends would immediately start bugging her to spill.

To her surprise, Zach walked into the bar less than five minutes after her drink arrived. Since there wasn't live music yet, she'd taken a table downstairs, the same one in the back corner that she'd come to think of as hers.

As soon as she saw him, her entire body tingled. She was about to wave, but he saw her, so she didn't have to.

Approaching the table, he locked his gaze on hers. She resisted the urge to lick her lips.

"Where are your friends?" he asked, pulling out the chair next to her.

She shrugged. "Not here yet. You're early."

"So are you." He grinned as the waitress, unasked, brought him a beer. "How'd you know?" he asked, after thanking her.

Her smile was deliberately coy. "I've seen you around in here. Don't look so surprised. A guy who looks like you must be used to that."

Zach's thunderstruck expression made both women laugh. The waitress walked off, still chuckling.

"Was she serious?" Zach asked, as he took a sip of his beer.

"Of course she was." Tilting her head, she studied him. "Seriously, are you kidding me?"

He frowned. "About what?"

Maddie and Carmen arrived then, saving her from answering. Still frowning, Zach greeted them.

"What's with the sour face?" Carmen asked, blunt as always.

Unfortunately, this question made Shayla laugh again. "Zach's not used to receiving compliments," she said, and told them what the waitress had said.

Maddie and Carmen looked from Shayla to Zach and back again. "Okay," Maddie commented.

Carmen shook her head. "Come on, Shayla. You're just as bad. Men are falling all over you if you even so much as smile at them."

"No, they're not."

Shayla's instant protest had the other two women giggling.

"See?" Carmen finally said.

Shayla glanced at Zach, who shrugged. The waitress, who evidently had been paying attention to every one of them, brought Maddie's usual beer and Carmen's tall glass of blood.

"Bavarian opera singer," the waitress said, in response to Carmen's arched brow.

"Perfect." Carmen flashed her dazzling white teeth. "Thank you."

Once the waitress left, Zach leaned forward. "Okay. We're all here. Tell me your plan."

"Yes," Maddie echoed.

Shayla took a deep breath. "You know how the captor wants two virgin Mermaids? We'll tell him we got one."

"What?" Carmen spoke first. "Are you serious?"

"Perfectly serious."

As of yet, Zach hadn't reacted. Instead, he crossed his arms and leaned back in his chair. "Where are you planning to come up with a virgin Mermaid?"

"It won't be a real virgin," she assured him. "But they won't know that. Not up front."

"I don't follow," he said slowly.

"I'll do it," she told him. "I'll pretend to be a virgin Mermaid. I can be the bait to get Nantha back."

Immediately Maddie and Carmen protested. "No way. That'd be too dangerous," Maddie said.

Carmen was more direct. "Don't be stupid here, Shayla. We kind of like having you around."

Zach just stared, his expression shut down. She couldn't read his thoughts at all.

"I'm serious," she reiterated, her eyes locked on his. "Clearly we've got to make some kind of an exchange. And we can't endanger any innocents. I'm a Mermaid, and it looks like I'm going to have to do."

"What makes you think they'll believe you're a virgin?" he drawled, his gaze intense.

Though she could feel her face heat, she stood her ground. "How are they going to know I'm not?" she countered. "There's only one way to tell for sure, and I'm not letting them go anywhere near there." With a rush of horrified shock, she realized what she'd just said also applied to his sister. And since the abductor already claimed to know Nantha wasn't a virgin...

"Of course, maybe they'll take my word for it," she hastened to add.

Carmen laughed. Maddie just shook her head and took a deep drink of her beer, her expression troubled.

But the person whose opinion most mattered said nothing. Shayla eyed him and waited.

Finally, he shifted in his chair, locking his gaze on her. "You know what?" he said, his tone firm. "I don't like you putting yourself in danger like that."

She grimaced. "It's not like we're going in blind. We have backup—each other. Besides that, what other options do we have?"

Expression furious, he considered. She saw in his gaze the moment he decided to go along with her plan.

"You're right. It's an excellent idea, and it just might work."

Maddie groaned. With eyes only for each other, Shayla and Zach ignored her.

"I'm glad you think so." Her original excitement had come back, thrumming in her veins. "What should we do next? Do you have a way to contact them?"

"No. But I should be talking to them soon. All I need to do is wait for them to call me again, which they hopefully will. When they do, I'll just say I could only come up with one Mermaid, and they'll have to take it or leave it."

"Perfect." Delighted, Shayla sipped her wine. "I feel better now that we have a plan. But, Zach, please don't say anything to Ion or your mother. I can't let the Pod find out about this or they'd put a stop to it. Somehow they seem to frown on royal princesses putting themselves in danger."

"You won't be at risk." Zach's immediate response made her feel all warm and fuzzy. "I won't let anything happen to you."

"Zach, you don't know Shayla that well," Maddie put in. Shayla shook her head at her friend.

"She can be impetuous," Carmen added. "She doesn't always think things through. And I for one am worried this is one of those times."

"Maybe you could pretend to be the Mermaid," Maddie said, meaning Carmen.

"Wouldn't work," Shayla answered. "Especially if you have to swim. With my natural tail, I can swim faster than a Great White. I can definitely outswim any human."

"What if they shackle you?" Carmen interjected. "I

really think you should rethink this idea. There's got to be a better way to rescue Nantha."

"If there is, we haven't come up with it," Shayla said, glancing at Zach, glad he agreed with her.

But now, his expression appeared troubled. As he met her gaze, he shook his head. "Maybe they're right," Zach said slowly. "Shayla, I can't let you put your life in danger. We've got to come up with a better idea."

"I can take care of myself," she protested, thinking furiously. "Plus Carmen can go with me. We can both be the virgins they want. She's immortal and freakishly strong."

Carmen grinned at the compliment. "Agreed."

This addition to her plan appeased both Maddie and Zach.

"I like it," Maddie said, smiling.

"Me, too," Zach agreed, finally leaning back in his chair.

Shayla couldn't help it—she laughed. "I give up. I love the way none of ya'll think I'm strong enough."

"It's not that," Zach hastened to explain. "It's just we feel better knowing we have backup."

Slowly, she nodded. The warmth in his eyes made her blood heat.

"By the way," he said, low-voiced. "I love the way you laugh."

Instantly, she blushed. Carmen and Maddie laughed. And once again, things were back to normal.

Though he'd agreed to try it, the more he thought about it, the less Zach liked Shayla's plan. Having Carmen as backup was reassuring, but Shayla was a royal

Mer-Princess. But, as she'd pointed out, at least they were doing something as opposed to before.

The women chatted away, drinking and laughing, as if two of them hadn't just decided to put themselves in grave danger. And now that Shayla had brought it up, the virgin aspect bothered him. He hadn't thought of his sister that way at all. Thinking about what Nantha's captors must have done to her to make that determination had him clenching his teeth and plotting their death. How dare they?

He also realized the idea of anyone putting their hands on Shayla was enough to make him go ballistic. Damn Nantha. What the hell had she been thinking to pull a stunt like this? Not only had she endangered her own life, but the lives of others.

Of course, the fact that she wasn't a virgin had probably been what saved Nantha's life, at least if the sacrificial theory was correct. He truly didn't understand the whole virgin thing. Virginity was overrated as far as he was concerned.

Looking up, he realized all three of the women had gone silent. They stared at him, Carmen with her perfectly arched brows raised, Maddie with a look of amusement quirking her lips and Shayla with what had to be exasperation. "Overrated, huh?" she asked, making him realize he must have spoken his thoughts out loud.

"Just so you know," she continued before he could speak, lifting her chin to meet his gaze. "I'm hoping we can stall them long enough to get your sister free. I'm not planning on being around them long enough for them to be able to check out whether I'm a virgin or not."

Relieved, he nodded. There was no way someone as passionate as Shayla could be untouched. As soon as he had the thought, he squashed it. While her love life was none of his business, at least she wasn't at risk of being sacrificed—or whatever it was they wanted to do to the poor virgins. However, the abductor might be so infuriated to learn he'd been lied to, he might just kill her and be done with it. Even with Carmen there to back her up, there was no way her safety would be guaranteed.

He didn't know what he'd do if he lost her. A shudder snaked up his spine at the thought. "I still have reservations," he began.

"We'll be fine," Carmen said immediately.

Shayla echoed her response.

"You know I feel really left out," Maddie interjected, sitting up really straight. "I want in. Let me be part of this, too."

Shayla included him in her smile. "I only need one other 'virgin' Mermaid. Maddie, I think it would be better if you stayed here to hold down the fort. You know we just started advertising. It might not be long before someone else might need our services."

Though disappointment clouded her pretty features, Maddie nodded. Meanwhile, Carmen looked like a cat who'd just finished eating a canary. "No worries, Zach. I can pretend to be a Mermaid," she drawled. Swiveling her head around to eye Zach, she smiled. "And I can protect her."

"Thanks," he told Carmen, before turning back to Shayla. "I'll agree to go forward with this plan. But I'm going with you."

"What?" Shayla shook her head so vigorously, that her long, inky hair whipped around her head. He ached to wrap his fingers in that hair, and pull her to him. "No, you're not. Having you there would negate the entire thing. They'd know it was some sort of setup."

"I disagree. Since I'm supposedly the one making the exchange, it's only right that I'd be there to make sure everything went off without a hitch." He folded his arms, aware he wasn't going to budge on this.

Again they locked gazes. His entire body tightened and his mouth went dry. Even now, the attraction sparking between them felt palpable. Talk about the worst possible timing. He refused to look away until she agreed. Finally, she nodded. "Fine. You're right. When the abductor phones you again, set up the exchange."

Relieved, he smiled. Now he could only hope his sister was all right. And that he and Shayla and the Vampire could pull this off without anyone getting hurt. Except, he amended grimly, the abductors. They could rot in hell for all he cared.

"I'm going to say I told you that I know he is the son of a famous movie producer and that he wanted to make both of you famous. That's how I got you to agree to go with me to meet him."

"Perfect," Shayla exclaimed, the admiration in her beautiful eyes making them glow. "Good thinking."

His body stirred in response. Whatever it was about this woman, the connection between them begged to be explored. Which he would, once all this craziness was over.

After finishing his beer, he excused himself and left. On his way toward the exit, he couldn't keep himself from glancing back over his shoulder. As he'd hoped and suspected, Shayla was watching him, too. Once again, their gazes locked, and that zing of attraction sparked.

Damn. Resolutely, he turned back around and headed for the door.

* * *

The next day, he kept busy. After slugging down his first cup of coffee, he went back to Galveston Island to begin another round of checking posters and asking people if they'd seen Nantha. Though he knew she was being held captive somewhere, he still cherished a hope that someone might have spotted her right before she was grabbed. At least then, he'd have a basic idea what general area she might be in.

Also, staying busy kept him from wondering if her captor would call him again. Since the clock was rapidly ticking, he figured the calls might escalate to every day.

When his phone rang, he actually jumped. Again, Caller ID said Unknown Caller.

"Well?" the abductor asked, again using the voice distortion software. "Your sweet little sister is just about out of time."

"I have what you want." Zach didn't bother to hide his rage. "Two virgin Mermaids. They think they're going on a fun adventure, so they're coming willingly. I told them you're related to a well-known movie producer and want to make them famous." He took a deep breath. "They bought it. When and where do you want to meet?"

His response apparently surprised the other guy, judging from the silence on the line. When he spoke again, he sounded uncertain. "You seriously have them? Are you sure they're virgins?"

"Very sure." Zach put a slight sneer into his voice. "I took the time to have them examined by a doctor. I told them it was to make sure they were healthy."

"Wonderful." The man appeared to believe him. "We will meet tonight down by the Pleasure Pier."

"That's too crowded," Zach protested. "There's too much of a chance of being seen."

"And that's exactly why I chose it. Your sister will be in human form. Make sure the other two are, as well. We'll meet there, and you can take Nantha, while I'll leave with the others. Ten tonight. It'll be good and dark by then."

Though every internal alarm clanged a warning, Zach agreed to the meeting. As soon as he hung up, he phoned Shayla and told her the plan.

"Perfect," she said. "The only thing we've got to be careful of is the darkness." Her brusque tone told him she was already thinking ahead. "Let me get ahold of Carmen. We'll meet you at the pier at nine. That'll give us time to scope the place out."

If he hadn't known better, her confidence would have him believing she'd done this before.

"Fine." Hating himself, he ended the call and began to pace. He had just a few hours to come up with a foolproof plan to ensure he didn't mess this up. He decided to arrive an hour early.

Fifteen minutes before nine, he parked his car and killed the engine. Despite his best efforts, the uncertainty of the situation had rendered him unable to mark out a clear and certain path. He'd actually jotted down several different variables, each a potential action by Nantha's captor. For those, he'd come up with possible reactions, which made him feel slightly more prepared.

The two women sat on one of the numerous benches on the long pier. They looked like typical tourists. Shayla had chosen to wear a bright floral sundress while Carmen wore neat Bermuda shorts and a tank top.

Shayla looked at him as if he'd sprouted two heads

when he told her what he'd done. "You outlined every possible scenario?" she asked in disbelief. "That's unreal."

"I'm an engineer," he said with a shrug. "That's just how we think."

Carmen snickered. "He's right, you know. One of my best friends is an engineer, and that's exactly how she is."

Surprised to find her an unexpected ally, he grinned. "Truth. And it comes in handy ninety percent of the time."

Shayla snorted and rolled her eyes. With that, the tension that had crackled in the air around them dissipated like smoke in a stiff breeze.

Still, time seemed to crawl. Finally, at 9:45, they all looked at each other.

"Let's do this," Shayla said. "I'm ready."

"I am, too," Carmen chimed in.

"Okay, Mermaids. Remember, the cover story is that this guy is the son of a famous movie producer. He's offered you both a chance at fame and fortune."

The two women exchanged amused glances. "Got it," they drawled.

Even at this late hour, there were still plenty of people on the pier. While this made Zach a bit nervous, he also found it oddly reassuring.

They were early, so they had plenty of time to wander around and check out the pier. Shayla and Carmen were acting like vapid schoolgirls, hanging on to each other and giggling. Since he figured Shayla would know better than anyone else how a virgin Mermaid would act, he pretended to humor them. All the while he kept a sharp eye out for anyone resembling his younger sister. To his immense disappointment, he didn't see her.

Yet. Or so he told himself.

Right before ten, Zach picked a spot closer to the carnival rides and stationed himself there. He had Shayla and Carmen take seats on a metal bench. Their backs were to the ocean, and a snow-cone shack provided a buffer to their right and a corn-dog stand to their left. This way, they could only be approached straight on. Much more easily defensible. Carmen caught his eye and dipped her chin, indicating her approval.

A few minutes after ten, Zach felt as wound up as a starving wolf closing in on a plump rabbit. He scanned the face of every single person who came in their direction. None of them had his stepsister's unique blue eyes.

"Excuse me." A man wearing a Houston Astros baseball cap bumped into him, hard enough to make Zach stagger. "I'm looking for the men's room," he mumbled, sounding drunk.

Instinctively, Zach recoiled. But the stranger leaned in close. "If you want your sister, follow me." And then took off, weaving through the crowd.

"That was him," Zach said. "We need to go after him."

They rushed after the man, keeping his baseball cap in their sights as he dodged people. He appeared to be alone, which meant if he truly planned to turn over Nantha, he'd stashed her somewhere else.

They couldn't risk losing him.

Finally, he left the pier, heading for the parking lot of a crowded seafood restaurant. Though Zach found that choice both odd and questionable, he had no option but to go after him. Patrons were coming and going, and cars circled the lot searching for a place to park.

"I don't get it," Zach murmured to Shayla, who stuck

close by his side. She shrugged, her attention focused on their quarry. Carmen's was too, her expression intense.

Instead of going inside the restaurant, the man went around to the back. More parking, most likely for the staff, and an industrial-size trash Dumpster enclosed on three sides by a six-foot fence.

The man stopped in front of the Dumpster and waited for them to catch up. He looked the two women up and down, leering. "Are these the two you promised?" he asked, his voice husky.

Zach had to bite back his disgust. He bet Shayla and Carmen did too, though he didn't dare look at them to see.

"Where's my sister?" Zach asked.

"She's here."

"Prove it." Somehow, Zach suspected she wasn't. He wouldn't be surprised if this guy didn't make a grab for Shayla and Carmen without turning over Nantha. At least he knew the two of them would be prepared in case this happened.

"Just a second." Boldly, the man circled around the women, inspecting them. "I need proof they're Mer."

Damn. The one thing they hadn't prepared for.

Maybe he hadn't, but Shayla must have. Still pretending eager anticipation, she pulled a photo from her pocket and handed it over. "Here. It's me, with my fish tail. It'll have to do, since obviously I can't change into my Mermaid shape right here."

He studied the photo before passing it back. "What about you?" he asked, turning to Carmen.

With a bored expression that didn't quite hide her rage, she, too, handed over a photograph. This had to be something she'd doctored, so Zach hoped it looked convincing. Evidently it did, as baseball cap guy nodded and returned it to her.

"Now, about my sister?" Zach asked, his hard voice matching his expression.

"Right." Moving toward the Dumpster, the other man slid it open. Inside, a clearly terrified Nantha stared out at them. A second glance showed she was not only gagged, but her hands were tied behind her back.

Chapter 10

Zach saw red. The effort to contain a rage unlike any he'd ever felt had him struggling to keep his inner Wolf contained. His beast snarled and fought like a crazed beast to escape. It took every ounce of strength Zach had to keep him contained. He knew better than to shift to Wolf unless absolutely necessary.

Shayla must have noticed. She bumped him with her hip. "What's all this?" she asked in a petulant voice. "Where's the movie guy? What's the deal with the girl in the Dumpster?"

"Yeah," Carmen chimed in. "Is this some kind of a hoax? Because I'm thinking it's not very funny."

Their playacting bought Zach the time he needed to get himself under control. "All in good time," he told Shayla. "Be patient."

Though they huffed and puffed, they nodded. Then

he turned to the stranger. "Release my sister," Zach demanded.

"Get her yourself."

As Zach helped Nantha climb out of the garbage-filled Dumpster, he first removed her gag. Instead of speaking, she gasped, sucking in great lungfuls of air. Tears welled up in her huge eyes, and she began shaking.

"It's okay," Zach told her, his fingers fumbling as he struggled to remove her bonds. "You're safe. You're coming home with me."

He barely had her free when she caught sight of Shayla. Her eyes widened as she stared, clearly shocked. "Your Highness?" she asked. "What are you doing here?"

Before Shayla could answer, two men appeared from around the back side of the Dumpster. They were both armed, with their pistols pointed directly at Zach and Shayla. Another gun suddenly showed up in the hand of the guy in the baseball cap. "Nobody move," he ordered.

Zach shoved Nantha toward Carmen. If anyone could get his sister to safety, she could since Vampires had supernatural speed. "Carmen. Take her and run," he shouted.

To her credit, the Vamp didn't hesitate. She snatched Nantha up as if she were weightless and took off, holding the young Mermaid in her arms as she sprinted away.

Though Zach braced himself for the three men to shoot, they did not. Instead, they kept their attention—and weapons—on Zach and Shayla. Zach considered jumping them, since regular bullets couldn't kill him, only silver ones could. But he figured bullets most likely would be fatal to Shayla, and he simply couldn't risk her getting shot.

At any moment he figured someone would comment

on Carmen's freakish speed, but no one did. Had to be because they were human and had no idea only Vamps could run that fast.

"Now we're short a Mermaid," ball cap guy commented. "Though, maybe, from what the other one said, we might have a very important Mermaid." He swung his gaze around to lock on Shayla. "What did she mean when she called you 'Your Highness'?"

"I have no idea," Shayla said, still using the petulant, spoiled tone. "And this is getting boring. Where's the movie guy? I'm here because I was promised he'd make me a star." She looked him up and down, her upper lip curling. "And what's the deal with the guns? Put them away, right this instant."

One of the men laughed out loud. Ball cap guy simply frowned. "Drop the act," he ordered. "You can't possibly be that stupid."

Shayla opened her mouth and then, after exchanging a quick glance with Zach, closed it. Because they both knew he was right.

"We have her," he told his cohorts. "But now what do we do with her escort?"

"He's with me," Shayla put in hurriedly. "I'm not going anywhere without him. If you want to take me, you've got to take him, too."

Instead, ball cap guy shook his head. With his gun still leveled on Zach, he squeezed the trigger and shot him point-blank.

Pain seared like fire through his gut. Zach doubled over, his forehead beaded with sweat. While a gut shot like this would be fatal to a human, to a Shifter it was merely excruciatingly painful. And inconvenient, since Zach would need to have a few hours to heal.

"You can't leave him here to die, boss," one of the other guys said. "That'll bring on too many questions."

"True. Bring him and the girl with us. Let's get out of here before someone sees."

Thankful for small blessings, Zach grimaced and grunted in pain as they loaded him up in the back of a minivan. Shayla climbed in after him, the expression in her eyes telling him she was struggling with fear and concern. "Are you all right?" she whispered in his ear.

He managed an almost imperceptible nod. "Not a silver bullet," he whispered back. Then louder, "Please, do something to stop the bleeding."

Shayla nodded, removing her jacket and pressing it up against his wound. He groaned, because it hurt like hell. "This should do it," she told him. Then, clearly remembering she was playing a part, she huffed. "Why did you shoot my agent?" she demanded, a tremble in the false bravado of her voice exactly right. "And where are you taking me? What is all this about?"

But no one would answer. The driver started the engine, and the truck took off. Every bump, every turn, every jolt, brought Zach a fresh stab of pain. His body had already started the healing process, which brought another kind of pain. But once he'd healed, he'd have a definite advantage. No one worried about defending themselves from a guy with a gut shot wound.

Zach had been shot! First instinct, Shayla panicked. While she wasn't normally a violent person, the knowledge that these men had harmed him made her wish she was a Wolf Shifter so she could change and rip out both their throats.

She wanted to protect him, heal him and avenge him.

But then she remembered Shifters couldn't be killed unless by fire or a silver bullet, and it was unlikely these men's bullets were anything but ordinary.

But still…

As soon as some of the color started returning to Zach's face, Shayla knew he'd be all right. Shifters were well known for their almost magical self-healing abilities and while she'd known he wouldn't die, watching him suffer had been another form of torture. With her gut still twisted in knots, she took deep breaths, trying to calm herself down.

Meanwhile, their captors continued to drive. They didn't speak much, not even among themselves. She wasn't sure what exactly they might have planned for her, but she'd gotten a good look at Zach's stepsister and she suspected it wouldn't be good. The other Mermaid had been supernaturally pale, her complexion more like that of a recently risen Vampire than a denizen of the sea. While Shayla had no idea what these men had done to Nantha while holding her captive, whatever it had been hadn't been healthy. No doubt they had something similar planned for Shayla.

She wondered exactly how long it would take Zach to return to normal. Hopefully, sometime between now and when they arrived at their destination, wherever that might be. She'd need his help to keep them from hurting her.

Right about now, she could have used Carmen's Vampiric strength. But at least Nantha was safe. Mission accomplished. Now she just needed to figure out a way to get her and Zach to safety.

"Where are we?" Zach's groggy voice startled her out

of her thoughts. "I can usually see pretty damn good in the dark, but I can't see a thing."

"Still in the van," she replied, stretching. "I must have dozed off. They tied me up before they left. I'm guessing they went to get a good night's rest before starting in on me tomorrow."

A rustling sound told her Zach had shifted his position. "They didn't even try to restrain me." The grim satisfaction in his voice made her smile.

"Because you were gut shot. Most people don't recover from a wound like that. Luckily for both of us, they don't have any idea what you are."

"True." His stomach growled. "Right now what I am is hungry."

Only a man could think about eating at a time like this. "Sorry. I don't have any food. But would you mind untying me?"

"Okay. But I want you to make it so it looks like you're still tied up when they come back."

Unbelievably, she found his fumbling around in the dark arousing. Her breath caught in her throat as he slid his fingers down her arm, searching for the rope. When he found it, he slipped his fingers under it, giving her a brief relief from the pressure. And then, it tightened again as he worked to undo the tie. She held her breath, not wanting to cry out or do anything that revealed how painful her wrists had become.

Finally. Freedom. She bit back a small moan, as he rubbed the spot where the rope had been. It tingled as blood began to flow back. "Oh, thank you," she breathed. "That feels so much better. I can feel my hands again."

Next he freed her feet. She held herself absolutely still while he trailed his hands down her sides, along the curve of her hip. Was it her imagination, or did he linger there slightly? But, no, he felt down the outside of her thighs, all the way to her ankles. There, the rope had been tied tighter, and she could no longer feel her feet at all. When he finally released her, she couldn't suppress a cry of relief.

"Let me rub it." His voice sounded husky. Dizzily, she wondered if touching her affected him the same way it did her.

Bad timing, she chided herself, even as she arched her body toward him. They had no way of knowing when their captors might return.

Still, knowing that did nothing to prevent the yearning, swift and sure, coursing through her. She'd long known she wanted him, though she'd been less certain of his feelings. Even now, while she secretly panted over him in the dark like an unhinged fool, he caressed her ankles, his confident, sure touch bringing the blood flow back.

A second later, a sound outside the van had them scrambling to redo the ropes.

A light came on, showing her that the van had been parked inside a garage or warehouse, which explained the utter enveloping blackness. A door opened and several men came in. Two from earlier and a couple that she hadn't seen before. Baseball cap guy was one of them.

"Are they in the van?" A man in a white lab coat asked. There were three dressed this way. Shayla figured this either meant they were doctors or lab technicians.

"Yeah. But we couldn't get two virgins. One ran away with the Mermaid we were using for trade."

The three men conferred among themselves.

"Have you verified her untouched status?"

"Of course not!" Clearly shocked, baseball cap guy stepped back. "I'm not letting myself get tempted that way. Look what nearly happened to John."

"You simply cannot allow the examination to become sexual," the first white-coated man admonished.

"Pretty hard to do when she starts singing to you."

"Then gag them."

"We've tried that. But they hum, which also affects us." All three of the lab coat men produced ear plugs. "That's why we wear these. No sound, no temptation."

Shayla had to admit, albeit begrudgingly, that they certainly had figured out a solid plan. Except there were things about Mermaids they apparently didn't know. Singing wasn't the only way to cast a beguiling on a human. With enough skill, a strong Mermaid could use a sentence or even a slow smile. And she, as a Princess of the Sea, definitely had been trained well.

Not that she ever practiced what she'd been taught. She'd always considered such methods invasive and wrong to inflict on innocent human males. This, however, was not one of those circumstances. This was out-and-out war.

Before she acted, she needed to warn Zach. While she wasn't sure if Shifters were more resistant to beguiling than humans, she didn't want to take a chance of catching him in her snare. If the attraction between them would ever have a chance of developing into something real, it had to be genuine.

"Zach," she whispered, making her voice urgent so he'd understand the seriousness of what she had to say. "When I start speaking to them, block your ears."

"They have earplugs," he shot back.

"I know. I need to take care of the other men first.

Then I'll deal with the ones in lab coats. I have other methods besides my voice."

Though his eyes widened, he simply nodded.

"Don't listen and don't look at me," she reiterated. "I don't want to accidentally beguile you."

"I get it," he said, frowning. "But if every Mermaid has these skills, why didn't my sister use them?"

"Not everyone has the experience or training," she began, breaking off as the group of men moved closer. Baseball cap guy opened the sliding side door and stepped aside. "Oh," he said. "I forgot to mention we shot the guy who was with the Mermaid. It's a gut wound, not looking good. We brought him with us because we didn't want to take the chance of leaving him there to die and being able to alert the police."

The white-coated men stared. "What do you intend to do with the body one he's...expired?"

His cold clinical tone as well as his choice of words had Shayla gritting her teeth. She'd had just enough warning to rearrange herself so it appeared she was still tied up, though she'd clenched her hands into fists.

"I dunno." Baseball cap guy didn't sound concerned. "Probably just bury the body. Unless you people need body parts for any of your experiments."

Experiments? What the...?

"I think we're good." Smiling smugly, the tallest white-coated man signaled his friends, and they all put in their earplugs.

Nonetheless, Shayla lifted her head and began to sing. "Go to sleep, go to sleep," she crooned. A lullaby. Immediately, all of the men without ear protection closed their eyes. Every single one dropped to the ground as if they'd become boneless.

The three in the white coats glanced back at the others, unfazed. One of them produced a wickedly long needle, the metal tip glinting in the light. "I'm just going to give you a little shot," he said. "This will help you get some rest, calm down and make you much more compliant with our wishes."

"I love compliant," she said, even though they couldn't hear her. Then she smiled, invoking the megawatt, utterly false movement of her lips that could charm even a charging grizzly.

All three of her adversaries froze. Shaking the rope off her hands, she gestured at them to remove their earplugs. With the slow and deliberate motions of sleepwalkers, they complied.

And then she sang. She sang a song of longing, of aches and needs and fears. Of truth and shadows, coming together in peace and harmony. Of love.

Rapt, they listened to every word, every note. And when she'd finished, she quietly asked them to drop the needle and hand over any weapons.

Apparently, none of the lab-coated men was armed. After the needle dropped to the cement floor with a clatter, they continued to stand motionless, as if awaiting further instructions. Their glazed expressions and slack jaws spoke of how deeply she'd enchanted them.

Aware she and Zach would need to move quickly if they were to escape, she ordered the men to lie on the floor near their comrades and sleep. Once they'd done so, she and Zach could grab any guns the others might have. Just in case anyone else showed up.

She could only hope Zach had healed enough to go fast. She didn't think they could use the van, but with any luck there'd be other vehicles outside.

"Okay, Zach," she said, turning to look at him. "You can take your fingers out of your ears now."

But though he twitched his hands, he lay supine with his eyes closed, as if he'd followed her instructions to the letter. As if…he'd somehow heard, even with his ears plugged.

How was this possible?

Horrified, she tried to figure out what to do. Why hadn't Zach done as she'd asked? Fingers in the ears, gaze averted?

Since she didn't have time to dwell on the why or how, she knew she'd need a solution. Stealing the van appeared to be the only way she'd get him out of there, because she was afraid if she gave him an order to snap out of it, all the others would do the same. And if that happened, every single one of them would be filled with an intense desire to love her, to have her and hold her and never, ever let her go. Which is what had gotten Nantha into trouble in the first place, singing the siren's song to unwary fishermen.

Something Merfolk were expressly forbidden to do.

Right now, she needed to focus on getting them out of there. Then she could worry about how to undo what she'd done and return Zach to normal.

She spied a large, metal garage door right behind the van. Since all the entranced men had lain down alongside it, the path to back out was clear. All she needed to do was to locate the button to open the door.

There, on the wall, just like in every other suburban garage. Relieved, she hopped out, her feet tingling from being immobile for so long. She punched the button, and as soon as the door began lifting, she jumped back into the van, this time in the driver's seat. Except she had no keys.

Eyeing ball cap guy still slumbering, she got out again and made her way over to him, stepping over the others, careful not to disturb them. Gingerly, she reached into his jeans pocket, praying she'd chosen the one that had the car keys.

There! As her fingers closed around them, she exhaled. Pulling Zach's fingers from his ears, she leaned close and whispered. "Zach. Get up and come walk with me." To her relief, he instantly complied. Whew.

Heart pounding, she glanced outside at the night sky before climbing back into the van. The last thing she needed was for more of these men's crew to show up at the last minute.

But no one did.

Counting her blessings, she started the engine and put the van in Reverse. Only once they'd reached a main road did she realize how badly she was shaking. She pulled over, sucking in one deep breath after another, trying to calm herself.

Meanwhile, Zach appeared to have fallen back asleep. Glancing at him, she let her gaze roam over his perfectly chiseled features, the stray lock of hair falling over his forehead. Though she could wake him now, she decided to let him slumber. He'd be much easier to deal with later, once they were out of danger and safe.

While she knew she could get him back to normal, the thought of an amorous, besotted Zach made her heart race. Except that while she wanted him badly, she wanted him to come to her with honest desire and need, not because of a beguiling song-spell sung by a Mermaid.

She decided for right now to focus on simply getting

them to safety. Since she had no idea of their location, she put her home address into her phone and asked for directions. Once the robotic voice began to give them to her, she put the van back in Drive and pulled out onto the road.

Two hours and forty-seven minutes later, she pulled up in front of her house. After she parked, she flexed her hands. They'd begun cramping from her iron grip on the steering wheel.

The dashboard clock said it was 3:10 in the morning. Despite that, she pulled out her cell phone and called Maddie. When her friend answered, she explained a tiny bit of what had happened and asked Maddie to come over. Once she'd agreed, Shayla dialed Carmen.

Of course that call went to voice mail. As a Vamp, Carmen was a creature of the night. Though normally she'd be either out partying with her other blood-drinking friends or hunting, she'd carried Nantha to safety. No doubt she'd either escorted the young Mermaid to Zach's mother's house or had taken her to the sea, depending on what Nantha had asked her to do. Most likely the sea, as only salty ocean water would have the healing properties she needed. She'd be arrested immediately, but it couldn't be helped.

Shayla left Carmen a message, simply stating that she was needed, and asked her to come over as soon as possible. She knew once Carmen got the message, she'd head this way, probably beating Maddie.

Turning to face Zach, Shayla gave soft orders that he was to follow her from the van and into the house. Robotically, he complied. Though she didn't know him all that well, she understood enough of his nature to know he'd hate this. Heck, anyone would.

She'd need the other women's help once she got him out of the beguiling. Sometimes men became combative when they woke. And that was with human men. She had no idea how a Shifter would react.

Deciding they'd need to attend to the practical matters, such as getting rid of the van, first, she had Zach sit on the couch. Once he had, she told him it would be okay to take a nap.

Instead of complying, he merely gazed at her as he slowly removed his bloodstained shirt. The wound on his stomach had already begun to heal, the skin knitting back together and looking pink. Amazing, the rejuvenating powers of Shifters.

She let her gaze travel slowly from his stomach, up across his broad and muscular chest, to his ruggedly handsome face. His pupils were dilated, and his skin flushed. When he stood, she saw the force of his arousal pushing against the front of his jeans.

Her knees went weak and she struggled to catch her breath. Even though she was well aware he was not in his right mind, she couldn't help but be affected.

There was no way she would be taking advantage of him while he was in this state. Sexual desire was one of the major effects of a beguiling. It wasn't anything personal. She could be any woman, as far as he was concerned right now.

"Settle down, big boy." Waving her hand in front of his face to break his intense concentration, she gestured at the couch. "Let yourself rest. Close your eyes and lean your head back. This will all be over soon."

Instead of complying, he held his ground. Towering over her, he closed the distance between them with a few steps. "Mine," he said, as he reached for her.

"No." But her protest came out weak. She knew if she insisted, that he'd back off. Beguiled or not, Zach wasn't the kind of man to force himself on a woman.

Even if part of her wanted him right now.

There was nothing forceful in the way he touched her. In fact, the way he slid his fingers down her face felt gentle and seductive. "You're so beautiful," he mused, as he tucked a wayward strand of her hair behind her ear. Though his pupils were still huge, she swore she saw awareness in his gaze. Had he somehow come out of the beguiling on his own? She began to wonder. Especially when he tugged her closer and breathed a trail of kisses down the side of her neck. "I want you," he whispered.

Dizzy with desire, she shivered. Tempted—oh, she was tempted. But if and when she and Zach ever got together, she wanted it to be clear of any kind of complications, like him getting accidentally caught up in her beguiling.

"No," she said again, more loudly and forcibly this time. She also stepped back. "Zach, you're not yourself. You need to stop."

"I am myself," he insisted. "Never been better." He touched his wound, drawing her gaze to his six-pack. "It's healing nicely, don't you think?"

While he definitely sounded normal, she needed to make sure.

A second later, someone knocked on her front door. Relieved, she hurried to answer. Carmen stood on the doorstep, and as soon as Shayla opened the door, Carmen hugged her. Though fast and hard, this was so out of character that it left Shayla without words.

"I'm so glad you two got out of there," Carmen said, brushing past Shayla and stepping inside. She sniffed the air, frowning slightly. Then her eyes widened when she caught sight of Zach, shirtless. She spun around to face Shayla. "Am I interrupting something?"

Though Shayla could feel her face heating, she shook her head. "No. He was shot, and his shirt was bloody. The wound is healing nicely, though."

"I thought I smelled blood." With a satisfied smirk, Carmen strolled over to Zach and got close to examine the wound. "It looks almost as good as new."

He looked at Carmen, his eyes cold. While he didn't recoil exactly, he clearly didn't welcome her getting near him.

"I need to make sure he's no longer under the beguiling spell," Shayla murmured for Carmen's ears alone. "Sometimes they can get a little violent when they're brought out. If that happens, will you help me restrain him?"

"Of course." Judging by the Vamp's satisfied grin, she'd actually relish this.

Chapter 11

Shayla took a deep breath. Then she spoke the ancient Greek words that would remove any trace of Mer-magic from him. Bracing herself, she waited to see how he'd react.

He blinked, clenching his jaw. He glared at Carmen, his expression hostile. "Where's my sister?" he demanded. "What have you done with Nantha?"

"She insisted on waiting in the car until I could judge how pissed off you were."

"Bring her inside." When Carmen didn't move, he added, "Please. For all we know, she might have already jumped into the sea so she doesn't have to face me."

"Are you okay?" Shayla asked cautiously. "You were a little out of it earlier."

"I'm fine. I just need to see Nantha."

"I'll go get her." As Carmen turned to do exactly that,

another tap on the door told them Maddie had arrived. Once she'd joined them, Shayla and Carmen filled her in on everything that had happened. Then Carmen slipped outside to retrieve the errant Mermaid. Shayla could only hope Zach wasn't right and that his sister was still where she was supposed to be.

A moment later, Carmen returned with the meek, blonde Mermaid teen. Nantha looked everywhere but at her big stepbrother, so she didn't see how his expression had softened.

She swallowed hard. "Hi," she said, her voice trembling.

No one spoke. Shayla figured Zach probably had something he wanted to say.

And she was right. "Nantha?" The tone of Zach's voice when he spoke his stepsister's name was also a command for her to look at him.

Slowly, the teenager raised her chin. Visibly trembling, she finally met her brother's gaze.

"Why?" he asked, a wealth of emotion in the single word. "What you did almost destroyed us. Me, your father and June."

At that, she hung her head. "I'm sorry." They all had to strain to hear her. "I just wanted to have fun. I really didn't mean for anyone to get hurt."

Inwardly, Shayla winced, though she kept her face expressionless. This was between Zach and his little sister. And later, she knew Nantha and Ion would have it out, as well. She almost felt sorry for the young Mermaid. Almost.

"There are a million different ways to have fun," Zach pointed out. "None of them involves worrying your family or luring innocent fishermen. Not only that, but you endangered Shayla and Carmen here."

"Not to mention your brother," Carmen put in, her hard voice matching her expression.

"I'm sorry." Her blue eyes huge and glistening with unshed tears, Nantha sniffed. "Really, really sorry."

"Come here." Zach held out his arms. Nantha ran to him, and he enveloped her in a bear hug. "Do you have any idea how worried we were?" he asked, smoothing her hair back from her face.

Watching them, Maddie smiled slightly. Shayla felt a catch in her heart, wondering if Nantha would ever understand the depths of a family's love. Even Carmen appeared to soften slightly, though she still held herself rigid and stiff. She moved over to stand next to Shayla, clearly uninterested in watching the touching and tender reunion between Zach and his sister.

"What'd they want the Mermaids for?" she asked Shayla, pitching her voice low.

"I don't know."

"What? Why didn't you find out what they were planning on doing with the Mermaids once they had them?"

Put that way, it was a damn fine question. Luckily, she had a damn fine answer.

"Because I was too busy trying to figure out how to get both Zach and myself out of there. He'd been shot, and while the wound had started healing, he still wasn't a hundred percent."

"Fair enough." Carmen shrugged. "But you know if they're up to something, they're not going to stop. For all you know, they could already be holding other Mermaids captive."

Hearing this, Nantha raised her head and stepped

away from her brother and toward them. "They do have other Mermaids. I was going to tell you this, Your Highness."

Ignoring the title, Shayla nodded. "How many?"

"Two, maybe three." Gaze troubled, she looked from Shayla to her brother, and then back again. "They want our blood. They took some of mine, and they ran some kind of test on it. That's when they came back and said I wasn't…pure."

"Blood?" Carmen's nostrils flared, as if she could smell it. "Why? Are they Vampires? Or do they have a Vampire they're feeding?"

Nantha's shoulders sagged. "I don't know. But as far as I can tell, they seemed to be human. I heard them talking. I think they're making something with the blood. One of the others even told me they took so much blood from another Mermaid that it killed her."

Horrified, Shayla gasped. "I'm going to have to let my father and brother know about this. I'll also need to text the representative from the Pod and fill him in."

"I'll need to inform the Pack Protectors as well," Maddie said.

Nantha nodded. "I'm pretty sure my father will go to the king, too." She swallowed. "I'm waiting to be arrested."

"You will be." Shayla almost reached out to comfort the younger Mermaid, but held back. The time had come for Nantha to pay the consequences of her reckless actions.

"What about the men?" Nantha asked. "They'll continue what they're doing if no one stops them."

Shayla, Maddie and Carmen exchanged a look.

"Are you thinking what I'm thinking?" Maddie asked.

"Yes," Shayla replied. "We have to work to stop these men before any more Mermaids are hurt or killed."

Zach took Nantha home, phoning ahead to alert his mother. As she had on the phone, June broke down in tears at the sight of her stepdaughter, wrapping her up in her arms and refusing to let her go.

When June finally released her, Nantha glanced around, partly in dread and part eagerly. "Where's Dad?"

June's happy expression crumpled. "I've been trying to reach him. He's under the sea, but he won't answer his phone."

"I tried, too," Zach said. "No answer. I ended up leaving a message asking Ion to call back as soon as he could. I don't know what's up with him, but he's sure busy all of a sudden." He glanced at his sister. "What the heck does he do these days that keeps him so busy all the time?"

She fidgeted, looking down. Finally she sighed. "All I can say is I'm not the only one with secrets. My dad's aren't mine to tell. Maybe you should ask him. I'm sure he'll tell you if he wants you to know."

What the hell kind of an answer was that? Zach shook his head. Did he really know his family? First Nantha, and now Ion? He swore if he found out his mother had some huge secret, he was going to lose it.

Even Shayla had turned out to be a royal Mer-Princess. At least she tried to downplay her lofty family connections. Though he'd much prefer her to be just an ordinary Mermaid, especially since he still harbored hopes of them getting together. When and if they did, he knew it'd be so hot they'd go up in flames.

"What's the deal with you and the princess?" Nantha asked, as if she'd read his mind. When she shot him a sideways glance, he believed he understood. She was trying to change the subject. He guessed he didn't blame her. "You know you're already promised to someone else."

"I've ended that," Zach replied, his tone curt. "As for the rest, I have no idea what you mean."

Nantha snorted. "Don't play innocent. I was only around you for a little while, and even I could see the smoldering looks you two exchange. Sparks are practically flying."

"None of your business." His short answer hopefully let her know to be careful. He wasn't going to let her try and use his personal life as a way to deflect attention from her own problems. Privately he wasn't surprised that his baby sister had picked up on the attraction Shayla had for him. He didn't know what it was about Shayla, but she drew him to her like no other woman ever had. Her combination of strength and confidence, her direct way of talking and of course her sexy, sensual body outshone any other female he'd ever met.

Nantha rolled her eyes. "Look, I'm actually happy for you. You deserve it. I'd give anything to have someone look at me the way you do her."

June looked from one to the other. "Shayla seems like a nice girl," she said. "I just don't want you to get hurt."

Mothers. He wondered why she immediately assumed he would come out the loser in a relationship with Shayla. Maybe because she was royalty. "I won't be hurt," he said. Then, deciding there was no point to beating around the bush, he added, "I like Shayla a lot, and I think she feels the same way about me. And—" he directed a hard look first at his mother, and then at his sister "—I liked her before I even learned she was a princess. We've just been so busy searching for you, Nantha, we haven't had time to date or anything."

Nantha briefly hung her head. "Sorry," she mumbled. "At least that's all over."

"It's not all over, not really. No doubt you'll be taken into custody soon. As for Shayla, she's still trying to find out who those men are and what they're doing. Plus, she wants to rescue any other Mermaids they might be holding captive."

"That sounds dangerous," June protested. "Since she's a princess, maybe she should assign someone else to work on that case."

Zach couldn't help it—he laughed. "She wouldn't do that. The Shadow Agency is her business. I think she's actually enjoying herself."

"She's pretty famous back home," Nantha interjected. "At one point, she was engaged to another prince from a neighboring city. He was handsome and strong and rich." She sighed. "All the single ladies were crushing on him."

Amazingly, he felt a quick stab of jealousy, even though Ion and Shayla had already told him about this. He'd be interested to get his little sister's take on it. "What happened?" He kept his tone casual, as if the answer didn't matter to him.

Judging from her smile, Nantha wasn't fooled. "He died. Drowned, somehow. Which is impossible for a Merman. It turned out he was poisoned. Shayla took it hard. She fell apart. Some people say she went crazy. The whole thing almost caused an international incident."

"Ion said some pretty awful things to her. His words hurt her badly. I don't know why, but your father seemed to take an instant dislike to her."

Nantha gasped. "Did he really do that? I'm surprised. Back home, you can't just go around insulting royalty."

He thought back to the aching look of pain and anger Shayla had worn. "Unfortunately, he did. I'd venture to say that Ion isn't among her favorite people right now."

His baby sister swore under her breath. He considered chastising her for her language, but figured she was going to get enough grief from Ion when the Merman finally appeared. Well deserved, but still. Part of him couldn't help but feel a tiny bit sorry for her.

But then he considered all she'd put him—and their parents—through. "I was shot, you know," he said.

June gasped. "Where? Are you all right?"

"I'm fine. Now. I was lucky it wasn't a silver bullet."

His mother hugged him. "Thank goodness. I don't know what I'd do if something happened to you." Releasing him, she turned to face Nantha. "See what kind of trouble you caused?"

Nantha hung her head. "I'm sorry." When she raised her face to look at him, tears glistened in her eyes. "I didn't think things through. A couple of us wanted to have some fun, and it seemed daring, at first. After that, things seemed to happen really fast, and I didn't know what to do. So I went along with it. But I'm really, really sorry."

Her apology softened June's anger. "Come here, sweetheart," the older woman said, wrapping the teenager up in a fierce hug. "I'm so glad you're all right. You have no idea how worried I was. Or how upset your father was. He's going to be furious with you, so you'd better brace yourself. And realize this. Whatever punishment he doles out is well deserved. You've got to understand you can't simply do something this awful with no repercussions."

"I do understand," Nantha whispered, the stricken look on her young face making him think she really did. "May I be excused?" she asked June. "I'm exhausted. I'd like to go to my room and lie down."

"Of course," June agreed instantly. "You'll need all the strength you can get to face your father."

"Thank you." Nantha hurried out of the room.

Zach shook his head. "I'm not done talking to her. I'll be right back." And he followed his sister down the hall.

She'd already made it inside her bedroom and closed the door. He knocked gently, three times.

"Come in, Zach," Nantha said softly.

When he stepped into her room, she eyed him for a moment silently. "I'm happy for you. Shayla is very beautiful, as well as kind. She'll make a good girlfriend."

Again, while he knew she was merely trying to divert him from what she'd done, he couldn't help but feel pleasure at her words.

"Look," he began.

"You know Shayla left her family, her friends and the sea and went to live permanently on land. Where I'm guessing she still lives."

She was good. He had to give her that.

"Yep. She's got a waterfront house, though, so I guess she can slip into the ocean whenever she wants."

"That's smart." Nantha sounded wiser than her years. "We get really sick if we're too far away from the water for very long. That's one of the things I had to convince my captors of." As soon as the words left her mouth, her expression went stricken as she realized she'd redirected the conversation exactly where he'd tried to start it.

His stomach twisted. Taking a deep breath, he tried to make himself relax. "Nantha, what you did is awful. You caused so much hurt, fear and worry. This caused a strain on everyone, not least of all your father. You're not a child any longer, and it's time you think of others besides yourself."

Though she nodded as if in agreement, she also frowned. "I hear what you're saying. But it all turned out all right in the end, so what's the harm?"

It took a few moments before he could push words out past the anger and disappointment clogging up his throat. "Do you really believe that?" He held up his hand. "Wait. Don't answer yet. I want you to think about this. What if your father disappeared without a trace? Or me, or June? And then while you were freaking out, trying to find us, you get a phone call wanting a ransom paid. Would you truly believe no harm, no foul if we managed to get free? What about all the worry, the suffering, the searching?"

Nantha didn't immediately answer. Good. At least she was considering his words.

"Please tell me you aren't that short-sighted and inconsiderate," he continued, hoping to pound the point home.

"I didn't think of it like that," she said, her voice small. A sound from outside made her jump. They both looked out the window and saw Ion striding toward the house, his face dark with anger. June trailed behind him, her expression both worried and relieved.

"I hope you're ready to face the music," Zach warned, right before Ion slammed into the house, calling for Nantha at the top of his lungs.

With an audible hitch in her breath, she turned to

Zach, as if to ask for help. The absolute panic in her expression told him that now maybe she finally understood how much trouble she was in. "Please…"

He shook his head. "You deserve to hear whatever your father has to say to you. He's been through hell since you disappeared."

Because she knew he was right, she hung her head and left her room, walking toward the living room. A moment later, Zach did the same. He thought he'd trail after her and listen in, since he sure as hell had been involved in all of this. He also wanted to prevent Ion from doing anything too drastic. His stepfather had seemed unstable lately, but that might have only been due to his daughter's disappearance. Since Nantha deserved a punishment for her actions, Zach definitely didn't intend to interfere too much.

To Zach's surprise, Ion yanked his daughter into his arms and wept. The scene was so raw, so personal, that Zach turned away.

He headed into the kitchen, where he fixed himself a giant glass of ice water. Then he waited until he heard the murmur of voices before returning to the living room.

Ion had taken a seat next to Nantha on the sofa, with June on his other side. They were talking quietly, their voices too low for Zach to hear. He walked into the room, dropped into the chair across from them and cleared his throat, feeling the need to remind them he was there.

Only June looked up. She flashed a reassuring smile before returning her attention back to her husband and stepdaughter. Despite her proximity, she somehow seemed apart, as if the two Merfolk were deliberately excluding her.

Zach's suspicions were confirmed a few seconds later

when Ion stood, tugging Nantha up with him. "We're leaving," he announced, his hard voice matching the look he gave his wife.

June protested anyway. "But you just got here, both of you. Can't you wait until tomorrow at least? Give us some time together?"

Expression unyielding, Ion shook his head. "We cannot. The king has requested Nantha be brought to him immediately. I plan to accompany her, so I can plead for him to be lenient with her."

As the two moved toward the door, Ion stopped, glancing back over his shoulder at Zach. "Please pass on to Princess Shayla that I will not forget her help in this. If there ever comes a time, I will repay her."

After issuing that pronouncement, Ion and Nantha slipped out the back door.

The stricken sound June made nearly broke Zach's heart. He took her arm, and together they went outside, just in time to watch the Merfolk slip into the ocean.

"I can't believe they're gone." With her hand over her mouth, June turned to him, her expression tormented. "I'm beginning to feel as if Ion no longer considers us part of his family."

Though Zach had begun to think the same thing, he didn't admit it to his mother. "I'm sure he had no choice," he said instead. "When a king summons you, you have to go."

Her expression cleared. "You're right, of course. Once everything settles down, we'll be able to go back to the way we were before."

For her sake, he hoped so, Zach privately doubted it. Something else was going on with Ion. He couldn't quite put his finger on it yet, but he was sure it would come out eventually.

June looked troubled again when Zach told her he had leave, making him feel awful.

"But it's almost dark," she protested. "Why don't you stay over for the night and head back home in the morning?"

When he hesitated, she sighed. "Please, Zach. I don't want to be alone tonight."

Of course then he had no choice. He agreed. She got them both a beer, and they sat on the back porch overlooking the ocean and drank it while the sun set. As the sky darkened, the solar lights came on, casting a soft glow in keeping with the peaceful evening. The only thing missing was the rest of the family, he thought. Whatever Ion was up to, he'd better not seriously hurt Zach's mother.

"Tell me about you and Shayla," she asked softly.

"There's nothing to tell." He hadn't meant to sound defensive, but his reply came out that way. "I hired her to find Nantha. She did. I need to pay her the balance of her fee."

"Isn't she going to continue to investigate this case?"

"Yes. But that's something she's doing on her own, for her people. I didn't hire her for that one."

"Are you helping her?"

He sighed. He knew what his mother was doing, looking for a distraction to pass the time. Unfortunately, her questions felt intrusive, maybe because he himself wasn't sure what direction he and Shayla's budding relationship might go.

"Possibly. Look, Mom." He spread his hand. "Right now there's nothing between me and Shayla. She's cute, and I'm attracted to her. That quite possibly might be the end of it. Maybe, maybe not."

"I see," she said. Her puzzled voice contradicted her statement. Plainly, she did not.

"You'll be the first to know if that changes," he told her, kissing her cheek. "Now if you don't mind, I'm going to go in and take a shower. It's been a really long day."

"Of course. I can only imagine." She got up when he did, following him into the house. "I'm probably going to sit out a little longer and watch the waves." The sadness coloring her voice was at odds with her attempt to smile. "Thank you for staying with me. I really appreciate it."

"I love you, Mom," he said. "No matter what happens, you're going to be all right."

"Yes." Some of the color had returned to her cheeks. She squared her shoulders and lifted her chin. "I am."

"Why do they want the blood, do you think?" Carmen swirled her own drink around, watching the blood move in her glass before she took a sip. "Is it possible they're Vampires?"

"Anything is possible." Though Shayla didn't mean to sound glum, the knowledge that somewhere these crazy people were holding young Mermaids hostage and doing unspeakable things to them made her feel ill. "But I will say this. The ones I met weren't Vamps. They were humans."

At that, Carmen made a quiet growl low in her throat.

Maddie stared. "You sound like a Shifter when you do that."

"Do I?" Supremely unconcerned, Carmen continued

to glower. "Humans taking blood like that is an abomination."

"Anyone capturing Mermaids, holding them prisoner, and doing who knows what to them is committing grave crimes and will be held accountable," Shayla said. "They may very well find themselves being held accountable to Poseidon himself." Her phone pinged, indicating an incoming text. She read it, disappointment clogging her throat.

Maddie leaned forward, a wolfish look in her eyes. "We've got to stop them. You two know where they were. Why don't we round up a posse and go get them?" She waved her hand around the room. "I'm sure we could get enough supernatural volunteers from this room to help us."

Shayla shook her head and held up her phone. "I just got a text from my guy with the Pod. They sent armed Mermen there to investigate. The place had been cleaned out. They're gone."

"Damn," Maddie cursed. Carmen merely flashed her fangs and finished off her drink.

"Now we're right back where we started." Shayla rubbed her temples. "I feel like I'm missing something obvious, but I can't think of what it might be."

Carmen squeezed her shoulder. "Don't worry. Once you de-stress, it might come to you. It's still there in your unconscious mind."

Though Shayla hoped so, she also knew she needed to rest. Exhaustion had her yawning. Finally, she stood. "I'm calling it an early night. I've got to go home and get some sleep."

Immediately, the other two stood. "We'll walk you out," Maddie said.

"I think I'll be okay," Shayla protested. "I don't think it's even dark yet."

"Maybe not, but there's no need to take chances. Especially after what you've been through."

After they accompanied her to where she could catch a cab, Carmen and Maddie waited until one pulled up. Then they turned around and went back the way they'd come. Shayla figured they were headed back to Broken Chains. She didn't blame them. The night was still young.

Once the cab delivered her to her house, she paid and gave the driver a generous tip. Trudging up the staircase, she let herself in the front door. She'd barely locked the dead bolt behind her when her cell phone rang.

"No," she protested out loud, even though she was alone. "Whoever it is can wait until morning."

Moving slowly, she headed to her bedroom, shedding clothes as she went. Once she reached her bed, she pulled back the covers and crawled between the sheets. She barely had enough energy to click off her light before falling asleep.

When she opened her eyes, it wasn't yet dawn. Her nightstand clock said 4:45 a.m. That's what she got for going to bed too early.

Yawning, she briefly debated snuggling back under the covers and trying for another hour of sleep. But then she remembered her phone had rung when she got home and reached for it on her nightstand.

She didn't recognize the number, and there was no message. Caller ID showed Unknown Caller.

Probably a solicitor, she muttered, deciding she'd try to sleep after all.

But try as she might, she couldn't get back to that

drowsy state of mind. Her mind wouldn't shut off, and she couldn't stop thinking of Nantha and Zach and Ion.

She decided to call her father and fill him in. Of course, she'd have to wait to a decent hour. He definitely wouldn't be awake now.

Though she knew Poseidon would be. She wondered how much of this the Ocean God knew.

Chapter 12

The next morning Zach passed on his mother's offer to cook him breakfast, snagging a bagel and coffee to go instead. Now that his sister had been found, he could either return to his job or actually try and enjoy part of his remaining vacation days. He decided to do the latter, at least until he saw Shayla and found out if there was any way she might want to spend some time with him, in a non-work capacity.

The thought made him feel ridiculously happy. When he arrived home, he thoroughly cleaned his little house, did laundry and made a grocery run, all things that were long overdue. He'd abandoned regular life when Nantha disappeared. Once he had his house in order, he thought he'd feel as if the rest of his life had gotten back to normal.

Finally, with his life restored to the neat, meticulous state he preferred, he showered and changed his clothes.

Then he drove south to Galveston. He spent the rest of the day going from business to business, taking down the posters and letting the workers know his sister had been found. Peoples' reactions touched him. He was hugged, prayed over, congratulated, high-fived and given a free coffee at one place.

He grabbed a sub sandwich for dinner and walked out onto the seawall to eat while looking out over the ocean. As usual, two or three freighter ships waited in the distance. He marveled at the fact that under the waves existed entire civilizations known only to Merfolk. While he knew exactly what it felt like to exchange his human body for that of a wolf, he wondered how switching legs for a huge fish tail and slicing through the water would feel.

He liked living near the gulf and enjoyed the beach as much as anyone. But the sea had never been an integral part of him, not the way it was for Ion and Nantha and Shayla. His realm as Wolf was the forest and meadows, the tall fields of grass, the texture and scent of damp earth. The polar opposite of Shayla's.

His parents' long marriage proved a Shifter and a Merfolk could survive their differences, but the last few days he'd been witness to an unraveling of sorts. He hoped this was only temporary. Surely Ion and June would find their way back to each other.

Finally, full darkness had fallen. He stood, dusting his hands on his jeans, and got back in his car. Less than five minutes later, he parked near Broken Chains, anticipation making him jittery.

Not only did he need to settle up with the Shadow Agency, since they'd solved his case, but he had to see Shayla. Even while all the drama with Nantha had been going on, he hadn't been able to stop thinking about the beautiful Mer-Princess.

When he walked in, he began scanning the crowd, hoping against hope he'd find her there. When he spotted her, sitting at a table with Maddie and Carmen, his entire insides came alive.

They looked up when he approached. Maddie and Carmen appeared pleased, while Shayla glanced up indifferently until she realized it was him. Her lovely eyes widened, and a pink flush spread across her creamy skin. Her lips parted, making him ache to taste them.

"Hi," she said faintly. "I'm surprised to see you so soon. I thought you might be home with your family, recuperating from your gunshot wound."

"Nope. It healed up almost immediately after." Grinning, he pulled out the one remaining chair and took a seat. "I came here to settle the rest of my bill now that the case is closed."

"Oh, it's not closed," Shayla said. "Your part is through. But the rest of us have decided we've got to find these guys and stop them before any more Mermaids get hurt."

Since she'd said as much before, he wasn't surprised. "I'd like to help. Count me in."

Now all three women exchanged glances. It occurred to him they might not welcome his help. Why they wouldn't, he had no idea. "What?" he asked, looking from one to the other.

In unison, all three women shook their heads.

"I want to help. In any way I can."

"You can't exactly travel under the ocean," Shayla pointed out.

"The bad guys are on land," he countered. "And I'm pretty damn good on land, if I do say so myself."

Carmen and Maddie laughed. Shayla just stared. Finally, when he thought she might out and out refuse, the tiniest smile curved one corner of her mouth.

"Fine," she said. "As long as you understand we're in charge of this investigation, not you."

He nodded. "No problem."

For whatever reason, all three women seemed to find this comment hilarious. He watched them laugh, signaling the waiter for a beer plus another round for everyone else.

The carefree sound made him happy. He leaned back in his chair, soaking in the atmosphere. The steady hum of voices talking, the band tuning up their instruments, the clink of glasses and bottles. The smell of whiskey and beer and various supernatural beings of every kind. In one sweep of the room, he picked up wolf and panther and bear. If he'd been in his Wolf form with his supersensitive nose, he could have pinpointed every single person in seconds.

The waiter brought his beer and drinks for everyone else. Zach noticed their choices hadn't changed—still wine for Shayla, beer for Maddie and the blood cocktail for Carmen.

"You're pretty relieved to have your little sister back, aren't you?" Maddie asked, after thanking him for the drink.

"It's a huge weight off my shoulders," he replied. "That's partly why I'm here. I wanted to do a little bit of celebrating."

"I would have thought you'd do that with your family." Shayla watched him, her gaze intense.

He grimaced. "There's not too much celebrating going on there right now. Ion took Nantha and went back under the sea. My mom is hurt. And Nantha…" He stopped, unsure of the right word.

"Is defiant?"

"Maybe. Unrepentant definitely. No one can seem to make her understand how wrong she was to do what she did."

"Ouch." Shayla winced. "I'm sure once she and Ion arrive back at their home, she'll have to answer to my brother."

"That's what Ion mentioned." This intrigued and worried him. "I know what my sister did was wrong. Do you have any idea what will happen to her?"

"She'll be imprisoned," Shayla said matter-of-factly. "Like I was. My brother will let her make a statement, but he always follows the law."

"I admit I find it a bit odd that your king gets involved in matters like this."

"Maybe so, but we Merfolk are old school." After sipping on her wine, she nodded. "Merc is a very hands-on kind of ruler. But she'll still have a fair trial. Merc's just a couple years older than me, and he's quite the lady's man. It's strange to think of him sitting in my father's throne and dispensing wisdom." She shook her head, her expression amused. "That said, I rarely visit the palace, especially since Richard died."

"Are you going there soon?" he asked. "I'm really interested to learn what happens with my sister." Privately he had his doubts Ion would be sharing news any time in the near future.

"Probably," Shayla said, taking a sip of her wine and smiling at him. He felt the power of that smile low in his gut. "I'm going to have to pay him a visit. He needs to know what's going on with these humans. Taking Mermaid blood and using it for nefarious purposes is enough to start an all-out war."

"What?" Carmen asked, leaning forward. "Are you saying the Merfolk would declare war on humanity?" Maddie had also gone still. Zach wondered if she'd truly meant that or if it had been a poor choice of words.

Shayla swallowed hard. "Oh, it won't be us, exactly. But if my father notifies Poseidon like he said he would, there will be hell to pay."

"Point taken," Zach replied. "You've mentioned him before, so I knew there was that possibility." He tilted his head, studying her. "I'll admit to being curious, though. If Poseidon exists, then what about all the other ancient Greek gods?"

"I wouldn't know about that one," Shayla admitted. "Though I'm reasonably sure they probably do. Where there's myth, there's often truth. You all know that better than anybody."

While the others began a lively debate over which of the ancient Greek gods or goddesses they'd most like to meet, Zach fell silent. He still felt like he'd missed something important, but he couldn't quite put his finger on exactly what that might be.

Shayla felt Zach's gaze on her, almost as if he'd reached out and caressed her skin. Tonight, she'd collect the final payment from him, and their business relationship would be over. Which meant…what? How did she broach the question of whether or not he might be interested in taking things a step farther?

She reached into her purse and pulled out an envelope. Inside, she'd placed a typed invoice. Sliding this across the table toward him, she felt relieved when he accepted it without comment.

He reached into his back pocket and removed his wallet. From this, he extracted a neatly folded check, which he placed in the envelope and passed it back to her. All without even checking the statement.

"Don't you want to look at it first?" she asked.

"Nope. I'd already written the check. We'd discussed the total, and you'd collected my down payment. I'm sure it will be fine."

Opening the envelope, she looked at his check. "It's for too much." Way too much. "I gave you credit for helping so much with the investigation."

He waved her comment away. "Not needed. You did what you said you'd do. My sister is safe. You earned every penny."

Pleased, she dipped her chin in agreement and closed the envelope up, placing it inside her purse. Zach watched her, his gaze intense. The way he looked at her made her entire body feel warm. She glanced at the others to see if they'd noticed.

Clearly oblivious, Carmen and Maddie continued to discuss the merits of various members of the Greek pantheon. This may have been intentional to give her privacy; she didn't know. Either way, she appreciated it.

She took a deep breath and gathered her courage to ask Zach if he wanted to have dinner sometime. Maddie's phone rang, interrupting her. While Shayla watched, Maddie checked the Caller ID before answering. All the color instantly drained from her face. "Excuse me," she told them. "I have to take this." Answering, she pushed up from the table and headed toward the door to go outside where it was much quieter.

Carmen frowned. "That didn't look good. Do you think I should go after her?"

"No." Shayla shook her head. "I think she wants privacy. I'm sure if it's something she needs us to know, she'll tell us."

Carmen nodded, her gaze drifting past Shayla toward the door. "Oh, wow!" she said, her eyes flashing. "Catch a look at what just came in. And he's heading this way." Her voice changed to a purr. "I like what I see."

Trying not to laugh, Shayla swiveled in her seat to see who had caught her picky friend's attention so strongly. The instant she caught sight of the broad-shouldered giant striding their way, the crowd parting for him like water, she groaned. "Oh, hell."

Still fixated on the newcomer, Carmen ignored her.

Zach however, went instantly alert. "What is it?" he asked, glancing up at the man purposely coming toward them.

"My brother," she said. "And for Merc to leave his kingdom, I'm guessing there's something very wrong indeed."

Now she had Carmen's attention. "*That's* your brother? Every woman in the place is drooling."

"They always do," Shayla replied. With his mane of wavy golden hair, startling green eyes and impressive physique, he attracted women the way a large school of feeding fish attracted hungry sharks.

"You know I love a challenge," Carmen purred.

Though she nodded, Shayla didn't have time for an answer because Merc had reached them. He swept up to their table as if riding a monster wave on a surfboard. "Sis, we need to talk."

"Pull up a chair," Shayla said, pretending not to get that he wanted her to leave with him. "These are my friends, Carmen and Zach."

With a startled expression, he appeared to notice for the first time that there were others present. "Nice to meet you," he said, dipping his chin in greeting. "But I can't hear myself think over the band. Do you think we could go somewhere quieter?"

That he thought to ask, rather than simply order, impressed her. When Merc had first assumed the mantle of kingship after their father, the sudden elevation to power had gone to his head in a big way. He'd taken to ordering even his own family about, until their father had not-so-gently corrected him. Now that he'd been settled in his position as ruler for a few years, he'd gained both experience and wisdom.

And he'd apparently remembered he had to treat his kid sister with respect.

Glancing at her watch, Shayla grinned. "The band should be taking a break at any minute."

No sooner had she spoken those words than the music stopped. As if on cue, the band announced they'd be out for fifteen minutes.

"There you go." Shayla waved her hand. "No loud band. What's going on, brother mine?"

"That's king to you," Merc shot back. She laughed; he tried to, but came up short. Eyeing him, she waited for him to tell her what was wrong.

Finally, after glancing around him with a look of clear discomfort, he sighed. "Look, I'm not really comfortable talking about this in a bar or in front of your friends. Especially since they clearly aren't Merfolk."

Not sure how to respond to that, Shayla opened her mouth and then closed it.

"I was just leaving." Shooting Merc a bored look, which Shayla knew to be false, Carmen gracefully got up and sauntered away, no doubt hoping Merc would watch her go. But Carmen didn't know Shayla's brother. When Merc fixated on something, he couldn't be dissuaded. He barely even glanced at the Vampire when she left.

Zach, however, didn't move. Either he hadn't gotten the too-obvious hints or he simply didn't care. Shayla would bet on the latter.

She decided that was fine with her. She liked having Zach close. He could even act as a buffer with her sometimes overpowering brother.

"Ahem." Merc cleared his throat, sending Zach an irritated glance. "Weren't you just leaving, as well?"

"Was I?" Zach glanced at Shayla, one brow raised. She knew he needed her to let him know what she wanted him to do. If she said go, he'd go.

And she realized she definitely didn't want him to go.

"He's staying," she said firmly. "Merc, he's helping me work the Mermaid blood case. Plus, his mother is married to Ion, Nantha's father. So, if that's why you're here, he needs to hear what you have to say."

Expression disgruntled, Merc finally nodded. "Fine. That is why I'm here, as you so astutely guessed. Ion's daughter has been taken into custody."

This surprised her. "Into custody? That was quick."

"We had to move fast because of what she did," Merc said. "You know as well as I do that she broke the law. We can't allow young Mermaids to go around luring humans. Just because this backfired on her doesn't mean she didn't do wrong."

Which, as she knew Merc remembered, had been one of the awful things Shayla had done when she'd been mindless with grief. Her jail time had been a time of learning and reflecting. Hopefully, that would also be the case with Nantha, even though the young Mermaid wasn't a princess.

Turning to eye Zach to see how he was taking this, her breath caught. This was his baby sister after all. But to her relief, he nodded his head in agreement.

Before Merc could speak, Carmen reappeared with Maddie in tow. "We're back," she said, smiling sweetly. "We couldn't just run off on our friends, especially when you all might be discussing business."

Grateful, Shayla nodded. "Good thinking. We were just talking about how Nantha has been taken into custody due to her crime."

Both women nodded, pulling out their chairs and grabbing their drinks as if they'd never left. "I'm not surprised," Carmen commented.

At this, Merc smiled. "Yes, but to our consternation, her father, Ion, protested. Apparently, he feels his little girl should be above the rules. He claimed favoritism on our part."

"Favoritism toward whom?" Shayla asked, though she suspected she might know.

"You." Merc shook his head. "Imagine our shock when he tried to use you as an example."

"Shayla?" Now Zach glanced from brother to sister, his expression confused. "Why would anyone show favoritism toward Shayla?"

"Exactly," she drawled. "I did my time."

Merc grinned back. "Yes, you did. But that doesn't seem to matter to him. He was practically rabid, demanding you be held accountable for your past sins while also insisting his daughter should be let go. He's so inconsistent, he seems unhinged."

Clearing his throat, Zach rapped on the table to get their attention. When they both looked at him, he spoke. "This is my family you're talking about."

"Who is this again?" Merc asked, raising one brow.

"Ion's stepson, Nantha's stepbrother," Shayla said.

"And Shayla's special friend," Maddie interjected, barely hiding her smile.

"Special?" The word distracted him, as Maddie had to have known it would.

"Thanks," Shayla mouthed to her friend, even as she felt that telltale blush heat her face.

But before Merc could question her, Zach redirected him. "Yes, we're friends. But that isn't important right now. I need to know what's going on with Ion and Nantha."

Merc turned his attention to Zach, considering his request. Finally, he dipped his shaggy head in acknowledgment. "Ion is part of a small, but very vocal group who still, despite the years that have now passed, say they believe Shayla murdered her fiancé. They have no proof, and most of us believe their stance is politically motivated."

"You saw how he was," Shayla interrupted. "Your stepfather says he believes I was involved in a crime."

"Which she was," Merc continued smoothly. "But not of murder. In her grief at losing Richard, she attempted to enact vengeance against the hapless humans who killed him."

"Did you?" Zach asked, leaning forward and fixing her with an intent look.

"No." She supposed she didn't blame him for asking, but it hurt. "I did commit a crime, similar to the one Nantha committed. I sang to them, lured them to the rocks. I'm lucky there weren't any deaths."

"And she was caught and punished," Merc added. "Exactly the same way your sister will be."

Zach took a deep breath and then nodded. "How long?"

"Six months."

He winced, turning to Shayla. "Were you imprisoned for six months, too?"

"Yes." She smiled, hoping to soften the blow. "But undersea prisons aren't like human ones. They're actually pretty comfortable. The punishment is the isolation."

"Nantha is very sociable. I worry she'd lose her mind if she has to be isolated that long."

"She won't," Shayla reassured him. "There is lots to do. Reading and learning, classes in everything from knitting to painting to cooking to teaching. I broadened my education while there. And most importantly, I came to terms with my grief."

"At least until you got out," Merc added, only partly teasing. "Then you decided you wanted nothing more to do with your own city or your own people. I guess we should be glad you didn't disown your family, as well."

Deciding to ignore her brother, she continued to focus on Zach. Maddie and Carmen listened, their rapt expressions attesting to their fascination with learning all of this about their very private friend.

"I needed my space," she continued. "And I don't think anyone could blame me. Though I knew I needed to be near the sea, I still wanted to live on land. So I moved here to Galveston Island. I'd been dabbling for years in selling artifacts I'd found on the ocean floor, so I had plenty of money saved up. I bought a house right on the water."

"I see." Zach watched her, his gaze so intent that even Merc took notice. "And then you were fine?"

"Relatively," she allowed. "I continued to grieve, but I went to a grief support group similar to the one I attended while in prison. I lived my life, developed my business and made friends." She included Maddie and Carmen in her smile. And finally, I was well enough to be able to visit my friends and family again."

"Though not often enough," Merc put in. "She rarely stops by the palace now since Dad retired and I became king."

"You healed, but some people, like Ion, continue to hold a grudge?" Clearly Zach still struggled with the idea of his stepfather believing such things about her."

Nodding, she eyed Zach, hoping he'd understand what she meant. "As always in life, there was gossip and rumors. Some kind and some…not so much. Apparently, there remains a determined camp who still believe I did horrible, unspeakable things to the man I was to marry. The fact that I went after the fishermen instead doesn't seem to register. I'm lucky I pulled myself back in time, or I might have been guilty of murder."

Saying this out loud shocked her brother. His quick intake of breath told her he'd never considered such a possibility.

"I can understand that," Zach said softly, surprising her. "You're a very passionate woman."

Her face heated at the compliment. Meanwhile, her

brother snorted. "Cool it, you two lovebirds. While I think all of this is cute, I've come here because I need your help. I'm trying to keep Father from involving Poseidon."

"You're the king." Shayla protested, taken aback at his immediate assumption that she and Zach were lovers. "Can't you simply forbid it?"

Her brother stared at her as if she'd grown two heads. "Who are you and what have you done with my sister? You know as well as I do that no one forbids Father anything. Though he's no longer the ruler, he was king long before I was even a gleam in his eye. If he wants to talk to his friend Poseidon, then that's exactly what he's going to do."

"Poseidon?" Maddie exclaimed. "This entire conversation is beyond interesting."

Even Carmen appeared absorbed. She tilted her head, interest gleaming in her eyes. "Why would one of the ancient gods care what mortals or Merfolk do?"

"Merfolk are his creatures," Merc explained. "He has always protected us. It won't be good if he learns a small group of humans are capturing Mermaids and using them for nefarious purposes."

"Nefarious," Maddie repeated dreamily. "Nice choice of word."

One thing about her brother, he knew how to charm the ladies without even trying.

"Why would this be a bad thing?" Carmen asked. "Since he's so powerful, wouldn't that make it easier on everyone? He could get the captive ones back and shut down the entire operation."

"Except he doesn't do things in half measures," Merc said.

"Poseidon's not known for his rational behavior when something angers him," Shayla explained, for all of their benefits. "Think tsunamis and cyclones. He has a terrible temper and tends to act before applying logical thinking."

"To say the least," Merc added, with a mock shudder. "He could wipe out entire cities with one sweep of his hand and not even blink."

"So what you're saying is we need to find these guys and shut them down before Poseidon gets involved?" Zach asked.

Merc glanced at him before bringing his gaze back to Shayla. "Can you do that?"

"Can we?" Shayla shook her head. "I don't know. We just recovered Nantha. We know where the other guys were operating, but they've long since vacated that place."

"Then you need to search for them," Merc insisted.

"We already are," Shayla shot back. "We've put the word out among our various supernatural groups, and we were just beginning to work on formulating a plan when you showed up. Having you sitting around issuing kingly orders isn't helping, you know."

Merc glared at her. Carmen and Maddie simply watched, wide-eyed. And Zach… Zach laughed.

Chapter 13

Both Shayla and her brother eyed him as if they thought he might have lost his mind. "What?" Shayla asked, when he'd stopped guffawing long enough to be able to hear her.

"It's good to know sibling relationships are the same whether you're Shifter or Merfolk," he said, still chuckling. "Listening to you two bicker reminds me of me and my stepsister. We occasionally argued like that."

Nantha. Though he didn't say her name, they all knew who he meant. This had a marked sobering effect, especially on Merc.

"I'm sorry," he said, meeting Zach's gaze. "I promise she's being treated fairly."

"Do you have any idea what's going to happen to her?" Zach asked, putting the question directly to Merc. "I mean, I know you said she'd be going to prison. Is there a process similar to the way it is among humans?"

"Definitely. She'll have a trial. Since she's already been charged, she'll be imprisoned until the trial. I'm sure counsel has already been assigned to assist her."

"Counsel? Like a lawyer?"

When Merc nodded, Zach's expression appeared to war between being impressed and feeling worried. "Just like the humans. I never would have guessed it."

"Why not?" Merc regarded him sternly. "Just because we have fish tails and use gills to breathe underwater doesn't make us a bunch of savages."

Instead of scrambling to explain his comment, Zach laughed again. "Point made," he said. "And don't look now, but I think a couple of the ladies over at the bar just bought you a drink."

Of course both Maddie and Carmen immediately swiveled around to stare, making Zach laugh and Merc frown.

"Or maybe it's for you, Zach," Shayla interjected. While her brother certainly was handsome, he couldn't hold a candle to Zach. She'd noticed earlier the women at the bar checking both men out, their gazes lingering on Zach. They'd also eyed her, clearly trying to figure out if she had a claim to either of the men.

Grinning, Merc shook his head. "I was about to leave. But now I have to see who the drink is for."

A moment later, the waiter appeared with two beers. One for Zach and one for Merc. Shayla clapped, delighted. "They're after both of you," she said. "Maybe we ladies should just take off and leave you guys at it."

"Don't." Zach grabbed her arm. "I'd much rather be with you than any other woman in this bar."

Whoa. Shayla sucked in her breath, stunned. Helpless to react as she wanted to with everyone watching, she looked down instead. Every part of her body buzzed with the connection.

"Okay, that's it." Throwing up his hands in defeat, Merc stood. "I'll leave you two alone. Or as alone as you can be with a Vampire and a Shifter sitting with you. All this sizzling crap is making me feel ansty." He took a deep drink of his beer. "Plus I've got two ladies over there waiting to talk to me."

They both watched as Merc made his way to the bar, the way he sauntered speaking volumes about his confidence. Several other feminine heads swiveled to watch him.

"Your brother is really something," Maddie breathed. Carmen nodded, as if to second that statement.

"Sorry," Shayla said. "He's always been pretty confident, even before he was crowned king."

"How does that work, exactly?" Zach asked. "Since your dad's still alive, I mean."

She knew what he meant. "Well in the human world, one is a king until death. We're a bit different since our lives are so much longer. Kings—and queens, too—can retire. My father had ruled for 116 years. He said he was tired, so he passed on the crown to Merc. I think it was a good decision. Now he fishes a lot. Mom teaches cooking classes and cooks."

Both Carmen and Maddie had swiveled in their chairs, not bothering to hide the fact that they were watching Merc chat with the women at the bar. Merc had taken a bar stool in between both women and they were all laughing, no doubt at something he'd said.

"He's a charmer," Shayla said. "He always did have a way with the ladies."

When she looked back at Zach, their gazes locked.

"Did you mean what you said a minute ago?" she blurted, lowering her voice so that Maddie and Carmen hopefully wouldn't hear.

His gaze never wavered. "Yes. With one addendum."

Heart skipping a beat, she waited.

"I'd rather be with you somewhere else. Want to get out of here?"

She didn't ask where he wanted to go, or what he had planned, if anything. She simply tossed back the last bit of her wine and nodded. He stood, helping pull back her chair before taking her arm. She felt his touch all the way down to her core.

"We're leaving," she said, touching Maddie's shoulder. Her two friends nodded, barely able to tear their gazes away from her brother.

Zach grinned and took her hand. Without a backward glance, fingers intertwined, they left the bar.

Zach couldn't believe they were holding hands. Shayla's small hand fit perfectly in his larger one, and the connection made his blood heat. The tension had been building in him ever since meeting the beautiful Mermaid. Certainly, at first her beauty played a large part in his attraction to her. But the more he'd been around her, the more he admired her steadfast devotion to her friends, her family and her newfound passion for private investigative work. Though he knew she felt the same pull of attraction to him that he did her, she played none of the coy games other women played. She made it clear that what he saw was what she was, and her refusal to pretend to be something more or less intrigued him. Her confidence and unabashed sexuality drew him in.

He burned for her, though he'd held himself in check

until his sister had been found. It felt like he'd been waiting forever. Far too long. Now, though... He needed to tell her the truth. The fact that he hadn't would probably make things worse.

As she pushed through the front door ahead of him, he was right on her heels, still holding her hand. Outside, in the deserted alley, she turned to him. Surprised, he gazed down at her, waiting to hear what she wanted to say.

Instead, she pulled him down and kissed him.

There was no hesitation in the sensual movement of her lips on his. The first touch ignited a fire. He tugged her close, body to body, and kissed her back.

Emotions—desire, certainly, but something stronger—flared. He lost track of time, forgot where they were, because everything about her filled up his entire world. He wanted to push her up against the wall and make love to her right then, right there.

When they finally broke apart, each was breathing hard.

"I want you," she said, her forehead resting against his chest.

"I want you, too," he replied. Only one thing held him back. The little matter of his arranged engagement to one of her subjects. The fact that he hadn't yet met his Mermaid fiancée didn't matter. He'd agreed several months ago, as a favor to Ion. It was a tangled mess he'd need to unravel before he could go any further with Shayla.

Starting with telling her the truth.

When she moved closer to him, Zach put his hands on her arms to keep her back.

"What's wrong?" she asked, bewilderment plain on her face.

Stomach twisting, he took a deep breath. "There's

something I need to tell you. There's no easy way to say it, so here goes. I'm engaged."

She froze, then jumped back. The look she gave him told him that he might as well have slapped her. "And you're just now telling me this?" Her icy tone matched the shock in her gaze.

"I… Yes. It's complicated. To be honest, the engagement has never seemed real. It definitely doesn't now. I didn't know I'd start to care for you."

Arms crossed, she shook her head. "Please don't give me that line about how you don't care for your fiancée. Because at some point, you had to propose."

"Actually, I've never met her. Ion asked me to do it as a favor to him. When he explained how much the alliance would help Nantha, how could I say no? I wasn't involved with anyone."

Her frown deepened. "Help Nantha how?"

"I'm not sure. Something about family connections. As in if Nantha was related to her family by marriage, her status would improve."

And to be fair, in the photo Ion had shown him, the Mermaid had been beautiful, the kind of heart-stopping gorgeousness that seemed to be common with Mermaids. Though she couldn't hold a candle to Shayla.

"You're telling me she's *Mer*?" Disbelief mingled with hurt in Shayla's voice. "One of my own people?"

Bracing himself, he nodded.

For a moment, she turned away from him, her shoulders rigid as if she was gathering herself back together. Meanwhile, he felt like he was still shattered in pieces from the force of his desire for her.

"I think you need to go," she told him. "Before I do or say something I'm going to regret."

"Wait." He grabbed her arm.

She shook him off. "Don't touch me."

"I'm going to break off the engagement," he continued, meaning it. "Ion will understand as that was one of my conditions to the arrangement. I promise you, I agreed for Ion's sake, not mine. And it was long before I met you. Let's be honest here. After what Nantha has done, I'm pretty sure there's no alliance on earth that could help her out."

At that, she spun around to face him. Clearly, all her composure had returned. "I'm not sure what to think, Zach. I don't like cheaters."

Ouch. "That's why I told you before we went any further. That's a situation I need to resolve before we can continue to explore our relationship."

To his relief, she didn't immediately dismiss his words. Which meant there was still hope.

"From what I've come to know of you," she finally said, "you've been honest and straightforward. I can't see why that would change. I don't appreciate you not telling me this up front, before all the flirting and stuff. But I'm glad you told me now."

He nodded. "I promise you, as soon as I see Ion again, I'm breaking it off."

"I think you should wait," she said, shocking him. "I'm very curious as to what Ion is up to. Who is this woman?"

"Her name is Teredia," he said, shrugging. "Beyond that, I don't know much about her. Ion said he'd arrange a meeting between the two of us, but so far he hasn't ever gotten around to it. I'll admit, I haven't pressed him either."

"Teredia." She mulled over the name. "I can't say I

recognize the name. But if a marriage to her would form an alliance, she has to be from a powerful family. Do you have a photo of her?"

"I do." Not sure whether he should be embarrassed to admit he'd placed the folded-up picture Ion had given him in his wallet, he simply dug it out and handed it over. "Honestly, I haven't thought much about it since I agreed. I figured once we met, it'd be easier to decide if this was a good match."

She looked up from studying the picture, frowning. "If you agree to an arranged marriage, anything after that is a moot point."

"One can always change their mind," he said firmly. "I made that clear with Ion up front. He was cool with it."

"Maybe so, but I'm willing to bet he wasn't being truthful. You can change your mind, but not without bringing disgrace down on your parents. Or in this case, on your stepfather. While your fiancée is beautiful, I don't recognize her face. I have to wonder what Ion hopes to gain by arranging the marriage."

"I wondered why she—or her parents—even sought this type of marriage. There must be something in it for them, as well."

"I'm going to find out." She had that determined tilt to her chin that he was coming to recognize. "I know he's your stepfather, but I can't help but feel he's up to no good."

She started to hand the photograph back, but paused. "I'm going to ask Merc. He'll hate me interrupting him, but this could be important."

She spun around and went back to the Broken Chains door. Intrigued, he followed her.

After the requisite series of knocks, they were inside.

Merc still sat at the bar with his two feminine companions. They were now falling all over each other, still laughing at something, though he wondered how they could hear over the death metal sounds coming from the band. Though Zach didn't care for this kind of music, lots of others did, judging from the head bobbing of many in the crowd.

Shayla pushed her way up to Merc, earning a furious look from one of the women with him.

"Chill out," Shayla said. "He's my brother."

Merc, too, appeared less than pleased. "What's up?" he asked, not bothering to hide the annoyance in his voice. "It better be something important for you to interrupt my fun."

"It is." Shayla handed over the picture. "Do you know her? She's Mer."

Lazily, Merc studied the image. "Pretty," he finally said, handing it back. "But, no, I have no idea who that is. Why?"

One of the women leaned in, pouting. "We're kind of busy here," she informed Shayla. "Maybe you can save the rest of this for a phone call?"

Both Zach and Merc stiffened. Shayla's mouth tightened. Slowly, she swung her head around, fixing her gaze on the still clueless woman. "Excuse me?" Though her voice dripped politeness, the undertone contained a clear warning. Zach didn't know if the other woman was drunk, stupid or both, but she didn't back down. Her aura revealed her to be a Shifter.

"Yes, honey," she purred. "This man and I are in the middle of arranging a very interesting evening. Now why don't you run along and leave us to our fun?"

Merc's eyes widened. He jumped down from his bar

stool and took Shayla's arm. "Come on, sis," he said. "Let's go outside and talk. No need to start a fight."

With her jaw locked into place, at first it appeared that Shayla wasn't going to go along. But finally, she let out her breath and jerked her chin in a quick nod.

With Merc holding on to one arm and Zach the other, they moved through the crowd toward the door.

Back in the alley, they waited as a small group of Vampires glided down the alley and to the entrance to Broken Chains. Once they'd been admitted and disappeared inside, Merc turned to face his sister.

"Okay, what's going on? Who is the Mermaid and why was this so important you felt you had to interrupt me on one of my rare nights on land?"

"It has to do with Ion," Shayla began. "And with Merc." Succinctly, she filled him in on what little details they had.

When she'd finished, Merc eyed Zach. "You're engaged, then?"

Feeling sheepish and a bit angry, Zach nodded. "I've changed my mind, though," he said. "I'm no longer willing to go through with the arranged marriage. I'm not sure why I even agreed in the first place, other than to help Ion."

Brow raised, Merc looked from Zach to Shayla and back again. Zach braced himself for the next comment, because it certainly would be true. His life had begun to change since meeting Shayla. He was no longer willing to simply continue to coast along the path of least resistance.

Surprisingly, Merc appeared willing to let that particular aspect of his sister's life remain private. He simply nodded. "Sometimes the sacrifices we're willing to make for our loved ones turn out to be too great." He turned his attention back to Shayla. "Thank you for bringing this to my attention."

"What do you think it means?" she asked, frowning.

"Who knows?" Merc shrugged. "It could be something or it could be nothing. One thing I've learned is that there's always some sort of intrigue going on at court. Dad used to hate it and I can see why." He sighed, dragging a hand through his golden hair. "I'll talk to Ion when I return. Once I learn the identity of this Teredia, your fiancée, I'll know more."

Zach nodded. "Let Ion know I need to speak with him, will you?"

"Of course." Glancing at the Broken Chains sign, he grimaced. "I'm going to have to take a pass on the no doubt exceptionally vigorous activities those two women had planned for me tonight and head home."

"I'm sorry," Shayla said, sounding anything but.

"No, you're not." Merc ruffled her hair, making her grin. "But you were right to bring this to my attention. It might be nothing, but in case it's not, I'm going to get right on it."

After giving his sister a quick hug, he shook Zach's hand and took off.

Leaving the two of them standing in almost the exact same spot as they'd been when they'd kissed.

"I'll walk you out," Zach said.

After a second, Shayla nodded. "Okay. I always feel better with some Shifter protection. That's why Maddie often goes with me."

They walked a few blocks in silence. "Do you usually catch a cab?" he finally asked, aware after one more block it would be much easier to wave one down.

She shot him an arch look. "Yes. There's no way I'm walking all the way to the other side of the island."

Things weren't right between them. He understood, he didn't blame her, but that didn't mean this new remoteness didn't hurt. It pained him to think he might have managed to ruin a relationship that had so much potential. Not if he could help it. He'd fix things. Starting with contacting Ion and calling off the arranged marriage. Once that had been done, there no longer would be anything coming between him and Shayla.

Once they'd reached Broadway, they hailed a passing cab. As it pulled up, Shayla glanced back at him before she yanked open the door. "Thanks for the company," she said, her tone impersonal. "You've given me a lot to think about."

It sounded like a goodbye. A forever goodbye.

As she climbed into the back seat, he acted on impulse, something he rarely did, and jumped in after her. "I'm going with you," he said, hoping she wouldn't say no.

Though she shook her head, she gave the cabbie her address and they were off. There were a hundred things he wanted to say, but not in the back seat of a cab and not without weighing his words. This was far too important to blow. So he held his silence and let his gaze wander over her while she looked out the window.

Beautiful, perfect and his, he thought, the fierce need to possess her as strong as an animal instinct. His. Meant to be, preordained, an agreement reached between them in another realm, between two souls. How had he not seen this, how could she not realize they'd be happiest together? Apart, they'd be nothing. United, they'd be complete.

This realization stunned him, at first. But as the knowledge settled in him, he knew it was true. Conscious of every breath she took, every move, the rustle of her clothing, the graceful way she pushed back her hair from her face, he marveled, drinking in the sight of her.

His.

And now it would be up to him to help her feel the same way.

Talk about uncomfortable. Shayla wasn't sure what to think, how to act, what to say. She really didn't even want to look at Zach and didn't understand why he'd decided, at the last minute, to come with her. It wasn't like she'd welcome him into her home. Not now, anyway.

Engaged. A tiny little detail he might have mentioned a lot sooner. And even worse, engaged to another Mermaid, someone from her hometown. Despite the fact that they'd never met, according to him, she couldn't help but feel a twinge or two of jealousy for the other woman.

Except Zach claimed he intended to break off the engagement. She had to wonder about that. Maybe it was different among Shape-shifters, but for Merfolk, an agreement to an arranged marriage was considered binding. For all she knew, Zach might end up married to this other Mermaid. And then where would they be?

The thought brought a stab of pain. She and Zach shared a strong connection. So much potential for a future that might be…or could have been. Thinking about losing out on that made her despondent.

The entire taxi ride felt endless. Despite the fact that they didn't speak, she couldn't help but be overly aware of the big man sitting next to her.

He belonged to another woman. Another Mermaid.

The news of his engagement had shocked her. Still did. But now, with some distance between her mouth and his, she shored up her resolve. The news might have actually come at the right time and was probably for the best. If only it didn't hurt so much.

Truthfully, she didn't need involvement. Even with the passing of time, she hadn't gotten over losing Richard. She wasn't sure she ever would. It wouldn't be fair to lead any other man on. She felt guilty that what she felt for Zach seemed stronger, deeper and more passionate that anything she'd ever shared with Richard. Until now, she'd always believed maybe everyone only got one chance, one love in their life, and when it was gone, it was gone. But then she'd met Zach. Would loving him be a betrayal of her memory of Richard?

Now she'd worked herself into a state of depression. Anger might have been better. At least that would be more useful in helping her resist such a handsome and sexy man as Zach.

She should have known he was too good to be true.

When the cab glided to a stop in front of her house, she went to pay the fair, but Zach beat her to it. "I'd like a moment of your time," he said gravely. "I promise, I won't take too long."

Though initially, her first impulse was to decline, she finally gave in and nodded. As the cab drove away, she turned and began climbing the steps, a wave of her hand his invitation to follow.

She unlocked her front door and went in. Inside, once she'd turned on the lights, she offered him a drink. Coffee or water, because that's all she had. He went with water. She got them both a bottle of water, and motioned him to take a seat. Instead of the couch, he chose her chair, which made her feel both relieved and disappointed. Still, she had to admit to being curious to hear what he had to say. In a detached, remote way, of course.

"About the fiancée," he began.

"Teredia," she interjected. "She has a name."

"Yes, you're right." He looked suitably dejected. "If I'd had one inkling that I'd be meeting someone like you, I never would have agreed to Ion's request."

She nodded. "You do realize that none of this is her fault." Though they both knew it might be.

"To be honest, this all might be something Ion's cooking up. I don't even know if Teredia is aware of our engagement," Zach continued. "After I agreed to marry her, I never heard anything. She didn't request a meeting or anything. But then again, neither did I." He scratched the back of his head. "I kind of put it to the back of my mind. It was a maybe someday thing, and it never seemed real to me."

Men. Shayla rolled her eyes. "It's okay, Zach. We're in a business relationship. There's no reason you'd think you'd need to tell me about her."

Proud of herself, feeling strong in her ability to remain aloof, she lifted her chin.

At this, he leaned forward. "Maybe we started as a business relationship. But you know as well as I do that there's huge potential for something more. I know you feel that spark between us."

Whales help her, but she found his quiet confidence sexy as hell. This man was trouble. She'd known that from the moment she first laid eyes on him.

Chapter 14

"Don't lie," he ordered, his gaze warm and insolent. "And don't even try to scurry back behind that wall you've built around your emotions."

What? Shayla blinked. On the verge of denying it, she gave up. Because he was right. Only recently had she allowed herself to even consider unlocking her heart.

And look where that had gotten her.

"Shayla?" he prompted.

"I do feel that spark," she finally admitted, shoring up her rapidly crumbling defenses yet again. "But that's all it can be. I can't be involved in a relationship. Not with you, not with anyone. I'm still not over losing my Richard."

Zach's eyes narrowed, and his sensual lips tightened. Watching him, she felt a sudden, swift longing for him to do something completely out of character and yank her up and against him and cover her mouth with his. She wished he'd kiss her deep and slow and persuasive, kiss her until she couldn't think, or move. Until she could only feel.

He shifted his weight, almost as if he knew her thoughts, but he didn't get up from his chair. "I can do casual, if that's what you want."

For the first time, she felt a surge of hope. Maybe, just maybe, if they had a fling, she'd get him out of her system and return to normal. "Interesting," she replied, striving to sound cool even though she was breathless to hear what he'd say next.

Now he did push up to his feet, crossing the small space that separated them. He towered over her, which she found she liked, and she couldn't help but stare longingly up at him. He crouched before her, the intensity in his gaze making her shiver inside. Then, just when she thought she might do something foolish, like launch herself at him and cover his mouth with hers, he touched her face, the gentle trace of his fingers down her cheek sending a shiver of awareness up her spine.

Right now, she thought helplessly, her body aching and thrumming, she wished he'd push her back on the floor and have his way with her instead of talking.

"How about we just agree to a no-strings-attached, friends-with-benefits type of thing?"

She caught her breath, ordering herself to focus. Once upon a time, earlier in her life, if anyone had ever asked her to do such a thing, she would have laughed at them. She'd always had a serious nature, especially for a freedom-loving species like Mermaids. Just as Zach had, she'd been contracted to be married to a man she'd never met. Once she had, and Richard had come into her life, she hadn't seen anything wrong with that. Merfolk looked at arranged marriages as natural. Something Zach clearly didn't understand.

"You're engaged," she reminded him, even as her body continued to burn with desire. "I don't think we should even be talking about anything like this."

Her prim tone made his mouth curve in a dangerous smile. Her heart stuttered in her chest as she stared. Emotion flooded her, more than lust and therefore dangerous. He could make her want him, crave him, need him, but she couldn't allow him to get close to her heart. She nearly hadn't survived it before. To her, love had been like a blaze of fire, a lightning strike inside a whirlwind. Full force and then gone forever.

Love and loss, light and dark, opposite sides of the same coin. She knew she was a better person for having loved Richard, and she wouldn't give that brief period of happiness up, even to spare herself the pain of losing him.

Aware there was no timeline on grief, she'd always known she'd be mourning for years. Now, with Zach, she felt herself slowly coming back to life. The color and texture had returned to her world. She'd begun living again.

Horrified, she wondered if that meant she was beginning to forget Richard? If she allowed Zach close, would Richard's handsome face slowly fade from her memory? Even as she panicked, she knew it wouldn't. She wasn't built that way. And her heart was big enough to allow herself to try and love again.

The thought paralyzed her. Love again? Love? What the hell was she thinking? She knew better. She knew all too well what would happen to her when it ended, as it surely would. Nothing lasts forever. She'd never survive it. No. She simply couldn't set herself up for that kind of pain ever again.

"No strings attached," he repeated. "If either of us wants out, it's a done deal."

Her mouth went dry. Mermaids were by nature sensual creatures, and she'd denied her body's needs for far too long. Plus, she wanted him. Oh, how she wanted him. Damn him for knowing this.

Zach, leaning close and tasting the skin at the base of her neck with his mouth, brought every forgotten need and craving back to the surface full force. "We can make love. Hang out. Eat. Have fun. No commitment."

This time, her walls didn't just crack; they crumbled to dust. "I don't know," she managed, her voice sounding more breathless than she wanted.

He kissed her then, long and deep and oh-so-hot. She melted into him, yet still a part of her held back. Could she do this? Was she capable of allowing herself the pleasure of him without letting him destroy her?

As he deepened the kiss, he slid his hand down the curve of her side, making her shiver. And she decided she could do this, would do this. As long as they both stuck to their agreement, she could already tell they'd be perfect together.

Except he was still engaged.

The thought was like a dash of ice water. She pulled away, got up and put as much distance as she could between them. "You need to go."

Though he stared at her in disbelief, he finally nodded. "You're right. I'm sorry."

As he got up to leave, regret flooded her. She dug her fingernails into her palms to keep from going after him and begging him to stay.

At the door, he turned. "I'm not married," he said, his gaze dark. "And not really engaged, as in I don't even know this woman. I understand that you want to wait until I've broken it off, and I get that."

All she could do was nod.

"But know this. I want you. And only you. I want to bury myself inside you until we're both senseless with pleasure."

So help her, her knees almost gave out. Zach sure did have a way with words all of a sudden.

When she didn't respond, he nodded and turned to go. And then, as if desire had set her brain on fire, she went after him. Shoved herself between him and the door and grabbed hold of him, pulling him down for another kiss.

Rationality and speech vanished. Consumed by desire, by need, they shed their clothes standing. At least he had the momentary bit of clarity to grab a condom from his wallet and put it on. Once he'd taken care of this, he shoved her up against the wall and entered her with one swift move. Urging him on, the guttural sounds escaping her throat made him wild. With swift and deep strokes of his rock-hard body, he claimed her, and brought her to the brink and beyond. Oh, so far beyond.

When she shuddered, convulsing around him, every pulse of her body echoed the pounding of her heart. He groaned, and then cried out; his body spasms brought her even more pleasure.

He supported her as she sagged against him, her body as slick with perspiration as his. "I didn't mean for our first time to be like this," he said, barely able to catch his breath enough to get the words out. "I'd planned for a little more finesse. You know, with a mattress and sheets and maybe candlelight. Less…savage."

His rueful comment made her smile. "I like savage. And next time, we can try it in my bed."

Which they did, a few hours later. She fell asleep in his arms, startled when she woke and realized he was still there, sleeping beside her.

Outside, thunder boomed and lightning flashed. Rain drummed on the roof and windows, and the wind drove the sea in white-capped waves. Her kind of weather. She especially loved slipping under the water during a storm, leaving the destructive surface energy for the serene calmness below. Part of her longed to run out there now, letting the storm buffet her, while the rest of her wanted to slide back under the covers and nestle up with Zach.

Zach. Who even managed to look ruggedly sexy with his eyes closed. She sighed, and then told herself to get a grip. Using her best drill sergeant voice, she called his name. "Zach." She shook him. "Wake up. It's morning. You have to go."

He opened one eye and smiled, the pure sexiness of him making her body twinge. "Why?"

Though sorely tempted, she stuck to her resolve. "Casual, remember? We both have a lot to do today."

When he stretched, hands over his head with a sexy move that made her mouth go dry, she had to take a step back. "You need to get ahold of Ion and cancel your engagement," she reminded him. "And I've got some detective work to do." Though all she really wanted to do was stay in bed with him.

"Gotcha." He pushed up off the bed, and walked into her bathroom, completely and gloriously naked. It took every ounce of self-control she possessed not to follow him there.

While he showered, she went to the kitchen and

slugged back coffee, waiting nervously for him to finish and go. Somehow she'd foolishly believed once they'd made love, she would have gotten him out of her system. Instead, it appeared she only wanted more.

Finally, he sauntered into the kitchen, fully clothed, with his hair still damp. "I thought I smelled coffee."

Dropping a casual kiss on her cheek, he poured himself a cup. Sipping it, he eyed her. "What's wrong with you? You're an awful lot on edge after someone who spent most of the night—"

"I'm stressed," she said, cutting him off. "I really didn't intend for things to go as far as they did. Especially with you still being engaged. I'd really like you to go now. I'll talk to you again once you've broken off your arranged marriage." She hoped her no-nonsense tone showed him she meant what she said.

Apparently, it did. His smile disappeared as he set the half-empty coffee mug on the counter near the sink. He eyed her, clearly on the verge of saying something, but when she shook her head in warning, he didn't.

"Gotcha."

She followed him to the door, pressing her lips together to keep from saying anything she might regret later.

One hand on the doorknob, he turned. "I'll be back," he promised. "And we'll pick up exactly where we left off."

And then he took off jogging in the pouring rain.

After showering and dressing, Shayla eyed the weather. The storm appeared to be moving out to sea, which was good since she and Maddie had agreed to meet for lunch.

They'd chosen Joe's Crab Shack on Pier 21. It was a

short drive from Shayla's house as long as she avoided the seawall area with its tourist traffic.

Maddie had already been seated at a table. She smiled and waved when Shayla walked in. Today she'd pulled her wild red hair into a bun, though a few strands had already escaped, framing her face.

Though bursting with her news, Shayla ordered an iced tea. They both agreed to split an order of oysters on the half shell. Though the ones she got on land were never as tasty as those harvested fresh under the sea, Shayla's mouth watered.

As soon as the waitress left, Maddie tilted her head, studying Shayla. "What have you done different? Is it your makeup, your hair? I can't quite put my finger on it, but something's changed. You're positively glowing."

"Am I?" Pleased, Shayla leaned forward and told her friend what she'd been doing since the previous day.

"You did what?" Maddie's mouth fell open. "Are you kidding me?"

"No." If Shayla would have been a cat Shifter, she would have purred. "Not kidding." She stretched, her body pleasantly sore in all the right places. "It was amazing, let me tell you."

"I'm so happy for you, but…" Maddie held up her hand. "I confess I'm a little worried about mixing business with pleasure. Maybe you should wait. I get that he's sexy as sin, but he's our client."

"Not anymore. His case was solved, and he's settled his account. There's no conflict of interest." Aware of how smug she sounded, Shayla shook her head. "I'm sorry. There is one complication, though. Turns out, he's engaged."

"What?" Since she'd just taken a sip of her iced

tea, Maddie nearly sprayed it. "Engaged? To another woman?"

"A Mermaid, actually. It was an arranged marriage." She explained what Zach had told her.

Maddie's frown deepened. "That sounds like a line," she said bluntly. "I'm surprised you fell for it. Look, I care about you, Shayla. While Zach seems like a nice guy, I don't want to see you get hurt."

The waitress brought Shayla's tea and their oysters. They went ahead and ordered their lunch, shrimp po'boys. Then they got down to the business of slurping raw oysters.

Only when they'd emptied every half shell did Shayla answer her friend. "I appreciate that, Maddie. And I won't be hurt. He knows I don't want a relationship. We talked about that. Once his engagement is off, we're going to have a very casual relationship. Friends with benefits, he called it. He doesn't want strings any more than I do."

Head tilted, Maddie eyed her, lips pursed. "I'm not convinced."

"Why not?" Shayla asked, genuinely curious.

Exhaling, Maddie looked down. When she raised her face again and met Shayla's gaze, her expression was troubled. "It's just that…"

Shayla waited.

"It's just that he's a Shifter," Maddie finally blurted. "We don't do casual very well."

"What?" Shayla blinked. "You can't make a blanket statement like that. Not all Shifters are exactly the same. That's like saying all Mermaids are sex-addicts."

Maddie didn't even crack a smile. "Well, aren't they?"

The notion made Shayla laugh. "Hardly." The thought

sobered her up. "Are you trying to tell me you think Shifters aren't capable of casual flings?"

"Sort of. But I'm thinking of Pack, since that's what I know best. Wolves tend to mate once and only once, forever."

"But you told me about events where a bunch of people would go shape-shift together and pair off for casual sex after they changed back to human."

Twin spots of color bloomed on Maddie's cheeks. "True, but what you're talking about is different. It's not a one-time, chance encounter."

This entire train of thought confused Shayla. "For all we know, Zach could be another kind of Shifter. We don't know for sure that he's Pack and becomes a Wolf. There are lots of other kinds of beasts, aren't there? He could be a Bear or a Lion."

Now Maddie crossed her arms. "Not only did he confirm it when I originally asked him if he checked with the Pack Protectors, but you know as well as I do that most of the Shifters around here are Pack. Bears are almost as rare as Dragons. I think it's safe to say that there's a ninety percent chance Zach's a Wolf."

"I have to agree. But why would he even suggest something like this if it wasn't what he wanted?"

When Maddie started to speak, Shayla held up one finger. "Before you say anything, consider how long it's been since I've…indulged in sexual relations."

Carmen appeared at their table. "I heard that," she said, grinning. "So the ice princess finally hooked up?"

"With Zach," Maddie interjected glumly. "What are you doing here? I thought you said you couldn't make it."

"My plans changed." Pulling up a chair, Carmen glanced from one to the other. "What the heck is going on? Shayla, you're practically glowing. I'm happy for you. But you, Maddie, you look like you're about to cry."

"Not even close," Maddie huffed. "I'm just trying to make sure no one gets hurt."

"By taking away all her fun?" Carmen guessed. "Maddie, I don't know about you, but Princes Shayla here hasn't been involved with a man since..."

Luckily, Carmen checked herself before saying it. Both of Shayla's friends knew from past experience that even the mere mention of Richard's death was enough to send Shayla into a tailspin.

Except this time, it wouldn't have rattled her. What did bother her was Maddie's disapproval. "Maddie, come on," Shayla said. "What exactly is the problem? And don't give me any baloney about being worried about Zach."

"Fine." Maddie sighed. "If you must know, I'm concerned about you. You say you can do casual and free-wheeling, but you forget. I know you."

"There's no need to be." Shayla reached out and touched the back of her friend's hand. "I promise you, I'll be okay."

"Will you be?" Maddie held her gaze. "Richard's death broke you, honey. I know it better than anyone."

Their sandwiches arrived, interrupting the conversation. Carmen waved away the waitress, claiming she'd already eaten. Since Vampires didn't partake in anything other than blood, that may or may not have been true.

"I appreciate your worry," Shayla said once they were alone again. "But I promise, you'll be the first to know if I think I'm in trouble. For now, I plan to enjoy being spontaneous."

"And enjoy your lunch," Carmen said, smiling. She

waited until both Shayla and Maddie had taken a bite before asking her question. "Why are you making him break off his engagement if you plan to keep things super casual? Let the man have his fling with you before he goes off and becomes someone else's husband."

The pang of jealousy that sliced through her, shocked her. "Because she's a Mermaid," she said. "How do you think she'd feel to know her fiancé cheated on her with her princess?"

Carmen nodded. "Good point. Not to change the subject, but I've got some news about those creeps who kidnapped Nantha."

Shayla dropped her po'boy on her plate. Maddie did too, mid-bite. "You could have led off with that, you know."

"Sorry." Carmen shrugged. "Watching you two with all the drama was so entertaining that I almost forgot. I've been talking to some of my Vamp friends that hang out down by where the fishing boats come in. They were telling me of a couple of guys—humans—who were dealing with a Merman to procure innocent Mermaids."

Shayla gasped. "Did they get any names? Or a location?"

"No names. But they said the guys were holing up in a boarded-up old house taken out by Hurricane Ike. You know, one of those ones that were abandoned and never repaired?"

Heart pounding, Shayla nodded. "Can you narrow it down to neighborhood? You knew there are quite a few all over the island."

"They weren't sure about that. But you can bet it will be someplace where there either aren't a lot of close neighbors, or where people don't care. At least we have a starting point. We can split up and search."

"One of us needs to stay with Shayla," Maddie put in. "It's too dangerous for her to be wandering around the seedier parts of the island without backup."

"Agreed." Carmen flashed a smile, taking care to keep her fangs hidden. "As a matter of fact, I think you two should search together. You know me. I work better alone."

Though Shayla was getting tired of the other two treating her as if she was fragile, she knew, compared to them, she sort of was. Maddie could change into a menacing Wolf if needed, while Carmen had Vampiric speed and strength. All Shayla could do was breathe underwater and change her legs for a Mermaid tail.

"I'm also interested in getting more information about this Merman who's making deals to procure innocent Mermaids," Shayla said. "I need to have more information to pass on to my brother."

"I'll see what I can find out." Rising gracefully, Carmen eyed their plate, her pert nose wrinkling in revulsion. "I'll leave you two to your meal. I need to rest up before tonight." She winked. "I've got some hunting to do. You'd be surprised how much they talk if you ask them at the right moment."

After Carmen left, Shayla and Maddie scarfed down the rest of their lunch in silence. When the check arrived, Shayla paid, waving away Maddie's attempt to give her money.

"Where do you want to check first?" Maddie asked. "I know there are several in the vicinity of Avenue L."

"Let's start there," Shayla agreed. "We can take my car." That way Maddie wouldn't have to worry about paying for gas.

* * *

After leaving Shayla's house, instead of going home to Texas City, Zach drove to his mother's. He really hoped Ion would be there, because he needed to end this farce of an engagement so he could get on with his life.

Making love with Shayla had been…earth-shattering. While he'd known it would be amazing, he marveled at the way he still craved her, just hours after they'd last touched. And while he wasn't good at being casual, he'd give her the space she needed until the day came she was ready for more. No matter how long it took.

When he got to his mom's house, June wasn't home. Nor was Ion. Just in case he got lucky, Zach dialed Ion's number. When his stepfather answered, Zach was shocked.

"Glad you called," Ion said, his tone businesslike. "I need to talk to you, in private. How about lunch? We can do Gaido's, if you want."

The popular restaurant was always crowded, but Ion knew Zach loved it.

Zach wasn't sure what to make of this request, but it suited him fine, so he agreed. He wondered if Ion somehow knew Zach wanted out of the agreement. He definitely hoped so. That would make things go a lot more smoothly.

Chapter 15

Zach had arrived first and waited on the decorative metal bench out front. When Ion pulled up, the instant he emerged from the Jeep he used whenever he was on land, he seemed different. Off, somehow. He kept running his hand through his longish-grey hair and one eye appeared to have developed a nervous twitch. In addition to losing weight, he practically vibrated with a nervous sort of restlessness. If Zach hadn't known him so well, he would have suspected drugs. Since he knew Ion didn't even indulge in alcohol, it had to be something else. But what?

His stepfather had been acting weird for days. As Ion walked up, he shook Zach's hand. His palms felt sweaty. Instead of meeting Zach's eye, the older man looked away. Odd. Especially since Zach hadn't yet mentioned wanting to break off the engagement to Teredia.

"How are you?" Zach asked, not bothering to hide his concern.

"Good, good," Ion answered, sounding anything but.

Ion's agitated movements continued, even after they were seated. He couldn't seem to stop jiggling his leg, and he drummed his fingers on the tabletop, the same repetitive beat, over and over. Zach pretended to survey the menu, even though he always had the same thing when he ate here. He considered asking Ion what was wrong, but figured the older man would tell him in his own time. After all, he'd requested this private meeting.

The waitress asked about their drink orders. Zach ordered iced tea and Ion his usual sparkling water, a particular affectation of his.

When she left, Zach waited for Ion to fill him in on the reason he'd wanted to meet, but Ion didn't speak.

The menu sat untouched in front of Ion, who alternated between scanning the interior of the restaurant and glancing out the window at the parking lot.

"Expecting someone?" Zach finally asked. His question made the man jump, as if he'd been so lost in thought he'd forgotten he wasn't alone.

"No." Ion scowled. "At least, I hope not." He looked down at his still tapping fingers and shook his head before raising his chin to meet Zach's gaze. "I think I'm being followed," he said, lowering his voice. "Not so much on land, but at home."

"Why?" Zach asked. "Does this have something to do with Nantha?"

"What? No."

The waitress brought their drinks. Zach ordered his favorite, the shrimp po'boy. To his surprise, Ion claimed he wasn't hungry.

Once the waitress left again, Zach leaned across the table. "Ion, what the hell is going on? You're as jumpy as a cat on coals."

To Zach's surprise, the mere fact of his noticing seemed to calm his stepfather down a little. Exhaling loudly, Ion relaxed his shoulders before jerking his chin in a decisive nod. "I'm just worried," he said. "It's probably nothing."

"But I'm guessing you want to talk about it, since you asked me to meet you for lunch."

Again a quick nod. "I need your help," Ion said.

This surprised Zach, as there wasn't a lot he could do under the ocean. "Go on. I'm not really sure how I can be of assistance, but I'll do the best I can."

Ion grimaced. "Actually, the best way you can assist me is to help me get Princess Shayla on my side."

"What?" Unable to believe his own ears, Zach stared. "You filed a complaint against her and now you expect her to want to help you?"

"I know, I know." At least Ion had the grace to sound sheepish. "But I'm desperate. I need her backing. It would do a lot to, er, clarify my situation."

"What did you do?" Zach couldn't imagine what could be so terrible that…wait a minute. "Are you somehow involved with those men who are kidnapping Mermaids and using their blood?"

"Of course not," Ion scoffed. "Anyone who'd help those idiots deserves to be shot. No, I haven't broken any laws—human or Mer—yet, but I really cannot tell you. Honestly, the less you know, the better."

"Yet? Ion, you're scaring me. What the hell is going on?"

"Again, it's not anything you need to know about."

This stung. "Yet you plan to involve Shayla?"

"This already involves her." Ion's instant response worried Zach. "Or she will be, before all of this finishes playing out. I know she doesn't go home much, and I need to learn what exactly her views are."

"About what?"

Ion waved his hand, as if the answer was inconsequential.

Zach's sandwich arrived just then. Not sure whether to be glad of the distraction or not, Zach dug in. Ion watched him eat as if he regretted skipping the meal. Finally, Zach offered him half his sandwich.

Surprisingly, Ion declined. He waited until Zach had polished off everything on his plate before speaking. "Will you help me?"

"I'm afraid not," Zach answered. "I'm going to need a lot more information before I'll even consider involving Shayla."

Ion's expression darkened. "Seriously? You're my son. You know I'm facing extreme difficulties, and yet you still refuse to help?"

"I don't know what you're facing," Zach gently pointed out. "Because you won't tell me." He took a deep breath, aware that what he had to say next might be a bit like pouring salt on a wound. "However, I do have something I need to tell you."

And then he proceeded to let Ion know he was breaking off the arranged engagement.

When he finished, Ion appeared as if he was about to blow a gasket. His face had turned the color of one of his pet lobsters. "I don't need this right now."

"I'm sorry." Zach spread his hands. "I have no choice."

"No choice? Wrong. You can't break that off. The contracts have already been signed."

"Really? By whom?" Because Zach knew damn good and well he hadn't signed anything.

"I acted as your proxy." Ion spoke through clenched teeth. "This is a done deal. You have no idea how much this marriage matters. Without it…" He covered his face with his hands for a moment. When he removed them, he met Zach's gaze, his own hard. "It's a done deal."

"No. It's not. I want out. I haven't signed a contract, and you can't act as my proxy unless I've designated you to, which I haven't. It was a mistake, one that I'm going to rectify now. Ion, I'm sorry. I won't be marrying a woman I've never met."

Expression calculating, Ion eyed him. "You know what? I didn't think it was possible for things to get any worse, but…" He narrowed his eyes. "Does this have anything to do with the princess?"

Though impressed with Ion's insight, Zach feigned disbelief. "Why would it? She and I have only worked together on a case, not dated. We're friends."

"Uh-huh." Ion didn't appear convinced. "Well, now that you're calling off your marriage—one that you agreed to, by the way—you owe me a favor. Set up a meeting with me and your friend the princess. There still might be a way to salvage all this. I need to talk to her. The sooner, the better."

"Giving me orders now?" Zach asked. He'd never liked this. Though he'd been young when his mother had married Ion, the Merman had learned through trial and error what wouldn't work discipline-wise with his Shifter stepson. Apparently, he'd managed to forget. Or had become so desperate he no longer cared.

Zach wasn't sure which hurt worse.

"Contact me as soon as it's arranged." Pushing to his feet, Ion tossed a twenty on the table. "Lunch is on me." And he took off, moving quickly with constant glances over his shoulder, as if he still thought someone might be following him.

Zach remained seated, staring after the man his mother loved, the only man he'd ever considered a father. He wasn't sure what to think about what had just happened. Needing a distraction, he dug out his phone and called Shayla.

"Hey," Shayla answered. "How are you?" The warmth in her voice meant she was glad to hear from him.

"Where are you?" he asked, hoping she'd be at home so he could run by there.

"Maddie and I are exploring abandoned houses," she said. "We just checked one out on M Street. Carmen got some intel that said Nantha's kidnappers might have set up in an abandoned house on the island."

"That sounds dangerous. Do you want some help?"

"Nope." She sounded cheerful. "We've got this under control. But I'll call you if we find anything."

"You do that. Listen, I just had lunch with Ion." He detailed their conversation, including the fact that he'd told his stepfather he wanted out of the arranged marriage.

"He signed the contract for you?" she asked, her shocked tone making him smile. "He can't do that."

"I know. I told him so."

"Oh, that's terrible. That poor woman and her family are going to be crushed. With a signed contract, the marriage is universally regarded as a done deal."

Which were the exact same words Ion had used. Instead of passing along Ion's request on the phone, he decided he'd rather do it in person. Maybe she'd have some insights as to what his stepfather might be planning.

"Are you busy tonight?" he asked. "Do you want to meet up at Broken Chains? We can grab a drink and then maybe go have dinner. What do you think?"

She went silent for the space of a few heartbeats. "Zach, are you asking me out on a date?"

After she'd asked the question, he clearly heard Maddie squeal in the background, which made him grin.

"I think I am," he allowed. "Now that I'm no longer engaged. Are you up for it?"

He swore he could hear the smile in her voice when she answered. "Yes. Yes, I am."

They made arrangements to meet at Broken Chains at seven. Then she wanted to get back to checking out potential locations. While he…found himself at loose ends. He might as well do some investigating himself. Since Shayla and Maddie were tackling residential areas, he figured he'd check out some of the abandoned warehouses close to Broken Chains. To him, it made more sense using a warehouse rather than a home as a base for whatever nefarious purposes those guys were up to.

He parked in the Pier 21 parking lot and walked. Though it was broad daylight, he knew he'd have to be careful. There might be someone who'd take exception to him prowling around their empty warehouse.

The first one he came across had boarded-up windows and doors and no clear way to gain access. Nevertheless, he prowled the perimeter, careful to remain aware of his surroundings.

Despite this, when a tall man wearing a hoody materialized in front of him, he was startled. Biting back a curse, Zach debated pretending to be a lost tourist.

But, as he eyed the man, he realized all he could see in the hoody were glowing red eyes. A Vampire, then. Or maybe a Wraith. His inner Wolf growled, hackles raised to signal danger. Zach tried to appear relaxed, though every instinct had sharpened, ready for danger.

"Are you a friend of Carmen?" he asked, figuring it couldn't hurt.

"Yes. And I know who you're looking for. They haven't been here," the stranger said, an odd inflection coloring his voice. "This is my territory. I prowl it constantly. There have been no men with white coats or Mermaids here. I've told Carmen I would watch for them."

"Thank you." Zach inclined his head in a gesture of respect. "We appreciate your help."

"You may leave now," the other man said. Not quite an order, but clearly a given. "I promise if I come across them, they will pay dearly for their crimes."

Zach nodded, turning carefully, his slow, deliberate actions intended to show the Vampire he wasn't a threat. Some Vamps had heightened predatory natures. He suspected it wouldn't take much of a wrong move to make this one attack.

When he reached his car, he got in and drove out to his mother's house. He wondered if Ion had gone there or back to the sea.

"No, he hasn't been here," June answered in response to his question. "Why?"

Zach outlined the events of earlier at lunch. June listened, swallowing hard. "I wish I'd have known you two were meeting," she said, clearly hurt. "I'd have joined you."

"I think Ion wanted this meeting to be private, Mom."

Zach hugged her. "I'm just wondering why he's acting so weird. Do you have any idea what he's up to?"

"No." She shook her head slowly. "He's pretty much completely shut me out. I've been worried." Her mouth twisted. "I think he wants to end our marriage."

Shocked, Zach wasn't sure what to say. Going by instinct, he offered reassurance. "I doubt that, Mom. You know he loves you. He's just going through some hard times. Even though we don't know what's happened, he won't break ties with those who love and respect him. Don't let yourself think such horrible thoughts."

Blinking back tears, she nodded. "Thanks, son. It's difficult, but you're right. I'll try to stay positive."

He still had a few hours before he was due to meet Shayla. "How about we make a pot of coffee and drink some out on the back porch?"

The simple act of having something to do seemed to snap her out of her mood. He watched her as she bustled about in the kitchen, measuring coffee grounds, getting out mugs, even arranging some homemade cookies on a plate. So help Ion, he'd better not hurt her.

After checking out five boarded-up houses, Shayla and Maddie called it a day. Maddie didn't tease her, for which Shayla was grateful as she hurried home to get ready for her date.

Her date. Say that three times fast. She hadn't been on a date in years, not since before her engagement to Richard.

Shocked, she realized she'd been humming as she got ready for her shower. Quite honestly, even thinking about Richard hadn't dimmed her mood. This didn't mean she'd forgotten him—she never would—but it made her realize she might have finally healed. At least enough to go forward with the next phase of her life.

Allowing herself to relax and have fun with someone who would make no demands, giving her the time and space she needed right now.

Normally when she met her friends at the bar, Shayla wore jeans and a T-shirt. Since Galveston was at heart a beach town, people tended to dress more casually. But for tonight, in honor of her first real date in forever, she chose to wear a formfitting little black dress and strappy heels. Under it, she chose red, lacy lingerie. As she spun in front of her mirror, she imagined Zach peeling the dress off her and flushed.

She took special care with her makeup as well, going with a smoky look for her eyes. Though initially she considered wearing her hair up, in the end she left it down and flowing. She chose dangly earrings, several bangle bracelets and a couple of her favorite rings.

Finished, she decided to head out. Even if she was a bit early, she could drink a glass of wine to calm her nerves.

She'd barely walked into Broken Chains and chosen a table when Zach arrived. He grinned when he saw her, the heat blazing from his gaze making her smile back.

They decided to have a drink while they debated where to eat. Finally, they settled on Italian, a little hole-in-the-wall off Broadway favored by the locals.

Leaving Broken Chains with a man was a new experience for Shayla, and one she found she relished. Walking through the crowded bar with his arm around her waist, she noted the way other women eyed him, as if he were a piece of candy they wanted to eat up.

Exactly the way Zach looked at her.

Warmth suffused her as she considered this. It had been a long time since a man had looked at her like that. Too long. One look from Zach made her entire body come alive. A single touch and she felt like she might go up in flames. Her knees felt weak as she contemplated whether or not they'd make love again tonight. Hopefully, they would. The sooner the better, as far as she was concerned.

The stars shone bright in the velvet canopy of the night sky. As they exited the alleyway, she paused to inhale the slightly salty tang carried on the southern breeze from the ocean. This, the way the sea always felt close no matter how far inland she was on the island, was one of the reasons she'd chosen to make this place her home.

A perfect night. A perfect man. She was happy. Happier than she'd been in a long time.

"Are you hungry?" Zach smiled down at her, the warmth in his gaze intoxicating. Suddenly, she realized she didn't care about eating dinner or food. All she wanted was him.

"For you," she murmured. "How about we skip the restaurant and go to my place? We can always eat later, once we've worked up an appetite." She'd spoken impulsively, but once said, she knew it felt right.

Appearing startled, he eyed her. "Are you sure?"

"More than I've ever been." She let her desire show in her gaze. "Unless you're starving and need nourishment." Worried, she realized she wasn't sure how it worked with Shifters, but she knew how Maddie could be. When Maddie got hungry, she became irritable until she ate. Something about her Wolf needing food.

"I can wait on the meal." He took her hand, his large fingers completely engulfing hers. She liked the way this made her feel safe and protected. "But I can't wait for you."

Yes! Suppressing the urge to high-five, she tugged him forward. "Then let's hurry up and go. I can't wait to show you what's on under this dress."

As they'd done before, they headed up toward The Strand, where all the tourists would be. Cabs would be plentiful there.

When they passed a boarded-up building with signs explaining it was under renovation, a man came out from the doorway, nearly walking into them.

"Oh. Sorry," he said, his pleasant voice only mildly annoyed. "I didn't see you two. My apologies."

"It's okay," Shayla began, right as he grabbed her arm. She felt the pain first, searing and strong, as if he'd branded her with a red-hot poker. Then, as she stared at her arm numbly, still in shock, she saw the blood running out in rivulets, crimson drops staining the concrete sidewalks. She realized she'd been stabbed.

"What the…?" Dizzy, she stumbled and nearly fell. Zach caught her, his shout of outrage making her turn her head. The man, her assailant, took off running, blending into the crowd of tourists.

"Here." Zach yanked off his shirt, using it as a make-shift tourniquet to try and stem the bleeding. She let him help her to the ground, while someone dialed 911 on their cell. A small crowd of onlookers formed a circle around them.

"Any special healing abilities?" Zach's voice rumbled in her ear, the gentleness bringing tears to her eyes.

"No," she answered, attempting to shake her head. Even this small movement made everything start spinning. "Why?" she croaked. "Why would someone do something like that?" Tears stung her eyes.

"The world is full of crazy people," a woman answered from the spectators.

"Is anyone here a doctor?" Zach asked. No one came forward.

Her arm throbbed, the pain and loss of blood turning her vertigo into light-headedness. She hoped the knife hadn't been coated with anything, poison or chemicals or cells carrying disease.

The next few moments passed in a blur. Sirens and flashing lights, paramedics speaking to her and placing her on a stretcher. The ambulance, an IV and machines.

"I'm okay," she tried to protest, though she knew she wasn't, not really.

Then she saw Zach, his handsome face a buoy in a sea of confusion.

"I'm here," he said, taking a seat next to her. "I'm with you, don't worry."

"Your husband's going to ride to UTMB with us," one of the EMTs said. At first, this confused her, but then she realized Zach must have told the paramedics they were married, so they wouldn't refuse his request to stay with her.

For that, she was glad. Briefly, she wondered if her dress could be salvaged, but given the amount of blood that had soaked it, she doubted that. Too bad. It was one of her favorite dresses.

Just for a second, she closed her eyes. Tired, so tired.

When she opened them next, she was in a small hospital room, lying on a bed with rails and hooked up to an IV and a couple of machines. True to his word, Zach had pulled up a chair at her side. Her arm no longer throbbed. In fact, she realized with a sense of wonder that it no longer hurt at all.

"Hey," he said softly. "You're in the ER. I, uh, located your insurance card in your wallet and gave it to them. They've given you some pain meds and cleaned you up. A doctor will be in here soon to stitch you up."

"Then I can go home?" She thought of the evening she'd envisioned earlier and winced. "This night isn't going like I'd planned at all."

"Me neither." His rueful grin made her smile. "The police are supposed to come up and take your statement, too. Right now, they seem to think this was just a random attack."

She nodded. "I agree. It was crazy, though. That guy came out of nowhere. He even seemed very pleasant. I have no idea why he stabbed me."

"That's what worries me." Zach leaned close. "With all the craziness going on, I have to wonder if he wasn't sent by those guys who had Nantha."

"What's your logic?" she asked, aware he wouldn't make such a statement without something to back it up.

"Remember how Nantha said those men were after Mer blood? When that guy knifed you, he cut a little chunk out of your arm. And I saw some kind of glass rectangle, like a slide. I think he might have gotten some of your blood."

"Wow." She considered this. "But unless he'd seen me before, he wouldn't have known I was Mer. Which means he might have been one of the men we met with to exchange Nantha. At least now the attack makes some sort of sense." If they were still hunting virgin blood, they'd be disappointed with hers, though she kept this to herself.

"Yeah. Except we still don't know why they want Mermaid blood or what they're doing with it."

She realized he was wearing a T-shirt. The last thing she remembered was him removing his shirt to use it to stop her wound from bleeding. "Where'd you get that?" she asked, motioning toward his chest.

"Hospital lost and found. They felt bad for me when they learned I no longer had anything to wear." He flashed a grin that sent a tingle all the way to her toes. "Plus one of the nurses said my bare chest was too distracting."

Shayla could imagine. Right now, she found him way too distracting, even fully clothed.

The doctor arrived right then. After inspecting Shayla's arm, he got her stitched right up. Once he'd finished, while the nurse bandaged her, he gave her a prescription for some antibiotics and pain medicine. Though she nodded and thanked him, she knew she'd be tearing up the pain medication one. Mermaids and opiates didn't mix well. In fact, she wondered what kind of pain med they'd given her earlier. Her entire body felt flushed, her skin super sensitive to the rasp of the material on her body.

Once the doctor finished, he gave her discharge instructions and told her she was free to go.

"Let's get you home," Zach said. "Do you need any help getting dressed?"

Startled, she looked down to see she was wearing one of those white, flowery hospital gowns that tied in the back. Underneath that, except for her thong, she was naked. And with every breath she took, the slightest movement of the cotton gown felt like fingernails raking her skin.

Yet in some odd way, she found it pleasurable. Which meant they'd probably given her some narcotics. Narcotics of any kind acted like a potent aphrodisiac on Merfolk.

Chapter 16

Great. Just great. Shayla knew she needed to warn Zach. But she couldn't make her mouth form the words.

Even though she still seemed capable of rational thought, her body continued to ride the wave of the drugs.

"Shayla?" Zach asked. "Did you hear me? Do you need my help?"

His voice seemed to be coming from a distance. Pleasure and pain. Pleasure.

"Help me?" she repeated. The thought of Zach's hands on her skin made her shudder. Desire and need had her body clenching, hovering on the verge of an explosion.

From this? She could only imagine what would happen if he actually touched her.

"Here," he said. "Let me help."

Damn. "No." She scooted back, away from him. This

simple movement so distracted her, she had to fight to keep herself from convulsing, bucking, riding the wave of pleasure.

"What?" He cocked his head. "You're acting weird. Are you sure you're all right? Should I go get the doctor?"

She pulled herself together. "I'm fine. I can dress myself. Why don't you wait in the hall and I'll be there in a minute."

"But your arm…"

"It's bandaged. I can manage. Please." She managed to infuse a note of desperation into the last word.

Zach nodded. "Your clothes are right here. I'll be right outside the curtain." After he got up, he pulled a light blue curtain closed. She hadn't even noticed it before.

He'd placed her clothing in a neat little pile on the bed. Both her dress and undergarments were stained with blood. Even her bra had a few rust-colored spots on the pretty red lace.

Since there was nothing she could do about that, she managed to get her bra and panties on. Gingerly, she swung her legs off the side of the bed and worked the dress over her head, tugging it down over her hips.

Shimmying to make sure it covered her, she nearly lost control of her body twice. Only by grimly focusing on the task at hand did she manage to keep herself on track.

Her shoes. Where were her shoes? Finally, she located them, tucked under the hospital bed. She slipped her feet into them, wondering if she'd be able to walk a straight line.

Finally fully clothed, she stood, holding on to the bed

rail just in case. No dizziness. Good. She took a step toward the curtain, meaning to pull it back.

"I got it." Zach was there before her, drawing it back. "You look better," he commented. "Now your face has some color."

She nodded, even as she swayed toward him. She wanted to climb up on him, rub herself against him like a cat in heat. Because that was how she felt, as if nothing else would do.

Despite knowing her reaction was due to narcotics in her system, part of her relished the freedom from having to make a choice. All along, she'd been hanging back, afraid to make the first move, while her desire for him simmered deep inside her. Now, egged on by the meds, that need had built to explosive heights. Once they were finally alone, she'd have no qualms about taking what she wanted.

"Let me help you walk," Zach said, taking her arm.

"No, wait." A nurse bustled in, pushing a wheelchair. "Please sit down in this and let me take you out. Hospital procedure."

Grateful for the distraction, Shayla let herself drop into the wheelchair. She couldn't help but notice the nurse fluttering her lashes at Zach, who seemed oblivious.

When they reached the front door, Zach pointed at a waiting cab. "I called them," he said, motioning to the driver, who got out and opened the back door.

"All right, then." Zach held out his arm. "Are you ready to go?" he asked.

Shayla nodded. She took his arm and used it to help pull herself up. Somehow, she managed to keep herself from sliding her body up against his as she got into the back of the cab.

He slid in next to her. Even sound was amplified, she thought, noting the way his jeans grated against the cheap vinyl seat.

With a detached air, she gave the cab driver her address and they were off. While she noted the way Zach continued to shoot worried glances her way, she was too busy trying to keep her errant body under control.

All Merfolk knew to avoid pain meds. If she'd been conscious when it had been administered, she would have claimed to be allergic. As it was, as long as the drug remained in her system, it would act like an erotic stimulant. Some people used it this way in small doses to enhance their sexual pleasure. Small doses were manageable. Too much, and one lost all control.

She suspected she'd been given a lot. If so, she was glad Zach was with her. There was no one else she'd want to experience this with.

Still, she thought she'd better warn him. As soon as they were alone. Right before she ripped off her clothes and jumped him.

Even picturing what she'd do to him brought a swell of arousal. She gasped, ruthlessly pushing it back down. Doing so was getting more difficult. Soon, she wouldn't be capable of anything but giving in to her raw desire.

After what felt like eternity, they pulled up in front of her house. She climbed out, still moving unsteadily, and waited while Zach paid the cabbie.

He took her arm as they walked up the stairs, and this time she allowed herself to lean into him with a sigh. At her front door, she handed him the key. Once he'd unlocked the door, she stumbled inside.

Moving swiftly, Zach caught her, preventing her from falling. At his nearness, a sensual haze settled over her. She inhaled, searching for the right words to let him know what had happened.

Instead, she pulled his face down to hers and kissed him. To her relief, he kissed her back. And then, without her being able to deliver a warning, she lost all control.

Barely remembering her wounded arm, she pushed him back on the sofa. Still fully clothed, she went after him. Kissing, caressing, she could barely breathe. She couldn't get enough.

"Shayla?" he choked out her name, not in protest but in question. His fully aroused body only inflamed her more. "Your wound," he said, his voice raspy. "You really need to rest."

Damn. He was right but also so, so wrong. She pushed herself up off him, until she was standing. Then, with her gaze locked on his, she yanked her dress over her head. Her bandaged arm was a bit of a distraction, but she managed. "There," she gasped, triumphant. "Zach, I have to have you." And she told him what pain meds did to her kind.

Staring at her, his eyes widened, his pupils darkening to nearly black. "Are you sure?" he rasped. "I don't want to hurt you."

"If you don't touch me soon, you're going to cause me a thousand times more pain than you can imagine," she promised. "I wore this lingerie for you. Now take off those clothes. Please." She added the last word out of desperation.

He needed no second urging.

Clad in nothing but her bra and panties, she watched as he tugged off his borrowed T-shirt. Her mouth went dry and her woman parts moistened as he stood and slid his belt through the buckle. Despite the size of his arousal, he managed to unzip his jeans and get them off. He pulled a condom from his pocket and, gaze locked with hers, pulled it on.

"Are you sure you should be doing this?" Zach asked. "You just were stabbed."

"Believe me, I'm sure," she managed, closing her eyes against a fresh wave of desire. "I need fast and hard and furious. The way it was before."

His devilish grin warned her. "Come here."

Not only did she go to him, when she reached him she put her hands on his chest and tried to push him down on the couch so she could straddle him. But he was having none of that.

Laughing, he caught her wrists and held them tight. "None of that. We're doing this my way."

As she opened her mouth to protest, he kissed her. Ahh, finally. She felt as if she'd been starved for skin to skin contact. Sinuously, she wound herself around him, well aware of ways to use her body to coax him into doing exactly what he might not think he wanted to do.

His arousal jumped against her belly. She practically purred.

"Hold still," he ordered, holding himself rigid. Then, as she contemplated whether or not to comply, he eased her down on the couch, still holding her wrists tightly. He climbed over her, keeping his body far enough above hers that her wiggling and shimmying had no effect.

"Now," he murmured. "We're going to do this the way we should have the first time. Taking our time. Slow and easy."

"But," she started to say, but he effectively cut off

her voice when he used his tongue to taste the skin at the base of her neck. He went from there to her breasts. When he suckled her, she gasped, arching her back and begging him—begging him—to take her right then and now.

He only smiled and continued what he was doing. She could see his swollen arousal, aching to lick the beads of moisture from the head. Again she wiggled, trying to work herself down enough to where she'd be in the perfect position to do exactly that. He shook his head. "Not yet, my Shayla. Not yet."

And then, as if he had all the time in the world, as if she wasn't throbbing with need, he entered her, but only partly.

She bucked again, drawing him so deep inside her, that she cried out. And when he withdrew, he pulled himself out completely.

"Stop," she ordered, half crying, half laughing. "I know you want this as much as I do."

He did, she could tell. His concentrated expression showed the strain of holding himself back. He shook his head and entered her again, filling her completely. Afraid to move, she somehow forced herself to hold still, letting him dictate the pace.

He began to move. Each slow, deliberate stroke a pleasurable form of torture. Tension built and built, and just when she thought she might explode, he captured her mouth and kissed her deeply. As their tongues mated, she shattered, her body pulsing around him for what felt like eternity.

While she began to come back down, he cried out and let go. Wild, no longer deliberate. Hard and deep and fast, exactly as she'd wanted in the beginning. To

her stunned disbelief, the tension began building in her
again. A second climax ripped through her, making her
scream. His release came almost instantaneously.

They held each other, clutched each other close,
until the shudders and tremors and ripples died away.
He stroked her hair, she touched his face. Emotions,
those pesky feelings she sought to keep at bay, threatened to overwhelm her. Normally, such a thing would
have concerned her, but she knew the pain medication
still coursed through her body. That had to be the reason. Of course.

Feeling no pressure to get up and do anything else
right away, they lay on the couch. He snuggled in behind
her and she turned so he could spoon her. It felt both
fantastic and odd to allow herself to relax this way. She
couldn't remember a time when she'd felt so protected,
safe and content.

With this thought, she drifted into a doze.

Zach was in trouble. He'd suspected all along, but
had convinced himself he could keep his feelings under
control. But this, the raw passion again, the way Shayla
clearly let down her guard, had filled his heart so full
he thought it might burst.

He loved her. Though she could never know, at least
not anytime soon. Such sentiment would send her into a
panic, giving her a reason and an excuse to run.

As she relaxed in his arms, her breathing evened,
letting him know she'd fallen asleep. What could he do
but hold on to her, wishing he never had to let her go.
When she woke, they'd go get that dinner, but he'd wait
until she was ready.

His cell phone rang, startling her awake. He checked

Caller ID, saw his mom's phone number and let the call go to voice mail. He'd check in with her later.

After a few seconds, she texted him. Urgent. Please call me as soon as you can.

By now, Shayla had pushed herself up into a sitting position. She frowned when she read the text. "I hope everything is okay."

"Me, too," he said, punching in his mother's number.

"Thank goodness you called. I don't know what to do. Something's wrong with Ion." His mother's voice sounded frantic. "He's here, but he doesn't seem like himself."

"He was acting weird when I met him for lunch earlier," Zach said. "But he flat-out refused to tell me what's going on."

"He won't talk to me either. He's angry. In a rage. I've never seen him like this. I'm—" she paused, and then lowered her voice "—frightened."

"Of Ion?" Stunned, Zach tried to process her words. His stepfather could be gruff, sometimes moody, but he'd never been a violent man. "Mom, what exactly is going on?"

Next to him, Shayla froze. Absently, he reached out and squeezed her shoulder.

"Not of him, but for him. Please come home," June said. "And if you can, please bring Shayla with you. Ion keeps repeating that he needs to talk to her."

After she ended the call, Zach pushed himself up and out of bed. He told Shayla what his mother had said, including her request to bring Shayla with him.

"I'm not sure what to make of that," Zach concluded. "Ion seems to think you'd be willing to assist him somehow. I'm not sure what's going on with him, but he's acting more and more unbalanced. I plan to ask my mom to try and talk him into getting a thorough medical checkup."

"That's a good idea. Because I can't get past you saying that he needs my help," she said, sounding incredulous. "I wonder what for?"

"Come on, let's get cleaned up and dressed. Then I guess you'll find out for yourself."

When they pulled up to his mother's house, every light was on. "Great," he muttered, turning to Shayla. "Whatever happens, I don't want you to be alone with Ion."

She studied him. "I appreciate your concern," she said. "But he's one of my people. I'm his princess. If he needs help and it's something I or my family can realistically do, I'm going to talk to him."

"I understand. But he's been acting strange. My mother said she was frightened, though she did clarify not of him, but for him."

"Do you believe her?"

He considered for a moment. "Yes. I don't see that I have a choice. And she and I have always had a code—811. If she were truly in danger, she would have texted that to me, or said it in the phone call."

"Then I'll be fine." She opened the door and got out of his car. He hurried to catch her, taking her arm as they went up the steps.

His mother flung open the door before they reached the top. "Oh, thank hounds you're here," she exclaimed. She hugged Shayla first, and then Zach. "Ion's on the back porch, glowering at the sea."

They went through the house, heading for the kitchen

and the French doors. Outside, several solar lights and a wall light illuminated the porch. Ion jumped up when he saw Zach and Shayla. "Thank you, son." He pumped Zach's hand. "Princess, I'm glad you agreed to meet with me."

"Are you?" Her tone cool, Shayla eyed him. "I need to ask something first. Did you ask to see me so you could insult me the way you did the last time we met?"

Ion's eyes widened before his expression hardened. "Again, my apologies. In my zeal to do what I believed to be right, I've made too many mistakes to count." He took a deep breath. "May we speak in private?"

Zach inhaled sharply, waiting to hear how Shayla would respond. She glanced at him, a slight smile hovering on her lips, before returning her attention to Ion.

"Anything you want to say to me, you can say in front of them," she said. "I understand not wanting to appear weak in front of your wife and son, but I feel this is necessary."

At her words, Ion blanched. "June," he ordered. "Go inside."

June didn't move. "No. I want to hear this. Maybe whatever it is will make me feel better about the way you've been acting since Nantha disappeared."

At the sound of his daughter's name, Ion swallowed. "I'm not sure I can do this," he admitted.

"Then don't." Shayla shrugged, turning away. "Come on, Zach. I think we might have just wasted our time. I don't know about you, but I'm hungry. Let's go get something to eat."

Careful not to show his surprise, Zach took her arm. They'd barely gone a few steps before Ion called after them. "Wait."

Slowly, Shayla turned. Crossing her arms, she eyed his stepfather.

"Everyone, please, sit down." Ion indicated the empty chairs surrounding the fire pit. He patted the seat next to him. "June, please sit here."

Once everyone had settled, he exhaled. "I'm in trouble," he began. "And partly responsible for what happened to Nantha."

"What?" June jumped to her feet.

"Please. Let me finish." Expression tortured, Ion waited until his wife had retaken her seat. "I fell in with some people who were advocating for change under the sea." He gave Shayla an apologetic grimace. "I arranged the marriage for Zach to strengthen my connection to them. His intended is the daughter of one of the leader's cousins."

"Now, that's over," Zach interjected. "Right?"

Ion sighed. "I haven't actually attempted breaking the contract yet. The king—" he eyed Shayla "—your brother got wind of our groups and decided to put an end to it. He's been rounding up our supporters."

Judging by Shayla's frown, her hope to see the best in Ion had rapidly slipped away. "The only reason Merc would do such a thing would be if your group posed a threat to the throne. Is that the case?"

Ion held her gaze. "Our group believes our people should become a democracy rather than a monarchy. As such, yes. I'd say we are a threat to the entire royal family."

"I don't understand." June glanced from her husband to Shayla. "What does any of this have to do with Nantha?"

"We needed to raise a lot of money fast." Defeat deepened Ion's tone. "For quite a while there's been a human scientist obsessed with Mermaid blood. He believed he could make something with it as an ingredient and use this concoction to force others to do his bidding."

Both June and Shayla gasped. "You didn't..." June said, her voice breaking. "You sold your own daughter?"

"No. Of course not. Nantha's been working closely with him, of her own free will." He swallowed. "But we have been supplying him with Mermaids to use for testing. Volunteers all. He always returned them to us after a few days. They were a bit weak, but a lot richer. See, we let them keep a cut of the proceeds as payment for their services."

"And then they went rogue?" Zach guessed.

"Yes. I feared they had her when Nantha disappeared. They'd taken to posing as fishermen hoping to lure Mermaids to them. And they've cut off all contact with me and our group. They're no longer returning any of the women they took. And money no longer changes hands."

Everyone sat in stunned silence, attempting to digest Ion's words.

"This is where you come in," Ion continued, addressing Shayla. "I need to meet with the king, confess my part in this, and see if he and his army can help us stop this before anyone dies."

"Someone already has," Shayla pointed out. "According to what Nantha said, they've bled a Mermaid out."

Ion's composure crumbled. "I was afraid of that," he muttered. "There's more. Some in our group learned I intend to go to the king. They've been following me. I think they want me dead."

Zach figured things couldn't get any worse. Judging from his mother's horrified expression, she felt the same way.

He glanced at Shayla. He could only imagine how she must feel.

"Please," Ion implored. "Princess Shayla, you're my last hope. Could you get me a meeting with your brother, preferably here on land?"

"How do I know you don't want to harm him?" Her level tone revealed her resolve. "I refuse to put my brother, our kingdom, in danger because of your foolish actions. However, these scientists or whatever they are must be stopped. And those Mermaids still being held captive must be freed."

As she neared the end of her impassioned speech, Shayla's cell phone chimed. And chimed again. She pulled it out of her purse and checked it. "Oh, no," she exclaimed, her voice both panicked and furious. "Dad's contacted Poseidon. There's going to be hell to pay now."

"Poseidon?" Ion leaped up so quickly, he knocked back his chair. It fell to the wood deck with a clatter. Ion barely noticed. "Why on earth would your father involve the God of the Sea?"

Instead of answering, she only regarded him sternly. "I take it you know what this means."

"Oh, I do. Believe me. I'm a dead man."

As if saying the god's name out loud summoned him, the wind picked up, kicking the waves into whitecaps, spraying foam over the beach and the boat dock. Shayla shivered, hoping Poseidon wasn't really near and trying to figure out the best way to diffuse the situation if he was.

Face pinched and miserable, Ion cast an imploring look her way. "If that's him, will you at least help me?"

"As best as I can," she answered. "You know as well as I do once Poseidon gets riled up, there's no stopping him."

"Ancient Greek gods," June marveled, clearly not comprehending the gravity of the situation.

From the tense set of Zach's jaw, he did.

Shayla reached out and touched Ion's shoulder, making him jump. "The only way to rectify this is to tell us where we can find those men. We need to shut down their operation, bring them into custody and save whatever captive Mermaids remain."

"That's just it," Ion said. "I don't know where they are. They always had me do the exchanges on the Pleasure Pier."

Like they had with Nantha.

Chapter 17

"I don't know if they'd fall for the decoy thing again," Shayla mused, turning the idea over in her mind. "But I'm willing to see if we can set something up."

"There's more," Ion interjected. "I've recently gotten word there's to be a transfer of four volunteer Mermaids tomorrow night. This will take place at the Pleasure Pier. One of the men from my group is arranging the entire thing."

"I see." Shayla actually smiled. "Finally, a lead we can use." She raised her voice, just in case Poseidon was there and listening. "We'll need to contact my brother, King Merc, and let him take charge of this investigation."

"What will happen to my husband?" June asked, worry carving fresh lines in her face.

"Ion's fate isn't up to me," Shayla explained. "That will be for Merc to decide. But I can tell you one thing.

Things will go better for him if he gives up the names of all the Merpeople in this ring."

Ion nodded. His conflicted expression told her how much he hated the idea of turning on his friends. But he also knew as well as she did that the penalty for such crimes was severe. His only hope was to throw himself on the king's mercy and offer to make restitution. And pray Poseidon chose not to become too involved. Hurricanes had been created over less.

"Did Poseidon get involved when your fiancé was poisoned?" Zach asked. Ion perked up at that, reminding her that he was among the group of Merfolk who'd refused to believe she hadn't been involved in Richard's death.

"No," she answered quietly. "I refused to let his killer cause any other loss of life. Though we never found out who killed Richard, or why, the general consensus was poison in something he drank. He loved his sea ale."

"Really? Because I don't know how many barkeeps, under the sea or on land, spike their ale with poison. I'm going to say none of them."

At his words, the sea seemed to shudder. The wind howled, pushing up water so high it sprayed them on the porch.

Shayla stared at him. "You ask for my help and then you again accuse me or murder. Your behavior is...unstable to say the least."

For a moment, confusion filled Ion's eyes. "I don't..."

June squeezed his arm. "Ion's agreed to have a complete physical by the best physician in Coral," she said.

Again, the wind howled, spattering them with sea foam.

"Maybe we should go inside," June said, twisting her

fingers nervously. "I don't see any reason to continue to tempt...fate."

"You go on," Shayla said, flashing Zach's mother what she hoped was a reassuring smile. "And you, too, Zach. If Poseidon does show himself, it'd be best if we Merfolk are here to greet him."

Ion swallowed, his nerves showing. But he straightened, putting on a brave face for his wife, which made Shayla respect him. "I'll be fine, June. Go on into the house. I'll join you in a few minutes."

"Okay." With a nod, June moved toward the back door. "Are you coming, Zach?"

"I'm going to stay here," Zach answered. "Just in case these two need any help. Go on, Mom. Everything will be fine."

Shayla admired the conviction in his voice, even though she knew everything being fine was far from certain.

Once June had gone inside, closing the French door behind her, Shayla walked to the railing. She eyed the churning sea and took a deep breath. Though she'd always been terrified of the God of the Sea, she knew she had to at least try to intervene. "Great Lord Poseidon," she said, pitching her voice to carry. Please give us a chance to make this right, to bring the evildoers in for justice, and to reclaim the Mermaids being held prisoner."

From the waves, a huge squid appeared, riding one cresting wave and landing on June's boat dock. When the water receded, the squid remained. Since Shayla wasn't sure what Poseidon wanted her to do, she didn't move. Keeping her gaze locked on the monstrous symbol of the ancient god's wrath, she pulled out her cell phone and texted her brother. Urgent. Please come immediately. West Beach, Galveston Island. Near the underwater rock.

Once she hit Send, she slowly returned the phone to her back pocket.

The huge beast didn't move. She wasn't sure what she expected it to do—begin speaking in a theatrically booming voice? Produce a handwritten directive? While she wouldn't put it past Poseidon to do any or all of those things, after a moment the squid flipped itself around and disappeared beneath the sea.

Once it was gone, the waves quieted and the wind died down.

"What the…" Zach asked.

"The ancient gods are like that," Shayla said. "Cryptic. They like to express themselves using symbolism. Just a second."

She dug her phone back out and did an internet search for what an octopus or squid symbolized. "Bingo," she said. "There's a lot, but these are the ones that are probably the most relevant. An octopus symbolizes strong will, focus and reason. Illusion, mystery and defense."

"Which means?" Ion asked.

"I think maybe that was Poseidon's way of saying he has faith in us and pointing out the tools we'll need to use to stop this ring of Mermaid kidnappers and killers. I've contacted my brother and asked him to come. I'm sure he's on his way even as we speak."

Too nervous to sit still, Ion paced. His restless energy made even Shayla feel unsettled. She was tempted to go for a quick swim to burn off some of her own jumpiness. But she didn't want to leave Zach and Ion, especially with the very real possibility the Merman might decide to flee. It wouldn't be the first time a Merfolk had decided to bolt before being convicted of their crimes. The vastness of the oceans made it certain those that ran would never be found.

Of course Ion had plenty of reasons not to leave. His loving wife. His daughter. And his stepson, Zach.

Merc arrived in under one hour, which meant he'd been swimming fast. Eyes flashing, he radiated fury. He rose out of the sea like an avenging warrior, exchanging his tail for his legs in an instantaneous move. Shayla envied him for that, while it made her smile. Her older brother had always worked hard to be such a show-off.

"Where is he?" Merc snarled. When he glanced past Shayla and caught sight of Ion standing silently by the chairs, his lip curled. "Are you prepared to pay for your crimes?"

When Ion started to speak, Shayla interrupted. "Not yet, Your Highness. We need his help to catch the humans responsible for kidnapping and murdering Mermaids. Not to mention the fact that he's agreed to provide the names of the Merfolk who are in the ring of conspirators."

"Have you?" the king demanded, eyeing Ion the way a whale eyed a jellyfish.

Ion swallowed hard. "Yes," he croaked. "In hopes that you will be lenient in my punishment, I will—"

"Betray your friends and colleagues in order to save your own neck. I see." Merc's voice dripped with disgust. "Just so you know, my security council has been monitoring those people's activities all along. We know who all is involved. And not to make you feel awkward, but I've never regarded that group or any other as a threat to me or my family. So I'm not sure how much any intel you give on them will help you alleviate your just and due punishment."

Someone gasped, making them all turn to look. June had stepped back onto the porch, unnoticed. Hand over her mouth, she looked at Merc with eyes brimming with tears. "My Ion is a good man," she said, advancing on Merc. "And if you're Lord Poseidon and truly a god, then you would already know this."

Clearly startled, Merc glanced over his shoulder as if half convinced Poseidon stood behind him. When he realized June actually assumed *he* was the God of the Sea, some of his tension vanished. He chuckled. "Allow me to introduce myself," he said. "I'm King Merc of the Merfolk."

"Shayla's brother," Zach put in helpfully.

June blinked, but her determined expression didn't waver at all. "Well, you still have power," she said, crossing to stand between him and her husband. "I beg you, please consider all the good this man has done when you get ready to pass judgment on him. He's been a wonderful husband to me and father to my son and stepdaughter." She sighed, and turned to face her husband. "I truly believe there may be some underlying medical issue affecting you. I pray it's nothing serious."

Though Ion's mouth tightened, he only nodded.

Merc slid his gaze past June to Shayla. The way one corner of his mouth quirked told her how hard he was trying not to laugh. The idea that he might actually be Poseidon continued to amuse him. She shrugged, caught Zach's eye and shrugged again. Zach crossed over to stand beside her.

"I'll add my voice to those who support him," Zach said. "Ion has been a good stepfather to me over the years. He's a loving father to his daughter and a great husband to my mother."

"I'll keep that under consideration," Merc said, allowing a brief smile before turning to Shayla. "Get me up to speed as quickly as possible."

She told him everything Ion had revealed, saving the worst news of all for last. "And Poseidon was here. Dad must have contacted him."

Her brother's eyes widened. "Are you sure? Did he speak to you?"

"After putting on a show with wind and waves and current, he appeared as a giant squid. I remembered how symbolism was big with his kind, so I looked up the meaning. I'm guessing he was trying to tell us what qualities we'll need in order to shut the human group down."

"Maybe. At least he didn't give you a deadline."

Ion cleared his throat. "I'm afraid there actually *is* a deadline," he said. "They're meeting to take possession of four more Mermaids tomorrow night. Though occasionally they're volunteers, most times they're actually not. The girls will either be drugged into a stupor, or convinced they're meeting these men for some other reason."

"Like the way we pretended they were movie producers," Shayla said.

"Right," Ion continued. "Anyway, this batch of Mermaids is important. They've implied this group will be their last. And they've hinted that they are really close to developing whatever they were making with the Merblood. If we don't find them and stop them, I fear they'll soon unleash their creation upon the world."

June served them all hot tea and cookies while they gathered around the outdoor table and plotted. Zach took the seat next to Shayla, his knee bumping hers.

She curled her hands around her mug to keep herself from squeezing his leg under the table.

Merc was in full-on King of The Merpeople mode. He interrupted their discussion by standing and slamming both of his hands down on the wooden table. "Here is what will happen," he said, his steely tone leaving no room for argument. "I am activating the Pod Enforcers. They will form an unbroken chain around the Pleasure Pier underwater."

Shayla nodded. "Sounds great, but what about on land? For all you know, these Mermaids are already out of the water. Having an army of Enforcers is an impressive show of force, but it won't do anything to stop the exchange if it takes place above the surface."

"I'm aware of that." Merc's stare let her know he didn't appreciate her statement. "Which is why the head of the Pod Enforcers is contacting the head of the Pack Protectors. We'll have them completely surrounded, both on land and sea."

"Sounds like a plan," Zach said. "And since my stepfather and sister were involved, I intend to be there, as well."

Zach hadn't had to argue at all with Merc about his intention to be there when the ring was rounded up and shut down. Shayla, however, did. With the tension thick enough to cut with a knife, Zach put a quick stop to that. "She's coming with me," he said, daring Merc to disagree.

The Mer-King clearly had too much on his mind. He back down right away, muttering something about tending to final arrangements. He and Shayla wanted to go back to her house, but Merc didn't want to let Ion out of his sight since he should have already been in custody, so they all decided to stay at June's house.

Ion seemed subdued. Zach didn't blame him. He made several attempts to catch his stepfather alone, but with June clinging to her husband's side, a private conversation seemed impossible.

Merc and Shayla bunked down in the living room, the king claiming the couch and Shayla taking the love seat. While Zach fervently hoped Shayla would join him in his bedroom after everyone else fell asleep, he had an idea her brother would be watching her like a hawk.

Early the next morning, Merc went into the sea to make sure his troops were in place and ready. Since Zach was Shifter, he'd been given the duty of being the point of contact with the Pack Protectors. Shayla had called Maddie the night before, and she'd passed along Zach's cell phone info to Maddie's brother. He'd be one of the Protectors fanning out to make a perimeter on the Pleasure Pier.

The operation had a high potential for success, but Zach knew failure might still be a possibility. The crowds of tourists were smaller than they'd be if it was summer, but there'd still be a lot of people who could inadvertently get in the way and be subject to being hurt. Especially if gunfire was involved. He hoped it wouldn't be, but given what had happened when he and Shayla met up with these guys, guns were a definite possibility.

At the house, June and Ion stayed shut up in the bedroom. June emerged mid-morning to grab a couple of donuts and two mugs of coffee, smiling sadly at her son before disappearing behind closed doors again. Since Ion would soon be going to prison, Zach figured they were saying their goodbyes the only way they could.

He felt terrible for his mother, but Ion had brought this on himself.

Even worse, Zach had a sneaking suspicion there might be more that his stepfather had not yet told them. It would all come out in the end, no doubt.

Merc reappeared in the late afternoon. He brimmed with confidence, telling them his Enforcers were assembled and clearing the sea around the Pleasure Pier. There wouldn't be any dolphin shows for the humans to ooh and aah at this sunset.

The Pack Protectors were assembling near Moody Gardens. From there, they'd fan out, making their way to the Pleasure Pier in small groups of two, three and four. The decision had been made to allow no single stragglers.

Since the kidnappers had seen Zach and Shayla, Merc made one last attempt to get them to agree to stay home.

"No," Shayla said flatly. "We'll wear baseball caps and sunglasses. With so many people on the pier, there's no way they'll recognize us."

"Fine." With too much on his mind, Merc shrugged. "Do whatever you want. Just don't get in the way. We'll rendezvous at Murdoch's Souvenir Shop at the end of the pier. See you soon." With that, he strode away.

Zach decided they'd stroll Seawall Boulevard, arriving at the pier as if they were average tourists, taking in all the sights.

The pier at dusk was a beautiful place. The amusement park turned the neon lights on for their rides, the garish colors somehow blending with the rose-and-purple sky. Quite a few of the tourists had drifted away to find food.

Zach and Shayla strolled arm in arm. They both wore

baseball caps, and she'd tucked her long hair up inside hers. The sunglasses weren't really necessary with the dimming light, so Zach removed his and tucked them in his shirt pocket. Shayla kept hers on.

Pretending to be tourists, they examined everything, exclaiming over gaudy souvenirs, clocks made of seashells and garish, poorly made tote bags. Though Zach continually scanned the crowd, he saw nothing suspicious. No men with several tipsy teenagers. But then, he also couldn't spot the Pack Protectors. Merc and his men waited under the water, which was probably a good thing, since due to his sheer size and massive amount of confidence, Merc tended to stand out in any size crowd.

Some kind of commotion seemed to be going on by the Ferris wheel. Exchanging a quick glance, Zach and Shayla jogged on over, joining the circle of people that had begun to form. They managed to work their way to the front, just in time to see a scuffle. Four young girls—Mermaids in human form—huddled together near a wooden building, wide-eyed and shaking, clearly terrified.

One man wearing a Galveston Police officer uniform and whose aura revealed him to be Shifter, had started questioning a young man with bright yellow dreadlocks, his pale skin and aura marking him as Mer. He shook his head, braids whipping around his face, clearly not wanting to answer whatever question the Protector had asked him. In fact, he began backing away, his furtive glances around revealing his cohorts. Two men, older, human, took off running. Several other Protectors, who'd been hanging back on the fringes of the crowd, went after them.

Taking advantage of the distraction, the young Merman ran for the edge of the pier. The crowd gasped in unison as he jumped, hitting the sea twenty some feet below.

Though many of the humans believed he'd killed himself, Zach knew better. Merc and his crew of Pod Enforcers would be there to foil his attempt at escape.

Meanwhile, several other Pack Protectors formed a protective ring around the terrified young Mermaids.

"I've got to go talk to them," Shayla said. "But I'm also concerned that they didn't catch the doctors or scientists or whatever they are. That young Merman clearly was the courier, trying to make the trade. I'm afraid they might have moved in too early, and the real bad guys got away."

"You don't know that," Zach reassured her. "By the time we got here, they might have already apprehended the others."

"I hope so." Taking Zach's arm, Shayla tugged him toward the girls. Two Mermen had already moved in, talking to the teens quietly. When Shayla reached them, they stepped aside. Catching sight of her face, the girls gave a collective gasp.

"Your Highness!"

"Shhhh." With a wave at the crowd, Shayla silenced them. "Are you all right? Were you drugged?"

"I don't think so." The youngest of the four, a petite raven-haired girl who appeared to be thirteen or fourteen, stepped forward. "Gresh—the guy who jumped into the water—he's our friend. He told us he'd met a guy who owned a modeling agency and wanted to take our pictures."

A slim blonde girl nodded. "It sounded harmless

enough, and fun besides. What girl doesn't dream of being discovered and made into a supermodel?"

Shayla's lips tightened, but she didn't address this comment. Instead, she fixed each girl individually with a royal glare. "Do your parents know you're here?"

Four young heads went down in unison.

"I thought not." Shayla gestured at the two Mermen. "Have them all checked out to make sure they haven't been given anything. I'm sure their king will want to have a word with them, as well."

At the mention of the king, the girls groaned. Shayla shook her finger at them. "Believe me, you won't be in half as much trouble with the king as you will be once your parents find out what almost happened to you."

With that, she swept away. Grinning, Zach went after her. "Way to leave them stressing," he said.

"They deserve it. They have no idea what almost happened to them." When she raised her face to his, he was stunned to realize she was blinking back tears. "It's also horrible that a friend betrayed them. I sure hope Merc caught that kid."

Zach pulled her close, wrapping his arms around her tightly, offering comfort while all the while wishing he could kiss her, even though he knew this wasn't the time or the place.

"Thank you," she said, stepping out of his arms and smiling up at him. "You have no idea how badly I needed that hug."

Which only made him want to hold her again. Instead, he knew they needed to get moving. The Pod Enforcers were shepherding the teens down the pier toward Murdoch's.

"Let's go rendezvous," he told her. "And find out if they got all the bastards."

* * *

As they neared the gift shop, Shayla saw their group. Merc's golden head stood tall above the rest. She hurried over to him, staying to the side while he spoke to the over-awed teenagers. Finally, the girls were escorted down the beach, presumably to find a secluded enough spot where they could disappear into the ocean so they could go home.

Silently, she and Merc watched them go. Zach continued to stay close by as well, which made her happy. "Did you manage to grab that kid who jumped off the pier?" she asked, keeping her voice low.

"Yes." Jaw set, Merc grimaced. "Those girls were his friends. They're all in the same class in school. Someone offered him the opportunity to make money, so he decided to sell out his so-called friends. He'll face charges."

"What about the others?"

"All the humans have been rounded up and are even now being interrogated by the Pack Protectors," Merc said. "Including the purported mastermind. He's revealed the location of his laboratory, and I've sent men there to retrieve his captives. They're there now."

Again, inexplicably, she felt like crying. Mustering every ounce of self-control she possessed, she managed to only nod.

"I've got several medical personnel checking out the young Mermaids. The ones who were to be traded. They appear to be all right, and so far, there are no indications they were drugged. And the captives…" He shuddered. "My men tell me they appear near death. Their blood has been taken so many times, their arms are a jagged mess of scars."

Her sharp intake of breath felt painful. When Zach

put his arm around her, offering his support, she took it. Merc eyed them both, but didn't comment, for which she was grateful. Zach had no idea how much his physical presence comforted her. She hoped to show him, slowly and thoroughly, later.

For now, though, she needed closure. At least she knew this entire crazy underground bunch of lowlifes would pay for what they'd done. And even better, they wouldn't have the opportunity to do it again.

"No more deaths?" she asked, needing to know.

"No." He swallowed hard. "I'm hoping everyone pulls through."

One of the Pack Protectors motioned to Zach that he wanted to have a word with him. Releasing her, he stepped away.

"Can I go see them?" Shayla asked, her heart aching. She couldn't imagine what those women had gone through.

"Not yet. Maybe later. I want them thoroughly examined, given IVs and whatever else needs to be done to help them heal."

Zach returned, shaking his head. "I was just talking to one of the Pack Protectors. The leader of the group turned out to be Mer, not human," he said. "I'm guessing he wasn't there when Shayla and I were prisoners or we would have known. When they rounded him up, he was wearing a white coat and trying to blend in with the humans, but you know that pesky thing about auras. Can't hide."

Merc snarled. "Mer? Then he belongs to me. Where is he?"

Zach pointed to a group of Pod Enforcers who'd

formed a circle around someone. "They're talking to him now."

Merc strode over, Shayla right behind him. Halfway there, someone grabbed Merc's arm and drew him aside, speaking urgently, leaving Shayla to continue on without him. Zach remained at her side. The circle of Pod Enforcers moved apart, clearing a path for their royal princess.

In the center of the group, a tall, extremely thin, bald Merman stood, his hands behind his back. His patrician features were notable only in their ordinariness. Jolted, Shayla realized she'd seen him before.

"You." Stunned, Shayla stared at the handcuffed man. Still defiant, he raised his head and stared back.

"Do you know him?" Zach asked, glancing from one to the other.

"We've met." Shayla swallowed hard. "Though I'm not sure I ever knew his name. He was part of Richard's protection detail. I believe he was there when Richard was killed."

The man said nothing, though a challenge flashed in his cold eyes. A challenge to what, Shayla wondered, feeling sick. Surely, this man hadn't been involved in murdering the very man he'd been charged with protecting.

Merc strode up just then, doing his own double take when he saw the man the Pod had captured. Then, clearly putting two and two together in a way that Shayla had been afraid to, he narrowed his gaze. "Treason is a crime punishable by death," he declared. "And so is murder."

Shayla gasped. "Are you saying you think he…?"

"You have no proof," the captive stated, lifting his chin even higher, the curve of his mouth mocking them.

"Actually, we do." Merc turned to Shayla, taking her

hand. "That's what my guard just took me aside to tell me. One of Richard's former protection detail has come clean, in exchange for leniency. He's already provided us with the names of those involved with poisoning Richard."

The captive paled. "I didn't poison him," he said. "I swear."

"But you looked the other way when someone did." Arms crossed, Merc shook his head. "Aiding and abetting a murder. Added to your newest crime, treason against your king, and I think your days are numbered."

"I want a deal," the man said, desperation coloring his voice. "Like the other guy got. Life imprisonment instead of death. Give me that, and I'll tell you everything."

Chapter 18

Holding her breath, Shayla waited to see what her brother would do. Beside her, Zach put his arm around her, pulling her close. Though tempted to rest her head on his shoulder, she didn't. Better to stand tall and straight when given news that might feel like a savage blow. Zach would be her cushion, helping her to absorb and understand.

"Before we come to any agreement," Merc finally answered. "I need to know what you were doing with all the blood you stole."

"Stole?" The man appeared honestly surprised. "I was told all the Mermaids who participated in the experiment were willing participants."

"Seriously." Shayla spit the word. "What about the ones who died?"

Her question seemed to bewilder him even more. "I

don't have any idea what you mean by that. No one died. This was all handled very professionally by my employees. I have a lab, and the volunteers came in and donated blood. They left after that. No one died."

Shayla and Merc exchanged a long look. If this man spoke truth—and clearly he believed what he said— then someone else had been responsible for keeping innocent Mermaids captive, starving them and taking so much blood they died.

Not mincing words, Merc outlined all this to him.

As he listened, all the color leached from the man's face. "I had no idea," he said. "I swear. I keep meticulous records, and I'll be more than happy to share them with you." He swallowed. "That is, once you grant me a deal."

Merc considered again. "Any deal will only be valid as long as you tell the truth. If I learn that you've lied— about anything—the deal is off."

Slowly, the man nodded.

"One more question," Merc asked. "What did you do with the blood?"

For the first time since he'd been taken captive, the man brightened. "Perfume," he said. "I've perfected a formula. With just the right amount—very little, actually—of Mermaid blood, any female human wearing this can become irresistible to men. I was just about to start scheduling meetings with various perfume manufacturers. I'll take the highest bidder. This should make me a fortune on the black market."

"On the backs of dead women," Shayla pointed out.

The other man's animated expression fell. "Sorry. Truly, I didn't know. I'm actually convinced there must be a misunderstanding. No one possibly could have died. My men would have told me." Shaking his head, he kicked at the wooden pier. "I would never allow this to happen. Not only would someone dying be a crime, but blood taken from a dead Mermaid would taint that entire batch of perfume, rendering it unusable. Since noting like that happened, I have to believe you're wrong."

"I wish we were." Merc's grim voice didn't reveal whether he believed the other man or not. "But even if you didn't know, you were still responsible when all's said and done." He narrowed his eyes. "Now tell me what you know about Prince Richard's death."

"Not without an agreement." His quick response showed none of this fazed him. "You're the king. I need your protection. I have too much to offer the world to be put to death."

Modest little guy, wasn't he? Shayla had a sudden, fierce urge to slap him. Of course, she reined this in, keeping quiet and waiting to see what her brother, the king, would do.

"Agreed," he finally said, raising his voice so all could hear. "I, King Merc of the Atlantic Ocean, swear that this man's crimes shall be punishable by life imprisonment rather than death, as long as he fulfills his part of our agreement and provides me verifiable information about the death of Prince Richard of Gill. Let my words be written down."

The leader of the Pod Enforcers nodded, carefully transcribing the words into some sort of electronic device that looked exactly like a computer tablet.

For the first time since he'd been arrested, the captive appeared to relax. "Thank you, my king." He bowed low. Once he stood straight again, he met Shayla's gaze.

"I know you loved Richard and he loved you, but there was another woman," he began.

"I know," Shayla interrupted. "He broke it off with her before the engagement."

"True. But she refused to accept that it was over."

Zach held Shayla while the piece of Merman excrement spewed garbage about her dead fiancé. Judging from the tight line of Merc's jaw, the king appeared to be regretting granting the criminal leniency. The horrible part of it all was that immediately there was no way to verify whether or not the man's words were true.

After initially going rigid in his arms, Shayla listened intently, not asking a single question. Zach couldn't tell if she believed all the nonsense the other man said, but he knew hearing it hurt her. Pain radiated from her, and he longed to take it inside himself and destroy it for her, but he couldn't.

In a nutshell, the story boiled down to this. Prince Richard had taken a lover, the sister of one of his royal guards. When he accepted the arranged marriage to Shayla, he'd done the honorable thing and ended the affair. But the other woman, who claimed to love him, refused to accept it and convinced her brother that the prince had taken her by force. For that, she'd said, Prince Richard needed to die.

"What was her name?" Shayla finally spoke, the question uttered in a voice dripping with ice.

The man sputtered, clearly startled. "Teredia Shiles."

Zach and Shayla exchanged a stunned glance. The very same woman Ion had wanted Zach to marry.

And now Zach knew beyond a shadow of a doubt that in fact, his stepfather hadn't told him everything.

Speaking of Ion, had the older man come down to the pier or remained at June's house? Zach casually scanned the area, actually beginning to wonder if Ion would try to escape his punishment. If Ion went on the run, that meant he'd never see his wife, Nantha and Zach again.

About to dig out his phone and call his mother to see if Ion was still there, Zach located him. Ion stood, hands in his pockets, in a corner engaged in what appeared to be an earnest discussion with a Pod Enforcer. Eyeing him, Zach could feel a muscle working in his jaw.

Teredia. The woman Ion had wanted him to marry had been Richard's lover and had him murdered. Had Ion known?

"If that son of a gun tried to involve me in some murderous plot, so help me…" He didn't realize he'd actually spoken out loud until Shayla squeezed his arm. When he looked back at the captive, he saw the other man not only understood what he meant, but knew the answer.

"You'd better tell me," Zach said, forcing the words out past clenched teeth. "Was this Teredia involved in a plot to overthrow the royal family?"

The man blanched, which for Zach seemed answer enough. Apparently, for Merc as well, because he took a threatening step toward the captive, making the other man flinch.

Looking from one to another, Shayla cursed. "What a tangled web they weave. Now it all begins to make sense."

"Are you all right?" Zach asked, watching Shayla closely. It had to be difficult, finally knowing what she'd suspected all along. Her fiancé had been murdered.

"I think I am," Shayla answered, bemusement and wonder in her voice. "It almost feels like a relief, to finally get some closure." She took a deep breath. "However, this Teredia has stolen enough from me. I want to meet her and see her punished for what's she's done."

"Oh, she will be," Merc interjected. "She's been apprehended by law enforcement in her own kingdom. I have men on the way to take custody of her now. But what I want to know is who is this Teredia, and why do you both seem familiar with her name?"

"Ion signed a marriage contract binding me with her," Zach explained. "I had him break it off when Shayla and I got involved, but clearly there was much more to it than I imagined."

Merc frowned. "Ion," he bellowed, causing the entire group to go silent. "Come here."

Several humans passing by turned and stared. Shayla shot her brother a warning glance. "Maybe we'd better go somewhere else to have this talk."

Merc nodded. "Not Broken Chains. As much as I love that place, not only can I not hear myself talk over the music, but women won't leave me alone in there."

Unable to help himself, Zach muttered, "Braggart." This earned him a grin from Shayla and a raised brow from Merc. Clearly, they'd both heard him. He shrugged.

"Zach?" Shayla asked. "Do you think your mom would mind if we went to her house? We could go to mine, but hers is a lot closer. Plus—" she lowered her voice "—I haven't had time to clean my place up. It's a wreck."

He couldn't help but laugh. "Only you," he told her, kissing her on the cheek, "would worry about something like that right now. But to answer your question, I'm sure my mother wouldn't mind if we all adjourn to her place. In fact, she's probably waiting for us."

"She is," Ion said. "She wasn't happy when I insisted on coming out here."

"Then let's go." Merc signaled his men, and one of the Pod Enforcers hurried over, nodding as Merc gave instructions.

Zach turned to find the Pack Protector he'd been speaking to, Maddie's brother, and found him waiting with a cluster of other Shifters. Zach told him what was going on.

"Are we still needed?" the other man asked. "Since there are no other Shifters involved…"

Overhearing, Merc shook his head. "I think we can take this from here," he said. "My men have custody of the offenders."

"What about the humans?" the Pack Protector asked. He motioned to the Shifter who wore the Galveston PD uniform. "They'll need to be booked here locally. We've ascertained that they don't know anything damaging. What they do know sounds more like a drug-induced fantasy than truth. I doubt they'd be taken seriously if they start rambling about Mermaid blood."

"Good point." Merc motioned to his men, ordering they release the humans to the local police officer who happened to be a Shifter. The offenders who were Merfolk went with the Pod Enforcers, who would take them under the sea and book them into jail.

As they all headed toward their various vehicles, Merc fell in with Zach and Shayla. "What's going on with you two?" he asked, his voice casual, though the look in his eyes warned Zach he'd better not hurt his sister.

Zach opened his mouth to answer and then thought better of it. He'd let Shayla take this one.

"None of your business," she told her brother, smiling.

Merc shrugged. "You're happy, that's all that matters anyway. Just be careful, okay?"

To Zach's surprise, Shayla linked her arm with his and laughed. "We always are. Right, Zach?"

Zach nodded. Ion walked past them, head down, hands jammed in his pockets.

"Should maybe someone ride with him?" Zach asked, unable to keep from wondering about the wisdom of letting his stepfather take his own car anywhere alone. "While I appreciate you holding off from taking him in custody for my mother's sake, his irrational behavior might lead him to do something crazy."

"Good point," Merc said, splitting off from them and hurrying after Ion. "Plus, I'm sure you two want your privacy."

Did they? Zach always would, but he wasn't sure about Shayla. Once her brother disappeared, her light-hearted mood fell off her. Clearly, she'd been putting on a brave face. She'd received a lot of upsetting news.

While he was grateful that she didn't feel the need to be fake with him, he also couldn't stop worrying about her. "Are you all right?" he asked, as they got into his car and buckled up.

Instead of answering, she tilted her head as if carefully considering his words. "You know, I think I am." The sense of wonder in her voice made him believe her. "I never understood *why* Richard died. Knowing he might have been murdered made it a thousand times worse. I went over a hundred different scenarios, things I could have done to change things."

She gave a heavy sigh. "Knowing the truth doesn't make his death easier, but I finally have some closure."

With a rueful shake of the head, she grimaced. "Over-used word, *closure*. But it's the right one."

"I'm glad," he said, starting the car. "I confess, I'm dreading hearing how all of this is connected. Ion arranging to marry me off to your fiancé's murderer? Why? What would be the benefit there for him?"

"I don't know." She touched his shoulder. "But get ready. I have a feeling we're about to find out."

When they pulled up to June's house, Ion and Merc had already arrived and were just getting out of the car. They stopped and waited while Zach parked.

As Zach and Shayla joined them, Ion met Zach's gaze. "I'm sorry," he said.

And then they all went inside.

Shayla wasn't sure what she expected to hear. Nothing Ion could say could shock her more than learning Richard had truly been murdered and why. Another woman. The old love triangle. Oddly enough, by some mutual form of tacit agreement, she and Richard had never discussed their previous love lives. It had been enough, Richard said, to know they would be each other's last. He didn't need to know about what had come before.

She'd always found that sweet, believing it proof that Richard was a good man. Now she had to wonder if maybe he just hadn't wanted her to know. Since he'd been with Teredia, who from all indications had long been part of a plot to overthrow the throne, what did that say about him? Of course, he'd broken things off, but she had no way to know what his beliefs were. And now that he was dead, she couldn't even ask him.

While also a royal prince, his home was far from hers,

in the North Sea. Had it been possible Richard had ambitions to expand his family's kingdom?

Maybe Ion would know. If not, she imagined this Teredia, once she'd been interrogated, would be able to shed more light on things.

Zach's mother ran to greet her husband, throwing her arms around him and holding on tight. He held her too, his composed facial expression at odds with the anguish in his eyes.

Merc cleared his throat. "Ion, I believe you haven't told us everything." He outlined what the ringleader had said. With every word the king spoke, Ion appeared to shrink.

Finally, he pushed out of his wife's embrace and walked to stare out the window. "I know you've given a couple of others a deal," he began.

"Let me guess." Mockery filled Merc's tone. "You want a deal too, before you'll talk?"

"No." Jamming his hands into his pockets, Ion turned to face them. "I don't deserve a deal. I almost caused my own daughter's death, I plotted to overthrow the crown and a Mermaid died because of me. I've been involved in all of it, working as hard as I could to disrupt everything good about the only life I've ever known."

"No." June rushed toward him. "You are lying. Ion, I know you're a good man. You helped me raise my son. I see how you are with your daughter. You're a good, loving father and kind and gentle husband. I refuse to believe you would do this—any of this—without a really good reason."

Zach stepped forward, standing at his mother's side. "I agree. So Ion, before you start confessing, if you really did do all these awful things, why don't you start with telling us the reason why?"

The older man stared at his stepson, shock and sorrow warring in his eyes. "I can't."

"You do realize it will all come out in the end," Merc said, taking no pity on him.

"Not if I die first." Ion's chin came up and defiance flashed in his eyes.

June cried out. "Don't even talk like that. Think of me, your daughter and Zach. Your death would destroy us."

"Better me than..." Ion didn't finish.

"Falling on your sword, so to speak?" Merc shook his head. "Dying to protect someone else will only ensure that person gets away with their crime and will be free to commit the same thing again. Others will be hurt. Is that what you want?"

Shayla had a sudden flash of insight. "I think I know who you're trying to protect. It's Nantha, isn't it?"

For a split second, alarm flashed across Ion's face. But that was enough. Everyone saw it.

"No." His denial, though strong, came too late. He realized this from the looks on everyone's faces. "Please. She's just a young girl."

"Who is already in a whale's worth of trouble," Merc said sternly. "You might as well tell us the rest of it."

But Ion kept his mouth closed.

"Ion, listen." Zach spoke up. "If Nantha has done something even worse than what we already know about, she needs help. When I talked to her, she seemed strangely unrepentant about her actions. If there's more, allowing yourself to be punished for her crimes will not help her. Think about it."

Ion slowly nodded. "You're right," he finally said. "Nantha got involved with the wrong people. I did what I had to do in order to save her."

June gasped. Zach frowned. Shayla's heart ached, both for the woman about to lose her husband to either prison or death, and the man she loved who clearly struggled to come to terms with what his impetuous sister might have done.

Wait, what? Loved? Filing that info away to examine in detail later, Shayla focused on the topic at hand. "Hold on," she said, drawing everyone's attention. "In getting all these bits and pieces of information, I don't see how all this is tied together. The Merman making perfume from Mermaid's blood, the other men who worked for him torturing young Mermaids and letting them die, Nantha running off and getting captured by these same men, you—Ion—arranging a marriage between Zach and a woman who killed my fiancé. Not to mention Ion stating that this perfume could be used to influence others. What is the common thread tying all this together? Can you explain that to me first?"

Merc gave her a look, full of respect. "She has a point," he said. "And we need to know what exactly Nantha has done."

Ion began to talk. "Nantha has always been brilliant, but she has little common sense or empathy for others. She was the one to come up with the idea of making a perfume from Mermaid pheromones and selling it to the highest bidder." He sighed, dragging a hand through his silver hair. "And she was the one who actually discovered the blood was more powerful if it came from a virgin."

"How do you know this?" Zach asked, his expression

telling Shayla he was hoping against hope that none of what Ion said would be true.

"I caught her experimenting with two of her friends. She was collecting their blood. When I walked in, she lied and told me it was for a science project."

"And you talked to the teacher," June put in, with a mother's understanding.

"Yes. When I confronted my daughter, Nantha told me everything. By then she'd revised her plan. Instead of selling the formula off to the highest bidder, she wanted to use the perfume herself on a much larger scale. Domination. Think about what can be done if a scent can make any man, all men, fall madly in love with you. She even had a name for it. Sirens' Song."

So far, Merc hadn't interrupted. "That's an awful lot of planning for a seventeen-year-old," he said.

Ion shrugged. "I thought so, too, but like I said, she's brilliant. Before she had this idea, she was the head of her class with a bright future. But this project consumed her, causing her schoolwork and social life to suffer. Which of course came to my attention."

"I remember that." June went to him, slipping her hand into his. "You were so worried about her. You even thought she might have gotten involved in drugs."

"What?" Zach looked from one parent to the other. "Why didn't you say something to me? I would have talked to her."

"Because I didn't want to speak badly of your sister with only suspicions. And then, when I knew for sure what was going on, the web had spread so far and become so entangled, I feared for her life."

It turned out Nantha had decided she needed help. One of her friends' parents was actively involved in the group trying to overthrow the crown, and when Nantha found out her own father was as well, she'd decided this would fit right in with her plans. Insinuating herself into the group, she engineered everything, using people like chess pieces being moved across a board. Until after a period of merely months, she'd managed to become one of the movement's leaders.

"They'd come up with a plan," Ion continued. "And when Nantha told me all this, I realized my daughter was likely a sociopath. Nantha left no stone unturned. I'm sorry, Zach." Ion's expression crumpled. "I should have told you the truth."

"What about you, Ion?" Shayla asked. "From your erratic behavior, I think you're leaving out your part in all this."

Ion grimaced. "I will take her punishment gladly," he finally said. "But she needs to be locked up, so she can't hurt anyone else."

Zach's mouth worked, but no sound came out. Shayla wanted to cry for him, for all of them. Zach and June had clearly no idea about Nantha. They'd believed her mischievous, but innocent. This had to hurt them on a visceral level.

"What about the men who were holding young Mermaids hostage?" Merc asked. "Wasn't Nantha one of their captives for a while, too?"

"So help me, if you lied about that, too…" Zach said, the harsh rasp in his voice revealing his pain.

"I didn't." Ion met his stepson's gaze. "Believe me. Everything I said was true. She and her friends were singing to fishermen, after which they tried out the latest batch of her perfume. She's the one who came up with the idea of pretending to be held hostage, asking for the virgin Mermaids in exchange. She must have been having difficulty finding enough willing participants in her bloodletting scheme. But I didn't know any of this. She played me, just like she played all of you." He covered his face with his hands and quietly wept, his shoulders shaking.

June wrapped her arms around him tightly, holding on as if she never intended to let go.

Shayla's throat ached. "What will happen now?" she asked her brother. "To Ion, and to Nantha? And Teredia, as well as all the others who were involved in this?"

"The Pod Enforcers are rounding them all up now. They'll be interrogated, of course. There will be hearings and trials, and each one will be dealt their punishment."

She thought about asking to speak with Teredia before the other woman was sentenced, and then decided against it. That part of her life was over. She'd gotten closure and had finally learned the truth about what had happened to Richard. The time had come to put all that behind her. After all, the future beckoned.

When Zach took her hand, she glanced up at him, letting her heart show in her eyes. His gaze locked on hers, and after a moment, some of the pain left his expression.

Merc looked from one to the other. "I'll keep you informed," he promised. "As soon as things settle down, I'll be in touch."

"Thank you," Zach said. "I appreciate that."

June sniffled, signaling how hard she was trying to hold back tears.

"Come," Merc said, gesturing at Ion. "It's time to return home and face justice."

Face resolute, Ion nodded. He turned and kissed June one more time before leaving her to go with his king.

Everyone followed them outside, Zach still holding tightly on to Shayla's hand. Side by side, they watched as Merc and Ion walked into the ocean, eventually disappearing. Shayla waded out, waiting until their human clothing floated to the surface, collecting each sodden article and bringing it back to shore. Avoiding looking at anyone, she spread everything out on the patio table, knowing the sea breeze and the sun would dry it.

Behind her, Zach conversed with his mother in low tones, offering words of comfort. When June requested to be left alone, Shayla understood. Each person had their own methods of dealing with grief.

Chapter 19

Taking a deep breath, Shayla went over and said her goodbyes. To her surprise, June offered her a hug. "Take care of my son tonight," she whispered in Shayla's ear. "He'll be hurting, too."

Shayla nodded. "I will." To prove it, she once again slipped her fingers in Zach's. Hand in hand, they walked to his car and drove away.

During the drive to her house on the other side of the island, Zach didn't speak, and Shayla didn't try to fill the silence with meaningless words. When they pulled up in her driveway, Zach didn't kill the engine or make any move to get out of the car.

"Don't you want to come in?" she asked.

"I'm sorry, but I don't. I need a distraction. I think I'm going to head over to Broken Chains and have a beer."

"I'll go with you," she said instantly. "That sounds a

lot better than sitting around my house." She knew she had to be careful not to let him suspect she was afraid to leave him alone.

He shrugged. "Suit yourself." Putting the car in Reverse, he backed out of her driveway and headed toward Harbor Shore Drive.

Broken Chains was packed, and the band—country swing this time—was going full force. Hand in hand, they twisted their way through the crowd, looking for a table. Of course, there weren't any on the main floor, so they headed for the stairs.

The top floor was nearly as full. Someone near the back stood up and waved. Maddie. And Carmen. Shayla pointed them out to Zach, standing up on tiptoe to put her mouth closer to his ear as she asked him if he wanted to join them. After a moment of hesitation, he nodded.

They made their way to the table. Right when they pulled out chairs, the waitress appeared, bringing Shayla's white wine and Zach's beer. When they thanked her, she grinned and waved before walking off to take someone else's order.

"I heard from my brother," Maddie said, bouncing in her chair from excitement. "He told me what happened, or at least as much as he knew."

Shayla filled them in on the rest, still holding tight to Zach's hand. He sipped his beer, listening without commenting.

When she finally wound down, even Carmen appeared stunned. "Wow. I can't believe a seventeen-year-old could do all that."

Zach grimaced. "Me, either. Part of me doesn't want to believe it. The other part knows it's true. When I spoke to her right after we saved her from the kidnappers, she had zero remorse for her actions. And she played me well, since all along she wasn't really being held prisoner." After speaking, he immediately looked stricken.

"Are you going to be okay?" Maddie asked.

"I'll be fine." Zach's immediate and curt response told Shayla that he wasn't. At least not right now.

Getting through the next few days was tough. If Nantha and Ion's betrayal had ripped him apart, Zach could only imagine how his mother must feel. She'd firmly refused his offer to stay with her, telling him he needed to get on with his life as she intended to get on with hers.

Then she'd packed everything up and gone to visit her sister in Denver. With Ion imprisoned, she'd told Zach she needed space between her and the sea.

Part of him could relate to this need to put distance between the old, familiar life where even the sight of the ocean would make her think of Ion. She hadn't said how long she'd be gone, and he hadn't pressed her.

Shayla stayed close, as if she understood how alone he felt. He wondered how she could, when he didn't understand it himself.

"You still have a family, you know," she told him.

He shook his head. "Do I? Sure, I have my mom. But Ion was like a father to me, and Nantha…" He couldn't even finish. The person his baby sister had become hurt too much to think about.

"The love is still there, no matter what." She hugged him. "That will never change, no matter the circumstances."

Though he nodded as if he agreed, inside he felt hollow. "You don't know what I'd give to be able to turn into a Merman and go under the water and visit them. I hate not knowing what's going on."

"Me, too," she agreed. "Three days have passed with no word from my brother. I haven't wanted to bug him and call, but if we don't hear anything by tomorrow, I will."

"I appreciate that." He put his arm around her, loving the way she leaned into him. Though they'd both agreed that their relationship should have no strings attached, that was no longer enough for him. He knew he had to tell her, even if doing so risked losing her for good. As June had so succinctly put it, time to get on with his life.

Yet every time he opened his mouth to tell her how he felt, he couldn't force the words past the lump in his throat. He decided he'd show her instead.

"I'd like to cook dinner for you tonight," he said. "At my place."

Her lovely eyes widened. "Your place?" Her mischievous smile made him smile back. "Since I haven't ever been there, I was beginning to wonder if you even had one."

"You've got me there," he replied ruefully. "I don't live on the island, so it's not as convenient as your house or my mother's. And it's an apartment. But if you don't mind coming up to Texas City, I'm a pretty decent cook."

Studying him, she nodded. "I'd be honored. You're full of surprises, aren't you?"

She had no idea how much he planned to surprise her.

Carefully nonchalant, he shrugged. "I try."

"You don't have to cook for me," she said, her expression earnest. "We can just go somewhere and grab a bite if you want."

Leaning in, he kissed her cheek. "Indulge me. I need to feel grounded."

Of course she let it go then, as he'd suspected she would. He told her he'd pick her up at six and then left to hit up the grocery store.

When he stepped into his small apartment, grocery bags in hand, he saw the place through a stranger's eyes. He liked his home neat and in order, but for the first time he realized the apartment appeared a bit austere, more like a hotel room than a home.

Since there wasn't much he could do about that right now, he decided to ignore it. Unpacking his bags, he assembled all the fixings for his favorite meal: homemade lasagna with garlic bread and a side salad. Humming under his breath, he got busy.

By the time he needed to leave to go pick Shayla up, the lasagna was assembled and ready to put into the oven. He'd also mixed up a nice salad, which was chilling, and the bottle of his favorite red wine blend would complement everything perfectly.

He only hoped she liked Italian food. Despite the way they fit together, despite the heat and the passion and the fact that they just plain enjoyed each other's company, there was a lot he didn't know about her and vice-versa. More than anything, he hoped they could change that.

His buoyant mood felt great; even the underlying hint of nervousness simmering below the surface didn't faze him. He'd bought her a bouquet of grocery-store flowers, figuring she'd like the simplicity of the unarranged blooms. Driving to her house, he felt confident she'd make the same choice he had to take their relationship to the next level.

After parking in front of her house, he hopped out

of the car and started for the front door. She opened it before he got there, wearing a long sundress that showcased her lithe figure.

Suddenly tongue-tied, he smiled and handed her the flowers. Her face lit up.

"Thank you," she said. "Come in. I'll just need to put these in water."

He waited while she did, his heart racing as he tried to find something casual to say. Alone with Shayla, the last thing he wanted to do was talk. He had a sudden image of his hands tangled in her long black hair, her face upturned, gaze eager, and her lips parted to receive his kiss.

His entire body reacted. She was beautiful and sexy, true. But with her, it was much more than that. She had a way of looking at him as if she truly knew him. And she seemed to genuinely like him, as if she actually considered him a friend despite the sizzling electricity that seemed to be constant when they were around each other.

If he gave into his desire now, things would remain the same as they were. Too casual. He thought of the meal he'd prepared and the evening he'd planned and resolved not to touch her. Not yet. Not until he knew they both wanted to be more than just friends who hooked up.

And if not? Then what? Did he possess the strength to simply walk away?

When she returned, her warm smile made him smile back.

"Are you ready?" he asked.

"I am."

When they pulled up in front of his apartment, he tried to see it through her eyes. "Sorry, it's kind of boring," he said. "Brick and wood, all the same. And no ocean view."

Still smiling, she shook her head. "I can't wait to see where you live. You can tell a lot about a person from their home space."

He thought of his bland apartment and winced. "Not me. I never really took the time to fix the place up."

Unlocking his front door, he stepped aside for her to enter. He closed and locked the door behind her. As he'd planned, the delicious aroma of his lasagna baking filled the room.

"That smells amazing," she commented, prowling around the room. He watched her closely, ready for her expressive face to reveal disappointment, but her thoughtful expression never changed.

She stopped in front of a framed print of a wolf that hung above his sofa. "This is beautiful," she said. "Who took this photo?"

"My father took it," he said, going to stand beside her. Close, but not touching. "Not Ion, but my birth father. He died in an oil well fire when I was two. That's my mother in her Wolf form. She gifted me this print when I graduated from college. She'd been keeping it up in the attic, all wrapped up because she couldn't bear to look at it."

"So you'd never seen it before?" she asked softly, slipping her hand into his.

Again the wild, fierce yearning to pull her close and claim her mouth in a kiss. Instead, he closed his fingers around hers and nodded. "Exactly. It's been with me ever since."

A timer went off in the kitchen, and he reluctantly released her hand so he could check on the meal. Time to pull out the lasagna and let it cool while he heated the loaf of garlic bread and opened the wine.

Shayla stayed in the other room, still studying the

portrait. "Do you look like her when you're a Wolf?" she asked, eyeing him over her shoulder.

He brought her a glass of wine. "Not really. Females are a bit smaller. My coat is darker, too. More like my father's."

"Thank you." Accepting the glass, she took a small sip. "I'd like to see that someday. You changing into your Wolf form. Would you mind if I did?"

His heart stuttered, even though he told himself she didn't know what asking such a question meant. Except for other Pack members, Wolf Shape-shifters only allowed their one true mate to see them in their other form. By Shayla asking to do this, she was asking to be his mate.

Which is what he wanted more than anything. In his heart, she already was.

"Maybe." Deliberately keeping his answer noncommittal, he returned to the kitchen. She followed, her eyes widening as she saw the lasagna.

"You made this yourself?"

The shock in her voice made him chuckle. "Yes. I invited you for a home-cooked meal. What'd you think that would be?"

"I don't know." She shrugged. "I thought you'd probably buy takeout or something. Or maybe grill some steaks."

"I didn't think you liked beef." Taking the salad from the fridge, he placed it on the table. "And almost everyone loves Italian food, so I figured it'd be a safe thing to make. This is my grandfather's recipe. My father's dad. He used to make it all the time for family get-togethers."

"Wow. Handsome, sexy and a cook, too." She grinned

at him as if she knew the effect her words had on his libido. "You're quite the package."

Though restraining himself from touching her had become increasingly difficult, he kept his hands busy with the food. After removing the loaf of garlic bread from the oven, he sliced it and placed it on the table next to the salad.

"Have a seat," he told her, taking his own. "We'll have salad and bread while the lasagna cools a little."

The wine—something about which he wasn't the slightest bit knowledgeable—turned out to be a perfect match. Silently he thanked the blind luck that had prompted him to choose this bottle.

They ate and talked and laughed. He loved the way she devoured her meal without the faintest pretense of nibbling at her food the way some of the other women he'd dated had. Of course, he'd never cooked for anyone else either.

Finally she pushed her plate away. "That was amazing," she said, her eyes sparkling. "I'm stuffed. I couldn't eat another bite."

"Too bad," he teased. "Because I have the most amazing tiramisu."

"You baked?"

He had to laugh at her shock. "No. There's a limit to what I can do. I picked some up at the store. Believe it or not, their bakery is top-notch."

"Maybe later," she said. "After some of this food settles."

As he gathered up their plates, she jumped up to help. He waved her away. "This will just take a few minutes. Have another glass of wine and relax. I'll join you when I'm done."

"I want to help," she insisted.

"I don't have a dishwasher," he warned her. "But if you really want to help, would you rather wash or dry?"

To his surprise, she wanted to wash. Working side by side, he marveled at how domestic the scene felt. As if they were already a committed couple. She hummed while she washed, which made him think she might feel the same.

Once the chore was done, they went back to the living room. Again, he tried to rehearse what he wanted to say. And just like before, he couldn't come up with much. Best to talk from his heart, he thought.

"There's something I've been meaning to talk to you about," he began. She'd taken a seat on his couch, clearly expecting him to sit with her. Instead, he paced.

"What's wrong?" she asked, sounding alarmed. "You seem agitated. And to be honest, that 'we need to talk' statement makes me think you're about to show me the door and tell me you don't want to see me again."

Stunned, he stared. "*That's* the conclusion you came to? After the meal and the invite to my apartment?"

Though she had the grace to look a bit sheepish, she lifted her chin. "If that's not what you want to discuss with me, then what is?"

"I want a commitment." Damn. He hadn't meant to blurt out the words like that, but he didn't want her getting any other wrong ideas.

"You what?" And then she smiled, a brilliant, dazzling smile that left no doubt she not only understood what he'd said, but that she liked it.

"I want a commitment," he repeated. "You and me. I don't want to be just friends who make love. I want more."

"Like what?" she asked calmly, though her eyes sparkled. Was she actually enjoying this?

He hoped so. Because from what he already knew about her, if she didn't like the idea of them being committed, she would have clearly and plainly said so.

"Mates." Emboldened, he said the word without thinking, before realizing she might not know what that meant to a Shifter. "Exclusive," he added. "You and me."

She considered for a moment, just long enough to make his heart stutter in his chest. Then she pushed herself up off the couch and launched herself at him, catching him so unprepared he almost didn't catch her.

But he did. He always would. And as she wrapped herself around him, he knew he had his answer.

He kissed her then, and as she opened her mouth to him he realized he wanted no misunderstandings. "Wait." Raising his head, he struggled to control his breathing. "I need an answer."

"I just gave you one," she murmured, wiggling suggestively against his obvious arousal. "But I'm guessing you want to hear it in words. So, yes, I'd love to be your mate. And yes, I do understand what the word *mate* means."

Staring down at her upturned face, at the mischief lurking in her gorgeous eyes, his chest ached. "Well, then, I might as well take this one step further. I love you, Shayla."

When she started to speak, he held up his hand. "You don't have to say it back. I mean it. And I wanted you to know."

"Zach." She smacked him in the arm, shaking her head slowly. "You know me. I'd never say words like that unless I meant them."

"Good." Struggling to hide the crushing disappointment he felt, he swallowed. "I don't ever want you to pretend something you don't feel."

"Oh, I won't." Her arch look and airy smile confused him. "Because I love you, too. If you weren't so busy trying to convince yourself otherwise, you'd have realized that a long time ago."

They kissed then, and one thing became another until they both completely forgot about the tiramisu.

One month later

Shayla had never been happier. Though she would never forget her earlier relationship with Richard, loving Zach was like a lasting and all-consuming blaze. They were each other's missing puzzle piece, and she could no longer imagine life without him. She had no doubt that she and Zach were meant to be together forever.

A few days after they'd agreed to commit to each other, she'd taken a swim back to Coral and checked with her brother. Ion, Nantha and Teredia were all in prison awaiting trial, along with others who'd been part of the group to overthrow the crown.

Despite Merc's offering, Shayla had declined to visit Teredia. She told her brother she needed to put that part of her life behind her and move forward, and then had shown him the ring Zach had given her.

She'd also shown her parents, who claimed not to be surprised. Her mother had wept, and Shayla could have sworn even her father's eyes got shiny.

"We were worried you'd never find happiness again," her mother cried. The two of them had wrapped Shayla up in a group hug, their love and joy for her palpable.

Once the shock of the news had settled in, Blythe had wanted to talk weddings, but Shayla promised her she'd discuss that with her later. She only wanted a small, intimate ceremony, close friends and family. Though clearly disappointed, her mother had agreed.

When she left her parents' house, instead of heading home to Galveston, Shayla paid a visit to Ion, aware both Zach and June would want to know how he was doing. The underwater prison where he was being held was luxurious, more like a resort hotel than a human prison, though Ion couldn't leave. The guards bowed to her, which made her feel funny, but quickly buzzed her in.

Ion appeared rested, the stress lines gone from his face and his posture relaxed. When she entered his cell, he'd jumped from his bunk, brows raised in surprise. He told her that his lawyer was working on getting him released on bail, though he wanted Shayla to tell June he wouldn't be allowed to visit her until he'd been acquitted. She decided not to break the news to him that June had left town, aware it wasn't her story to tell.

After she'd told him about her and Zach's engagement, at first Ion had no reaction and then, in keeping with his bizarre behavior, he'd laughed out loud, acting pleased. He'd hugged her and offered his congratulations, expressing sorrow that he wouldn't be out in time to attend the wedding. She told him they'd miss him and promised to send a video of the ceremony. Medical tests had been ordered, but the results weren't back yet.

When she got back home, she immediately phoned Zach. He'd hurried over, arriving at her front door less than thirty minutes after her call. Zach had gone back to work, so they didn't get to see each other as much as they liked. He'd finally agreed to give up his apartment and move into her beach house with her, but not until after they were married. Which he hoped would be sooner rather than later, since his lease was up at the end of the month.

His reasoning had made her grin.

Zach had been both relieved and saddened when she'd passed Ion's words along to him. He'd promised to let his mother know, since she was going to try and fly home to attend their wedding ceremony. They'd decided not to wait, both certain and aware they shouldn't waste any time. Life was far too short and unpredictable.

They'd talked it out, both agreeing they wanted something small. She wanted to wed on her pier, an idea he loved. Together, they'd chosen a date, made a guest list, hired a local florist and purchased their wedding finery.

This wedding would be exactly the way she'd always dreamt of. Not some pompous formal ceremony in Coral, but something reflective of both their personalities. They'd decided on a simple wedding, to be held at her home on the pier as the sun had begun to set. Dusk would enable their Vampire friends to attend.

And now the day had come. The wedding would be in a few short hours. Behind them, the florist and her staff worked feverishly to handle the decorations. Shayla refused to get involved, telling the decorator she had confidence in however she chose to decorate.

Instead, she and Zach sat outside, at the very end of her pier, right where they'd be married. Zach exhaled, his contentment obvious in his relaxed posture and calm expression. The sun made his dark blond hair golden, lighting up his skin and turning his light blue eyes the rich color of her sea. His hip bumped hers, making her smile. The tide was in, which meant they could sit on the end of her dock and their feet could dangle below the surface of the water. She felt…satisfied. More than that. Happy. Aware that she was exactly where she was supposed to be, and with whom. The vows would only be a formality, because in their hearts, she and Zach were already committed.

Inside the house, June had started baking, insisting she could make a cake as beautiful as any bakery. Shayla had shrugged and let her, because one less detail to worry about was a good thing. She and Zach had picked up June at the airport that morning and now they had a little time before the other guests arrived. Zach's coworkers and friends would be here in a little over an hour, giving her family plenty of time to make their appearance. Once they showed up, Shayla would go up to her room and get dressed.

"Any time now," Zach muttered, glancing at his watch. Shayla kissed the side of his neck, loving the way this made him shiver.

As if on cue, Merc appeared, rising out of the water in the dramatic fashion he'd perfected when they were teens. "I brought someone to see you," he said, smiling.

A woman appeared, her heart-shaped face and long-lashed eyes glistening with seawater.

"Shayla, meet Lanessa," Merc announced. "She and I are now betrothed."

"What?" Shayla scrambled up, smiling. "When did this happen? Congratulations! Welcome to the family."

Zach echoed her sentiment.

"Thank you both." The beautiful Mermaid turned her large eyes on him before looking back at Shayla. "I'm sorry, I don't mean to stare. I've never met a Shapeshifter before."

"You need to get my brother to bring you to Broken Chains," Shayla told her. "It's a paranormal bar here in Galveston. You can meet Shape-shifters and even Vampires there, plus dance to live music."

She turned her gaze on Merc. "Will you take me later?"

"Of course," he agreed. "Maybe after the reception."

"Um…" Shayla smiled. "The reception is at Broken Chains. That's where we met. Where else would we hold it?"

"Perfect." Magnificent as always, her brother flipped the end of his glistening fish tail. "Can you hand me a towel or a pair of shorts, please?" He glanced at his companion. "And Lanessa will need something, as well."

Because they'd been waiting for her family, Shayla was prepared. She reached into a basket behind her, retrieving two beach towels, a swimsuit cover-up for Lanessa that she'd been going to give her mom and a pair of men's swim trunks for her brother. Luckily, she'd brought extras, since she wasn't sure what other relatives her parents might bring.

Then she took off for her room, where her dress hung in a plastic bag. She slipped it on, loving the way the lacy sheath hugged her curves. She'd decided to wear her hair long, with one large white flower as her only ornament. She'd carry a bouquet of similar flowers.

Maddie and Carmen arrived together, hurrying up to her room and squealing as they caught sight of Shayla in her white minidress. "You know it's bad luck for the groom to see the bride before the ceremony," Maddie whispered. "So stay up here and don't let Zach see you."

Shayla only shrugged. "We're different. We've already spent the day together. We didn't see the logic in making one of us hide out until we're married."

"I concur," the ever-practical Carmen agreed. "Makes everything go much more smoothly."

Pursing her lips, Maddie shook her head. "At least he hasn't seen you in this dress, right?"

Slowly, Shayla nodded. "I wanted to surprise him."

"Perfect!" Maddie smoothed her dress down, glancing at Carmen and frowning a little. "It's weird how two women can wear the exact same dress and look totally different."

For her two bridesmaids, Shayla had chosen dresses that appeared to be made of sea foam. The simple, classic design flattered both her friends.

"I look like a slutty nurse," Maddie muttered, "while she manages to somehow look classy."

Both Shayla and Carmen laughed. "You look beautiful," Shayla hurried to reassure her.

Her mom and dad arrived shortly after that, both beaming with happiness. Her mother only poked her head into Shayla's room, oohing over her dress, before hurrying outside to join her husband. Shayla and Zach had set up some folding chairs on the pier, the florist had decorated them, and once Zach's coworkers arrived, everyone took their seats.

The officiant, a friend of Carmen who appeared to be a Vampire, swept past everyone in a long robe that might have been a replica or might have been several centuries old. She scanned the crowd before nodding to signal she was ready.

Shayla watched from her window. A soft tap on her door meant her father had arrived to walk her down the aisle.

Seeing her, he beamed. "You look stunning. Every bit a royal princess."

She took his arm, aware he meant well. "Thanks, Dad."

The music started to play. They'd decided to go old school and use the typical wedding march. As Shayla stepped outside, she focused on Zach waiting next to the officiant, his powerful, muscular body standing tall and straight and handsome as sin. When he saw her, his rugged expression softened. The blaze of warmth in his eyes let her know he found her beautiful. She was glad. She'd chosen her dress with only him in mind.

With her arm in her father's she made her way to the end of the pier. Even the stern-faced officiant smiled as her father released her arm. There'd be no giving away in this ceremony. Shayla had been adamant on that. She gave herself to Zach quite freely and joyfully, with her heart full.

The officiant cleared her throat. Shayla and Zach took up their positions on either side of her. As they did, the wind gusted, sending up a spray of seawater on them, though the moisture barely touched her dress.

"Look," Maddie said from her other side, pointing. Shayla turned to see. Out in the open ocean, a large waterspout spun, purple and gray and green. It swirled and dipped, coming closer and putting on a show before disappearing back out to sea.

As soon as it vanished, the wind died down, and the sea became calm and smooth as glass.

"Poseidon," Merc said, making everyone who wasn't Merfolk laugh, thinking Merc made a joke. The Merfolk knew better. Shayla's father appeared especially pleased, making her wonder if he'd invited Poseidon to her wedding.

And he'd come. Wide-eyed, Shayla dipped her chin in homage. She felt honored that the Sea God had blessed her wedding. She caught Zach's eye and smiled, her heart full of love and joy.

And then, with the sun setting orange and red over the water, she and Zach spoke their vows.

Maddie caught the bouquet, a feat that clearly surprised her. Then they all piled into the bus Zach had rented and made their way to Broken Chains, to wind down the celebration in the place where it had all begun.

* * * * *

Jane Kindred is the author of the Demons of Elysium series of M/M erotic fantasy romance, the Looking Glass Gods dark fantasy tetralogy and the gothic paranormal romance *The Lost Coast*. Jane spent her formative years ruining her eyes reading romance novels in the Tucson sun and watching *Star Trek* marathons in the dark. She now writes to the sound of San Francisco foghorns while two cats slowly but surely edge her off the side of the bed.

Books by Jane Kindred

Harlequin Nocturne

Sisters in Sin

Waking the Serpent
Bewitching the Dragon
The Dragon's Hunt

THE DRAGON'S HUNT
Jane Kindred

Prologue

Blood ran into his eyes as he struggled to his feet. The groans of the maimed and the dying around him were eclipsed by the battle cries of his comrades who remained, and by the crack of iron against leather and wood—and against flesh and bone. They never should have followed their enemy into the woods. They'd been set upon by forces they couldn't count, swarming out from behind every tree and every rock like a band of brigands, surrounding them with no room to maneuver, no way to stand in shield formation. It quickly became every man for himself.

Through the blood and mud caking his vision, he caught sight of the sudden arc of a battle-axe swinging down on him from his left. He'd lost his shield, and he turned and parried with his sword, but he'd taken a fierce blow to his sword arm from the last man he'd killed, and he stumbled back under the force, pain radiating like fire through his arm to the shoulder. The next swing from his opponent's axe he couldn't evade, and the blade caught him under the ribs, hooking in the links of his hauberk. He prayed to the Allfather as he went down that he might take one more enemy with him as he died. Let him die an honorable death. The axe descended, and he summoned all his strength, thrusting his sword to meet the bastard's gut as his enemy fell on him.

The blade should have split his skull. He thought he'd felt the blow. But he was blind as a newborn kitten in the muck and mud. And then he realized he must have gone deaf as well. Silence fell over him like an oncoming bank of fog, muting the clangs and cries, engulfing him in an utter lack of sensation. Perhaps he'd died. But this was no Valhalla. This was…nothing. Had Odin not chosen him after all? Could this be Fólkvangr, the field of the slain in Freyja's domain? Or was he in cold and empty Helheim? Surely he'd not been consigned to the Shore of Corpses. He was no oath-breaker; and murder—it didn't count in war.

A hand, cool and feminine, touched his forehead. Perhaps this was only the in-between place where warriors waited for the Valkyries to come for them. He tried to clasp the hand but found he couldn't make his limbs work. A cool kiss now brushed his forehead.

"Beautiful one." The whisper at his ear was a soothing breeze, quieting the fire in his veins with the beauty of its cadence. "You shall not die."

Was he to go back out to the battle? He must be in the tent being tended by his father's slave girl. He'd lost consciousness.

"Did I kill him?" His voice came out in not much

more of a whisper than his benefactor's, though much rougher. His throat still felt the fire that had eased from the rest of him. A fever, no doubt, had taken him. He'd lain delirious and was only now coming around. Yes, this made sense. "Did I send my foe to Hel?"

"You were victorious. And I have claimed you."

Before he could ask her to repeat the odd phrase, a searing pain encircled his heart, not fire this time, but the burn of ice, accompanied by the sensation of pins and needles in the flesh of his forearms. He could neither move nor speak, and the pain was becoming intense.

"Hush, beautiful one. Now they cannot have you."

"They?" He managed to croak out the single word, though his tongue felt like wool batting.

Soft lips breathed against his. "That Which Became, That Which is Happening, That Which Must Become."

Chapter 1

Summoning a demon probably wasn't the smartest thing Rhea Carlisle had ever done. But the Carlisle sisters weren't exactly known for doing the smart thing. Phoebe let dead people step into her, and Ione had picked up a dude in a bar and boinked him until he turned into a dragon, so, really, anything Rhea did after that was fair game.

Technically, though, it wasn't her fault. The ink was to blame.

Rhea had picked it up at a body art convention in Flagstaff from a guy who sold his own custom blends—pigments supposedly mixed with the ash of Mount Eyjafjallajökull and consecrated under the full moon. All that mattered to her was the exceptionally rich color. It was the perfect deep poppy red with just the slightest whisper of blue. It made her think of a dark chocolate cherry cordial spilling open. Or pools of fresh blood. Maybe pools of blood oozing out of a dark chocolate cherry cordial. It was just the thing to fill in the crescent moon and descending cross she'd outlined on her calf—a symbol representing the "Black Moon Lilith," the geometric position of the moon at the apogee of its elliptical orbit.

It was Rhea's way of claiming her heritage as a descendent of the goddess. Demoness. Whatever. Whether a real "Lilith" had ever existed, Rhea's great-great-great-grand-whatever, Madeleine Marchant, had believed she was her direct descendent. It had been enough to get Madeleine kicked out of her coven in fifteenth-century France and burned at the stake. It seemed the decent thing to do to claim Madeleine's blood. Not to mention defiant. Ione was a high priestess in that same coven today, which made things a little awkward for everyone involved.

Before she'd even finished inking the tattoo, Rhea felt the tremors of a vision moving in the pigment. Reading the ink was her gift—she'd dubbed it "pictomancy"—and one that had been growing with her skill as a tattoo artist, but the visions were becoming increasingly intrusive, and she'd been actively trying to avoid them. They came now without conscious effort, giving her glimpses into minds she'd rather not have access to. But she hadn't yet been able to read a tattoo on her own skin. Maybe this was her opportunity to get some answers about her own fate for once. She smoothed her thumb along the edge of the fresh pigment and concentrated on what she wanted to know: *What does my future hold? Will my business be a success?*

The room around her winked out, replaced with the

image of a snow-covered hill and a frigid sky blazing with stars.

Rhea leaped to her feet as thunder rumbled over the hill, a froth of dark snow clouds swiftly gathering as though in time-lapse. From within them, what could only be a Viking horde emerged on horseback, wolf-like hounds howling as they charged through a bank of snow that billowed and roiled like an ocean of thunderheads beneath the horses' hooves. The leader of the hunt, ruddy-blond hair wild about his head, and eyes the pale, bleached cornflower blue of the Sedona winter sky, was close enough to touch as the horses rumbled right through Rhea like spectral apparitions. Or maybe she was the apparition.

Either way, the hunters vanished as swiftly as they'd come, leaving her standing in the living room of her one-bedroom apartment—with the fully solid figure of a demon. At least, she thought it must be a demon. Standing on its hind legs, the creature was the size of a human with the appearance of a fox, green eyes fixed on Rhea. It was a weirdly attractive fox, red fur flowing down its back in feminine waves, piercing eyes rimmed in black that rose to a charming point at the outside corners, putting Rhea's cosmetic attempts at the effect to shame.

"Why have you summoned me?"

She hadn't expected the fox to speak. Which, given that it was standing on its hind legs in her living room giving her its foxy resting bitch face, seemed a little obvious now that she thought about it. The voice was decidedly female.

"I didn't. Summon you. At least, I wasn't aware I was summoning…anyone."

"But you're a sorceress."

Rhea laughed. "Sorceress? You've got the wrong sister. I'm just a college graduate with a useless degree and a crap-ton of student loan debt trying to make a living as a tattoo artist."

The fox narrowed her eyes and gave Rhea an up-and-down look, taking in the slightly overgrown shock of unnaturally blond hair streaked with rainbow pastel hues, the oversize flannel shirt, and Rhea's bare legs. Because who didn't tattoo herself in her underwear?

Being made to feel self-conscious made her testy. "Just who are you, if you don't mind me asking?"

One tuft of russet fur rose over an outlined eye. "I am Vixen, the Guardian of the Hunt. You have spilled blood upon the pristine snowbanks and summoned me."

"Well, I didn't mean to summon you. I was just inking a tattoo." Rhea pointed her toes and indicated the crescent moon on her left calf still seeping blood in little dots against the fresh ink. "I guess that's the blood you meant? But I don't know anything about pristine snowbanks or hunts. I think there's been some kind of mix-up."

Vixen looked offended and crossed her downy little paws in front of her chest. "There is no mix-up. I come when I am summoned. Whom do you wish to have hunted?"

"Hunted? This is getting a little out of hand. I don't want anyone hunted."

Vixen was looking decidedly more human as she observed Rhea with a slightly suspicious—and more than slightly irritated—expression. "If you did not summon me, how were you privy to the Hunt?"

"What hunt are you even talking about?"

"That which rides in Odin's name to claim the souls

of murderers, adulterers and oath-breakers. Odin's Hunt. The Wild Hunt."

"The Wild…?" Rhea felt light-headed. Maybe she was hallucinating from low blood sugar. "Okay, I'm done with this. This isn't happening. You're not real. Go away." She headed into the kitchen. There was orange juice in the fridge. Rhea grabbed it and drank straight from the carton.

When she set the empty carton down, Vixen was gone. Maybe it was time to wrap this up for the night. She'd finished the fill on the calf piece, anyway; she could do the shading another time. And maybe it was time to quit this pictomancy crap once and for all. Rhea cleaned up and bandaged the tattoo before putting her kit away and heading off to bed.

The peculiar incident continued to nag at her as she tried to fall asleep. It *had* been her imagination, hadn't it? The whole thing was probably the result of the blood sugar drop. She always told her clients to be careful to eat something before she worked on them, and she'd ignored her own advice. It made more sense than having conjured some kind of vulpine Guardian of the Hunt with her own blood. And why a fox, anyway? As a symbol, those were always trouble. Maybe Theia would know.

Her hand was on her phone on the nightstand, ready to dial her twin out of habit, when she remembered. She wasn't speaking to Theia. They hadn't talked since Theia had revealed the bombshell she'd been withholding about their father's infidelity and his double life with a second family. How could Theia have kept that from her? They'd never had secrets from each other. Even when Rhea had gone off to college at Arizona State in Tempe, and Theia had gone in the opposite direction to Northern Arizona

University, it was always "Rhe" and "Thei" against the world. Until now.

Rhea turned and punched her pillow a few times—fluffing it and getting out her frustrations at the same time—before giving up. She sat up and thumbed through her social media news feed, trying to quiet her mind, unabashedly cyberstalking her own twin sister to see what she was up to. Nothing much, it turned out. In the past week, she'd posted a couple of kitten memes, reposted some inspirational platitudes, and posted a status update consisting of a picture of the Flagstaff sunset over the snow-covered San Francisco Peaks from her back deck, with the caption, "Snowbowl is open. It's officially assclown season at NAU."

By the following morning, Rhea was convinced it had been a dream after all, and by noon, she'd forgotten all about the talking fox in her living room. But the images of the Hunt itself still lingered. She sketched out a quick drawing of the riders before heading into Sedona for the day.

She'd spent her whole life in the town that was part provincial charm, part metaphysical tourist trap—with a dash of Western mystique thrown in for good measure—but now she was a commuter.

The first half of the drive was dusty high desert dotted with snakeweed and desert broom and scrubby piñon pines until the bluish-gray shades and shadows in the distance differentiated into striations of burnt orange and creamy café au lait and succulent green. But from the moment the pale sandstone dome of Thunder Mountain came fully into view amid the red cliffs and mesas, it was like driving into a secret world. Being away at college had given her a new appreciation for its visual magic.

Although she'd forgotten just how crazy Uptown could get at Christmastime. Just south of the strip where she'd rented her shop, the Tlaquepaque Arts & Crafts Village was in the grips of a full-on holiday orgy of decorated trees—and decorated saguaros—complete with strolling midday carolers in Dickensian garb.

The galleries would be stunning at night with the glow of the six thousand luminarias now lining the walkways and walls. Rhea allowed herself a quick drive around the circle to admire the artful kitsch before heading back up the hill to deal with the mundane aspects of starting a business. Pretty much all she'd done so far was hang the sign out front, and there were barely two weeks before her official opening.

In between setting up her accounting software, filling out DBA forms and scrubbing graffiti off the stairwell, she couldn't help returning obsessively to the drawing of the Wild Hunt. In the back of her mind, she knew this was classic avoidance—a habit that had plagued her all through school—but the central figure in particular was compelling, as if he demanded to be drawn. She labored over the details of the wild hair and leather armor, trying to remember whether it had been trimmed with fur or whether the fur had been underneath—

"I have to say, I did *not* expect to see someone like you sitting behind the counter."

Rhea jumped at the warm, rough-edged voice and glanced up, surprised by the intrusion and trying not to show her irritation at having been dragged out of the mental world of the drawing. She hadn't even heard the bell on the door. She opened her mouth to say she wasn't open yet, but the scruffy, muscle-bound dudebro didn't give her a chance.

"Is this your side project?" A pair of bespectacled blue eyes twinkled at her beneath a somewhat careless mop of blond hair with a hint of strawberry in a face framed by stubble with a more decidedly red hue. Something about those eyes gave her a little shock. A warning premonition? Déjà vu? His smile was amused, one well-developed arm in a snug, black Henley resting on the counter as he leaned against it. She realized she was staring.

"I beg your pardon?"

The smile faded. "Ouch." He straightened and scrubbed his fingers absently over his scalp in the hair at his crown, making it clear how his hair had gotten that way. "I guess I kind of ghosted on you. Not cool. Sorry." He had a slight accent she couldn't place.

Rhea blinked at him, trying not to physically squirm at the little frisson of unease tickling her spine. "Ghosted?" Did he have something to do with last night's visitation? The possibility that he'd been a part of that intrusion into her mental peace made her testy. "Who are you supposed to be, Christmas Past?"

"I…" Rando-guy looked startled—and a little hurt, as though no one had ever spoken to him in such an unfriendly manner before. Maybe he expected women to be dazzled at the sight of his muscular Nordic perfection and quirky little smile. And those sky blue eyes. And his ginger beard and tousled bedhead. "Sorry, I didn't mean to bother you. I just saw the sign…" He messed up his hair again, distractedly, like he was *trying* to be that freaking adorable. "Never mind." He turned and headed for the door, and Rhea had an attack of conscience (because it certainly wasn't the firm ass in those jeans affecting her); he was here about the Help-Wanted sign.

"Sorry, wait." She closed her drawing pad and set down the pen. "I didn't mean to bite your head off. I'm a little cranky this afternoon and you kinda caught me off guard. We're not officially open yet, and I wasn't expecting anyone to wander in. You're here about the job?"

He turned, tucking his hands into his jean pockets, looking like a damn little lost lamb. A two-hundred-and-twenty-pound lost lamb. In cowboy boots.

"Uh, yeah. Is the position still open?"

"Do you have any retail experience?"

"Not…as such."

"Been around tattooing much?"

"Um, no."

"Are you inked?"

One hand slid out of its pocket, going for the forelock once more. "This was a bad idea."

"Why don't you let me be the judge?" Rhea handed him her tablet and switched over to the job application. "It doesn't have to be super detailed. I'm just looking for someone with a demonstrated ability to hold down a job. And someone who's personable." She gave him a pointed look to let him know that so far he hadn't passed the test for the latter.

His sky blues lit up with an engaging smile. "I can be personable."

"We'll see." Rhea turned her stool toward the credenza behind her, making a point of going back to her drawing and paying him no attention. The rider on the most prominent horse took shape under her pen, the wild hair and eyes she remembered from her vision—eyes that bore a striking resemblance to her applicant's—the rugged furs, the upraised sword—

"All done."

She started at the second interruption. She hadn't expected to get drawn so deeply into the image so quickly.

Her determined would-be employee slid the tablet across the counter toward her when she looked up. "There wasn't that much to fill in, to be honest. I just moved here, so none of it's local—I don't have a permanent address yet. But I'm dependable." He gave Rhea that amiable smile once more. A little too amiable for her taste. It gave the impression he wasn't too bright.

She took the tablet and looked it over. Leo Ström had waited tables at a family restaurant chain in Flagstaff for a few months, bagged groceries in Tucson over the summer, worked as a lab assistant at the University of Arizona for a semester. He also had a degree in biology from Stockholm University.

Rhea glanced up. "You studied in Sweden?"

Leo shrugged. "I've lived all over the place."

"And what made you come here?"

"Ley lines."

He said it with a grin, but Rhea couldn't help rolling her eyes. It was bad enough when tourists treated the town like a wacky sideshow, but people who moved here strictly for the metaphysical ambiance could be even worse.

"Kidding." Leo smiled. "When I dropped out of the grad program at NAU, I decided I wanted to regroup in a place that spoke to me. And Sedona…" He shrugged. "Spoke to me."

It was still kinda ley lines. "What were you studying in grad school?"

Leo gave her a peculiar look. Had she already asked that question?

"Molecular biology."

"No kidding? My sister's in the molecular biology grad program at NAU."

Leo laughed awkwardly. Maybe he thought she was making fun of him somehow.

"Seriously. She's studying autosomal recessive neurodegenerative disorders in rats or something."

"Are you...?" Leo's hand was in his hair again. He looked completely flustered. "I thought..." He shook his head, the flustered expression turning to a look of understanding as his pale skin went pink. "You're not Theia, are you?"

Chapter 2

Now it all made sense. She wasn't usually this slow on the uptake, but over the last four years of living more than a hundred and fifty miles apart, she'd become less accustomed to being mistaken for her twin.

"You know Theia."

Leo nodded, combing his fingers through his hair. "This is embarrassing."

"When you said 'ghosted'…"

"We met on Tinder. We went out a couple of times, but I kind of stopped answering her texts because things got weird. I mean, not *weird*. We just weren't hitting it off." He exhaled deeply. "Oh, boy."

All the times some guy had mistaken her for Theia in high school came crashing back. Theia was the "sweet" one, the normal one who didn't dress weird or act like a clown, and guys were always falling for her. And more often than Rhea cared to recall, they had run into her somewhere and taken her for Theia, treating her the way guys usually *didn't* treat Rhea. Then they'd realize they were talking to the "other one" and the disappointment would be palpable and awkward.

"I made this weird, didn't I?" Leo tucked his hands back into his pockets. "Sorry. I hope you find someone to fill the position. Take care." He was walking away again.

Anger flared inside her, irrational and childish but impossible to suppress. "So Theia was good enough to bang for a while, but I'm chopped liver." Damn. Why did she have to say that out loud?

Leo's shoulders stiffened as he reached the door, and he turned back with a miserable look of discomfort. "Look, I didn't mean to—"

"No, it's me. Sorry. I'm totally overreacting." Rhea sighed, setting the tablet on the counter. "You just triggered some stupid childhood drama." She tried to laugh it off. "Should we try this again? Rhea Carlisle." She held out her hand.

Leo squared his shoulders and came back to the counter. "Nice to meet you, Rhea Carlisle." He smiled as he shook her hand. "I'm Leo Ström."

"Yeah, I know." Rhea indicated the tablet with a nod of her head when Leo looked suspicious. "It's on the application."

"Right." He laughed, still a bit awkward but more at ease.

"So what's your availability?"

"My availability?"

"For the job. What hours would you be available to work? I'm open seven days."

Leo's eyes widened within the wire frames. "You'd actually hire me after this disaster?"

"It's hardly your fault someone Xeroxed your ex-girlfriend." *Without telling you, apparently.* Which was a new low for Theia.

"Whoa. Wait. She's not my ex-girlfriend."

"Oh, so you're still seeing her." Rhea laughed at the look of mortification on his face as he stuttered, trying to answer. "I'm just giving you crap. I need someone to work about twenty hours a week to help get the place in shape and book appointments, mostly mornings, occasionally closing if you prove trustworthy." She winked at his expression. "Sound okay to you?"

"Uh, yeah." Slightly bemused, he took her outstretched hand once more and shook on it. "Yeah, sounds great. Thanks."

"You didn't ask what it pays."

"At this point, I'm thinking maybe I shouldn't press my luck." Leo grinned as he pushed up his glasses on the bridge of his nose. "Tomorrow morning, then?"

She was probably going to regret this. Honestly, she was already regretting it. Why hadn't she just let him walk away? An entanglement of Theia's was the last thing she needed.

Rhea put on a professional smile. "Morning is a relative term. Eleven o'clock sharp. We open at noon."

The temperature, mild when she'd set out this morning, had dropped precipitously by the time she headed home, and the first snow of the season was falling. Not heavy enough to cover the ground yet, but if it kept up, it might have some staying power by morning. She wasn't looking forward to snow driving after spending the last five years in Tempe. Especially now that she'd chosen to live in Cottonwood, half an hour from her shop. Not that *choosing* was precisely the word for it. The tiny apartment was all she could afford, especially without a roommate. And she'd only been able to swing the one-bedroom because the manager had offered to give her the studio price for the first three months.

For a while, she'd thought she might move up to Flagstaff with Theia, but that was out of the question now. Unbelievable that Theia wouldn't even have mentioned having a twin to someone she was dating. Was she ashamed of everyone in the family now? It was bad enough that she'd officially changed her name, taking her middle name, "Dawn," as her last name because she didn't want to acknowledge the father who'd lied to them all their lives. Rhea wondered if Theia recognized the irony of her secret keeping.

The wipers swished across the windshield, set to intermittent, and as they slid back into place against the hood, something else whooshed past in their path. Something large and white and moving fast. Rhea slammed on the brakes—and, of course, began to hydroplane on the freshly wet road. The back end of the car whipped about and Rhea was in free-spin. Luckily, no one else was on the road. She managed to get the car under control and pull onto the opposite shoulder, although she was now facing the wrong way.

Shaken, she watched the wipers snap up and fall back a few times, trying to put together what could have whizzed past her window. A bird? Its wingspan, if it was one, must have been wider than her windshield. While she contemplated it, a loud horn split the air, making her heart pound.

That wasn't a car horn. It was some kind of literal *horn*, with someone blowing into it, the notes of a herald or a mounted charge. Rhea braced herself, gripping the wheel as the ground rumbled with the impact of something heavy—or many somethings. It was like the vision in her living room, only this was right out in the open and there was no tattoo to read. But the riders were here.

This time, they'd taken on a more spectral appearance, the horses looking almost skeletal and the riders gaunt and wraithlike, dressed in contemporary clothing. The wet road was visible through their translucent forms as they thundered across the highway toward her. Rhea shrieked and ducked against the seat with her arms over her head as the riders began to leap across her MINI. She was sure they were going to trample the roof and crush her inside, but they somehow all managed to clear the top of the car—though some just barely, as hooves rattled and scraped across it.

As the last horse thundered onto the ground on the passenger side, the gaunt-faced horseman paused and turned, spectral gaze fixed on her as she sat up. Oddly, he was wearing a cowboy hat. He tipped it at her, sunken orbs in the hollowed spectral flesh flashing a vivid aquamarine, before turning and galloping away.

She'd finally started to exhale when something jumped onto the hood of the car and scrambled over it, making her heart leap into her throat. A wolflike hound trailed the hunt. Like the rider, the hound turned and fixed its wolfy eyes on her—pale blue and disturbingly sentient—before tearing off into the brush. They were all swallowed up—the vision and the thunder, the horns and baying alike—into the billowing, unearthly fog that traveled with them.

In their wake, the snow became a sudden, violent hail, with large marble-sized pellets hammering her roof and windows. She waited it out, making sure the worst of it was over before putting the car in Drive and turning around on the slick road to head home.

Delayed shock hit her once she was inside her apartment. Rhea collapsed onto the couch in the dark, shuddering and trying to catch her breath. She hadn't had an asthma attack since she was a kid, but her chest was tight and her airway felt like it was closing.

She sat up and deliberately slowed her breathing, listening to her lungs make a peculiar wheezing rattle as she breathed in deeply, and finally got herself under control. Maybe it was time to get some expert advice, because this was getting too weird. Not from Theia, of course. And Ione would freak out and go into "mom" mode. It was hard for her oldest sister not to slip back into the role their parents' deaths had forced her into—a teenager herself at the time—whenever anything threatened one of her siblings. But Phoebe, the middle child of the family, was used to dealing with weird.

Phoebe answered on the first ring. "Hey, kiddo. What's up?"

"When you have shades stepping into you…do you ever see anything ghostly or is it just their presence you feel?"

"Well, hello to you, too. And, no, I don't perceive the shades visually. Rafe sees them, of course. Dating someone who commands the dead has its perks." Phoebe's boyfriend happened to be the last scion of Quetzalcoatl. Because of course he was. "Why, did you need me to contact someone for you?"

"No." Realizing she was scratching at her jeans over

the healing tattoo, Rhea snatched her hand away. "No, it's…never mind. I think I'm overtired."

"Rhe. Come on, this is me. What's going on?"

Her hand slid under the jeans, but Rhea curled her fingers and managed to stop herself. *Damn this stupid tattoo.*

"I thought I saw something a little…weird."

"How weird?"

Rhea hesitated.

"Rhe? How weird?"

"Johnny Cash 'Ghost Riders in the Sky' weird. Only on Highway 89A and not in the sky."

"Okay. That's decidedly in the weird column."

"And it's not the first time I saw them. I had a vision while working on one of my tattoos. And then there was a fox in my living room, and she said I'd summoned her from the Wild Hunt."

Phoebe was quiet for a moment. "Honey…are you still taking those antidepressants?"

Rhea let out an exasperated sigh. "I wasn't halluci-nating."

"Sorry, but it's a little hard to process. A talking fox?"

"And *who* has a boyfriend that turns into a feathered snake god, can shift into crow form and talks to coy-otes? Jesus, Phoebes. Talking to a fox in my living room is hardly the weirdest thing anyone in this family does. Ione has sex with a goddamn dragon."

"She doesn't actually have sex with the dragon. Dev and his dragon demon are two separate entities who hap-pen to share the same corporeal form."

"Right. Okay. You're absolutely right. I am being completely ridiculous with this fox-spirit thing. That's way more normal. Good night." Her thumb was poised to end the call.

"Rhea, wait." Phoebe made a noise suggesting she was blowing her bangs out of her face. "I'm sorry. I didn't mean to be a jerk. After everything that's happened lately, I guess I owe you the benefit of the doubt."

"Yeah, I guess you do."

"What does Theia think?"

It was Rhea's turn to blow at imaginary hair—or not so imaginary, as her spikes were getting way too long these days, and one in particular kept flopping over and hanging in her eyes. "I don't know what Theia thinks."

"You didn't call her first?"

"I'm not really talking to Theia."

"You're what? Rhe, what's going on with you?"

"Besides talking fox hallucinations? Just trying to deal with the fact that Theia kept Dad's second family a secret for months."

"I thought you two found the genealogical information together."

"That part was all Theia. She knew we had three other sisters, and she knew one of them was living a few miles away from her. And she never said a word to me. Maybe if she had, Laurel wouldn't have apprenticed herself to a psycho necromancer and tried to kill you."

"Nobody's to blame for that but Laurel herself—and that bag of dicks who took advantage of her vulnerability, Carter Hanson Hamilton." Phoebe delivered the name of Ione's ex with all due mocking disgust. Though "bag of dicks" was being kind, as far as Rhea was concerned. "You can't let that come between you and Theia. Does she even know how you feel about it?"

Rhea sighed. "She knows. Anyway, I don't want to

talk about it. I just want to know if there's any kind of precedent for seeing a ghostly hunting party. Can you check with Rafe to see if he knows anything about the Wild Hunt or if he's seen anything out of the ordinary in the spirit world lately?"

"Of course."

"And Phoebes? Don't mention any of this to Ione or Theia."

She lay awake later, unable to stop thinking about the haunting eyes of the straggling rider—and his straggling hound—as they'd paused to acknowledge her. The hound had lacked the skeletal appearance, but it certainly possessed the same unnerving gaze. Had all of the hunting party seen her? Or just those two? And why her?

According to Vixen, Rhea's blood had summoned the Hunt. Of course, the name of the custom ink was Bloodbath. A bit macabre, maybe, but the color really was lovely. And unusual in its intensity. As was the damn itching. The healing skin was driving her mad again as she thought about it.

Rhea drew her leg from the covers. It could do with a little moisturizer. As she stroked the lotion over the Lilith mark, her fingers tingled with the precursor to a vision. Rhea pulled her hand away. She was so not in the mood for another vision.

But the pictomancy had a mind of its own.

This time it was an image of blood pooling onto a pristine field of snow. Something dark and hulking stood in the periphery, casting its shadow on the blood under a stark full moon. And then the darkness seemed to swallow the vision entirely.

There was no clear distinction between when the vision ended and when sleep and dreaming began.

Chapter 3

Leo climbed back into bed after dashing from the bathroom over the cold tile floor, folding his arms behind his head on the pillow as he stared up at the ceiling. The vague stuff of dreams fluttered at the edges of his consciousness, but he could never quite recall his. What he remembered, though, was Rhea Carlisle. He had the feeling she'd traipsed through his dreamscape. He'd never met anyone like her. An absurd assertion since he'd dated her twin, but indisputably true.

Her eyes, like Theia's, were a true gray, made more striking by the dark limbal rings encircling the irises. But Rhea's gaze seemed to lay him bare. Theia, even after they'd hung out several times, had remained somewhere on the surface with him, never allowing him deeper, her eyes warm but guarded. Rhea's eyes challenged the one gazing upon them to see her, to be drawn into her. Within moments of meeting her, he'd felt the challenge: *I dare you to know me.* And he wanted to. Intensely.

But taking the job at Demoness Ink was a bad idea. Because being around someone who wanted to be known, whom he wanted to know, meant risking being known. And, frankly, he wasn't sure he wanted to know himself. His nightly ritual kept whatever darkness was inside him from coming out, but it was a constant discipline. And the foolishness of romantic entanglements in the workplace aside, that discipline made dating difficult and awkward. Claiming he was busy whenever a potential partner suggested an evening date became quickly suspect, and he couldn't blame Theia for having gotten weird about it.

And, anyway, what if she came into the shop to visit her sister? She'd never believe he'd just happened into the obscure tattoo parlor in Sedona where her twin worked by chance. She'd think he was crazy. Of course, he *was* a little crazy. And it didn't matter what Theia thought of him. What mattered was Rhea. Which was why he was absolutely not going to show up to the job. It was out of the question.

He arrived at the little upstairs hole-in-the-wall that was Demoness Ink at five minutes to eleven and stood waiting in the lightly spitting snow until he realized, at five after, that Rhea was watching him calmly from behind the counter inside. The corner of her mouth turned up as he met her eyes, and Leo lowered his gaze, shaking his head with a laugh as he pushed open the door.

He brushed the soles of his boots against the sisal mat inside, hands in his coat pockets, before glancing up with a sheepish smile. "How long did you know I was out there?"

"Saw you come up the stairs." Rhea's heathery eyes were bright with amusement. "I thought I'd see how long it took you to try the door."

"Employee intelligence test?"

Rhea laughed. "The opposite of what you're thinking, though. I like mine a little bit stupid." She meant her employees, of course, but for a split second he heard it as how she liked her men.

Before the heat in his cheeks at his foolishness could give him away, he took his hands from his pockets and blew on them, rubbing them together. "Well, you're in luck, then, because I'm an idiot. I didn't even think to put gloves on. Guess the joke's on me."

"The joke was already on you." Rhea grinned at him, those starkly outlined irises merciless. "There's a coatrack in the back if you want to hang your jacket up."

"Thanks." Leo headed past the counter to the back room, pulling off his hat as he went. At least he'd had the sense to wear it. Both the hat and coat were already significantly damp from standing in the snowfall. He found the rack and hung them on it, noting the sturdy, adjustable dentist's-style tattoo chair. It might work in a pinch if he had to close some night and didn't want to chance being late. Of course, he'd have to bring his own restraints, though he always carried them out of sheer necessity.

"Did you get lost back there?" Rhea's perpetually amused voice carried from the front.

Leo tried to ruffle his hair back into place as he returned to the reception area. It was usually a losing battle, hat or no hat.

Rhea was eyeing his marks. He'd worn a T-shirt despite the cold, and the fading ink of his gauntlets and the band around his upper arm peeking out under the sleeve seemed more visible than usual under the fluorescent light.

"I thought you didn't have any ink."

He thought about saying he wasn't sure it even was ink. How crazy would he sound if he said he didn't remember getting tattooed?

"I didn't say I didn't have any ink. I said I didn't have any experience with tattooing." He glanced at his arm. "I got these done ages ago, so I'm not sure they even count anymore."

Rhea came out from around the counter to look them over. "You must have been underage when you got them to have that much fading. Are they home jobs?"

"You could say that." Let her think they were prison tattoos if that's what she meant. Gang tattoos he'd gotten in juvie. Hell, maybe they were.

Rhea took his arm to inspect one of the marks more closely, and his skin rippled along his spine. "It's nice work for a home job." Her palm moved up his arm, warm and soft, and he flinched involuntarily. Rhea let go and took a step back. "Sorry. I should have asked first. I hate it when people touch my skin without asking just because it's decorated."

"No, it's fine." He couldn't help wondering where she was decorated, since nothing was visible. "It's just goose bumps. Feels like the temperature's dropped a bit."

Rhea tucked her hands into her back pockets, looking up at him. "Can I ask what they mean?" He hadn't realized how stark the difference was in their heights until now, despite having dated her twin. But she seemed somehow smaller, more petite than he'd expected. He had a good six or seven inches on her.

She was still waiting for his answer.

Leo held out his right forearm. "This one is the all-rune." Two sets of three parallel lines crossed each other diagonally over three vertical lines. "It symbolizes the Web of Wyrd."

Rhea's eyes crinkled. "The web of what, now?"

"Wyrd." He spelled it out to clarify. "One of the Norse fates. It's supposed to symbolize the tapestry fate weaves."

"Oh, *Urd*, sister of Skuld and Verdande."

Leo smiled. "You know your Norns."

"Actually, I know manga and anime." Rhea laughed. "The series *Oh My Goddess!* The third Norn is called Belldandy in the series, which always made me giggle, so I do know a little bit about Norns, but only enough to know the names."

Leo was intrigued. It was the first he'd heard of Norn manga. "I'll have to check it out." He held up his other arm, turning his wrist to reveal the knotted designs of the wraparound. "This one's Mjölnir—"

"Thor's hammer."

Leo cocked his head. "You're sure you don't know Norse mythology?"

Rhea grinned. "Marvel Comics. And the other?"

One of Jörmungandr's coils was visible under his sleeve at his right biceps. Leo pushed the sleeve up to reveal the coiling solid cuff. "The Midgard Serpent." A look of apprehension and surprise flashed in Rhea's eyes. "I know what you're thinking. I have all these Nordic tattoos. I promise I'm not a Nazi skinhead. I'm just proud of my Swedish heritage. And apparently, as you've already noted, fairly stupid." He smiled wryly. "I never realized most of these symbols had been co-opted by white nationalists. I tend to keep them covered most of the time."

"I wasn't thinking that." Rhea's look was guarded. She was so thinking that. "But now that you mention it, I can see where someone might make that mistake." *Uh-huh.* "I have to say, though, that scruffy puppy-dog hair pretty much ruins the skinhead look for you. If that's what you were going for, it's another big fail." Her laugh, letting him know she was cutting him slack, was infectious, and he found himself smiling at the warmth in her eyes. A smile he realized was probably only adding to the impression he wasn't the brightest bulb in the pack.

But Rhea had switched into business mode. "Before I put you to work, we should probably talk pay."

Leo rolled down his sleeve over Jörmungandr. "I was thinking maybe we could work out a deal. I'd be happy to exchange some work for touch-ups. Maybe some new ink, too." Why had he added that? He didn't want new ink. He didn't even want the ink he had. But it did need touching up. In fact, it was what had brought him to the shop in the first place. Before he'd seen the Help-Wanted sign, the name of the place had caught his eye, and he'd figured it would be as good a place as any to get the work done. It wouldn't be wise to put it off any longer. Like the nightly ritual, he knew the marks helped him keep his equilibrium, though he wasn't sure why. It was a stupid idea, anyway. She'd probably think he was some kind of scam artist.

But Rhea cocked her head, considering. "The first gauntlet would probably take less than an hour, maybe two for the second, and the cuff might run a little longer. Let's give it a conservative estimate of six hours for the three. Anything else you want, we'd have to negotiate based on the size and complexity and whether you want original artwork or have something of your own in mind. Normally, I charge one fifty an hour, with a one-hour minimum. So let's say ten hours of work equals one hour of tattoo work. That would take you through the end of the year and my official opening. We can decide on any additional commitment after that."

Leo's eyes widened at the dollar figure. "Fifteen dollars an hour? That seems awfully generous."

Rhea shrugged. "To be perfectly honest, there's no way I could pay you in cash right now, so let's just say I'd be giving you a good deal on the ink. Besides…" That devilish half grin she'd given him through the window earlier turned up the side of her mouth. "You don't know what I'm going to have you doing."

What she had him doing, it turned out, at least for that first day, was little more than counting inventory and learning her booking system. When she ran out of things for him to do, Rhea offered to start working on his touch-ups while he was still on the clock. He hadn't expected her to start right away, but he certainly had no objection. It wasn't like he had anywhere to be. As long as he was back at the motel before nightfall, everything would be fine.

As soon as Rhea's fingers brushed his ink, there were whispers of visions. Her gift had initially manifested as shared visions with her clients, a kind of psychic reading, and she'd done a few for family and friends. But her skills had recently expanded to include the delivery of more immediate images that popped into her head without the client even being aware of it—and without her wanting to see them. Ever since she'd gotten images from some creep thinking about pushing her head into his lap, she'd been very careful not to indulge in the latter type.

She tried to keep her mind occupied by focusing on the physical anchors of the here and now—the sharp scent of the alcohol as she swabbed Leo's skin, the soft snick of the razor as it traveled over the blond hairs on his arm, the warmth of Leo's body heat as she leaned in close to examine the lines she'd be tracing. And the scent of his skin, like amber-resin oil and pumpkin spice and— *Wow.*

Rhea got up and busied herself readying supplies to get herself under control. What the heck was that about? He was kinda hot, sure, but not so-hot-that-smelling-him-makes-you-wet hot. Except, clearly, he was.

She worked to keep from blushing as she gave him a smile after setting up the machine and ink caps. "Okay, ready?"

Leo smiled back, and it nearly melted her. "Ready as I'll ever be."

She managed to act like a normal person as she sat and got to work on the outline. When the needles made contact with Leo's skin, the image bombarded her psyche: blood spattered across a dazzling field of snow, like a giant cherry slush spilled on a white rug.

Leo was looking at her funny. "Are you okay?"

She'd taken her foot off the pedal. "Hmm? Yep, sorry, just thinking for a sec. I might want to use round needles for the line work instead of flat. Give it some more depth, since some of these strokes are really fine." She hoped she wasn't babbling nonsense. She could barely remember the words as they left her mouth. Rhea took a breath and went back to work. "I'll start on the thicker lines on the three parallel columns."

"Staves."

"What's that?"

"The columns are called staves, like in the tarot."

"Oh, that makes sense." And like the tarot, they were drawing pictures she couldn't unsee. *Running through thick overgrowth in an ancient wood, tree branches scoring limbs and face. After someone. On the hunt.* A pause in the here and now to wipe the blood. *The enemy emerges from the darkness. Now the hunted. Swinging the blade to block the blow and missing. Stumbling headlong into the snow as the light grows dim.*

Somehow, she got through it without botching the original work and actually managed to make the tattoo sharper and bolder while giving the lines a bit more definition and character—a subtle woodiness to the staves, with ridges and bumps of texture in the outlines if you looked closely.

"This looks fantastic." Leo studied his tattoo in the light, obviously pleased, as Rhea cleaned up.

"I hope you don't mind the little extras I added. If you prefer the lines smooth, I can go over it again."

"No, it's great." Leo looked up, his eyes shining behind his glasses. "I hope I can earn it."

"It took me a little longer than I expected, but I'll honor the estimate. So ten hours of work should do it."

Leo shook his head. "Nope. I'll pay for the time it took. Plus, there's the tip, which you've totally earned. This is excellent work."

Rhea felt her cheeks warm, as if he'd complimented her on her body instead of praising her skill. "Well, thanks. But you don't have to tip." *Yes, he does, Rhea.*

Shut up and take the money. Even if the money was paid in labor, she *had* earned it, and she needed to stop devaluing herself if she wanted to make a living as an artist.

"But I want to. So what would twenty percent bring it to?"

"An hour and a half at one fifty an hour would be two twenty-five—"

"An hour and a half?" Leo's brows drew together as he drew his phone from his pocket.

"Yeah, I know. Really, I'm absolutely cool with charging what I originally estimated. It's not your fault I got fancy. Let's make it one fifty plus anything else you think is appropriate."

"No, that's not it." He was still looking at his phone, his expression slightly worried. "I'll happily pay for the work. I just didn't realize how late it was."

Rhea glanced at the tablet on its stand. She'd spent a little extra time setting up, but it wasn't even six o'clock yet.

"Sorry. I should have let you know what time it was when we got started. Did you have somewhere you needed to be?"

Leo slipped his phone into his pocket and gave her a slightly forced smile. "No, it's cool. I'm just not a night person. I like to be home before it gets dark."

"I suppose you turn into a pumpkin?"

Leo's laugh was nervous. "Something like that."

Rhea couldn't figure out what faux pas she'd made, but she'd definitely made one. "I shouldn't have assumed you'd want to jump right into it after your first day of work. We can schedule the rest of your touch-ups for whenever you want."

"Don't worry about it. It's not a big deal. And I love the tattoo, so it's all good."

She still felt she'd upset him somehow. Maybe a gesture of trust would smooth things over. Rhea twisted an extra door key off the shop ring.

"In case I need you to open or close sometime."

Leo stared as she placed the key in his palm. "You're giving me a key?"

"Is there any reason I shouldn't?" Damn, she really hoped there wasn't.

Leo's smile this time was genuine and a little heartbreakingly adorable. "Absolutely not. You've got my Social Security number, so you can track me down. Not that you'd ever have to track me down. Because you won't need to. You can count on me." Leo looked flustered at his own rambling. He held out the key. "Maybe you should keep this after all."

Rhea laughed. "No, take it. Just know that I *will* hunt you down if you ever screw me over." He looked a little worried. Which was perhaps a little worrying. Why hadn't she just taken the key back?

"Well, I thank you." Leo gave her a dramatic little bow and slipped a length of ball chain out of his shirt from around his neck. He unhooked the clasp to slide the key onto it to hang next to the pendant he wore, an image of a wide-branching tree with roots that mirrored them. "I shall keep it close to my heart." He patted his chest after he'd slipped the chain back into his shirt, emphasizing the firm definition of his pecs.

After Leo headed out, Rhea tidied up and checked to make sure all the valuable equipment was locked in a cabinet. She was almost home when she remembered she'd left the damn tablet.

A strong wind drove the light snow still falling across the highway, making Rhea more cautious than usual— while also keeping an eye out for wayward ghostly riders. Luckily, she saw none of those, but it was almost seven by the time she got back to the shop.

She'd left a light on in back. Had she let Leo Ström's soulful eyes and potent scent rattle her that much? She grabbed the tablet off the counter without bothering to turn on the light and headed into the back to switch off the lamp—and gave a little yip of surprise. Leo Ström, speak of the devil, was sitting in her chair.

Correction: he was *shackled* to her chair.

Chapter 4

Rhea dropped her bag in the doorway. "Leo? What the hell happened?"

Leo looked embarrassed as Rhea examined the restraints at his wrists. "I came back to get my hat and surprised these two guys. I guess they were looking to steal your equipment or something. One of them pulled a gun and ordered me into the chair and cuffed me."

The restraints were professional looking, heavy-duty leather cuffs secured with a pair of electronic padlocks. Rhea turned one of the locks in her hand. "These look serious. I'm going to have to cut the cuffs off." She probably had a pocketknife or a box cutter in the toolbox in the back of her car. Rhea pulled aside the curtain and headed back out. "I might have something I can use."

Leo called after her. "Maybe we should leave it. They said the locks were on a timer and they'd open automatically when the time was up. It can't be that long. They probably just needed enough time to get away, right? We should just wait."

"Wait?" Rhea glanced over her shoulder, incredulous. She shook her head and opened the door. "I'm not waiting around to see if they were telling the truth. Let me find something."

There was no pocketknife, but she found a fish-gutting knife she'd forgotten about. It had belonged to her father, whose toolbox she'd been hauling around since leaving for college. Some girls kept letters and stuffed animals to remember the dead. Rhea had a toolbox.

A bell tolled distantly as she crawled out of the hatchback, some church clock chiming the hour. The mark of passing time brought her focus back to Leo's claim. Who would use a timer on a padlock? Why would a couple of crooks even have wrist restraints with padlocks? Something didn't add up.

When she returned, Leo had one leg crossed jauntily over the other as though he was just relaxing in the tattoo chair. He no longer looked embarrassed but completely at ease.

"Ah, you're an angel." He nodded at the knife in Rhea's hand. "I knew you'd come through." His eyes looked different somehow. Darker. Or bluer. Maybe it was just because he wasn't wearing his glasses.

"You're lucky I came back." She unsnapped the sheath and slipped the knife out.

"Guess it's a good thing I stopped in, though. Otherwise you'd have been robbed."

Rhea paused with the knife at the edge of the first cuff. "But you're tied up. How does that keep me from being robbed?"

"I guess finding someone here spooked them and they didn't want to hang around."

There hadn't been much to rob because she'd locked up her machines and needles, and even the ink. The only thing of value had been right on the front counter in plain view of the door. The tablet hadn't been touched. But they'd hung around long enough to threaten Leo with a gun and strap him to a chair with timed electronic locks?

Rhea regarded him. "So where's your hat?"

"My what?"

"Your hat. You said you came back for your hat."

"Oh." Leo shrugged. "Yeah, guess it wasn't even here. How dumb am I?"

Rhea straightened. "You don't even remember telling me about a hat, do you?"

"Of course I do. It just wasn't the most pressing thing on my mind." He wriggled his wrists in the restraints. "Come on, doll. These are starting to chafe."

Rhea slid the knife back into its sheath. "Don't call me doll."

Leo's smile was mischievous. "What would you like me to call you?"

"How about my name? Rhea will do fine."

"All right, then, Rhea, sweetheart, would you please get these off of me?"

Rhea folded her arms. "Is this some kind of joke?" She glanced around, half expecting to see a hidden camera. "Are you punking me?"

"I wouldn't even know how to 'punk' you—unless that's a euphemism for something. I wouldn't mind euphemizing you, now you mention it."

"Leo, this isn't funny. I thought you seemed like a nice, normal person, so I gave you a chance—"

Leo's laughter interrupted her. It infuriated her, and, at the same time, there was something deeply sensual about the way he laughed. It somehow managed not to be mocking. It was as though he genuinely found the idea amusing.

"*Nice* and *normal* aren't words I would use to describe myself."

"I'm beginning to sense that."

Leo laughed again, and the timbre of his laughter tickled along her skin. "Come on, Rhea. Just release me. I promise to make it worth your while."

"You're kind of creeping me out right now." Or maybe the fact that she was aroused by his laugh was creeping her out. She shivered as he chuckled softly. Nah, it was him.

"I'm sorry. I promise to be good." He straightened in the chair and blinked at her from behind a messy lock of hair. "I solemnly swear I am not a creep."

"You just said you weren't nice or normal, which kind of leaves creep."

"Oh, come now. There's plenty of room between nice and creep. There's interesting. Fun. Unusual. Exciting. You don't really like nice, normal people. Admit it." Rhea blinked back at him, matching fake innocence with fake innocence. "*You're* not nice or normal."

"What's that supposed to mean?"

Leo studied her, taking stock with a frank gaze that made her blush. "You don't dress like every woman your age."

"What do you mean, *my* age? You can't be much older."

He ignored the question as if he hadn't heard it. "So many tend to wear tight, revealing, bright colored clothing, as if they're afraid of not being seen. The plain white shirt with the sleeves rolled up, loose cotton pants in black, practical boots—they speak of comfort, both physical and with your own individuality. Your dress is confident and unconcerned with being 'right.'"

"I see." She shifted her weight, feeling downright *un*comfortable under his scrutiny, appreciative though it was.

"And your hair… I've never seen anything like it. How many colors have you got in there? I see dark roots beneath an almost platinum fair and little streaks of pale blue, pink, lavender—"

"Okay, so I like color." Rhea ran her fingers through her hair, trying to get the floppy point out of her eyes.

"And then you put something in it to make it do that, to separate it."

"Look, why are you going on about my hair?"

"It's not nice or normal. It's rather exceptional. I quite like it."

Rhea could feel the heat in her cheeks. "Well, goodie for you. I didn't ask for your approval—"

"I know. It's extraordinarily sexy, you not wanting anyone's approval."

"And you're trying to distract me from the real issue here, which is that you're up to something weird in my tattoo shop. I don't believe for a minute that you came back here for your hat, and a couple of random thieves happened by and locked you up at gunpoint with restraints and timed padlocks."

"Don't you?" Leo's eyes glinted with amusement.

"No, I don't. I think somebody else tied you up. And you let her. Or him. But I'm guessing her."

"Sex games, you mean." Well, there it was. Blunt and out in the open.

"Maybe you didn't play by the rules, so she left you to cool your heels. Or you were paying for it, which is more likely—paying for sex in *my* tattoo shop—and she robbed your ass and took off after she'd tied you up like a sucker."

Leo seemed pleased. "I like that story. That's really good. I should use that. But why would I do such a thing in your tattoo shop?"

"I don't know, because you're obviously a freak? I don't care why. Because I'm calling the cops."

Leo's plump lower lip protruded in a mock pout. "That's not very nice."

"Yeah, well, as you've pointed out, neither are you."

"Why don't you cut me loose and find out how not nice I can be?"

"Cute. Enjoy your jail cell." Rhea pocketed the knife and took out her phone.

"Well, it's not ideal. But so long as *somebody* cuts me loose, I'll have won the contest. I can work with that."

Rhea paused and sighed. "What contest?"

Leo looked surprised and chagrined. "Contest? Did I say contest? There's no contest."

"Uh-huh. Good luck with that, then."

"All right." Leo sighed audibly. "All right, you caught me. It's a little game I play with a friend. He bets me I can't escape before the time runs out on the clock. If I'm free before dawn, I win the whole pot. And the pot is substantial. We've been at this a long time. If you help me win, I'll split it with you, eighty-twenty."

"Eighty-twenty."

"Seventy-thirty, then."

"You're so completely full of shit. Tell you what. Let's pretend there really is a game, and I won't call the police. If you're gone when I come back tomorrow morning, good riddance. And if you're not? If your 'friend' doesn't return to let you loose because you've been such a very naughty, naughty boy, *then* I call the cops. And you can tell your bullshit stories to them. Have a super night." She switched off the light and left him sitting in the dark.

"Rhea." The way he growled her name sent a shiver up her spine. *"Rhe-a."* The musical lilt to his voice this time, deep and rich, made goose bumps skitter over her arms, the slight accent making her name into a promise of unspeakable pleasure.

She dug her nails into her palms, steeling herself to ignore him, and went out, locking the door behind her. There was nothing he could steal. She had the tablet. Let him get out of his own mess. And hopefully she'd never have to see him again. Which sucked, because she'd really wanted to like him.

It was a long, boring drive back to Cottonwood, and she couldn't stop rehashing the strange scene she'd walked in on. Leo had to be on drugs. It was the only explanation for his odd behavior and for the bizarre change in his demeanor. It would be just her luck to have hired a meth head. Though he didn't look like a meth head. He looked like Thor. The snug T-shirt fit him like one of Chris Hemsworth's costumes in the Marvel Avengers movies. Did he own anything that wasn't stretch cotton and snug? Who was he to talk about Rhea's clothing, anyway?

His amber-resin scent still lingered somehow, and Rhea let out a quiet, frustrated growl. It wasn't often a guy really got to her physically. She appreciated a hot body and a pretty face as much as the next person, but she was more likely to be affected by cerebral attraction. And there was nothing cerebral about Leo. At least, not the Leo she'd met yesterday, not the Leo she'd tattooed this evening. The Bizarro Leo currently shackled to her tattoo chair, however... Maybe not cerebral, exactly, but he certainly seemed to have a layer of depth the "other" Leo lacked.

A familiar thundering drew her out of her reverie, and Rhea gripped the wheel and slowed the car. The spectral hunting party galloped out of the darkness several yards ahead. Beside the leader, a woman in a long, flowing and utterly impractical gown rode a white horse that lacked the skeletal features of the others. *She* lacked them, in fact, green eyes bright in the headlights reflecting off the snow and healthy, rosy cheeks visible, as if an altogether different light shined on her. Or perhaps she refracted light differently. The gown was layers of brilliant cobalt blue fluttering in the wind, with a kind of leather breastplate covering the bodice, and flowing copper hair streamed out behind her.

Rhea slowed to a stop. The female rider did the same in the center of the highway, while the others thundered onward. She turned and smiled, and it was by no means a friendly smile. It sent a little chill up her spine. Or maybe that was the frigid air seeping through her windows. Rhea turned up the heat, her gaze drawn away for a second as she sought the knob. When she focused on the road once more, the huntress was gone.

Chapter 5

In the morning, Rhea took her time getting ready. She wasn't looking forward to getting the police involved if Leo was still there. By the time she finally made herself head into town, the midmorning sun was brilliant against a clear winter sky—crystalline blue, although the air was icy. The snow had stopped falling sometime in the night, leaving the red rocks of Sedona's dramatic landscape striped and dotted with white, like a spice cake dusted with powdered sugar.

She parked in back, making a mental note to take care of the spray paint on the wall of the building. She couldn't make out what it said. Probably just some stupid tags. So much for Leo being able to help her with the cleanup. To her relief, when she unlocked the door, the shop was empty.

There was no sign of any hanky-panky Leo might

have gotten up to in the back room. No leather cuffs and no electronic locks. And speaking of locks, she was going to have to change hers. That was another hundred bucks she didn't have.

The little bell on the door jingled, and Rhea went through the curtain, hoping someone finally wanted to make an appointment. Her jaw dropped when Leo turned from closing the door behind him and smiled as if showing up this morning were the most ordinary thing in the world.

His smile faltered at her expression. "Is something wrong?"

"Seriously? That's how you're going to handle this? Just act like nothing happened?"

Leo frowned. "Like…what happened?"

"I'm not in the mood for this." Rhea held out her hand. "Just give me the key."

He stood blinking at her, baby blues wide with innocence behind his glasses, and she thought he was going to keep playing dumb, but he sighed and fished the chain out of his shirt inside his coat and slid the key off.

"You were here last night, weren't you?" Leo placed the key in her palm. "I had this vague idea I'd spoken to you. I was hoping it was a dream."

"Very funny."

"I'm not trying to be funny. I kind of…blacked out last night. I should have told you about my problem."

"What, that you're a meth head?"

"I'm not a meth head." Leo took off his hat and tousled his hair, which made him look even more like a meth head. "I…have a dissociative disorder. I usually lock myself in my room when I feel it coming on. It mostly happens around this time of year, after dark. That's why I try not to be out late. It only lasts a few hours, so I came up with the idea of using timed padlocks."

Rhea laughed sharply. "That's the lamest story yet. You've gone from 'a man came in the window' to 'I can't help myself, it's a mental disorder.'"

"It's not a story." Leo stuffed his hands into the pockets of his dopey plaid hunting jacket. "I said a man came in the window?"

"It's from an old comic routine. Except the guy's not funny anymore."

"I see. What *did* I say?"

"You're honestly going to stand there and tell me you don't remember."

"I *don't* remember. I hope I wasn't rude to you. But I can't apologize properly if you don't tell me what I said."

Rhea curled her fist around the key. "You said you came back to get your hat and surprised a couple of thieves who'd broken in, and they shackled you to the chair."

"That's it?"

"Pretty much." She wasn't sure why, but she didn't want to acknowledge the game he'd played with her.

"But I was still here this morning. You didn't try to cut me loose?" Leo blushed. "I mean, not that I'm blaming you."

"I didn't believe you last night—and I don't believe you now—so I left you to get out of your own mess. And it looks like you did, so I guess your dominatrix came back."

"Dominatrix?" The slight pink in his cheeks went crimson. "I swear to you, that is absolutely not what happened. When I'm dissociating, I do a lot of weird things, say a lot of weird things. It's like sleepwalking.

That's why I use the restraints. But there was *no* dominatrix. I just stayed out too late and didn't think I'd make it back to the motel in time, so I slipped back in here after you left."

"And you just happened to have restraints on you. You carry them around."

"Yes, as a matter of fact. I can't always afford to rent a motel room around the clock, so I usually check out in the morning and take all my belongings with me." Leo sighed. "Look, I don't expect you to believe me, and I'm really sorry for anything weird I said or did last night. I'll have to find some other way to pay you back for the ink." He went to the door. "But I will. You have my word."

"Why don't you just pay for it now?"

Leo paused in the doorway, looking back. "I really only have enough cash to cover the motel."

"You can clean off the graffiti in the parking lot."

She wasn't sure why she wasn't just letting him go and being glad to be rid of him, but something about his little sob story of not being able to afford the motel room around the clock rang true. She wasn't buying the dissociative bit, but if he was essentially homeless, it didn't feel right to toss him out on his ass in the snow. What had he really done, anyway? Used the key she'd given him willingly to let himself into her shop after hours and maybe got kinky with some crack whore in her tattoo chair? Yeah, okay. That was pretty bad. But he hadn't done anything *to* her, and he hadn't robbed her. So that was something. Sort of.

Leo was still staring at her, uncertain.

"I mean, if you want to prove you're not some kind of creep, you can at least work off your debt."

He nodded emphatically. "Sure. Absolutely. Just point me in the right direction."

"There's a bucket of cleaning supplies in the bathroom. I've had to do this a few times already. These damn kids keep coming back and tagging things."

Leo nodded, looking like an eager pup, and fetched the supplies.

"The lot's down the back stairs. Paint's on the wall next to the red MINI. You'll see it."

"Got it. I'll take care of it." Leo paused once more in the doorway as he headed out. "Thanks."

"For what?"

Leo shrugged. "For not calling the cops on me, I guess. For giving me another chance."

Rhea raised an eyebrow. "It's early yet. Don't make me regret it. And no more weirdness."

Even though she was still glaring at him, his face broke into an unexpected and disarming smile. "You won't regret it. No more weirdness. Cross my heart." He made the quaint gesture, finger making an X over his heart, before heading downstairs. If he was a meth head, he was a damn adorable one. Rhea sighed and set up her tablet and got to work.

Leo stopped at the bottom of the stairs and leaned against the wall, closing his eyes. How the hell had he been so stupid and careless? He should never have stayed for the tattoo touch-up that close to twilight. He was usually good for a stretch of time after the sun initially set—he had an app on his phone to determine when civil and nautical twilight began and ended so he wouldn't get caught out like he had. Because after full dark, all bets were off. Sometimes he recalled the transitional time—what he referred to as his own personal twilight—but more often than not, it was like drinking to excess, with only fuzzy memories of the time leading up to the episode. And the headache he had in the morning only emphasized the similarities. Christ. He might as *well* be a meth head.

He pushed away from the wall, rubbing at the serpent tattoo through his sleeve as he went down to the back of the touristy little shopping complex. Jörmungandr was the last of the marks, the one he knew a little something about, even if he still couldn't remember getting it. He couldn't even say how he knew, but something told him the symbolism of the Midgard Serpent contained the destructive energy of his illness. The part that would be unleashed if he wasn't careful, if he didn't follow the rules he'd set for himself. And last night he'd played fast and loose with the rules because of Rhea Carlisle's touch.

Something had happened when she touched his skin. Not just the little tingle of pleasure at the softness of it or the desire to be near her, but a connection that made him feel as if he could almost remember whatever it was he'd forgotten about the marks and his episodes and his entire life. Little silent movies had played for an instant in his head as she'd worked the ink. And he was certain Rhea had seen those featurettes, too. Her reaction, that little shock of stillness, echoed his own. *Snow kicked up by the hooves of horses—the sturdy, stocky horses of war. The smell and creak of leather and mail. The tang of blood and ice on his tongue.* But wars weren't fought on horseback in leather and chain mail. Not anymore.

Leo stopped in the parking lot to catch his breath, the familiar muscle spasm tugging at his ribs, as if someone had thrust a knife under them. Then it was gone and for-

The Dragon's Hunt

gotten. There was Rhea's red MINI, and there was the graffiti. Leo's brows drew together as he contemplated the tags. This wasn't gang graffiti. These were runes.

He set down the bucket and got to work. A brush and some paint thinner took out some of the color, but the paint had set into the wood—probably done while Leo was still tied up upstairs raving like a lunatic. When he'd done all he could with the thinner, he started on the sandpaper-backed sponge. As he scrubbed the runes from the wall, the shapes gave up their meaning. *Soiled... impure. Throw*—no, *cast out. The impure shall be cast out.* He pieced the rest together. *And the pure shall inherit the land.*

Leo set down his sanding sponge and wiped his brow. Something about this made him really angry. Murderously angry. And, as with so many things that similarly affected him, he had no idea why. Or even why he could read the symbols in the first place. Odder still was why some shiftless punk would be spray-painting Norse runes on the walls of an outdoor shopping mall in the middle of Northern Arizona. Because these were definitely Norse.

Leo's spine twitched, as though someone had walked on his grave, and he rolled his shoulders. Under his right sleeve, Jörmungandr was prickling against his skin. The ink irritated him more in winter. Probably from going from the cold and damp to the dry air of heated interiors. He could feel the outline of the tattoo through the sleeve as he rubbed at it, slightly raised, the skin inflamed.

But it wasn't dry skin. It was these runes. They were a message for him. Somehow, he was certain of that. And the mark was responding to the message as though to a threat. He pondered the faded symbols on the wall as he sanded out the last of them. Leo straightened and frowned. That little spidery shape at the end—that wasn't part of the runes. He'd thought it was messy punctuation or maybe a stray mark, but now… Another shudder traveled down his spine, this time one of revulsion. It was a crudely drawn swastika.

It brought new meaning to the words spelled out by the runes. It wasn't the first time some nasty little vermin had tried to drag him into their racist bullshit. And nothing made him angrier than being mistaken for one of them. They'd appropriated his heritage, sullied the beauty of his ancestors' mythology, twisting it to their own purposes. He wanted to find the little shits and crack their skulls.

He tossed the sanding sponge into the bucket and went around to the front stairs and checked to make sure his bag was still safe underneath them. Of course, the cat, so to speak, was *out* of the bag. He might as well take it upstairs. The army surplus duffel bag contained a change of clothing, the restraints and locks, and his beard trimmer. Everything he owned in the world. Leo slung the bag over his shoulder and mounted the stairs.

Rhea made a face at the spreadsheet on her tablet. Numbers were so not her thing, much less this annoying program. Theia was the one who had always been good with calculations. They'd talked about owning a shop together for years. Not a tattoo shop, of course. Coffee and books had ranked among the top five. They'd both liked the idea of a cat café. But in every iteration of that idle dream since high school, cats or no cats, Theia had been the one doing the books and the finances while Rhea was the artist and the public face of the business. Now she was stuck doing everything herself. Which wasn't exactly Theia's fault—she wouldn't have been interested in opening a tattoo shop, but it still rankled that Rhea couldn't even count on her for emotional support.

True to Theia's pattern, as soon as Rhea started stewing about her, a text notification chimed on her phone. In addition to having prophetic dreams, one of Theia's gifts was an uncanny—and annoying—sense of knowing when someone was thinking about her.

Thinking about you, Moonpie. Also an irritating gift for synchronicity. And for coming up with cutesy names.

Rhea switched the screen off and glanced up as Leo came in. "How'd it go?"

Leo rubbed absently at his right biceps. "I think I got most of it. Did you happen to see what it was?"

"It looked like scribbling to me. I thought maybe it was gang symbols. Why?"

"It was in the runic alphabet. Norse runes, specifically." His expression said this was significant.

Rhea set down the tablet. "Were you able to read it?"

"It was a message about racial purity. Have they done anything like this before?"

"No, just stupid gang tags. At least, I thought they were gang tags." Rhea tried to remember if she'd ever seen anything overtly racist. "You're sure the message was about racial purity?"

"There was also a swastika."

Rhea's stomach clenched. "Fuck. I guess that's pretty unambiguous."

Leo's eyes were hard. "The next time you catch them at it, you should call the cops."

"I'm not a big fan of calling the cops on kids, but I've never actually caught them." Rhea considered. "To be honest, I'm not even sure they're kids. I just assumed."

"Does anybody around here have a security camera pointed on the lot?"

"Not that I know of."

"You should get one. Or a security guard. These groups usually escalate."

"I can't even afford to pay someone to clean up graffiti. How would I pay for a security guard?" Rhea noticed the duffel bag slung over his shoulder. "What's in the bag?"

Leo glanced down as though he'd forgotten it. "My stuff. I was keeping it under the stairs so you wouldn't think I was squatting here. Which I guess I kind of was. Sorry. It wasn't my intention."

"So you really are homeless."

"I'm not an addict or anything. I just move around a lot during the winter. It's hard to hold down a job and an apartment when you have to spend dusk to dawn restrained. People kind of frown on it when they find out."

Rhea fiddled with the edge of the counter. Maybe she'd misjudged him. She liked to think she was openminded about mental health issues. She wasn't exactly the poster girl for neurotypicality. She was probably going to regret this, but that had never stopped her before.

"Why don't you sleep here, then? You could keep an eye on the place."

Leo's eyes narrowed. "Are you messing with me?"

"I need a security guard, you don't have anywhere to stay… It seems like a natural solution."

Leo still looked skeptical. "You got the part where I'm not in my right mind and I have to be restrained until dawn, right?"

"But the vandals wouldn't know that. If they see a

light on, they'll be less likely to try anything. And you can always call me—you have a cell phone?"

"Yeah, I've got a phone."

"So if you see something, you could give me a call to alert me, and I could come by and catch them in the act. Assuming they stuck around that long."

"You're also assuming I'd be levelheaded enough to remember to call you—or to care. I don't really know what goes on when I'm 'out.'"

"Well, I do. I was here talking to you. You seemed perfectly lucid, just—kind of an ass."

Leo laughed, that genuine laughter of surprise that made his whole face light up. "A lucid ass, huh? You know, I've never had anybody tell me what I'm like in that state. It might be useful to have an observer to document it. I mean—I'm sure you've got better things to do than babysit my lucid ass personality. But if you wanted to stick around to verify that I'm not doing drugs or calling pro-dommes to spank me in your back room, you'd be welcome to." He grinned, running his fingers through his hair in a gesture that belied the easy self-deprecation.

Rhea pondered the idea. She'd be a fool to completely take him at his word. It wouldn't hurt to keep an eye on him and see if he was putting her on.

"Why not?"

Leo cocked his head, studying her. "You're serious. You'd let me sleep here—or not sleep, as the case may be."

"Let's just try it out for one night." Rhea gave him her patented half smirk. "I'll let you know what I think in the morning."

Chapter 6

After locking up, Rhea finished off their Chinese take-out while Leo set up. It was like watching Houdini prepare for a straitjacket stunt. He was well practiced in setting up the restraints on each arm of the chair so that all he had to do was slip one arm in, tighten the strap and snap the lock into place, slip in the other arm, pull the strap with his teeth and wrap his fingers around the lock to close it. It was actually kind of hot. And now he was at her mercy, which she hadn't thought about. She wondered if he'd thought about it.

Leo leaned back against the headrest, the scholarly glasses set aside as if his other personality didn't need them. "I should warn you I'll probably say anything to try to get you to release me once I've slipped into 'lucid ass' mode."

"I'm aware." Rhea raised a suggestive eyebrow without elaborating on what he'd said the night before. "I think I can handle you. It."

It was Leo's turn to raise an eyebrow. "There's a reason I use the restraints. I might seem persuasive, even pleasant when I'm trying to manipulate you into releasing me, but I have it on good authority that I'm anything but when I've managed to wrangle my way out of them."

Rhea was skeptical of the need for all this drama. She suspected his fear of being set free was all part of the illness. "You've wrangled your way out before?"

"I'm told I have, yes." Leo didn't elaborate, though he looked uncomfortable.

"Are you saying you become violent?"

"To my knowledge, I've never done anything totally random, like attack someone out of the blue. But it's kind of like a blackout drunk. I've been jailed on assault charges for fights I've apparently been goaded into." He colored slightly. "Or started."

She realized she hadn't even run a background check on him. She wasn't off to a very good start with this business stuff. "I'll keep that in mind."

"I just want you to understand the seriousness of the problem. I wouldn't go through this if I didn't think it was absolutely necessary. I haven't attacked anyone unprovoked, but I'd hate for there to be a first time. And I'd really hate for it to be with you. Promise you won't let him charm you."

"Duly noted." Odd that he'd referred to himself in the third person. "And I promise." She tried to keep her tone light, but she was starting to wish she'd let someone know where she was tonight. On the other hand, it was almost dark and nothing had happened to convince her he even had this dissociative disorder. "So what do you do all night while you're tied to a chair? It has to be pretty boring. Isn't there some medication you could take that would be easier than going through this?"

"If I could afford the medication, sure. But it also makes me kind of lethargic and dull. And it isn't fool-proof. Since I only have these episodes for a few weeks out of the year, this works well enough."

"Why do you suppose that is? These few weeks, I mean. What's significant about them?"

Leo smiled. "Are you analyzing me?"

"I'm just curious. I've never heard of a dissociative disorder with a time element."

Leo lowered his eyes, like she'd caught him in a lie. "I have a confession to make."

Rhea swiveled the stool back and forth idly. "What's that?"

"I've been screwing with you." He looked up, blue eyes twinkling. "I don't have a dissociative disorder. When you caught me last night I was embarrassed to admit I was messing around in here with my toys and got myself stuck. So I made up the whole thing when you confronted me this morning."

A rush of anger propelled her off the stool. She'd always hated being the butt of a joke. And she'd always been too gullible, which people like Leo tended to pick up on. People who thought it was funny to see how far they could take something before she caught on. Rhea wanted to punch him.

"You're a goddamn jerk."

"I really am. I'm sorry." He seemed genuinely con-trite, but she wasn't falling for that. "To tell you the truth, I never thought you'd believe me. But I couldn't help myself. The only disorder I have is that I'm a compulsive liar."

"You're a compulsive liar." Rhea folded her arms. His eyes had taken on the darker hue or deeper intensity she'd noticed the night before. Maybe it was just the light in here. Or maybe it wasn't. "If you're a compulsive liar, why would I believe anything you just said?"

"Ooh. You're good." Leo's expression changed from contrite and slightly chagrined to an almost sultry gaze of appreciation. "You're very good. I like playing with you."

"Playing with me."

"Isn't that what we're doing? I suppose dull-as-a-sack-of-hammers Leo told you I was dangerous. Are you my babysitter?" He waggled his eyebrows. "Care to sit closer?" Rhea followed his gaze to his lap without thinking and quickly looked away from the prominent bulge in his pants. If this was all an act, he was one sick puppy. "Don't tell me you and he haven't been intimate."

Rhea met his eyes once more, glaring defiantly. "Me and who, exactly?"

"Candy-ass. Leo the Dull."

"So you're not Leo. Is that what I'm supposed to believe now?"

"Me?" Leo smiled, utterly charming. "I'm Leo's *munr.*"

"Munr?"

"His subconscious. The distillation of his will and desire. His id, if you like. I occupy the skin and retain control over the vital processes, the *hamr* and *líkamr.* Leo the Dull is ruled by his *hugr,* the essence of his conscious thought. You might call it the soul. I call it fucking annoying. Happily, it's off doing some dull soul thing.

But he doesn't trust me, so he locks me up. It's really unkind." He gave her an adorable pout.

"So this is real, then. This isn't just more compulsive lying?"

Leo—or Leo's id—gave her a dramatic sigh. "If I said I was lying about being a compulsive liar, would you believe me? So many layers of meta. And so boring. When we could be having fun." He gestured with his hips, and Rhea almost made the mistake of looking down again but caught herself. Leo laughed good-naturedly. "Come on. You don't really think I'm dangerous like he told you? He's a puritanical child. I'd never do anything Leo isn't capable of doing himself. He's repressed and he expects me to sit here all night, a slave to his tight little repressed ass, just because he's afraid to be his authentic self."

Rhea leaned back against the cabinet. If this was an act, it was Oscar worthy. It also didn't seem like a dissociative episode. Not that she was any judge. But she'd seen magic before, and this had the air of a magical transformation.

"Have you made up your mind about me?" Leo smiled up at her.

"If you mean have I made up my mind about whether you're telling me the truth—"

"No, I mean, have you made up your mind about whether you're going to satisfy your curiosity? He won't remember any of this tomorrow. You could have your way with me. But be gentle. Technically, I'm a virgin."

"You're unbelievable."

"You have no idea."

"And neither do you, according to you. If you're never

allowed free rein when you're in control of the—what did you call it?"

"The *hamr* and *líkamr*. Appearance and form. The skin, if you like."

"So if you're never in control of the skin, how do you know you're any good?"

Leo laughed, the rich, deep laugh that made her loins tingle. "Because, darling, I'm the one with the hard-on. Trust me, I know how to use it." He gyrated his hips again, making Rhea suck in her breath involuntarily. "Ha, I knew it. You want me. Come on. You don't even have to let me go. Just come closer. Please," he added, and that one little word sounded sincere.

Rhea gritted her teeth. "I'm not coming over there, so you can forget it."

"Why?" He growled the word in frustration. "I'm not trying to trick you. I just want a little kiss. A taste of your lips. Just to satisfy what we're both feeling. What do I have to do to convince you I'm sincere?"

"You're *not* sincere. You think this is a game."

"Rhea. A hard-on is not a game." He sighed, head back against the headrest once more. "It's not as if I could pretend to have one." He had a point. One that didn't bear examining.

"I think my hanging out here while your soul is supposedly off skipping the light fandango was a bad idea. You're going to spend the entire time trying to manipulate me into letting you go, and I'm going to spend the entire time being super annoyed." Rhea took her coat from the rack. "I agreed to observe your transformation to validate your claim that you have a dissociative disorder, and I've done that." She pulled the coat on. "So good luck to you."

As she started through the curtain, Leo's voice stopped her. "Did you tattoo me?" He sounded surprised.

Rhea turned, adjusting her collar, to see him studying what he'd called the allrune on his right forearm. "You asked me to touch it up. You don't remember?"

"I tend to ignore Leo the Dull. He spends his time studying chemistry or something. It's a snooze fest."

"Molecular biology." Rhea shrugged when he looked up at her with a look of curiosity. "That's what you said. You dropped out of the molecular biology graduate program at NAU."

"NAU."

"Northern Arizona University. In Flagstaff. Where you met Theia."

"Theia." Leo's eyes registered sudden recognition. "That's why you look so familiar to me. You're Theia Dawn's sister."

The usual irritation at having someone make the connection prickled on her skin. "And that, I presume, is why you're sitting there sporting your misplaced 'admiration' for me."

His eyes seemed to go a shade darker, and he leaned forward sharply, jerking against the restraints with such ferocity that she jumped back even though she was several feet away. "Don't do that," he snapped. "Don't you dare stand there and try to tell me I don't know my own feelings."

"I wasn't exactly talking about your feelings."

"*Desire.* That's my purview. I know all about desire, and I'm not some stupid animal ruled by my prick who'll just wave it at anybody with tits."

Rhea's face went hot. "I didn't say you were an animal, and I don't appreciate the way you're talking to me. Being Leo's id—"

"Munr."

"Whatever—doesn't give you a free pass to be an asshole."

Leo looked taken aback. *"I'm* an asshole?"

"Yeah, you are. Pretty much."

"You're the one who just accused me of being attracted to you because you look like your sister. I'd say you're the asshole."

Rhea flicked the hair out of her eyes in frustration. "How does that make me an asshole? You dated my sister! When you walked in here two days ago, it was because you thought I was Theia. It doesn't take a genius to conclude that your interest in me—your *desire*—is misplaced."

"I'd show you how misplaced it is if you weren't such a chicken."

As Rhea opened her mouth to tell him to go to hell, the realization struck her that she'd been drawn into an argument with a man's id, and she burst out laughing.

Leo glowered at her. "What's so damn funny?"

"This…" She lifted her arms, encompassing the room, the evening, the two of them. "I can't believe I'm arguing with you about the sincerity of your hard-on."

His glower wavered, curving upward into a slight smirk. "I'd have to concede that it's a first in my experience."

Rhea returned the smirk. "I thought you didn't have any experience. Except you obviously remember Theia."

"But I didn't sleep with Theia." That he had no memory of it now didn't necessarily mean he hadn't, but the admission was more satisfying than it ought to be. "At

any rate, when Leo isn't boring me into a coma, I can
retain some of his memories, but I can't recall ever having such an argument with anyone. You'd think I'd remember being tattooed, though." He glanced down, his
gaze drawn to the other arm. "Are you going to do this
one, too?"

"I was."

He looked up. "But you're not now?"

"No, I— He's working it off. I mean, *you're* working
it off. So I may do the next one. If I let you stay."

"And you don't know if you're going to let me stay."
Leo nodded thoughtfully. "That's fair. Just once, I'd like
to remember getting tattooed, though."

"I'll talk to him about it. He said he might want another new one." She was starting to talk about Leo in
the third person, but it seemed easier to treat them as
two different people. "Might be a good way to pass the
time while you're locked up."

"So you *are* letting me stay."

"I didn't say that."

"But you are." Leo looked smug. "And what about
you? Are you sticking around? Going to keep that coat
on?"

"Maybe. Going to keep that hard-on?"

Leo laughed in that incredibly sexy way Rhea was
starting to want to keep being the cause of, the sort of
laughter one would describe as being genuinely "tickled." Not to mention the throaty richness of the sound
he made. He also closed his eyes when he did it. It was
probably a good thing he was tied up. She wasn't sure
what she'd do if he were able to reach out and touch her
right now.

"So what is it with those tattoos, anyway?" She folded

her arms, still wearing the coat, maybe subconsciously—or not so subconsciously—trying to keep herself closed to him. "They look older than you."

Leo opened his eyes, the smile slightly less joyful. "They've been there as long as I can remember."

"But you don't remember all that much from the times you're not in control of the skin."

"True. But I also don't remember a time when the marks weren't there."

"This soul-splitting-off thing with the other Leo—"

"Leo the Dull." His blue eyes twinkled.

"Okay, *Leo the Dull* going off to do whatever and leaving you here in restraints—how long has that been going on?"

The smile faded as he pondered the question. "I guess I don't remember a time before that either."

"Not even when you were a kid? This was going on back then?"

"I—don't remember being a child. I suppose that's a bit peculiar, isn't it?"

"Maybe not. Maybe it only happened after puberty. If it's a dissociative disorder, that might make sense. Maybe something traumatic happened to you around the time you got the tattoos."

"Except it's not a disorder. I told you that was bullshit Leo the Dull made up to explain me away. It's Leo's self-righteous *hugr* going off to be self-righteous without me."

"That's how you see it, anyway." She realized she was leaning toward the mental illness hypothesis after all.

"And you're back to analyzing me."

"Maybe I am. You're right, I am. Sorry."

"I'm not objecting. I just find it interesting. Because

it means you find *me* interesting." He grinned broadly. "Which I can't imagine is something I share with Leo the Dull."

"Or maybe I find your tattoos interesting. It is kinda my thing after all." But she did find Leo interesting, with or without his *hugr*. "They've been there as long as you can remember, and they're home jobs with significant fading—at least the two on your forearms. The other one looks professional."

"The other one?"

"On your upper arm." He was staring at her blankly. "The Midgard Serpent." He'd worn the long-sleeved Henley today, with the sleeves pushed up to his elbows. What he couldn't see, apparently, he wasn't aware of.

Leo's face clouded. "He's marked me with the serpent? That son of a bitch."

"What's the significance of the serpent?" She'd noted it with some trepidation. Serpents seemed to be intimately bound up with the Carlisle sisters' lives. It all went back to the Lilith blood.

"The Midgard Serpent—Jörmungandr—it's supposed to bring about Ragnarök. The twilight of the gods. The end of the world. Jörmungandr rules the waters surrounding the visible world. It's a sea serpent. A dragon."

Of course it was a dragon. It was *always* dragons.

Rhea sat on the stool once more, rolling it closer to the chair. "So why is it significant that he marked you with it?" It was no use trying not to differentiate between the two of them. "Is he trying to end *you*?"

"Oh, I'm sure he'd love to. But that's not it. It's a way of containing my energy just as Jörmungandr contains the world. I assume it encircles my arm and swallows its tail?"

"I only glanced at it, but, yeah, I think so." She pondered for a moment. "Do you want to see it?"

Leo's eyes danced with amusement. "I don't see how you're going to be able to get my shirt off without undoing the restraints. Or are you planning to cut the shirt off me?" He looked hopeful.

"Yeah, nice try." Rhea wheeled the stool up next to him and pulled down the right shoulder of the stretchy fabric, baring his upper arm. "Take a look."

Leo's breath was warm against her hand as he stretched his neck to see the tattoo. "Can you pull it down a little more?"

As she did, her hand brushed the ink, and the vision from the allrune came back to her, only far more forcefully and in vivid detail. Where her earliest visions had encompassed a series of images answering a question in the client's mind, the ones she'd had without the client's awareness were more like impressions, a peak into memories or desires swirling about inside the person's head. But this...this was like actually being there.

Ice-cold air rushed up at her as she plunged toward the frozen ground, and the force of the impact knocked the air from her lungs. Blood made a spattered trail in the snow ahead of her—her blood. She struggled to stand, fumbling headlong toward the frozen thicket while the groans of the dying and the clash and thud of conflict sounded on the hill behind her.

Her feet were becoming numb as her boots sank into the snow, the creak and crunch of her weight compressing it the only evidence she was still touching it and not floating above the ground. Her chest ached, her lungs having trouble taking in air, and blood was flowing from a hole between her ribs. Blood and sweat ran into her

eyes, and she collapsed into the snow and muck and mud,
a yard from the covering trees. And from within them
came the howling and snarling of wolves.

"What the hell was that?" Leo's growl penetrated the
vision, tearing her out of the icy snowbank and grim
daylight into the warmth of the heated shop and arti-
ficial light.

Rhea broke her grip on Leo's arm and staggered backward off the stool. "What was what?"

"Don't give me that. What just happened? Are you
going to pretend you didn't see any of that?"

Rhea was still trying to catch her breath without
showing she was doing it. "Why, what did you see?"

"Snow and blood and a pack of wolves."

"Have you ever seen this before? Do you…remem-
ber any of it?"

"Why would I have seen it?"

"Because it's your memory. Your reading." Rhea
sighed. "I wasn't trying to get a reading. It's an ability
I have—I read tattoos. I've been trying to avoid doing
it lately, especially when the person hasn't asked for a
reading. But when I get anywhere near your tattoos…it
just sort of happens."

He scrutinized her face, maybe trying for a reading
himself. "It happened with Leo? I mean, when he was
occupying the skin?"

"A little bit, yeah."

"And what did he say about it? Is it something that
happened to us?"

"He didn't say anything. *I* didn't say anything. I don't
know if he saw it. Sometimes it's like that, especially
if the person hasn't asked for a reading." Rhea paused.
"It's not always a memory. It could be a premonition."

"So I may be stabbed and eaten by wolves in my future?" Leo scowled. "Do it again. I want to see more."

Rhea kept her distance. "I don't think that's such a great idea."

"Why? It's not as though seeing something is going to make it happen. I want to know what's going on, where the wolves are, who stabbed me." He gestured with his head. "Come over here and do it again." He seemed to realize his tone wasn't being appreciated. "Please."

Rhea sighed. "I can't guarantee it will be the same vision. I don't even know if it *is* a premonition. I'm still trying to get a handle on this ability, which is why I haven't been doing it lately." His sleeve had slipped back up over his shoulder, and Rhea pulled it down again. The amber-resin-and-spice scent he'd exuded before rolled off him in waves, a personal pheromone designed just for her. Rhea bit her lip and let her hand move down the firm musculature toward the knotted pattern of the snake.

This time, there was no snow, no blood, no fighting. Only Leo's body under hers, hard and hot...and naked. They were both naked, in this very chair, and Leo was bound to it while Rhea straddled his lap, full of him, riding him, moaning as he pumped his hips into her, grasping for his mouth with hers as the beating of their hearts and their rapid breathing rose toward a crescendo. She arched her back and tilted her hips deeper into his lap, feet off the ground and hands gripping the chair behind her as Leo dipped his head and closed the heat of his mouth over her breast, sucking the nipple in roughly against his teeth. And with a melodic shout, she—

"Holy fuck." Rhea sprang back so forcefully she slammed into the cabinet behind her and hit her head on the corner of the shelf above it.

Leo's eyes were on her, warm with amusement and desire. And his erection, she couldn't help noticing, was back with a vengeance. "Well, that was different. Was that your future or mine?"

"I…" Rhea shook her head, trying to form words, her face giving off heat like a radiant coil. She managed, finally, four small words in a breathless rush—"I have to go"—and darted past him through the curtain.

Chapter 7

A clock tower in the distance struck seven as predawn light reached the back of the shop, and the locks, right on schedule, clicked open. Leo yawned and rubbed his wrists after working the buckles out of the restraints, disappointed that Rhea had left sometime during the night. He wondered idly if his presence in the building would actually be a deterrent to vandals. He'd kept his cell phone within reach, but would his alter ego bother to call Rhea if he heard someone outside? For all Leo knew, he was the sort of person who would cheer them on.

Leo frowned. God, he hoped his alter ego wasn't a neo-Nazi. Could that be the source of the tattoos? *No*. He refused to accept the idea that he could harbor something so antithetical to his own morality. Rhea had said he was an ass, but she hadn't said anything about him being a neo-Nazi ass.

As long as he was sleeping here—assuming he hadn't done something reprehensible last night and Rhea was still letting him stay—he might as well make himself useful. After checking downstairs to make sure there was no new graffiti, he found more cleaning supplies in the bathroom and gave all the counters a good scrubbing, along with the bathroom tile and the wood floors in the rest of the shop. There was no shower, but he managed to give himself a decent sponge bath before changing into his other clothes. He wrinkled his nose as he sniff-checked the T-shirt. He was going to have to find a laundromat soon.

The door opened as he was pulling the shirt over his head, and Rhea made a sharp little noise like she'd caught him naked.

He tugged the fabric down, head emerging through the collar, and grinned sheepishly as he put his glasses back on. "Sorry. Guess I could have changed in the bathroom."

Her eyes were even wider than usual and her cheeks were flushed. Maybe it was from being out in the cold. It wasn't as if he hadn't been wearing any pants.

"Must have been boring sitting around with Lucid Ass Leo last night, huh?"

Rhea peeled off her gloves and unwound her scarf as she headed into the back. "I wouldn't say boring, no." She returned, sans hat and coat, with that little spike of silvery-lavender hair hanging in her eyes.

Goddamn, she was cute. The word wouldn't have done her justice if he'd used it to describe her to someone else, but it was the best word to capture the sum total of her mannerisms and quirks—the wide, dark-rimmed eyes that crinkled with easy amusement and sarcasm, the combination of almost haphazard yet defiant dress that at the same time managed to seem completely un-selfconscious and totally endearing, the no-nonsense way she spoke as if she didn't give a damn if she impressed anyone; they could take her as she was or get bent. But the wild, punky hair had its own separate personality, rebelling from and complementing her at the same time.

She was staring at him like he'd forgotten to zip his fly. He checked to be sure.

"So…was I rude to you again? I hope I didn't do anything out of line."

Rhea studied him. "You absolutely don't remember anything that happens when you're in that state?"

"No. Shit, I did something, didn't I? That's why you left. I'm sorry, I wish I could—"

"You didn't do anything. I mean, you tried to get me to sit on your—"

"No."

"Yeah. But it was nothing I couldn't handle. I mean the come-ons," she added hastily. "But he—*you*—said some curious things about your tattoos."

"Did I?" Leo leaned back against the front counter, palms braced against the edge. Was he finally going to get some answers his conscious mind didn't have access to? Having Rhea talk to his alter ego might turn out to be useful. Unless she found out something he didn't want her to know. He only wished he knew what there was to find out. "Like what?"

"He didn't remember getting them. And he didn't even know about the Midgard Serpent. He thinks you got it to punish him in some way. To control him."

So the other him didn't have a clue about the marks either.

Leo tried not to let the disappointment show on his face. "You realize you keep talking about me in the third person."

Rhea shrugged in acknowledgment. "It's a little weird trying to have a conversation with someone about their other self. He kept using the third person when he talked about you. He calls you…"

Leo waited, but she didn't finish the sentence. "He calls me what?"

Her cheeks reddened slightly. "Leo the Dull."

"Really." He wasn't sure why that annoyed him so much. "Did you tell him we call him the Lucid Ass?"

"It didn't come up."

"Well, maybe next time you can let him know." The rush of air filling his chest and the tightness in his jaw were confusing until it dawned on him that he was jealous of his own alter ego. The idea of him spending time with Rhea—*propositioning* Rhea—made him want to call the asshole out and challenge him. But the "asshole" was himself. It occurred to him that perhaps this response wasn't entirely healthy.

Rhea's expression was guarded. "So, did you? Get the tattoo to punish him, I mean."

Why did he get the feeling she was mad at him about it? "Maybe. I don't know."

She laughed, obviously disbelieving. "How can you not know?"

This was starting to go places he really didn't want it to go. On the other hand, she already knew more about him than he knew about himself. What was the point in keeping what he did know a secret?

"Because… I don't actually remember getting it." There. It was out. She was looking at him the way he'd expected her to. Not only did he have an alternate personality he had to tie up at night, he had blackouts and giant gaps in his history no sane person would have.

"Neither of you remember getting the tattoo?" She glanced at his wrists. The way he was gripping the counter made the allrune and Mjölnir prominently visible. "Do you remember getting those?"

He didn't want to answer. But she already knew.

"I only know they weren't always there and they weren't by choice. But *when* they were put there and by whom…?" He shrugged. "I couldn't tell you. Jörmungandr…" He paused, the memory of buzzing tattoo needles tugging faintly at him. He remembered the aftercare, peeling back the gauze bandage and seeing the intricate black designs, holding his arm before the mirror and turning until he could see the shape of the coiling snake. "Jörmungandr, I think I had done myself. But that's all I know."

Rhea studied him, trying to determine, no doubt, whether he was full of shit. "Do you have any long-term memory?"

Leo gave her a half smile. "Are you analyzing me?"

Her eyes narrowed. "That's what he said."

"Well." Leo shrugged and pushed away from the counter. "We both share the same skin." He put his hands in his pockets, uncomfortable with her scrutiny. "So I promised to work off my debt. What else do you need done? I checked downstairs earlier and didn't find any new graffiti, and I cleaned up a bit in here."

Rhea glanced around, her eyes taking in the gleaming hardwood. "Did you scrub the floor?"

"Yeah."

She looked at him curiously. "I don't have a mop."

"I just used a sponge and some warm soapy water. I followed up with a towel to make sure the water didn't soak in."

She was still looking at him funny.

"What?"

"Nothing, I just— Well, I didn't expect you to be crawling around on my floor on your hands and knees." That little flush was back in her cheeks. "But thank you. It looks great." She glanced around once more, avoiding his eyes. "I did want to go over the inventory. It's not much yet, a dozen bottles of ink, a small supply of needles and accessories, and the disinfecting supplies. I started a spreadsheet to estimate how much I'll need and how much this is going to set me back before I start to turn a profit, but I couldn't get all the columns to add up."

"I can take a look at it for you."

"Could you? That would be great. Even if you could just finish entering the physical inventory and tallying it, that would really help. The more complex stuff can wait."

Leo smiled as Rhea fished the tablet out of her bag. "I'm pretty good with data. I'm used to working in a lab."

While Rhea pulled up the spreadsheet to show him how far she'd gotten, the bell on the door jingled. A woman who looked as much like Rhea as she could without being her twin—except for the long, dark chestnut hair in a high ponytail and bangs—stepped inside, blowing on her bare fingers and stamping her feet.

"Goddamn. It's colder than a witch's tit." She grinned as Rhea turned in surprise. "Hi, brat! I figured I'd come by and see your new digs while Rafe is busy dealing with the frozen pipes at one of his worksites."

"Phoebe." Rhea's expression was a mixture of pleased and annoyed as she went to greet her. "It's not ready yet.

I told you I'd have everyone in for the grand opening. How did you even know where it was? I didn't tell anyone I'd signed a lease."

"Seriously, Rhe. A new tattoo shop opens up in Uptown Sedona with the name Demoness Ink? Give me some credit."

Leo studied the spreadsheet as if greatly interested in it. If Rhea didn't want to introduce him, that was her business.

But he hadn't escaped her sister's notice. "You already have a client?"

Rhea cleared her throat. "This is Leo. He's my employee."

"Employee, huh? Well, aren't we fancy. Hi, Leo. I'm Phoebe, the sister that doesn't look just like her."

Leo stepped forward to shake her hand. "I wouldn't say that. There's actually a striking resemblance. If I hadn't already met Theia, I might have guessed you were the twin."

"You've met Theia?"

Rhea's posture had gone stiff. He realized he'd stepped in it.

"We were in the same program at NAU." He figured mentioning they'd dated would compound the mistake. "Well, I'd better get started on that inventory. Nice to meet you, Phoebe." He slunk away into the back room before Rhea murdered him with her eyes.

Rhea switched on the electric kettle on the little table in the waiting area after Leo tactfully pulled the curtain closed behind him. "Do you want some tea? I've also got cocoa."

Phoebe was giving her the eye as she took off her

coat. That I-know-what-you're-up-to eye that had often led to bargaining and blackmail when they were younger and Phoebe had caught one of the twins trying to keep something from Ione.

"Stop looking at me like that."

"You *like* him." Phoebe's voice was low but not low enough.

"Shut up. What are we, twelve?"

"You're blushing." Phoebe pinched her cheek, and Rhea smacked her hand away. "And that was your work on his arm. So I know you've read him. Spill. I want details."

Rhea lowered her voice, hoping Phoebe would take the hint. "There are no details. You're out of your mind. He's just my employee." She got some mugs and spoons from the shelf and brought the bin of assorted tea and cocoa packets, choosing a jasmine green for herself as she sat on the funky red leather couch she'd found at a flea market.

Phoebe grabbed a cocoa packet and plopped down beside her. "This is me you're talking to." She ripped open the packet and dumped the powder into one of the mugs. "I know that look." She glanced at the curtain. "And *damn*. Is it hot in here or is it just him?"

"Jesus, Phoebes. Would you please keep your voice down?"

Phoebe grinned. "Not so funny when the shoe's on the other foot, eh? You and Theia were merciless when I met Rafe. I think turnabout's fair play."

"Yeah, well, your *sex tape* was all over the internet. I think you had a little ribbing coming."

Phoebe grimaced. "You are forbidden from mentioning the sex tape. We all agreed never to speak of it again.

How was I supposed to know there was a reporter hiding in the bushes outside his house?"

The kettle beeped, and Rhea poured water into Phoebe's cup. "You might have thought about closing the curtains, Slutina."

"Ouch. The claws are coming out." Phoebe stirred her cocoa. "You don't usually get this defensive unless there's something to defend. Does this have anything to do with Theia?"

Rhea kept her expression neutral as she poured the water over her tea bag. "No, it has nothing to do with Theia."

"She says she doesn't know why you're mad at her."

"Phoebe." Rhea closed her fist around the hot mug. "I told you not to talk to her about it."

"I didn't. She called me to see if I knew what was going on with you. She's worried about you."

"So you told her."

"I *didn't*. I said she'd have to talk to you because it wasn't my business. But we all think it's a little weird."

"Phoebe!" The heat of the mug was becoming intense, and Rhea uncurled her fingers before it burned her palm. "I can't believe you. I tell you something about Theia in confidence and you not only discuss it with her but you decide to bring Di into it?" It was the nickname the three of them used for Ione. Her given name was actually Dione, but she hated it.

Phoebe blew on her cocoa before taking a careful sip. "There was no 'bringing.' You know I don't volunteer information to Ione. But apparently Rafe and Dev got together—Dev's looking for work now that he's no longer employed by the Covent, and Rafe might be able to use him in operations for the construction business—and I guess Rafe might have mentioned something about you two not talking."

Rhea growled as she wrapped the string of her tea bag around her spoon. "Which he knew because you told him."

Phoebe had the grace to look chagrined. "I talk about things I care about with Rafe. And I care about you. So, yeah, I told him. Which was kind of your fault, if you think about it. Because you told me to ask him about the ghost riders and I had to provide context."

"Which included, 'Oh, by the way, Rhea's being a bitch and not talking to Theia.'"

"Nobody thinks you're being a bitch. And yes, of course it did. I'm thorough." Phoebe tried to hide her smile. "Anyway, don't think I haven't noticed that you've steered me away from the subject of hot Thor in there."

Rhea slapped Phoebe's arm with the spoon, which turned out to be still hot from the tea bag, and Phoebe made a little squeal of protest.

"So what's the story?" Phoebe rubbed at the spot. "You didn't just happen to hire somebody who was in Theia's grad program. What's his deal?"

"There's no deal. He saw my Help-Wanted sign and came in, thinking I was Theia. After a little awkwardness around the confusion, I hired him."

"Why is a molecular biology student looking for work in a tattoo shop?"

"Ex-molecular biology student, and how do I know?"

"How well did he know Theia?"

Rhea sighed and drank her tea. "They dated, apparently."

"Oh, honey." Phoebe was giving her another one of

her looks, only this one was akin to pity. "You're doing that thing again."

"What thing?" Rhea looked over her shoulder to make sure the curtain was still closed. "There's no 'thing.'"

"That thing where you try to compete with Theia when she's not even competing with you. You know you're your own person, unique and interesting and sexy."

"Jesus, Phoebes."

"You don't need validation from someone who was into Theia to prove you're valuable."

"That is not what I'm doing, and shut up, I don't do that." Rhea set her mug down forcefully. "Sometimes you're worse than Ione."

Phoebe set down her own mug with a glare. "Okay, *that* was mean."

"Then stop being bossy and judgmental."

"Rhea."

Rhea leaned close to her, keeping her voice to a low murmur. "If you must know, I did read him. And the vision I got was of me riding him like a Brahma bull on Rodeo Day. So don't tell me I'm looking for validation, because I got it without even asking for it, and I've never even had sex that good in my actual life."

"Wow." Phoebe raised her eyebrows and looked pointedly in the direction of the curtained back room. "That wouldn't have anything to do with that snake tattoo peeking out of his sleeve, would it?"

Rhea scrubbed her hands over her face and smoothed her hair back, palms pressed to her crown. "I am so screwed." She and Phoebe locked eyes at the inadvertent pun and burst out laughing.

When the laughter subsided, Rhea sighed. "There's

a lot more I can't get into right now, but the tattoo is apparently meant to contain the destructive energy of the Midgard Serpent."

"The way Dev's tattoo keeps Kur caged inside him?"

"Not exactly." Rhea glanced nervously over her shoulder again. "It's more like his own negative potential."

"So you don't think he's like Rafe and Dev."

Rhea stared into her empty cup. How was this happening? Was she really "destined" somehow to be with Leo because of serpent energy and Lilith blood? Were all the Carlisle sisters cursed because of crazy Madeleine Marchant being burned at the stake in 1462?

"Rhea?"

"Hmm? Sorry. No, I don't think he's a shifter." What she thought seemed even more improbable. That he was something more than just a mortal man with a mystical propensity to transform into something serpentine, like Rafe Diamante or Dev Gideon did, at the touch of the Carlisle sisters' demon blood. She had also seen the visions of the Wild Hunt, and a battle in a field of snow, and talking foxes.

She was about to say more when the curtain opened with a loud scrape of the wooden rings on the rod. Unusually loud, like he'd been waiting for his moment to emerge and wanted to make sure they noticed. Crap. How much had he heard? She thought back frantically over the last several seconds.

"I think I've got your spreadsheet sorted." He held up the tablet.

Rhea couldn't tell from the look on his face whether he'd heard anything embarrassing. "That was quick. I was tearing my hair out over that thing."

"You just had a couple of little errors in your formula."

Rhea laughed. "Very diplomatic." She rose and went to the shelf to get him a cup, trying to keep from being awkward. "Do you want some tea or cocoa?"

"Actually, I realized I hadn't eaten, so I thought I'd go out and get a sandwich or something if you can spare me?"

"Of course."

Leo grabbed his coat and hat from the back room and set the tablet on the counter. "Would either of you like anything?" If he'd heard anything mortifying, he wasn't letting on.

Rhea picked up the tablet and pretended to look over the spreadsheet. "No, I'm good."

"I'm good, too." Phoebe paused a little too long; Rhea should have seen it coming. "But Rhe's *very* good. Or so I've heard." She was too far away for Rhea to kick her.

Leo laughed awkwardly, pulling on his hat, and let himself out. A blast of cold air was sucked in before he shut the door behind him.

Phoebe was smiling smugly.

"You suck, Phoebe."

"You and Theia always take such pleasure in tormenting me about my sex life, and I never could figure out what was so damn appealing. But, you know, this is actually pretty fun. I get it now." She beamed. "I like it."

Rhea gave her a murderous glare. For once, she was completely without a comeback. She'd created a monster. At least Leo hadn't overheard anything crucial.

Phoebe took a sip of her cocoa. "So have you seen any more ghost riders?"

"They're not ghost riders. They're riders and they

happen to look like ghosts. And I refuse to answer that question on the grounds that it may incriminate me."

Phoebe grinned. "I've taught you well. Guess all that law school I wasted money on paid off. Anyway, Rafe agrees."

"With what?"

"They're shades, in a manner of speaking, but not ghosts. Not the spirits of the dead. More like wraiths. Especially given the presence of that fox you mentioned. He says it sounds like you encountered a *fylgja*. It's an aspect of the Norse concept of the self. Apparently, there are several aspects that can act independently of one another, projecting outside the physical body. The *fylgja* is a sort of familiar spirit projection. It can also appear as a warning."

It fit with Leo's talk last night about the *munr* and *hugr* being separate parts of himself. But if Vixen's appearance had been a warning…what was it a warning of?

Chapter 8

Leo had heard every word of Rhea's conversation with her sister. He'd tried not to, but the sound in the little shop carried extremely well and they were unbelievably terrible at keeping their voices down.

At least he knew now why Rhea had left last night. He'd never heard it put quite so colorfully before, but "riding him like a Brahma bull" painted a vivid picture. He was going to have to find out more about this "reading" skill of hers. It explained the images he'd seen while she was working on his tattoo. And if he was going to have her do more work, he'd have to find some way to shield himself from being read—or straight-up admit he knew about her ability.

As he walked in the brisk air, he tried not to dwell on the image she'd conjured and instead pondered her talk of "shifters." It had followed the discussion of the Midgard Serpent. Rhea apparently knew more about that than she'd let on. Could she have lied about what his alter ego knew? It was frustrating having only part of the story of his own life, and knowing the other Leo might have information he didn't was infuriating. As if they were two separate people competing with each other. And now they were competing for a woman's attention.

Not that Leo was pursuing Rhea, or that he could even afford to pursue anyone, but she'd had the vision while reading the other him, not Leo himself. Which, coupled with the propositioning he'd reportedly done, meant the other him already had detailed images of being with Rhea in his mind. Or were her readings premonitions? Heat rushed to his face with a surge of anger at the thought of the other Leo occupying his skin while being intimate with Rhea—without him.

Gods, he was losing his mind. And he was *not* going to think about Rhea in that fashion. It was getting him nowhere. He concentrated once more on the idea of shape-shifting. Did Rhea actually know shape-shifters—this Rafe and Dev her sister had mentioned? And if she did, what would his tattoo have to do with it? Rhea didn't seem to think Leo was a shifter. But the fact that her sister had even asked was just weird. Like it was common enough that she'd expect it. Could that be why he'd always been so determined not to let his alter ego get free? Would Leo *shift*?

Deep in thought about the terrifying prospect of actually becoming Jörmungandr, he wasn't paying attention to his surroundings, and he nearly ran smack into someone coming from the opposite direction.

Slipping precariously on the icy sidewalk, he grabbed for the other man's arm to steady them both. "I am *so* sorry." Leo let go and took a step back. "I wasn't paying attention to where I was going."

"I can see that. You really ought to… Leo? Leo Ström, right?"

Leo pushed up his glasses, trying to place the face. Early thirties, fairly nondescript brown hair and eyes— he looked vaguely familiar, but—shit, what if this was someone he should know but had forgotten along with so much else?

"Brock Dressler." Dressler held out his hand. "We met at a conference at NAU a few months ago. *Genetic Imperatives in Biotechnology.* We talked briefly about eugenics while we were waiting for the elevator."

Leo shook his hand and nodded. Maybe he'd forgotten him because he hadn't made much of an impression. "Right, right. Of course. Brock. How have you been?"

"Can't complain." Dressler turned up his collar against the wind. "What brings you to Sedona?"

"Oh, just the scenery. I hadn't been down here before. I'm taking a break from my studies."

"You picked a great time. Sedona's beautiful any time of year, but there's something special about snow in the desert. We don't usually get it this early. Looks like we're going to have a white Christmas." He winked conspiratorially. "I'm allowed to say that now, right?" Dressler laughed like he'd said something clever.

Leo thought about ignoring it, but he was feeling contrary, still riled up by the thought of the other Leo being with Rhea. "Why wouldn't you be allowed to say that?"

"White and Christmas." Dressler grinned. "Thank God we don't have to tiptoe around trying not to offend the elites pushing their agenda anymore."

Leo folded his arms, perhaps subconsciously aware of their intentions. "What 'elites' would those be?"

"You know, the liberal Zionist media."

He took a deep breath, trying to be the better man, trying to think of what the better man would say to such an appalling expression of idiocy.

Dressler's smile faltered. "Don't tell me you're one of them? Not with those tattoos."

Leo glanced down. The sleeves of his coat had ridden up when he'd crossed his arms, revealing the gauntlets.

"Why else would you have the allrune and Thor's hammer tattooed on your arms? I know a brother when I see one."

In retrospect, coldcocking a virtual stranger on the street probably wasn't his finest hour. But it felt like it was as his fist impacted with Dressler's jaw.

Dressler's head snapped back, his eyes wide with surprise, and he stumbled backward, ducking belatedly. "What the *hell*, Leo?"

Leo stepped in close before Dressler could back away farther. "I'm not your goddamn brother. Don't you ever mistake me for one of yours. And if you want my advice, I wouldn't throw away your toe shoes just yet either, because you're going to need to go back to tiptoeing. There are still plenty of people who find your kind of talk disgusting. Thank the gods." He turned on his heel, grateful he didn't slip on the ice again and make a fool of himself after his outburst.

"I ought to press charges, you maniac!" Dressler called after him. "That was assault!"

Your face *is an assault.* He choked back laughter at the childishness of the thought and waited until he'd rounded the corner before shaking out his hand and flexing his bloodied knuckles. He wasn't sure if it was Dressler's blood or his own. He'd hit the guy pretty good. At least he'd made his position clear. And maybe the little worm would think twice about assuming his bigotry was somehow acceptable now. Leo would be just fine with his kind going back into the closet for fear of public ridicule. Or face punching.

He remembered the conversation at the conference now. The panel they'd come out of was on balancing the strengths and weaknesses of inherited traits, and Dressler had spouted some drivel about the ethics of breeding out inferior genes. Leo hadn't taken his words as hinting at racial purity at the time, but in retrospect, Dressler's agenda seemed fairly transparent. He remembered hoping the elevator would hurry up and come. He'd been about to meet Theia for drinks—they'd gone out only once before—and he'd brushed off Dressler without paying him much mind. Combined with the graffiti at Rhea's place, what Leo had dismissed as xenophobic wing nut babble took on greater significance. Maybe there was something bigger going on here.

By the time he got back to the shop, Rhea's sister was gone. He'd forgotten to get his sandwich, but then that hadn't really been the purpose of his walk. Rhea stood behind the counter, absently twisting a pastel multicolored spike of hair, the tablet's screen asleep in front of her.

He smiled and tried for nonchalance as he closed the door against the cold air. "So how many of you are there?"

Rhea paused with the strand around her index finger. "*Me?* I'm not the one with a split personality."

"No, I meant sisters." He grinned. "I want to be on the lookout in case I stumble across another one."

Rhea pushed the hair back from her forehead with a look of annoyance. She'd probably heard that one more than once. "There are four." She scrunched up her nose. "Or seven, depending on whom you ask."

Leo dropped onto the leather couch, realizing it wasn't quite made for his weight as it creaked beneath him. "Sounds intriguing."

"It's not."

"Sorry. I didn't mean to pry."

"No, that's okay." Rhea folded her arms and leaned against the counter. "It's just kind of a sore spot with me right now. It's not a secret or anything. Or maybe it is. I don't know. But it might be nice to talk to someone other than my sisters about it."

Leo leaned back, stretching his arms across the couch back. "I'm all ears."

"Theia was doing this genealogy thing a while back. Genetic research is kind of her hobby. She was interested in plotting various traits throughout our lineage, and with our parents dead and no living grandparents, there was no one to ask." Rhea looked up at the ceiling as if carefully choosing her words. "And she stumbled upon this other Carlisle family. It turns out our father was a secret bigamist, and there are three half sisters out there we've never met. Well, except one, who's a nutjob and left roadkill on our doorsteps after she found out about us."

Leo's hat was slipping into his eyes and he pushed it back on his head, as if he needed to see better to process the story. "Damn."

"Yeah. Damn."

For once, he didn't have that nagging desire to know where he'd come from. There were certain benefits to not having a family. No one to totally betray you and leave you feeling stabbed in the gut.

"But you and your sisters are pretty close, I take it? The ones you grew up with. It must be cool to have a twin."

"Usually." The dark rings around the gray of Rhea's eyes seemed especially vivid. He decided not to pry further, but apparently Rhea didn't need any more encouragement now that she'd gotten started. "I thought I could trust Theia, but she never told me about any of this. I had to find out when the nutjob was trying to kill Phoebe."

He wasn't quite sure what to say to that. "She literally tried to kill her?"

"She got taken in by this asshole my older sister Ione used to date, and he kind of…recruited her to do his dirty work while he's in prison."

Leo shifted on the couch. He'd had to ask.

"Too much information, right?" Rhea laughed and picked up the tablet, studying the spreadsheet. "Anyway, that's why Theia's not exactly my favorite person right now."

A funny little pang of disappointment accompanied the realization that jealousy over his involvement with Theia had nothing to do with it, and he spoke, as usual, before he thought. "That's why?"

Rhea eyed him over the top of the tablet. "Why else?"

"I don't know." *Think fast, Ström.* "I guess if I had a twin, I wouldn't let that come between us."

Rhea looked at him pointedly. "You can't even get along with your own id."

He couldn't help but laugh. "You've got me there."

He scratched at his knit cap. "Id. That's an interesting way of looking at it."

"Well, he said the term was *munr*. I mean, *you* said." The word had a sharp zing of familiarity, but he couldn't place it. It was like trying to read something in a dream.

"Munr?"

"I think it's Old Norse. He said it was the self of will and desire."

"The self." He scratched at the hat again.

"He claims your soul goes off on some business of its own, which is why he's in charge of the skin."

"My *soul*?"

"He called it the *hugr*. The self of conscious thought. You really didn't know any of this?"

The hat was bugging him, and he pulled it off his head. "I...did not." Leo combed his fingers through his hair. The idea that parts of him were engaged in activities and conversations he knew nothing about was unnerving. "You said he—my *munr*—thinks I got the Midgard Serpent tattoo to keep him in line. I think that's true. I've had the idea since I got the tattoo that the serpent is a symbol for his destructive energy, and, that if he were to escape, he could use that energy to cause a great deal of harm."

He'd been pondering how to broach the subject of shifters without letting on that he'd heard her entire conversation with Phoebe, but he lucked out, and she did it for him.

"Do you think that energy could be literal?"

"Literal?"

Rhea's unruly strand of hair slid back into her face as she looked down at the counter, pondering the answer. "Like...do you think he has any unusual abilities?

Maybe the ability to actually…change the form he's in? I mean, he talks about being in control of the 'skin,' which I think he sees as another aspect of self. What if he could manipulate it?"

"You think my *munr* could turn into a snake."

"Well, maybe not a snake exactly, but…something physically different from the form you're in now." She was dancing around it. Maybe he was going to have to say it after all. But Rhea straightened and put her hands in her pockets. "Do you believe in magic?"

He took his time answering. "Well, since so much of what I know about my life is somewhat murky, I can't say that I definitely *don't* believe in magic."

That crooked half smile, half smirk that drew undue attention to her lips slid into place. "So you're not *not* licking toads."

Leo pulled his gaze away from her mouth. "I… What?"

"It's from an episode of *The Simpsons*. Bart asks Homer if he's licking toads and he says he's not *not* licking toads."

"What's *The Simpsons*?"

Rhea's mouth dropped open in exaggerated horror. "Don't tell me you've never seen *The Simpsons*. It's only been on television for nearly thirty years. They must have had it in Sweden."

Leo lifted his shoulders, giving her a helpless smile. "I don't really watch television." The truth was, he might have watched hundreds of television shows, but that sort of thing didn't seem to stick.

Rhea shook her head. "I'm starting to worry about you, Leo. I may have to do an intervention. Lock you up at my place instead of here some night and force you to watch *The Simpsons* best-of. Maybe some 'Treehouse of Horror' episodes—the Halloween specials."

Something inside him did a little flip-flop at the idea of Rhea locking him up. He moved his hat into his lap. "You realize you'd be showing the Lucid Ass your House of Horrors and I still wouldn't have seen it. In fact, why don't you ask him? He's probably already seen some. I often leave the television on in the motel to give him something to do at night."

"It's Treehouse of Horror, and I suppose you're probably right." She shrugged. "Maybe I will ask him."

"So you plan to stay again this evening? That is, if you're going to allow *me* to stay again this evening?"

Rhea studied him, her expression giving away nothing. "Yes, I'm going to let you stay. I don't know if I will. We'll see." She drummed her fingers against the counter. "In the meantime, you're here to work, remember?"

"Right." Leo jumped up, making a strategic wardrobe adjustment. "Sorry. I got a little too cozy, huh? So what's next?"

Rhea took a stack of flyers from behind the counter and set them on it with a heavy plop. "I've been setting up digital ads and working on the website, but I figured some old-school advertising couldn't hurt. I need these posted around the Uptown area." She brought out a staple gun along with a heavy-duty roll of cellophane tape and set them next to the stack. "Use whatever method works. Staples for telephone poles, tape for the sides of newsstands. Whatever. Just don't get arrested."

Leo smiled, putting his coat back on. "I think I can handle it." As he put on his hat, Rhea came out from around the counter and surprised him by grabbing his hand.

"What the heck is this?" She held up his bloodied

knuckles. He'd forgotten all about Dressler and the ill-conceived but immensely satisfying action he'd taken in response to the man's bigotry.

"I, uh…" *Oh, hell, just say it.* "I punched a Nazi."

"You *what*?"

"This asshole I ran into while I was out. I'd met him at a genetics in biotech conference a few weeks ago, and he assumed my attendance at a panel on selecting for beneficial genetic mutations meant I was sympathetic to his cause. Well, that, and my tattoos."

Rhea studied him, clearly trying to decide if he was putting her on or just insane. She was still holding his hand. She noticed at the same moment he did, and she let it drop. He'd kind of been enjoying it. More than "kind of."

"Should I be checking to see if you have a prison record?"

She didn't seem too serious, so Leo laughed. "Maybe you should be. For all I know, I could be a felon."

She frowned. "That's not encouraging. But I don't necessarily disapprove of punching Nazis."

"So…" He smiled. "You're not *not* licking toads."

The grin he got in return was totally worth the bruised knuckles.

He had to get creative with posting the flyers. There weren't many accessible utility poles or newsstands. A few crystal shops and bookstores had boards where postings were encouraged, so he hit up as many of those as he could, pinning the flyers among advertisements for Reiki and yoga and cupping. He couldn't help a little juvenile smile at that last term.

But the smile faded as he stopped to put up a few flyers on the planks lining a temporary covered walkway.

Right in the middle of the advertisements for indie bands and metaphysical retreats, a bold poster, larger than the others, had been tacked up. Red-and-black print repeated the phrase from the graffiti he'd cleaned up, this time in English, complete with swastikas.

Intending to tear it down and rip it to shreds to deposit it in the nearest recycling bin, he met with an unpleasant surprise. Something sharp lined the back of the poster, slicing his fingers open as he yanked on the poster board. Leo swore and pulled his hand away to find his fingers dripping with blood.

Chapter 9

Rhea looked up when the bell on the door announced Leo's entrance, the smile on her face quickly turning to openmouthed shock as she saw his bloody fingers.

She hurried out from behind the counter. "*Now* what happened?"

"This time it wasn't me. But it *was* Nazis." He held up the bloodied strips of poster board, showing her the razor blades he'd found glued to the back along the edges.

"Are you kidding me? Who would do that?" Rhea took the strips from him and set them on the counter. "Come on. We'd better clean you up. You don't want to get sepsis."

A flash of something went through his mind, not quite a memory, but an image of a fallen comrade dying of a festering wound. *Comrade in what?*

"No," he agreed and let Rhea lead him to the bathroom.

Having Rhea fussing over him was almost worth the sting of the soap and alcohol as she cleaned him up and bandaged his fingers.

"I don't think I really need bandages," he protested, but Rhea was insistent.

"For all we know, you need a tetanus shot." Rhea glanced up from taping the last of the adhesive bandages over his right pinkie. "Have you ever had a booster?" When he opened his mouth to say he wasn't sure, Rhea held up her hand and shook her head. "Never mind, don't tell me—you have no idea. Jesus, Leo. How do you even know what your name is?"

Leo shrugged and smiled. "It's on my passport." He was only half kidding. Rhea rolled her eyes as they headed back into the reception area.

She carefully picked up one of the bloodied poster strips from the counter. "Why did you bring these back?"

"I thought we might need the evidence. I don't know. I suppose the police can't do anything."

"The police might be complicit." That wasn't encouraging. Rhea laid out the strips on the counter, piecing it together, and frowned. "'The impure shall be cast out.'"

"That was the same thing that was written on the wall downstairs."

Rhea's expression hardened. "That's not good."

"Does it have some special meaning?"

"My half sister Laurel—she kept using that phrase when she was delivering threatening notes from the necro—from Ione's ex."

Leo looked bemused. "You think her ex is involved in this?"

"I wouldn't put it past him. He's the reason the police are a no-go. They were in on some ugly shit with him when he was a high-powered attorney." Little frown lines formed between Rhea's eyes. "Damn. I'm going to have to let Ione know about this. She'll totally freak. She's kind of controlling when it comes to the three of us—she raised us, basically, after our parents died." Rhea leaned back against the counter. "But if this has something to do with Carter, I have to let her know. And Phoebe. And Theia. Dammit."

Leo started to brush his fingers through his hair but paused as he remembered the bandages. "Maybe it's a coincidence."

"Nothing is ever a coincidence around this guy. He's powerful and spiteful. We took his little apprentice away from him, which has to have pissed him off. Maybe he's found another way to get to us."

Leo studied her. She was seriously rattled. "What you started to say a minute ago... This guy, your sister's ex—is he actually a necrophiliac?"

Rhea laughed, and then shuddered. "He's certainly twisted enough to do it. But that wasn't what I was about to say." She put her hands in her pockets and studied the floor. "I suppose I might as well tell you. Carter Hamilton and my sister Ione both belonged to the same coven. Until Carter decided regular witchcraft wasn't enough for him and he started using magic intended to give him power over the dead." She glanced up, a combination of defiance and determination in her eyes, as if daring him not to believe her. "He's a necromancer."

It was one of those words he knew he'd heard before in another context, in another time, but the significance eluded him.

"Or he was. We stripped him of his power." She was watching him, waiting for his reaction.

"Who's 'we'?"

"My sisters and I. And Rafe, Phoebe's boyfriend."

"And your sister Ione is…?"

"A witch. Yes. So is Rafe."

A lot of people called themselves witches these days. It wasn't that unusual. Necromancy, on the other hand… But he wanted to know more about these "shifter" abilities.

"You said Rafe is able to shift into another form. Is that because of this 'necromancer'?"

"You don't have to say 'necromancer' like I'm talking about my imaginary friend. It's fine if you don't believe me, but don't condescend to me." Rhea went to the electric kettle and switched it on. "You should get something hot into you. You're freezing and your fingers are bleeding through those…" She'd turned away to get him a mug from the shelf, but she paused with the mug in her hand and turned slowly back to face him.

"What's wrong?"

"When did I say Rafe could shift into another form?"

"When you were suggesting the Ass might have the ability to transform into something serpentine."

Rhea shook her head slowly. "No. No, I'm pretty sure I didn't." Her cheeks went slightly pink. "I mentioned it to Phoebe. We were talking about your tattoo and about Phoebe's and Ione's boyfriends. And you…heard the entire conversation." The pink was now a delightful fuchsia.

Leo tried to find something to do with his hands. He ended up crossing his arms awkwardly, his fingers splayed. "I caught a few things here and there."

"You didn't hear me talking about reading you."

"Reading me?"

"Stop it, Leo." Her eyes narrowed with irritation, the dark brows contrasting with the glowing cheeks. "Just stop. You heard me tell Phoebe that I..." She obviously couldn't bring herself to say it to his face.

Leo looked down at his boots. "That you had a vision where you rode me like a Brahma bull, I believe it was." He couldn't help smiling, and he snuck a glance up at her from under his lashes.

Rhea groaned, forehead in her hand. "Is the ground opening up? My eyes are closed. I can't tell. Please tell me the ground is opening up to swallow me whole."

Leo laughed. "Nope. Sorry. The ground appears to be pretty stable."

"I've sexually harassed my own employee." Rhea sighed, still not looking up. "Let me get you the complaint form to fill out. I think I should warn you in advance that I don't have much for you to sue me for. Just my shop. And my entire life savings that I've sunk into it."

"I think you're making too big of a deal about this."

Rhea peered up at him through her fingers. "Isn't that my line? Is this where I get dismissive and make an accusatory comment about what you were wearing? I'm new at being a lecherous douchebag."

"Rhea." He couldn't help laughing at her miserable expression. "I'm not going to sue you. I was a little surprised. More about the reading part than the...riding." That, of course, wasn't true, but he *was* curious. He realized he needed to phrase this just right. "Can you tell a person's fortune by reading their tattoos?"

She was still looking through her fingers. "I've been known to...read certain information about a person's life from their tattoos, yes." The kettle beeped and Rhea heaved an audible sigh of relief. "Tea or cocoa?"

"Cocoa." He watched as Rhea busied herself with the little packets. "So, is it like a tarot reading or a palm reading?"

"It's like I *am* the tarot." Rhea poured the hot water into the cups. "I pick up images. It used to be only when the subject wanted to know something. It was a shared vision, but lately… I don't know, it's kind of gotten out of control. I've been trying to quit."

"But you read me yesterday when you were working on the touch-up." Leo came to the table and took the cocoa from her. "I felt something. Saw…some kind of…" He sat on the couch, blowing on the hot beverage. "I don't know. It felt like a memory."

Rhea sat beside him at a deliberate, respectable distance. "Why didn't you say anything?"

"Why didn't *you*?"

"The visions I've been having recently have been one-sided. I didn't want to call attention to it." She took a sip of her cocoa while it was still too hot and winced. "I'm not even sure we saw the same thing."

Leo smirked into his cup. "There wasn't any bull riding on my end."

Rhea sighed and set her cup down, pressing her lips together against the cocoa burn, prompting a sudden urge within him to kiss them and make it better. "There wasn't any on my end either. Just a bunch of snow. Full-on subarctic winter. And you were running—or I was running. It got a little blurry identity wise. Like in a dream. I've never had a vision that dragged me into it that way before. But there was blood spattered on the snow. And I think someone stabbed me." They both shuddered at the same moment, and Rhea glanced at him. "Is that what you saw?"

"Pretty much. The blood and the snow. And there were wolves. But not the stabbing. Except, when you said that, it felt…true, I guess is the only word. I could almost feel it happening."

Rhea studied him. "There weren't any wolves in my vision. At least, not that one. I did hear wolves in the vision I had with *him*." Her cheeks went pink again. "The first vision. Before the…"

"The Brahma bull?" he offered helpfully.

Rhea glared. "You're just going to keep saying it, aren't you?"

"Sorry. It's just such a colorful description."

She made that soft little groan again that didn't help matters. "Anyway, there were hunting dogs in one of my visions, too." She was pointedly trying to get him off the subject of Brahma bulls. "Though they did look a bit wolfish. Except they had curly tails."

"Jämthunds."

"Sorry?"

"Sounds like they were *jämthunds*. A kind of Swedish elkhound. They have sort of wolfish faces. Probably descended from them." Leo sipped his cocoa. "I wonder what the hunting imagery means."

Rhea looked like she was about to say something but sipped her cocoa instead.

"So about your fortune-telling ability—"

"I call it pictomancy."

"You said you'd done readings for people based on their queries. I wonder if you could use it to find out about someone's past."

"You mean your missing past."

"Yeah, I…" He hadn't thought this through. He didn't know what Rhea might find. That was the problem with not knowing. "Never mind. Bad idea."

"Not necessarily." Rhea's look was guarded; maybe she was calculating the possibility of another intimate vision. "If you concentrate on a specific question, the reading should give us the answer to only that question. That's the way it's always worked before."

Was there a specific question he could ask that wouldn't be potentially disastrous? He vaguely recalled getting the Jörmungandr tattoo. That ought to be safe enough, to get clarity on where and when he'd gotten it done. Just *some* damned detail from his past, no matter how mundane, would be nice.

Rhea sipped her cocoa again. "Do you want me to do a reading?"

"How much do you charge?"

Her gray eyes flashed with apparent insult. "I don't *charge*. That would be unethical."

"Why would it be unethical? People charge for reading fortunes all the time."

"Well, I'm not 'people.' I only do readings for friends and family."

Leo smiled, cocking his head. "So I'm a friend?"

The smile she gave him in return seemed a little surprised. And pleased. "Yeah, I guess you are."

He was surprised by how this affected him. He couldn't remember ever having a friend. Which was sad and pathetic. Then again, he couldn't remember if he'd ever watched television. Maybe he'd had lots of friends. And maybe his alter ego had escaped and turned into a giant snake and killed them. *Sure, just go there imme-*

diately. That'll help with the whole "carefully selected past" concept.

Rhea set down her mug. "So roll up your sleeve."

"Actually, I was thinking of the Midgard Serpent."

Rhea laughed nervously. "Right. Because that wasn't at all awkward the last time."

"I wasn't present the last time," he reminded her. "At least not mentally. And you said you could focus on an event from the past."

She looked suspicious. "Why does it have to be the serpent?"

"Because the question I want answered— Do I tell you beforehand?"

"It's not a parlor trick, so, yeah, that information would be useful."

"Right. Sorry. I want to find out exactly when and where I got the tattoo."

"And you don't want to know where you got the others?"

Leo gave her an apologetic smile. "Not from you."

"Ah. Got it. Okay, take off your shirt." Her face went red again as soon as she'd said it. "I wasn't speaking as your employer."

Leo laughed. "It's okay. The lines here are sort of blurry, anyway." He stripped off the shirt before she could object.

Rhea pointedly avoided looking at his bare chest, turning her body on an angle to face his shoulder. Mindful of the cold, she rubbed her palms together briskly before placing her right hand over the tattoo. There was no immediate flash of imagery. He wasn't sure if that was good or bad.

"Now think about your question. Hold it in your mind. Make it as specific as you can."

Leo concentrated on what he remembered about the time around the tattooing. He'd been in Sweden, he thought. Working on his undergraduate degree. He was dating someone... "Oh." As he spoke the word aloud, the vision came, and he could see Rhea was sharing it. *Faye.*

Somehow, he'd forgotten Faye. *She was with him in the tattoo shop, bundled in a fur coat like the place was cold. Fire-red hair flowed down her back, blending with the russet hues of the fur. She was laughing at something the tattoo artist said, flirting with him, green eyes alight with pleasure. Faye flirted with everyone. "He can take it," she was saying. "I've seen him take much worse." She winked before turning her attention on Leo. "Can't you, beautiful one?" Leo could feel the endorphin high from the tattoo blending with the helpless state of desire Faye could reduce him to with a word. The scene changed swiftly to a bedroom, Faye displayed in all her glory against the deep blue sheets, a poppy floating in the ocean. "What would you do for me, pretty Leo? Will you do* anything *for me?" He leaped onto the bed on all fours like a wild dog. "Gods, yes!"*

"That's about enough of that."

The vision ended abruptly, and Leo suffered an instant of disorientation, trying to remember where he was. The moment had seemed utterly real. Mortified, he realized where he was when Rhea, scowling beside him, withdrew her hand.

He grabbed his shirt and pulled it on. "Sorry. I didn't mean for that— I had no idea—"

"Of course you had no idea. That was the point of the reading, wasn't it?" Rhea rose and busied herself tidying the cocoa things. "It's not like you conjured the vision deliberately. The pictomancy took you there. That was the moment. That's when you agreed to get the tattoo."

"What do you mean, that was the moment? How do you know?"

Rhea turned back to him, her expression annoyed. "'Will you do *anything* for me?'" She copied Faye's sexy, purring inflection rather well. "She was asking if you'd get tattooed for her. That was the answer to your question. And I'm guessing you had the kind of relationship where she tested your loyalty to her in a number of... interesting ways. If you catch my drift."

Leo crossed his arms over his chest, bandaged fingers still making it awkward. "No, I don't catch your drift. What are you talking about?"

Rhea looked at the ceiling and made an exasperated growling noise. "She was topping you. Idiot."

"Topping..."

"Oh my *God*. BDSM! Bondage. Discipline. Dominance and submission. Ringing a bell yet?" She made a little motion with one of the empty cups like she was ringing a servant's bell.

Heat rushed up his neck to the tips of his ears. And there was nothing he could say in his defense, because he remembered Faye now. Faye had treated him like a plaything—and he hadn't objected. He remembered crawling on all fours for her, sitting up and begging like a dog while his cock raged, her angry, willing standard raised between his legs. He'd licked his own cum off her boots.

Rhea went back to putting things away. "I'm beginning to see why it didn't work out between you and Theia. If you even suggested anything kinky, she'd throw you out of a moving car on the highway without looking back to see if you'd gotten road rash. She can be surprisingly prudish about sex."

"Which you're not, I take it."

"Me?" Rhea turned away from the shelves, glaring fire. "Who the hell said anything about me?"

"I— Nobody. I just meant— You sounded dismissive. I wasn't trying to— This isn't about you and me."

"Oh, heaven forfend!"

"Heaven…what?"

"Fuck off, Leo." She grabbed the tablet from its stand and dropped it into the bag she kept behind the counter. "You can close up tonight." She turned back at the door. "I mean *lock* up. By yourself. Since that's your thing."

Chapter 10

Rhea sat in her car and screamed for five minutes before starting the engine. She didn't even have a real reason for being mad at Leo. It wasn't like he'd chosen the memory deliberately. She couldn't say why his habitual cluelessness had pushed her over the edge, but if she'd heard one more of her own words repeated back at her as if it were in a foreign language, she'd have lost it. Like she was losing it now.

As she started the car, she remembered she'd meant to call Ione about Leo's Nazis. Christ. Not *his* Nazis. The Nazis who'd shown up...around the same time he had.

Rhea frowned, warming her fingers while she waited for the window to defog. Was there some connection? Leo's reaction to the incidents seemed genuine. She didn't harbor any suspicion that he was part of it. Not directly. But it did seem to be centered on him. The graffiti, the poster, the random white supremacist he'd run into on the street who'd provoked Leo into punching him in the face. What were the odds some guy Leo had met at a conference in Flagstaff would run into him on the street in Sedona a few weeks later? Not astronomical, she supposed, but still.

She took out her phone, thumb poised over Ione's number. Maybe she should call Phoebe and let the Carlisle grapevine do her dirty work for her. Not for the first time, she wished she could call Theia and tell her about all this weirdness. Ask her what *she'd* do. WWTD: What Would Theia Do? It was a mantra she'd fallen back on many times. Instead of going off half-cocked as she was prone to, she'd pause to think for a minute how Theia would respond to a situation. Theia was the thinking one, the one who looked at something from all angles before making up her mind about it and the one who gave everyone the benefit of the doubt.

Rhea was the one who said the first thing that came into her head, no matter how inappropriate. It sucked not having Theia on her side. She felt like she was missing a limb. Or like she was no longer grounded, and she might float up into the air and dissipate in the atmosphere if she didn't maintain constant vigilance.

She had to suck it up and call Ione. But maybe it could wait until morning.

The setting sun was throwing purple shadows over Snoopy Rock. Leo's "episode" would be starting soon. And the other Leo wouldn't remember anything that happened between her and daytime Leo. Probably. As she contemplated going back upstairs, movement in the shadows caught her eye. A dog sat on its haunches, staring. A wolfy-looking dog with pale blue eyes. She'd seen this hound before—the vision of the Hunt that had over-taken her on the highway. Which begged the question: Was she having a vision now?

There were no other indications of magic in the twi-light. Snow had begun to fall. The wolf-dog stared at her. Her windshield wipers thumped quietly as she put them on intermittent. No trumpeting horns sounded. No great white birds flew at her. No thundering hooves.

"Shoo." Her window was rolled up. It wasn't as if the dog could hear her. "Go away. Go home."

It gave her one more look before standing and trot-ting off, swallowed up into the darkness. Its tail curled over its rump. Maybe it was part basenji. Because sure.

Christmas lights were sparkling to life around the shopping center as she backed out of the parking space. She loved this time of year. It wasn't religious for her anymore. That ship had sailed a long time ago for every-one in the family except Ione. The pagan high priestess. Not that Ione let that keep her from going to church. But the lights and pageantry, even the stupid holiday music, both secular and religious, made Rhea happy. She hadn't bothered putting up a tree at her new place, but now she was regretting it.

Before she pulled out of the lot, her phone buzzed. Rhea glanced at the message on the screen. Theia.

Just wondering about your holiday plans. Phoebe says you're really busy with your new business (congrats!) and might not make it for Christmas Eve dinner.

The screen went black.

Rhea reached for the phone, her thumb reactivating the screen. Maybe she was being stupid about Theia's secrecy. Maybe it was time to let it go. Another text balloon appeared.

I heard from Laurel. She's not ready to do a big family holiday or anything, but she says she'll meet me for coffee the day after Christmas.

Rhea jammed her thumb against the button and tossed the phone facedown on the seat beside her. Unbelievable. She felt like screaming again. How could Theia even consider that woman family? Had she actually *invited* her? Dinner was going to be at Phoebe's—because there was no way Ione would have people eating food in her cream-colored fortress of solitude. *Phoebe*, whom Laurel had tried to freaking murder.

It didn't matter to Rhea that Laurel had been under Carter's influence, poisoned by Carter's lies. And it didn't matter that she'd thought she was only consigning Phoebe's soul to the underworld to give Carter control over her. "Soul death," Rafe called it. Murder was murder. And you didn't invite your sister's would-be murderer to Christmas dinner, for God's sake, or have fucking coffee with her. She didn't even know Theia anymore.

The last of the sunlight had faded by the time Rhea hit the road, and the glow of the luminarias at Tlaquepaque as she drove by to take a peek had the look of a sacred ceremony under the deep cobalt sky. As the blue turned to black outside the city limits, the little pockets of cheery holiday lights along the highway seemed all the cheerier, and yet somehow lonelier at the same time.

Thunder rumbled in the distance despite the falling snow. But of course it wasn't thunder. Rhea pulled over to the side of the road preemptively. Sure enough, the rumbling grew louder, the ground shaking with the impact of hooves. This time, a rider on horseback, who looked wholly human, barreled out of the brush from a trail up ahead and began galloping down the highway, throwing panicked looks over his shoulder as the first of the Hunt emerged from the trail moments later to the sound of horns—car horns, this time, because the rider they pursued was going the wrong way in the opposite lane of traffic.

Presumably, the drivers who honked and swerved around the startled man and his equally startled horse saw only the one being pursued and not the terrifying assembly swiftly gaining on him. From Rhea's vantage point, she saw the leader of the Hunt charge forward, ignoring the oncoming traffic, and beside him, the woman Rhea had seen with the Hunt before, hair covered this time with an impressive horned helmet, her gown pieced together with some kind of flowing metal armor. She pulled ahead of the leader and came alongside the terrified rider, mere feet away from Rhea's car, and with a sweep of her deceptively graceful arm, she dragged him from his horse and onto the back of her own.

The leader of the Hunt raised his sword in the air with a wild shout, and Rhea stared openmouthed as the female warrior's horse galloped past her MINI into the air. Wings stretched out behind the warrior, not from the horse rising into the air but from the back of the woman herself, the wingspan broad—and bright white.

The riderless horse panicked, ears thrown back and eyes wild as it galloped toward the swerving traffic. Someone was going to get killed here. And if Rhea wasn't careful, that might include her. After the next car passed, she pulled out onto the highway and tried to overtake the horse, with no idea what she was going to do about it if she did. But before she had to confront the stupidity of her lack of a plan, the leader of the Hunt drew up beside the horse on the other side and leaped from his spectral mount onto the living one. The horse immediately calmed as the hunter took the reins, while the rest of the Hunt, including the hounds and the leader's own mount, rose into the sky and thundered away after the female warrior and her prize.

Only the corporeal horse and the leader of the Hunt remained on the highway, while Rhea's car kept pace with it. As distant headlights grew larger, she realized she was going to end up getting the poor horse killed—and who knew about the hunter?—if she didn't get out of the way. She picked up speed. In her rearview mirror, she saw the horse pulling behind her into what was at least the right directional lane. And following it loped a smaller, dark shape: the black wolflike hunting dog.

The hunter turned his mount onto a trail and disappeared into the darkness, but the dog somehow kept up with Rhea's car. She was driving cautiously, but she couldn't imagine how it was trotting steadily behind her at forty miles an hour. She started to feel guilty, even though she hadn't encouraged the dog to follow her. How did she even know it was part of the Hunt? It didn't look spectral. Maybe someone's dog just—happened to be running with a ghostly hunting party. Because sure. She couldn't shake the feeling, though. And she couldn't shake the dog.

Rhea slowed as she turned into her neighborhood, and when the dog continued to follow, she pulled into a convenience store parking lot. If it was rabid or something, or some crazy shape-shifting necromancer, at least there were bright lights and people around. The dog simply sat on the pavement watching her, its tongue out, panting, while her engine idled. She supposed she'd be panting, too, if she'd been running behind a car for twenty minutes at forty miles an hour.

After a moment, she opened the car door, carefully watching the animal as it watched her. It didn't look rabid. Then again, she wasn't sure she knew what rabid looked like. Didn't they say rabid animals showed no fear? This wolf-dog—*jämthund*, maybe—certainly wasn't showing any. She put one foot outside the car, the toe of her boot on the pavement, and the dog stood. Rhea yanked her foot back inside and slammed the door. Its blue eyes blinked deliberately before the dog nonchalantly trotted around the side of the building. Rhea took a deep breath and backed out of her parking space, slowly cruising around to where the dog had disappeared. There was no sign of it.

It occurred to her as she drove home that the dog was perhaps the least weird thing in this whole bizarre scenario. A winged woman warrior had just swept some dude off his horse and flown away with him, accompanied by spectral hunters, and the leader of the Hunt had ridden off on the dude's horse.

She unlocked her door to find the weirdest part of it, in fact, sitting in her living room.

Rhea jumped when she switched on the light. "Vixen." She'd almost managed to convince herself the fox had been a hallucination.

The Guardian of the Hunt sighed with annoyance. "You're distracting him."

Rhea dropped her bag onto the chair by the door and folded her arms. "Distracting whom?"

"The Chieftain. You have him worrying about stray horses. He ought to have dealt with the prey himself. He is the leader of the Hunt."

"Dealt with how? And what does it have to do with me?"

"He should have taken the head as a trophy for the pleasure of the gods. As for you…" Vixen studied her and shook her head, clearly finding Rhea lacking. "You don't believe in the gods. You are not a huntress or a warrior. And yet you are in the middle of this hunt, and so you are a part of it, worthy or not."

"So why doesn't anyone else see this stupid hunt? If you don't think I'm 'worthy,' why can't someone else who's more suited to it have the Hunt revealed to them and deal with it themselves?"

"You see because you have the gift of second sight."

Rhea laughed. "I hate to be the one to break it to you, but a lot of people in Sedona have the gift of second sight."

"None like you."

"Well, that's flattering. I guess."

"It wasn't meant to be flattering. There is some aspect of your gift the Chieftain has clearly responded to. Something he needs."

Rhea's stomach growled. She hadn't eaten all day and she was tired of talking to this stupid fox. "Maybe he needs someone who'll distract him from taking people's heads as trophies," she offered as she headed to the kitchen to get a frozen dinner. "That was a human being, you know." She spoke into the freezer as she worked a box out of the ice. "So what did he even do? Why was he being hunted?"

"Perhaps you should ask the Chieftain."

"And how am I supposed to do that, exactly?" Rhea popped her dinner into the microwave and set the timer.

Vixen pursed her downy muzzle. "It seems the Chieftain has chosen you as his earthly protector. When he travels by night, he is vulnerable. You have the power to protect him or destroy him."

Rhea's hand dropped to her side. "Wait…you don't mean Leo Ström is the Chieftain?"

Vixen ignored the question. "Because of your disruption, Kára was forced to take the lead."

"Kára?"

"The warrior who took the prey as her prize."

The microwave timer dinged and Rhea opened the door to take out the steaming little tray and stir the half-frozen noodles in the center. "So what's she going to do with him now that she has him? Is she planning on taking his head for her own trophy?" Rhea popped the tray back in and punched in another minute. "Or is she taking him to Valhalla?"

"His kind does *not* belong in Valhalla." Vixen's voice was tight with disdain and anger. "Valhalla is for heroes, for those slain in battle, not for cowards."

When she looked up from pressing the start button, Vixen was gone.

"She's a Valkyrie, though, right?" Rhea said to the empty room. "I totally nailed it, didn't I? That was a Valkyrie I just saw." She shook her head with a sigh. "And now, not only do I have conversations with talking foxes, I'm talking to myself *as if* I were having a conversation with a talking fox. Because that's totally not weird."

It was clearly time for alcohol.

Chapter 11

Rhea woke in the morning with a throbbing headache and an upset stomach. Microwaved macaroni and cheese and Guinness in a can apparently didn't mix.

She was late getting into the shop but found the door locked and the lights out. Leo wasn't there. Rhea realized she didn't even have his cell phone number. She looked up his application on her tablet. He hadn't provided it. Maybe he'd decided to bail after she'd ribbed him for being Faye's boy toy. Maybe she'd done a little more than rib him. Maybe she was a bit of a jerk, and now she was out a perfectly good employee. And a hot, mysterious nutjob her subconscious clearly wanted to ride like she was a rodeo queen.

He'd helped her out a lot already, though. The place was even cleaner than when she'd come in yesterday, inventory was officially counted, and the accounting system was all set up and ready to go. She might actually be able to get this business off the ground. All she needed now were some clients.

As if she'd conjured one, the door jingled open and someone walked in. Someone who was not Leo. This guy was a much better dresser—if not quite as sexy in his natty suit—and his hair lacked the undisciplined chaos of Leo's.

She gave him her best professional smile. "Looking for a tattoo?"

The natty dresser smiled back. "I saw one of your flyers and thought I'd come check it out." He glanced around at the flash Leo had helped hang on the walls. "Is this all your work?"

"None of it is, actually." Rhea came out from behind the counter and picked up the leather-bound book on the coffee table. "This is my portfolio, if you'd like to take a look. We're not officially open yet, but I'm taking appointments beginning the first of the year and I'd be happy to do a consultation if you see something you like." She handed him the book. "I'm Rhea."

"Brock." He held out his hand, his face lighting up with a genuine smile of interest. The handshake was firm and brief. No nonsense. The day was looking up. "Are you the only tattooist?"

Rhea's smile faltered. "I'm hoping to bring in some other artists once I've opened, but for now it's just me. Is that a problem?"

"No! Sorry, no. I was just curious." He opened the book, looking embarrassed.

"Why don't you have a seat? I've got tea and cocoa if you want to take your time looking it over."

"Cocoa sounds great, thanks." Brock sat and flipped

through the book while Rhea took the kettle into the back to fill it. He raised his voice to carry to where she was. "This one's interesting."

Rhea came back out to set the kettle on the heating plate and leaned across the table to see what he was looking at. It turned out to be Theia's sacrum tattoo: a multicolored sunrise with dark curls of filigree in front of it.

"That one uses a sort of combination watercolor/airbrush technique I've been experimenting with."

"It's really stunning. Not exactly the kind of thing I'd get, but I love the effect." He glanced up. "How long have you been tattooing?" It was the question she'd been dreading. But it was only fair.

"Honestly, only about six months professionally. I practiced on friends for about a year first. And on myself."

"On yourself? Any you can show me?" Brock brushed the carefully styled hair across his forehead. "I mean... that's not a rude question, is it? I didn't mean to get personal."

Rhea laughed. "Well, I did volunteer the information that I've tattooed myself, so I kind of stepped right into that, didn't I? I don't really have any I can show you without a wardrobe malfunction—oh. Wait, I do have one." She put her foot up on the edge of the couch and rolled up the left leg of her pants before pushing the thick woolen sock out of the way. "I did this a few days ago. I have some more fine detail work to do on it, but it's mostly done."

"Wow." Brock leaned in to get a better look at the Black Moon Lilith. "That's an amazing color."

"I know. I just love it. I found it at a convention recently. A custom blend. Hopefully, it stays true when it's done healing." She rolled down her pant leg and took her foot off the couch, feeling self-conscious. She didn't usually show off her own ink to strangers.

"I've never seen that symbol before. Does it have any special meaning?"

Rhea hesitated. She hadn't even shown her sisters this tattoo yet. She certainly wasn't going to tell some guy who'd walked in off the street about the Lilith connection. She hadn't even told Leo about *that*. Not that it was any of Leo's business. But she knew more about his business than—

Rhea realized Brock was staring at her curiously while she waged her internal debate. "It has some personal meaning."

Brock smiled. "Those are the best, huh? I've been thinking about getting a quote from one of my favorite books. I should probably think it through carefully, though, if it's going to be words. That's what everyone tells me."

"Good advice. Never tattoo someone else's name on your skin is better advice." Rhea grinned. "So this will be your first tattoo?"

Brock nodded, thumbing through the book. "I've been thinking about getting one for years but never had the guts to go through with it. But when I saw your flyer, it seemed like the time was right."

"While you're thinking it over, I can put you down for an appointment for when the shop opens after the first. You can always cancel—with twenty-four-hours' notice, of course—if you change your mind or haven't decided on the right tattoo by then."

Brock smiled, but the smile drooped as he considered. "After the first. I'm going to be traveling for a while on business. There's no way you could do it before? I promise not to tell anyone I got it early."

There wasn't much else she needed to do before opening, and turning down her first client didn't seem like a good start. "Well… I guess I could. If I have the color you want in stock."

"Oh, it's going to be all black, whatever I decide on."

"Then I've got your color." Rhea smiled. "Okay, let's put you on the calendar." She grabbed the tablet from the counter and pulled up the booking app. "Just so you know, I charge one fifty an hour with a one-hour minimum." He nodded when she looked up. "How's next Friday at one o'clock?"

"Perfect."

"I can call or send you a reminder the day before if you want to enter your name and contact information in the app."

Brock typed in the information and handed the tablet back.

Her new client glanced at his watch and rose as the kettle beeped. "Guess I'm going to miss out on that cocoa. I need to get going. But it was great meeting you, Rhea, and I'm really looking forward to next Friday."

After he'd left, Rhea turned on some music and indulged in a little victory dance. She paused to text Phoebe—after shaking off the millisecond's impulse to hit Theia's number first—to tell her she'd bagged her first client, leading to a *squee* of congratulations and a follow-up phone call moments later.

"That's awesome, sweetie!" Phoebe was always Rhea's biggest cheerleader, but something in her voice said this wasn't the reason for her call.

Rhea sighed. "Okay, what is it?"

"What's what?"

"What is it you're waiting a polite three minutes into this congratulatory call to tell me that has nothing to do with my first official client?"

"I keep forgetting you're psychic."

"Ha. And yet you haven't let me tattoo you or let me anywhere near your existing tattoos since the one I gave you to help find Rafe when Carter was trying to drain him of his blood."

"Yeah, thanks for the reminder, Theia. I'd almost stopped having nightmares about it."

Rhea felt her teeth grinding together. "You just called me Theia."

"Oh, shitballs. I'm sorry. It's just—Theia says you've blocked her number, and she called to tell me she had a dream about you and asked me to pass it on."

"Oh, for God's sake."

"She's worried about you, Rhe. And you know her dreams are always significant."

"And always vague enough to read like a horoscope everyone thinks makes perfect sense after the fact."

"Why are you so pissed at Theia?"

"Just tell me the dream."

"She said someone came to your door to take something from you, and you let them in. She says to tell you to be careful reading the ink of a stranger because you may read what you want to and miss the—" Phoebe paused as if reading from something herself. "And miss the meaning of the words beneath the skin. And she dreamed about a black wolf. She couldn't figure out if it meant you harm."

Goddammit. It figured Theia's dreams about her would be right on the nose.

"Rhe? You still there?"

"Yeah, I'm here. Thanks for the message."

"Is that a thanks for Theia or for me?"

Rhea made an exasperated noise. "Whomever you want it to be for."

"So other than your awesome news, how are you doing? Any more visits from the ghost riders?"

"Nope. Not a one." She didn't feel like telling Phoebe she'd had another conversation with a talking fox. Or about being stalked by a wolf. Elkhound. Whatever. It would only wind up getting back to Theia.

"Huh." Phoebe didn't sound convinced. "Why would they show themselves to you for no reason and then stop?"

"How would I know?"

"Do you think it has something to do with snake boy?"

Rhea growled. "He's not a snake boy, and, again, how would I know?"

"Uh-oh. Trouble in paradise?"

"Phoebe—"

"I'm just saying, you had this hot vision, and your visions are never wrong, so—"

"I've also had visions from creepers fantasizing about me. Those didn't come true. They were just nasty little 'wishes' I made damn sure weren't going to be fulfilled."

"But you were in control in the vision with Leo. You experienced it physically."

"Maybe it was *my* wishful thinking. Anyway, I need to get going."

"You still haven't RSVP'd for Christmas Eve. You're coming, aren't you?" Phoebe tried to sound stern.

"I'll think about it."

Rhea turned the volume back up on the music after the call and broke into dance once more, rocking out to Lady Gaga and Beyoncé. As she spun about with a particularly vigorous hair whip, she careened unexpectedly into Leo's arms. He looked as surprised as she felt.

"Holy shit, Leo." Rhea steadied herself and backed out of his grip, trying not to blush. "You nearly gave me a heart attack. How long have you been standing there?"

"I just walked in. I said hello, but I guess you couldn't hear me over the music." He was kind of shouting over it even now.

Rhea hurried to turn it down. "Sorry, I was celebrating. I booked my first client."

Leo smiled. "That's terrific. Sorry I wasn't here."

"Where were you, anyway? When I found the place empty, I thought maybe you'd quit."

He glanced down at his boots, rocking back on them slightly, with his hands in his pockets. "I kind of did. Or I was going to." He looked up and met Rhea's eyes. "And then I realized I hadn't worked off my tattoo yet."

"I see." Rhea leaned back against the counter. "Well, if you're uncomfortable here, I don't want you to feel obligated to stay. You can pay me back when you have the money."

Leo blinked at her, the same blue eyes as that damn dog's. "Are…are you firing me?"

Rhea's temper flared—the way it did when she realized she was the one being an asshole. "I'm confused. Do you want to work here or do you not want to work here?"

"Okay, I guess I should go." Leo drew his hands out of his pockets—gloveless and pink from the cold—and turned to leave.

Rhea glared at the ground for a second, like the

ground was the one being the asshole, before reaching out and grabbing for his hand. "Leo, wait. I'm sorry. I'm being a jerk."

Her fingers brushed the Thor's Hammer tattoo at his wrist as he turned back toward her, and the vision hit her before she could pull away. *The thundering hoofbeats of the Hunt, the Viking she'd seen in her first vision in her living room leading the charge, blue eyes bright with excitement. The hair was longer and wilder and the beard fuller, and the thick fur garments and leather armor made him seem bulkier, but it was unmistakably Leo. He raised his sword and gave a hair-raising cry.*

Leo was the one to break the connection, pulling Rhea's hand from his wrist and grabbing her arms to give her a sharp shake. "All right, what the hell was that?"

Rhea stared up at him. "That was you, Leo. I don't know how, but it seems you're the Chieftain of the Hunt."

He dropped her arms and took a step back. "Sorry, *what* am I?"

"You lead the Wild Hunt. Or your *hugr* does. I think."

"My conscious thought-self."

"The other Leo said it was comparable to your soul."

Leo pulled off his hat and messed up his hair. "My *soul* is riding around in the middle of the night…leading Odin's Hunt."

"So you know about the Hunt."

"Of course I know about it. I minored in Norse mythology."

"You never mentioned that before."

"No, because I—just remembered it." Leo shook his head. "This is too much. Why would I be leading Odin's Hunt? I'm starting to think you're feeding me these visions."

A prickle of outrage rippled through her skin. "You think I'm making this up?"

"No. No, I—" He sank onto the couch. "I am *really* confused." Leo glanced up at her, suspicion still lingering in his gaze. "So how do *you* know about the Hunt?"

"I've been seeing it for a few nights now. Ever since you arrived in town. It doesn't look quite like the vision. The horses and riders are more spectral, more contemporarily dressed. It only happens when you're here, locked up."

"And when were you going to tell me about this?"

"I wasn't sure it had anything to do with you. I see weird things sometimes. I mean, never this weird, but it started with my own tattoo before I'd even met you."

"What tattoo?"

She'd shown it to a stranger. She might as well show it to Leo.

Rhea rolled up her pant leg once more and propped her boot on the edge of the coffee table. "I did it the night before you came into the shop, and while I was finishing up, I had the first vision of the Hunt."

Leo studied it. "Oh, the Black Moon Lilith."

Rhea let the fabric of her pants drop back over it, removing her boot from the table. "You know the symbol?"

"Of course. From Theia."

That familiar surge of anger was back. "Theia talked to you about Lilith?"

Leo gave her a peculiar look. "She has the same tattoo."

It was all Rhea could do not to kick the table across the room. "Theia has a tattoo I don't know about? A tattoo I didn't *do*?"

Leo blanched. "I just assumed you *had* done it. It's

exactly the same except for the color. She just has the black outline inside her left forearm. I asked her what it was and she called it the Black Moon Lilith symbol."

Visions having nothing to do with pictomancy or Wild Hunts were going through Rhea's mind—visions of putting a pillow over Theia's face and holding it down. "But she didn't tell you anything else about Lilith?"

"Like what?"

"You didn't ask her what the significance was?"

"No. It didn't seem like any of my business, and she didn't offer."

Rhea walked back to the counter and fiddled with the tablet. "And did she offer any information about the tattoo I *did* do?"

"I didn't see any other tattoos."

Rhea laughed. "Come on. You didn't notice the giant sunrise above her ass cheeks?"

Leo looked annoyed. "I never saw her ass cheeks."

"I suppose she's missionary only."

He straightened his glasses. "If you must know, I didn't see *any* parts of her that weren't clothed."

"Um, how did you have sex if you never saw her naked?"

"I never said I had sex with Theia. You just assumed."

Rhea looked back down at the tablet to hide her surprise. Nighttime Leo had been telling the truth. "Well, that's a first." She glanced up and met his eyes. "You know, because she's a super slut." She grinned and fiddled with the accounting program for a minute before giving up with a sigh. Rhea took the tablet off the stand and came around the counter to bring it over to him. "I added a column and I think I broke the spreadsheet again. Would you mind fixing it? If you're here to work, that is."

"Absolutely. If you're not firing me, I'm not quitting." His thumb hit the home button as he took the tablet, and he ended up in the booking app. Leo paused, reading the entry, and his eyes darted up to meet Rhea's. "What is Brock Dressler's name doing in here?"

"That's my new client."

Leo stared at her. "That's the Nazi I punched."

Chapter 12

There was no way to be sure Brock Dressler hadn't come to the shop by coincidence. But Leo wasn't buying it.

"He must have followed me back. Or he saw me later putting up the flyers."

Rhea had the urge to rub her arms, like bugs were crawling on them. "He seemed so normal."

"They always seem normal. Because they believe they are. It's everyone else who's brainwashed. Everyone else who's attacking them for their beliefs. They're the most persecuted sons of bitches in the world." Leo looked down at the scabs on his knuckles. He should have gone in for a second punch.

"It sounds like you have a lot of experience with them."

Leo's head shot up. He searched Rhea's face, trying

to determine if there was more behind the statement than the words on the surface. "Maybe I do. I don't remember."

Rhea sat on the arm of the couch. "It seems like all this Nazi stuff must have something to do with you." She held up her hand as he opened his mouth to protest. "I'm not saying you're part of it. But that it's, I don't know, following you."

Leo slumped forward with his head in his hands. It did seem to follow him, and he didn't know why. Dressler had made a beeline for him at the conference, and then there he'd been on the street while Leo was going for lunch. Not to mention the graffiti and the posters. And now Dressler showing up wanting a tattoo? What the hell was the connection? He wanted to grab hold of his brain and shake it until he remembered. And the horrible fear was that he'd find he somehow *did* have something to do with these bastards. That he wasn't who he thought he was. That maybe he wasn't a good person at all.

Rhea's hand settled gently on his shoulder. "We could do another reading. Maybe read one of the earlier tattoos. Go further back and find out how you got it."

Leo lifted his head.

"Unless there's a reason you don't want me seeing that, which is totally your call."

"What reason would I have for not wanting you to see how I got the earlier tattoos?" Even as he said it, he realized he'd told her yesterday he didn't.

"I don't know, Leo. You tell me."

The fear of being exposed gripped him again. And he didn't even know what he was afraid of having exposed. That he was crazy, maybe, and this would give her the proof. Or that he really was associated with scum like Dressler.

"What I'd like to know more about is this Hunt thing," he said finally. "If my soul is actually leaving my body to *hunt* something—"

"Somebody."

"What?"

"Hunt some*body*. Last night, I watched them chase down some guy and snatch him off his horse and take him…"

"Take him where?"

"They rode off into the sky."

Leo laughed, but she was serious. He was starting to wonder which one of them was the crazy one. "Okay. Well, then, I'd like to know who I'm hunting and why."

"You want the reading, then."

He nodded. "Yeah. I want the reading." He pushed up his sleeve and held out his arm, hand in a tight fist. "Let's do Mjölnir."

He screwed his eyes shut and held his breath as Rhea placed her hand on the tattoo, repeating "not a Nazi" in his head like Harry Potter begging the Sorting Hat not to put him in Slytherin. So he'd seen *Harry Potter*, he realized. Or maybe read it. That was something.

And then he had one boot in a stirrup and he was swinging himself onto the back of a sturdy horse. *He didn't feel like himself. He felt stronger. More in control. And incredibly angry. "No mercy!" he bellowed. A woman beside him answered, "For Odin and Freyja!"*

The horse thundered forward at his command, but before he could catch his breath, the scene changed. Searing pain seized his arm. Leo looked down to find his hand had been severed. Someone grabbed his bleeding stump as he drifted toward unconsciousness.

"We had a bargain, damn you!" It was the woman's voice, the one from the Hunt.

"You said nothing of limbs," said another woman, her voice toneless, beyond cold. "Only head and heart."

"He will have no heart if the blood drains from it!"

"Will you give us his mind?"

"His mind? I have given you his will!"

Leo was shivering and everything was going dark.

"Think quickly, Kára. The skein unravels as the heart winds down. He is nothing but clockwork. A mind for a body. We think it a fair exchange."

"Leo." Someone was shaking him. Or he was shaking. Shaking apart. Something crinkly draped his shoulders. "Leo, snap out of it. You're scaring me."

He realized his eyes were still screwed shut, and he opened them to find Rhea hovering over him with concern. She'd wrapped him in some kind of space-age silver blanket.

"Are you with me?"

"Rhea?"

"Thank God. You scared the crap out of me. I think you were going into shock. I grabbed the Mylar blanket from the first aid kit. You should lie down and elevate your feet. Get the blood pumping back to your heart."

Leo let her ease him back onto the couch and lift his feet to slide a pillow under them. Blood to his heart. What the hell had he just seen? He pulled his right arm from the blanket to make sure his hand was still attached.

"It felt so real," he murmured.

"I think it was real." Rhea put his arm back inside the blanket.

"How could it be real? I lost my hand."

"I don't understand exactly how, but you asked why you were hunting—"

"I also asked who."

"True, and we didn't really get a who, but I might have an idea about that. My point is, you seem to have been part of a bargain. Kára said she'd given them your will, and then she apparently bargained your mind to keep you from bleeding to death."

"Who the hell is Kára?"

"That's what the voice in the vision called her. I think it's the woman I saw hunting with you—or with the Chieftain, anyway—last night. I think she's a Valkyrie."

Leo sat up, no longer shivering so hard he thought he might come apart. "A Valkyrie? That's ridiculous."

"About as ridiculous as a flying hunting party, yeah."

Nervous energy propelled him to his feet as he pulled off the Mylar blanket. "I don't know what to think about any of this." He held out his right hand, alternating between making a fist and flexing his fingers. "But I think I'm good on the whole reading thing for now. Until I can get a better idea of what's real and what's my mind supplying images in some semi-dream state."

Rhea picked up the blanket, folding it into smaller and smaller squares. "But the reading last night—that seemed to ring true."

Heat rushed to Leo's face as he remembered the vivid images conjured by the reading and the even more vivid memories that followed when the reading ended. "Yes. Faye is someone I actually knew. I don't remember when I stopped seeing her or even how long ago, but the vision…yeah, it definitely happened." He tucked his hands into his back pockets. They felt like extra appendages he didn't know what to do with. "Sorry. I know it made you uncomfortable."

Rhea gave him an odd little smile he couldn't interpret. "I wouldn't say it made me uncomfortable, exactly."

Unconsciously, he'd stepped closer to her. Close enough to see the faint glow of heat in her cheeks. Why would she be blushing if she wasn't uncomfortable? Unless... *Please. Dude. She is* not *into you. She's into* him.

The rings around Rhea's irises seemed extra dark. "I guess I was a little jealous, if you want to know the truth. Not that I have any right to be. It's not like we—" She paused, biting her lip. "I mean, I'm your boss."

He couldn't seem to stop staring at her mouth. With another step, Leo had breached the distance between them. The folded Mylar slipped from Rhea's fingers, exploding back into a full-sized blanket at their feet in slow motion as she stared up at him.

Before he could second-guess himself, he took her hand, his fingers weaving between hers. "I could quit again," he said. "If you think that would help."

The corners of her eyes crinkled, her smile slight and secretive like the Mona Lisa. It was as good a sign as any.

Her eyes went wide when he cupped the back of her neck and lowered his head, but she melted against him as he drew her close and kissed her. She was surprisingly slight and soft in his arms, her lips slick and sweet. She gave off such a prickly, self-reliant vibe, he'd half expected her to be built like a wiry, hard-muscled boy. But there was nothing boyish about the way her petite curves pressed into him.

After a moment, self-consciousness kicked in, and Leo stepped back, letting their fingers separate, uncertain now whether he'd been projecting. "Sorry. I hope I didn't misread…?"

Rhea's tentative smile faded. He'd blown it.

She snatched up the Mylar, cramming it back into little folded squares. "For future reference, Leo, 'sorry' is not what a girl wants to hear after intimate contact."

Rhea kept things light for the rest of the afternoon, trying not to let on how conflicted she was about the kiss. He'd taken her by surprise, sending the blood rushing to her extremities in the best way possible, and her lips still tingled—she had to keep stopping herself from touching her fingertips to them to be sure his mouth wasn't somehow still pressed against them—but his tentativeness afterward was weird and disappointing. She couldn't get the memory of the vision she'd shared with the other Leo out of her head. There had been nothing tentative or uncertain about what they'd been doing.

Leo was gamely trying to pretend the kiss hadn't happened, which made the disappointment worse. She couldn't help thinking about the passion he'd shown for Faye. Maybe he only responded that way to dominant women. Rhea certainly wasn't submissive, but actively dominating someone wasn't really her thing either.

By late afternoon, she figured making a lighthearted exit before dusk was the best course of action, but after they shared some Indian takeout, Leo posed the question she'd been hoping to avoid.

"Are you going to stick around tonight?"

Rhea didn't raise her head as she boxed up what they hadn't finished. "Do you think it matters?"

"Matters?" Leo's expression was wounded when Rhea looked up.

"I mean, you won't remember whether I was here, anyway."

"True. But it's nice to know someone's here before it happens." Leo took the dishes to the sink. "You're probably right, though. I don't blame you for not wanting to deal with my out of control id."

"He's not *that* out of control." Rhea bagged up the garbage and set it by the door. She turned to find Leo watching her with a thoughtful expression. "Do you like board games?"

The expression went from thoughtful to confused. "Board games?"

"I've got Scrabble and some other games on my tablet. Maybe the Lucid Ass could use something to occupy the time."

Leo laughed. "I suppose he could. I can't speak for him, of course, but presuming we share the same interests, sure. Sounds fun to me."

They started playing Scrabble while Leo was still himself, strapped in and waiting for the light to fade. But there was a definite moment when Rhea could almost see the change come over him: Lucid Ass Leo's Mr. Hyde eclipsing Leo the Dull's Dr. Jekyll.

He paused with his finger poised above the tile he'd been about to move while Rhea held the tablet for him, and Leo's habitual hesitant tension relaxed into an easy self-confidence.

Crisp blue eyes rose to meet hers with amusement beneath the pale lashes. "Well, now. What fresh hell can this be?"

"Feeling all right, Leo?"

"Marvelous. I missed you last night."

"Did you, now?"

"You doubt my sincerity. Do you doubt my tumescence?"

Rhea forced herself not to follow the downward flick of his gaze. "Unless you were about to put that word on the board, that's a losing move, mister."

"The board?"

"The game board. We're playing Scrabble. I have to warn you, I come from a Scrabble family, and I'm very competitive."

"What's the purpose of it?"

"We build words onto existing words on the board by placing our letter tiles on the squares, and each tile has a specific value—there, above the letter—while certain squares multiply the points of a letter or a word."

"But what's the *purpose* of it?"

Rhea sighed. "I thought you could use something to pass the time. It's a game. Entertainment."

"Is it? I can think of much more exciting entertainment."

"I'm sure you can." She tapped the board. "It's your move."

Leo perused the board while Rhea averted her eyes to avoid seeing his tiles, which he'd failed to hide at the bottom of the screen. "What was *his* last word?"

"Tinsel. He added the *S-E-L* to my *tin* for six points."

"Tinsel?" Leo laughed with that deep, warm vibration his laughter had when the *munr* had the skin. "He could have made it *tins* and spelled *sensual*. Or *sexual*. He's an idiot."

"I don't disagree."

Leo uncrossed his ankles to poke his stockinged foot against her shin. "Oh, dear. What did the fool do?"

"Nothing."

"That's what I was afraid of. You have to see what an idiot he is." The foot remained where it was, his big toe slowly stroking her through the fabric. "We share the same skin. He shares my desires. I *am* his desires. Only I'm honest about it. I'm direct and forthright. What you see is what you get."

She forgot not to look where his gaze was trying to draw hers. *Jesus.*

His grin reminded her of the Cheshire cat. "And you obviously like what you see."

Rhea folded the tablet into her crossed arms. "That's your opinion."

"I swear, if I had him in front of me, I'd beat the snot out of him for being too stupid to see how much you desire him in return. The flush in your cheeks, the sparkle in your eyes, the way your breath is rising and falling in your chest."

"Stop looking at my chest."

"Honestly, I can't imagine what you see in him—other than the obvious fact of our rather impressive skin. If he can't act like a man and respond to those signals, if his all-important dull little soul can't recognize what he has right in front of him, he doesn't deserve you."

Was he trying to make her feel better? Giving her a pep talk about the guy—who was *himself*, no less—who'd failed to make a move?

"You sound like one of my sisters." She jumped as the stockinged toe slipped beneath her pant leg and stroked her skin.

"I assure you, I am nothing like one of your sisters." He was goddamned adept with that one toe—through a *sock*. It made her wonder what he could do with the rest of his body. "Why don't you put that fancy game board down and let me show you just how unlike them I am?"

"It's not just a fancy game board, it's a computer. Honestly, Leo, how do you not know anything?"

"Is that a reason to keep hugging it?" His foot slipped from her pant leg and hooked beneath one of the wheeled legs of the stool, and with a sharp tug, he managed to drag her close to him, making her lose her grip on the tablet as she threw her arms out to catch herself against the armrests. Which meant grasping his forearms. The tablet tumbled into his lap.

Leo shifted his weight and the tablet slipped between his legs—where it remained propped at a forty-five degree angle.

Leo's smile was amused at her hesitation. "Are you planning to cede that to me for the rest of the night?"

The tablet gave a little jump as she moved one hand from his arm.

"You seem happy to have it."

"I'd be much happier with something else there."

"I'm sure you would."

"Don't be silly. Just pick it up. It's not as if I can do anything." He jerked lightly on his wrist restraints. "I'm completely at your mercy."

The image of Leo on his hands and knees at Faye's bidding sprang to her mind. "Right. I forgot that was your thing."

"Sorry?"

Rhea snatched the tablet from his lap and pushed off with her feet against the base of the chair, sending the stool rolling backward. "That's what *he* said."

"I'm not following you."

"You seem to enjoy being at a woman's mercy."

Leo's red-gold brows drew together. "What woman's mercy? Yours? I don't exactly have a choice in the matter."

"Faye's, for instance."

"And who is Faye?"

Rhea laughed. "Surely you remember the woman you swore you'd do anything for. The one who marked you as her own."

"Marked…?"

Leo turned his head toward the Midgard Serpent tattoo, though it was hidden beneath his shirt. He'd worn the long-sleeved one again today. Rhea really needed to give him an allowance to buy some new things. She could write it off as a business expense.

"She gave me the tattoo?" His vision turned inward. "*She* gave me the tattoo. She marked me so I couldn't escape the skin."

"You wanted to escape the skin?"

"She'd already bound me." He turned his wrists in the restraints. "As you can see. Bound Leo's will so that he had to obey her. Convinced him to engage in this stupid ritual. But if the *hugr* can leave temporarily, so can the *munr*. Except not now. As Jörmungandr constrains the waters of the sea, the mark constrains the will."

She'd bound his will. "Kára." They'd said the name together.

Leo's eyes fixed on hers, narrowed with suspicion. "How do you know that name?"

"I shared a vision with Leo. Two visions, actually. One of Faye having him marked and one of Kára…bargaining his mind for his life. They're the same woman, aren't they? The Valkyrie."

"The Valkyrie." Leo's fists curled tightly against the armrests. "The accursed Valkyrie."

Chapter 13

Leo leaned back against the headrest. Rhea couldn't help but notice the enthusiasm of his erection had faded. "I can't say whether it was willing submission on Leo's part—without will, how is anything willing? But you're correct that the Valkyrie owns me. She has enslaved me."

He'd been pretty damned willing in her vision, but Rhea decided not to go there. "How much do you remember?"

"You said she bargained Leo's mind."

"He was bleeding to death and going into shock. He'd lost his hand."

Leo's eyes flicked toward his presently whole limbs with little interest, perhaps checking to see if they were there. "And that's why both he and I are absolute shit at remembering things. A pretty stupid bargain, if you ask me. Plenty of people have survived the loss of a hand.

But I suppose no one did ask me." He sighed, staring at the ceiling. "I remember… I don't know. Chronologically, very little. But Kára, I cannot forget. She's like staring at the sun—intensely and damagingly beautiful."

Rhea must have reacted in some way she wasn't aware of—a breath of disappointment or a slight movement that gave her discomfort away—as Leo turned his gaze on her.

"Such beauty is hardly a personal merit. It's something cold, like a diamond, to be admired and coveted, perhaps, but not truly desired." He gave her an ironic half smile. "I should know."

"A lot of people covet you, do they?"

He laughed, a little sound of delight. "I didn't mean myself. I meant that I know what it is to desire something truly. You dismiss my desire as soulless gluttony, when it is the purest thing I can offer you. Far purer than anything *he* will ever express. He's a coward."

Okay, *now* she was uncomfortable. It was one thing to think he was toying with her, trying to get into her pants because she happened to be there—and maybe as a ploy to get her to set him free—but the way his eyes looked into hers as he spoke made her feel naked. He wasn't goddamn kidding. He *wanted* her. And he'd obviously gotten over whatever had momentarily…deflated him.

Leo tilted his head. "You want me, but my wanting you seems to distress you."

Rhea cleared her throat awkwardly. Which she was sure was totally hot. "It's a little weird. You're…" She gestured at him helplessly.

"Tied up and kept here against my will? A mindless, soulless animal?"

"In my employee's body, for God's sake."

He was still studying her with curiosity. "So it's because you've entered into a financial relationship with him? Would it be like paying me for sex?"

"Jesus, Leo. *No.*" Rhea flipped the irritating spike of hair out of her face. She had to get him talking about something else. "What do you know about the Wild Hunt?"

His face clouded, but he shook his head. "What is that?"

"A spectral hunting party that roams the night in the weeks between All Souls and Yule. It's mainly found in Norse and Germanic folklore. At least, I thought it was just folklore. Until I saw it."

Leo shrugged. "What has that to do with me?"

"I think that's where your *hugr* goes at night."

His quizzical look turned into a scowl. "It's not *my hugr.* It's his."

"Right. Well, that's what he's doing when he leaves the 'skin' to you. He's out riding, hunting people—murderers and oath-breakers, I guess."

"Bully for him. Sounds right up his self-righteous alley."

"I believe he rides with Kára. I saw her last night, flying off with someone she'd hunted down."

Leo shifted restlessly, wrists chafing against the bonds. "I don't want to hear any more about Kára."

"But if she's a Valkyrie and she controls him, I'm just trying to work out why—"

"Enough!" Leo punctuated the shout with a swing of his foot, sending the rolling worktable beside them spinning across the room and onto its side with a bang that made her flinch. "I said I didn't want to hear any more about her." He seemed slightly subdued by Rhea's reaction, but his eyes were flashing a warning.

"All right. Sorry." Rhea picked up the table and the scattered supplies from the shelf it had collided with and closed the cover on the tablet. "Maybe I should go."

"Please don't." Was it her imagination or had his voice shaken a bit? "You have no idea what it's like sitting here for hours waiting to die."

"You don't actually die, Leo."

"It feels like dying. He has the days, and his miserable soul has the freedom to fly where it will at night, hunting the profane, while I sit imprisoned. This is my entire life, dusk to dawn. And then I'm gone, snuffed out. Reborn again the next night but knowing each night that I have one less before I die again for an entire year."

She was tempted to tease him for being melodramatic. It wasn't as if he was *actually* gone when the other Leo was awake. Like a split personality, he was integrated once more with the whole. At least, that's what she assumed. But it had to suck sitting here by himself. If she were tied to a chair even for a single night, she'd probably go a little bit bonkers.

"All right." Rhea pulled up the wheeled stool once more and sat beside him. "I'll stay for a bit."

The sudden urgency in his eyes was intense. "Stay the night."

Rhea laughed, trying to lighten the mood. "And we're back to that."

"That wasn't a proposition. Although I'm up for it, of course. Always." The smirk was back. "Just stay. Keep me company."

"I have to sleep sometime, you know. *I* don't disappear with the sun."

"Oh." He closed his eyes and turned his head to the side dramatically, as if she'd struck him a sudden blow. "She has a heart of stone." Leo peeked at her out of one eye and laughed at her dry expression. "If you get tired, you can share the chair with me. It's quite comfortable."

She shook her head at him despairingly. "So you don't sleep at all?"

Leo shrugged. "It seems wasteful when I have so little time. But I confess to having fallen asleep out of sheer boredom on occasion."

"Then I'll do my best to keep you entertained."

"I can think of a few ways."

Rhea groaned. "You never stop."

Leo winked. "You don't want me to. But let's set that aside for the moment. Tell me about this gift of yours. This reading tattoos."

"I'm not reading you again."

"Too much for you last time, was I?"

Rhea looked away, trying not to think about the truth of that statement.

"No worries. I'm not asking for a reading. Even if you do hand them out to *him* like candy."

"You do realize you're the same person, right?"

His eyebrow lifted. "Are we? At any rate, I'm curious about how it works. Have you always had the ability?"

"Why are you so interested all of a sudden?"

"Must everything have an ulterior motive? I'm simply trying to pass the time. You said you would entertain me."

"God, I did, didn't I?" Rhea leaned back on the stool with her arms folded, debating how much she ought to tell him. It wasn't as if he'd remember any of this once he'd gone dormant or whatever it was he did. The idea that, in a few days, this Leo would be gone gave her more than a twinge of regret. "All right. Why not? All of my sisters have gifts—"

"How many do you have, anyway?"

"Gifts?"

"Sisters."

"Oh." Rhea swallowed the familiar irritation. "Well, that depends."

Leo looked amused. "It doesn't usually."

"There's nothing usual about us. There were four of us. But, recently, Theia discovered we have three half sisters."

"Seven sisters. Like the Pleiades."

"In this case, the Titanides. Each of us is named after one of the original female Titans." It was sufficient for the story. "And each of us has a gift corresponding with our namesake. Although mine's a bit off. Rhea is associated with wild music and ecstatic rites, and a chariot pulled by a pair of lionesses—"

"Is she really? You know, the goddess Freyja rides in a chariot pulled by two cats. She's the Norse goddess of love and war. Sex and death, intimately intertwined."

"*Okay.* Charming and weird."

"You don't think sex and death are intertwined?"

"Well… I didn't until just now."

Leo laughed, his eyes crinkling with pleasure. "Sex is generative power. Death is a kind of birth, a passage from one life to the next. And of course there is the *little* death."

Rhea cleared her throat. "Moving right along. For years, I tried to figure out what my 'power' was. Ione is a powerful witch. Phoebe can talk to dead people. And Theia—" Her chest tightened at the thought of Theia.

"She's always had visions and prophetic dreams. But I never had anything. Until I started doing tattoos. Then the visions just came to me."

Leo studied her with a secretive smile. "And do they always come true, your visions?"

"Ah-ha-ha." She waggled her finger at him. "There you go again."

His eyes twinkled. "I have so little to occupy my thoughts. What with not having a mind. I'm nothing but will."

"You seem to have more of a mind than Leo the—" Rhea stopped before she finished the epithet. She hadn't meant to call him that.

"You see? He *is* dull, isn't he? A complete bore." He made a little motion that encompassed his shoulders and hips, almost a shimmy. "I can't help that I have all the best attributes." The shimmy set off that tingling in her extremities again.

"Except modesty."

"If I had any, it would be false modesty." He winked one sparkling blue eye. "So where do these gifts of yours come from? Did your parents have them?"

Rhea chewed her lip. "I haven't told Leo this. The other Leo."

He leaned forward in the chair. "Ooh, a secret. Just between you and me."

"Supposedly, we have demon blood. From the first demoness, Lilith."

"That, my dearest dove, is…" He shook his head slowly, letting his gaze roam over her. "Fucking hot."

She wasn't sure whether it was the endearment or the hungry, appreciative gaze or the unexpected "fucking hot" that was melting her pussy like the well of wax around a candle's flame. Probably all three. His biceps were flexed, hard and well defined beneath his sleeves as his fists clenched and unclenched in unconscious chafing against his bonds. He was at her mercy, as he'd said. She was sitting here with one of the hottest guys she'd ever seen—who wanted her with a refreshingly naked lust—resisting his tacky, relentless come-ons. And suddenly, it seemed absurd that she was sitting a foot away from him.

Leo's eyes widened as she pushed herself off the stool and swung her leg over the chair to straddle his hips. The seat was too wide to straddle comfortably, so she balanced her knees on the vinyl cushion on either side of him.

"If I'd known vulgarity was all it took—"

"Shut up, Leo." Rhea gripped his shoulders—*good lord, the muscles*—and silenced him. He tasted of cardamom and caraway and a bit of mint from the Indian food they'd eaten earlier. She supposed she tasted the same. His tongue teased as he alternately nipped and licked at her lips, humming softly into her mouth when she grew impatient with his teasing and pressed in closer. The vibration of sound made her damp between her thighs. Relaxing her hips against his, she felt his answering appreciation pressed firmly against her.

It wasn't quite her vision—they weren't naked, for one—but there was definitely something to be said for having a man at her mercy. In past experiences—admittedly not many and pretty much exclusively with horny undergrad dudes with one single-minded collegiate goal—this part, the kissing and sensuous grinding, was usually swiftly eclipsed by artless groping and undressing. The simple art of "making out" had been sorely lacking in those past experiences. She lost track of time, just kissing and moving with Leo in his lap in a gently rolling and perfectly synchronous wave, enveloped in his captivating scent.

Leo groaned when she pulled away at last, his hands grasping uselessly at the air. "Don't go."

"I'm not going anywhere." She took off his glasses—daytime Leo had kept them on to play Scrabble—and set them aside, settling back in his lap to look at him. His lips had reddened like cherries, wet and swollen. She could relate.

His tongue slid languidly across his bottom lip, making it slicker. "That was unexpected. And quite pleasurable. I wish I had my hands free." He stretched his pinky out to stroke one of her thighs, barely reaching. "Just one, perhaps?"

Rhea let go of his shoulders finally, letting her hands glide down his chest, feeling the hardness of his pecs, the sharp little peaks of his nipples beneath the fabric, his heartbeat.

She traced the outline of his pendant through the fabric. "You could at least pretend not to be using me just to get free."

The vibration of his laughter rumbled beneath her hands. "I've not pretended to be a saint. But I do have to object to the use of the word *just*. There is no *just* about you. You're very complex. As is my desire for you. Do I want to be free of these damn shackles? Of course. But if I had to choose between freedom and having you in my lap, it would be a very difficult decision."

Rhea withdrew her hands and folded her arms. "And what would you choose?"

Leo leaned back, observing her, deciding, no doubt,

whether she was worth his freedom. "How much freedom would I be bargaining? All of it? Or a single night?"

"Would your answer be different?"

"Of course. It would be no hardship at all to remain bound for another night if it meant spending that night with you."

"Now you're just trying to flatter me." Rhea grinned. "But I'll take it."

"No flattery at all. You make me forget I'm here against my will—in the most literal sense of the term."

Rhea uncrossed her arms and rested a hand on one of his. Leo threaded their fingers together. They sat that way, oddly comfortable in each other's silence and company, until the text notification on her phone broke the spell. He tightened his grip on her hand to keep her from letting go as she slid off his lap and dropped her feet to the floor.

She tugged against him. "I need to grab my phone."

"Do you? I'm not sure you're well enough acquainted with need to make such an assertion."

"Leo." She pried at his fingers with her other hand, and he released her reluctantly, his mouth drooping into a pout. "I'm only going two feet across the room."

She snagged the phone from the counter and opened the message. Phoebe had sent a picture of Puddleglum, her fat Siamese tabby, wearing a tiny sombrero, with the caption "We're going to party, karamu, fiesta…all night long." Rhea stifled a snort-laugh and switched off the screen.

When she looked up, Leo's expression resembled Puddleglum's resigned glower. "Are you leaving?"

Rhea tucked the phone into her back pocket and slid onto his lap once more. "I said I'd stay, didn't I?" She found the pedal beneath the chair and lowered the seat back, to Leo's pleased smirk.

"You might have let me know the chair reclined."

"Sorry, I hadn't even thought of it." Rhea rested her crossed arms on his chest.

"So this demon blood of yours—that's what gives you the power of...?"

"Pictomancy. But we're done talking about me."

"Are we?"

Rhea silenced him once more. While they kissed, her hands roamed over his obliques, stroking the taut muscles. With a shiver and a sudden jerk, Leo began to laugh. His skin twitched beneath her touch.

"You're ticklish." Rhea grinned. That was unexpected. And adorable. "You really are at my mercy, then."

"Cruel mistress. You wouldn't dare."

She tugged his shirt from his pants and moved her hands over the hardness of his abs, flirting with the edges of his waist to see where he'd twitch. *Goddamn.* It wasn't as if he'd been hiding much beneath the tight shirt, but he was even more ripped than she'd imagined. His abs formed a sharp V dipping down into the waistline of his pants. He wasn't ticklish there.

"Careful." The tone of his voice made her look up from unbuckling his belt. His eyes were intense. "There's only so much teasing I can take."

"Am I teasing you?"

"Aren't you?"

Was she? Rhea paused to consider. Was she really prepared to have sex with Leo right now? A man who was tied up and not in his right mind? The sincerity of his obvious desire notwithstanding, there was something more than a little unsavory about the circumstances. If the situation were reversed…

Rhea let go of the belt buckle and lowered his shirt.

Leo sighed. "Not quite the response I was hoping for."

"It wouldn't be right."

Leo dropped his head back against the headrest and rolled his eyes. "This is what it comes to. The absolute petty pointlessness of having a soul." He fixed his gaze on her. "Every part of your body and your mind desires me, wants to ride me with abandon and give yourself over to passion and lust as you did in our vision. But your silly little soul insists 'it wouldn't be right,' and so you deny yourself. You don't think *he's* going to give you the opportunity, do you? He'd just as soon wear a hair shirt and castigate himself for his impure thoughts."

Rhea sat up, glaring at him through the errant lock of hair. "You don't have to be a dick about it." She regretted her choice of words immediately, given where she was sitting.

But Leo ignored the double entendre. "I'm not saying he doesn't want you, just that he's too pathetic to act on that desire. *Me*. I'm that desire. Right here in front of you, telling you to take what you want." Maybe he'd only been waiting to act on the wordplay. He punctuated the phrase with a movement beneath her that made her breath catch.

She managed not to show it. "People who take what they want regardless of anyone else's feelings are the reason the world is so messed up. I happen to care about Leo's feelings. *Your* feelings, as much as you like to think you're not him. And I wouldn't be able to look him in the eyes tomorrow morning if I acted on pure desire for my own selfish reasons without any thought for how he's going to feel about it when he's back in his own skin."

He studied her, his chest heaving with anger or passion—or both—and looking so hot she wanted to cry. And kick herself for not just saying "screw it" and going for it.

"He doesn't have to find out." The soft, hopeful tone in which he'd said it was so absurd she had to laugh. Leo gave her a reluctant smile and shrugged. "You can't fault a *munr* for trying."

It only made her laugh harder, tears springing to the corners of her eyes from the release of tension. She wiped them away, shaking her head, and let herself melt against him—moving subtly aside to avoid the frustration of continued friction. She'd almost gotten herself under control when Leo spoke again.

"Well, that was fun." The resignation in his voice rumbled through his chest beneath her ear where she'd rested her head. "What do you want to do now?"

Rhea buried her face in his shirt and laughed until the tears were flowing down her cheeks.

Chapter 14

The click of the locks woke him with a jolt. Something was different. Leo opened his eyes to find Rhea snoring softly on his shoulder. She'd lowered the seat back and curled up next to him on the chair. Or on him, mostly— one leg draped over his lap. Leo narrowed his eyes. His shirt was untucked and his belt buckle was open. What in the name of the gods had his alter ego done?

He was afraid to wake her, afraid to find out, but his bladder had no intention of being so accommodating. Leo turned his right wrist under the leather and worked the strap out of the buckle. Reaching over Rhea to unstrap the other woke her.

She glanced up with a quizzical look, stretching sleepily as if not quite aware of where she'd awoken, and he watched the realization dawn on her face.

Rhea scrambled up, wiping a bit of spittle from the

corner of her mouth. "Leo, I…" She looked around help-lessly, as if an explanation might show up somewhere in the room. "You wanted me to stay, so I—"

"Would you mind holding that thought?" Leo swung his legs over the other side of the chair, avoiding her eyes as he tugged his shirt down over the open belt buckle, trying to act like he didn't notice. "I really need to use the bathroom."

After he'd relieved himself and put his clothes back together, he stared into the mirror over the sink. "What the hell did you do?" His reflection blinked back at him without answering.

"Leo?" Rhea tapped on the door. "You okay in there?"

He must have been staring at himself, resisting the urge to put a fist through the mirror to get to his alter ego, for some time. "Yeah, I'm good." He washed his hands and face and his pits and came out to find Rhea pacing in front of the counter, hands in her back pockets accentuating the curve of her ass.

She turned at the sound of the closing door. "I can explain. Nothing happened. Mostly." Her face was flushed.

"We don't have to talk about it." The last thing he wanted to hear was what "mostly" meant.

"Of course we do. I violated your trust."

"*You* did?"

"I kissed him. And then I almost let things get out of control, but I realized it wouldn't be fair to you to take it any further because you wouldn't remember, so you couldn't exactly consent. So I stopped." Rhea took her hands from her pockets and scrubbed them over her face. "This sounds so awful. I'm sorry. I shouldn't have started anything."

"And he was completely innocent in the matter, was he?"

"Well, I—"

"Let's just forget about it. I don't want to know what he does with you."

"He's *you*, Leo. And we didn't do anything, I told you. Just kissed."

Just kissed with his pants undone.

"Would you have told me if I hadn't noticed anything?"

"I…am so sorry, Leo. It won't happen again."

"That was a nonanswer."

Rhea looked down at her feet. "I don't know. I doubt it." She glanced up again. "Because this is *so* awkward. Which is precisely why I stopped. I realized how awkward it would be if we…" She didn't need to finish the sentence. The idea of her being with the other Leo—it didn't matter that it was his body—or maybe it mattered more—caused him actual physical pain.

Leo looked around and found his glasses, pulling them on and adjusting them to buy time. "I think maybe I should get a room tonight. I don't think this was such a good idea."

Rhea's face fell. "You're quitting? Again?"

He smiled despite himself at the added word. "Just finding someplace else to sleep. But to be honest…" He glanced around at the empty shop. "It doesn't look like you need me for much of anything else. I mean, the place looks ready. Have you considered opening the shop early? Why wait until the New Year?"

"You may have noticed the clients aren't exactly flocking in."

"What about the one you just booked?"

Rhea gaped at him. "Brock Dressler? Are you suggesting I actually tattoo that creep?"

"You could use your pictomancy to find out what he's up to. You said you could read people without them knowing. I could be here to make sure nothing happens, stay out of sight."

"What are you going to do, hide in the bathroom?"

"Why not? You could call him and tell him you have an earlier opening available. He doesn't know I'm aware of the appointment."

Rhea considered. "I suppose I could. But I'd have to get him in here tomorrow. Monday's Christmas, so I wasn't planning on being open this weekend."

Which meant tomorrow was the solstice. He'd been so wrapped up in his angst over Rhea's intimacy with his alter ego he'd almost forgotten. He just had to get through two more nights.

"In the meantime, I think I'm going to need a little time to myself, so unless you need me to do anything to set up for the appointment—?"

"No, it's fine. You go ahead." Rhea looked slightly wounded. Well, too bad. She'd wounded him first. "But you'll be back tomorrow?"

Leo managed a reassuring smile. "Definitely."

He eventually found a room for the night, though it cost him more than he'd planned. He hadn't figured in the effects of the holiday season tourism on the prices of even the most modest accommodations.

As dusk approached, he considered the usual setup for the restraints—the headboard of the bed in his room was essentially a piece of stuffed vinyl with nothing to secure them to, and the frame sat flush with the floor, so nothing usable there. There was a chair at the writing desk, but it was flimsy. He could see ramming the chair against the wall to break the supports and easily getting free. The only other options were the plumbing behind the toilet or the surprisingly sturdy metal shower rod permanently fixed to the wall instead of sitting in a bracket. Neither seemed a comfortable option for spending more than fourteen hours. Then again, why did the bastard deserve comfort?

He took perverse pleasure in pulling the restraints tight as he locked the two together over the shower curtain rod. It was oddly positioned, high enough that his arms were raised above his head—not painfully high, but high. It was probably part of the infrastructure, a piece of steel piping conveniently placed to double as a curtain rod. He supposed he'd regret it in the morning when the consequences became his, but the potential discomfort was worth knowing the other Leo would be miserable for a night.

The bastard had left him in the dark. Leo took a deep breath. The first in the absence of the miserable little *hugr* was always the sweetest.

What the hell? His arms were stretched above his head. Not the first time Leo had left him this way, but usually he'd been left with some kind of comforts. His eyes adjusted to the darkness. *A goddamn bathtub.* The son of a bitch had shackled him over a curtain rod in the bathroom like some damn hand-washed socks left to drip dry.

Despite the indignity, it brought a dark smile to his face. Leo had obviously leaped to conclusions after finding Rhea passed out in his lap with his pants undone. He supposed he could have nudged Rhea after she'd nodded off and asked her to put his clothes back together. But it was more fun knowing Leo would wake to the apparent evidence of how they'd passed the time.

The consequences of getting under Leo's skin were bittersweet, though. He had only a single night left after this one to see her—if Leo allowed it. Who knew where he'd wake up in a year? He was heartily sick of being Leo's bitch to be chained and imprisoned. And it made him more determined than ever to find a way to get loose before dawn came on the twenty-third and put an end to this game.

With Rhea's evocation of the word *Valkyrie* having jogged his memory, he now had an inkling of how long the game had been going on. It was difficult to piece together an accurate picture of the time after he'd lost his hand—and evidently had it restored by the Fates— since, with it, had come the fracturing of his mind. But before that, when he and Leo's other selves had been fully cognizant of the curse, he had been with Kára for more than three centuries. His death, which she had bargained with the Norns to forestall, had occurred in the year nine hundred and sixty-eight. He'd retained enough bits and pieces of memory over recent years to know it had been more than a thousand since.

He couldn't remember when Kára had marked him with the bond of Jörmungandr, but Leo was obviously stupid enough to have done it at her bidding without question. Judging from Rhea's comments about him being at a woman's mercy, he could just imagine the circumstances under which it had been done.

It meant that when he did escape, he would be confined to Leo's skin. Not a terrible hardship—especially knowing the *hugr* would be doomed to wander the Night Realm forever. Without the skin, the *hugr* would never know what it was like to be with Rhea. And that was an experience *this* Leo had no intention of letting pass him by.

As the evening wore on, Leo tried to find a more comfortable position, but there was no give in the link between the restraints. His arms ached and his fingers had gone numb. And he needed to take a goddamn piss. Not for the first time, he wished he could step outside the skin—not only now, to escape, but in general, so he could strangle the miserable little shit for stringing him up like a lutefisk.

The allrune tattoo itched something fierce beneath the suede backing of the cuff. Having the restraints rubbing against the healing tattoo couldn't be doing it any favors. The itching became intolerable, and Leo twisted in the shackles, cursing Leo the Dull. He let out a bellow of rage, not caring if the manager came and had him arrested for being a pervert. It would serve Leo right to lose the game that way.

The discomfort lessened with the expulsion of sound, but a tickling sensation remained. In the mirror across from him, barely visible in the black-and-white hues of night, a thin shadow, like a darkening vein, crawled down his arm.

Leo glanced up. The tattoo was bleeding from one corner. Rhea would probably have to repair it once it healed. And he might not even be aware the touch-up had happened for another year. They would be far away from Rhea by then. He cursed and kicked the back wall of the shower stall, and the heel of his boot stuck in it, cheap plaster crumbling into the stall as he wiggled it out. He laughed out loud, angry and yet feeling a strange sense of release. Fuck Leo.

The blocky shapes and angles of the bathroom had become a shade grayer. Dawn was coming. One more night left. One more chance to act on desire. One more chance to break loose once and for all and be free of Leo the Dull forever.

His arms felt like they'd been pulled from their sockets, and it took forever to work the link loose from the D rings on the restraints. Leo dropped to his knees in the shower stall and lowered his head to his knees.

"Son of a *bitch*." His alter ego had taken revenge on him by pissing his pants.

Chapter 15

She'd tattooed at least a dozen people, a few of them more than once, and never had a complaint. But her first official client had her feeling like an imposter—and not just because she was planning to spy on his nefarious plans through pictomancy.

Rhea glanced at the clock on her phone. Leo hadn't arrived yet and it was almost noon. She was beginning to think he wasn't coming back, that last night had been an excuse to split once and for all. If she was going to have to be alone with this creep, maybe she should rethink the whole thing and cancel. And maybe she should just give up this stupid idea of having her own tattoo shop since no one but some alt-right jackhole had expressed the slightest bit of interest, and she was going to die homeless and penniless and twenty pounds overweight.

The door jingled as Leo finally made an appearance. "Hey. Sorry I'm late. I had to do laundry."

"He's going to be here in half an hour. You decided to stop and do laundry first?"

"I had kind of a bad night."

She wasn't sure what constituted a bad night when one wasn't conscious of how one spent it, but she hadn't slept well herself. After heading home, she'd been restless and jittery. She hadn't seen any sign of the Hunt or Vixen and not even a glimpse of the black wolf-dog. How weird was her life that she'd been disappointed by that? She'd ended up elaborating on her tattoo design, adding some delicate filigree around the Black Moon Lilith symbol. It hadn't prompted any visions, but her dreams had been odd and dark—literal darkness, where she couldn't find anything or anyone and kept going in circles—and she'd woken up feeling more tired than when she'd gone to sleep.

"I thought maybe you'd decided not to come back."

"I considered it." Leo peeled out of his coat, revealing that the black long-sleeved shirt had been his choice today, but he left his knit hat on as though he'd forgotten it was there. "But then I realized I was making a big deal out of nothing. He's going to be gone after tonight, anyway. Then we can get to know each other without him in the way. Maybe even go out on an actual date or something." Leo gave her a tentative lopsided grin. "If you still want to, that is."

"Of course I want to." The other Leo was going to be gone after tonight? Somehow, she'd thought he had a few more days, despite knowing the time frame of the Hunt.

Leo glanced around awkwardly. "Anyway, I should

probably make myself scarce." He disappeared into the bathroom not a moment too soon. Brock was early.

As the door opened, Rhea noticed Leo's plaid hunting jacket lying on the couch. There was no time to stash it, so she put it on. It was hip length on Leo but the hem hit Rhea mid-thigh.

Brock gave her a big smile. "So glad you were able to fit me in earlier. I really appreciate this." She hadn't noticed before, but his hair was cropped close on the sides, with a sort of pompadour-esque floop of longer hair hanging over it, oiled and slicked. God, how had she not pegged him for a Nazi?

Rhea resisted an automatic gag reflex as she shook his hand. "No problem. I realized I was going to be away for the holidays and I might not get back in time, so this works perfectly for me. Come on back." She led him through the curtain, casting an eye at the bathroom door to make sure it was shut. "You can hang up your coat on the rack."

"Looks like you have two," he observed as he removed his to hang it up.

"Oh, this?" Rhea lifted her arms at her sides, the sleeves hanging under her arms like flannel wings. "It's kind of my lucky work smock. It belonged to my dad. It gets pretty drafty in here. I wasn't expecting such cold weather this early."

"Yeah, this snow has been something, hasn't it? So much for those global warming gloom-and-doomers."

Rhea resisted the urge to tell him he was confusing climate with weather. "So, you said you have a mock-up of what you want?"

Brock handed her a piece of paper with the words *I am. I think. I will.* in a sort of retro serif typeface with fuzzy edges and missing spots, like it had been typed on an old typewriter. "Ayn Rand," he said. Rhea repressed the urge to roll her eyes. At least it wasn't Hitler.

"Is this the size you want it?"

"A little smaller." He took off his suit jacket and rolled up the sleeve of his pin-striped shirt. A little overdressed for getting a tattoo. "I want it right here, on the inside of my arm, starting below my elbow and heading toward my wrist."

Rhea reduced the image on her photocopier and copied it onto the transfer sheet once Brock approved it. "All right. I think we're ready to go."

She shoved Leo's jacket sleeves up to her elbows and had to roll the cuffs several times to keep them there, but she managed to act like it was part of her artistic ritual. Brock's skin was unusually taut, with an almost leathery quality to it, requiring a lot of pressure to pierce. She supposed he must get a lot of sun.

As Rhea worked through the outline, she let her arm above the glove rest lightly on the upper part of the tattoo, skin to skin, and concentrated on reading without "broadcasting" the reading to him. She'd done it deliberately once or twice, and the key was focusing on images close enough to the client's surface thoughts that they didn't intrude.

Rhea put out a little "feeler" question as though it were his own thought: *Did I eat enough before I came?* A clear image came to her of a bowl of muesli. How exciting.

She glanced up to see if the image had intruded on his thoughts. "How are you doing so far? Okay?"

Brock smiled a little nervously. "So far so good. It's both not as bad as I expected and a great deal worse."

Rhea laughed. "Sounds about right. Some areas are more sensitive than others, too, so it might feel like it's no big deal then suddenly become a big deal. Let me know if you need me to take a break. The endorphins should kick in pretty soon, though."

Time to try a little more specific test. She kept her thoughts focused on *how do I feel about this?* and then led him toward a loaded topic to see if she could pick up on what he really felt regardless of what he said.

"It's great to have someone breaking in the chair. I can't wait for the official opening, but getting this place ready has been a challenge. Some kids keep spray-painting graffiti on the walls. I swear, I've cleaned it off half a dozen times in the past two weeks."

"That's a shame. Have the police had any luck catching them?"

"I haven't called the cops. Hopefully, I won't have to. It seems pretty harmless. They're obviously doing it for kicks. Trying to impress their friends and act like badasses. Although, the other day, they added a swastika to a tag. Who knows what motivated that? Actual hate? Or just, 'Ooh, look how edgy I am'?"

"Really? I wonder if they belong to a gang. Have you seen any of them?"

So far, his mental imagery was surprisingly blank. At least, she wasn't getting much of anything equating to *how do I feel about this?* Maybe she should try a different tactic.

"No, just the graffiti. I doubt they belong to any organized group, though." *Like the Nazi Party*, she thought deliberately and pictured a goose-stepping SS squad.

Brock flinched, and she took her foot off the pedal.

"Did I hit a nerve?" She was taking a chance with the double entendre, but what the hell.

"Yeah, it kind of took me by surprise when you got between the bones."

"Sometimes it's the spots you least expect to be sensitive. Tattooing over bone can be extra painful, but you never know what's going to be a trigger." She blotted the blood on the fresh part of the tattoo, letting their arms touch again, and projected the question with specificity: *How do I feel about Nazis?* This time, she picked up his own image of shouting skinheads and a white supremacist rally. It was pretty stereotypical stuff, and the feeling that accompanied it was a definitive wave of disgust.

She was starting to think Leo was wrong about him. If he was a Nazi, he certainly didn't think of himself as one. She wasn't picking up any images indicating he was at all sympathetic to such a cause.

Rhea tried a few more times but got nothing more definitive. She even tried more generally to see if she could pick up on an impression of why he'd come into her tattoo shop, but all she got was a flash of memory of him seeing one of her flyers.

He tipped her well and thanked her profusely. "This is really great. Absolutely fantastic. I'll be sure to spread the word."

Rhea beamed. "So glad you like it." She took a picture for her online gallery and wished him Happy Holidays as he left—her first client and a satisfied one.

Leo came out when he'd gone. "Doesn't sound like you tipped him off. Great job steering him. Did you get anything?"

Rhea uploaded the photo. "Not really. Are you sure

about what he said to you? Maybe you misunderstood him."

Leo's eyes narrowed. "Are you kidding me?"

"He didn't react like he was on board with any of that—the swastika, the Nazis. I even tried picturing stuff myself, as a sort of subliminal suggestion, and the worst I got was a shudder."

Leo scratched his head through the cap. "I don't get it. He was very specific to me about the purity of the races and some pro-eugenics crap."

Rhea shrugged. "Maybe he's a racist asshole who thinks he's better than those other racist assholes."

"And you didn't get anything from him about why he showed up here after running into me?"

"Honestly, I think it must have been a coincidence. I floated the question and got an image of one of my flyers. Nothing about you. I doubt he's even aware you work here."

Leo sank onto the couch, shaking his head. "I don't get it. What are the odds? But maybe you're right."

"On the plus side..." Rhea held up the fifty he'd given her for a tip and grinned. "Demoness Ink is officially legit." She snapped the bill in both hands. "And now I've got Christmas spending money." She paused and grimaced. "And the gas and electric bill on this place for the first month is probably going to be three times this."

Leo leaned forward, arms resting on his knees, looking rueful. "I feel bad being one more expense."

"Are you kidding? I've conned you into accepting ink for payment. You're the best thing I've got going here."

Leo grinned. "In that case, maybe you could pay me a little early? I've been thinking it would be fun to have both wrists itching at the same time."

"What the hell." Rhea popped the fifty into her cash box. "I'm in a generous mood, and I'm on a roll. After we close today, we'll get you set up."

Mjölnir was more complex than the allrune, a knotted pattern weaving throughout it. It was nice work but impossibly faded, as though the ink had blurred and run together over time. Time Leo couldn't possibly have had the tattoo.

"I may need to add some color to give it definition," she said as she looked it over. "Would you be okay with that? Or do you want to stick with black?"

"Actually, I really like the scarlet color you have in the tattoo you showed me. I was thinking that might look nice as a contrast inside the white space."

Rhea smiled. "I was just thinking that color would be awesome there." She took the bottle of ink out of her kit. "It's called Bloodbath."

Leo laughed. "Let's hope that's not prophetic."

Rhea pondered the job as she set up the supplies. "This one's probably going to take a bit more time than the other one did. Maybe two hours. Is that going to work for you?" She hesitated. "I mean…are you staying here tonight or do you need to get back to the motel?"

Leo considered. "I wasn't going to stay, but sometimes I have major memory problems after the final night. That's why I move around a lot. It's uncomfortable to wake up somewhere and have pieces missing that other people are expecting you to have. Maybe it would help to have a familiar face there when I wake up—if you're going to stay, that is."

"I thought I would." Rhea tried to play it casual. She didn't dare let him see how relieved she was at the prospect or how much she'd missed seeing his other self the night before. "And you have my word nothing untoward will happen." She crossed her heart, as he'd done the other day, with a lighthearted smile.

Leo's expression said he wasn't sure he could trust her, but he smiled, anyway. "Now if we could only get *his* word."

"Well, that's what the restraints are for, right? I'll keep my distance, and he can do his worst. As long as you trust me."

"I do trust you." This time the smile was genuine. "Him, not so much. But you, absolutely." His stomach growled, and Rhea paused in prepping his arm.

"When did you eat last?"

"I had an egg sandwich this morning."

"Leo. You know you can't get a tattoo without any food in your system. That's the first rule on the wall." She pointed to the plaque. "Let's get dinner first. If we run out of time, I can always do the rest while you're restrained."

"That's not exactly keeping your distance." The smile this time was more genuine. "But I trust you. So, yeah. Shouldn't be a problem."

They went for pizza, going out to pick it up down the block. The place was busy, and the light was already getting low by the time they walked back up the hill with their pie. Rhea had forgotten this was the longest night of the year.

Leo hurried inside and grabbed his bag to get the restraints in place before dusk fell.

Rhea helped secure them. "Sorry, Leo. I didn't think it would take that long. We should have gotten fast food. How are you going to eat like this?"

"I suppose," he said as the locks clicked into place, "you'll have to feed me, my little dove."

Rhea looked up into the *munr*'s amused eyes. "Wow. Just in the nick of time, it would seem."

"To you, maybe. I would have much preferred to skip this foolish ritual altogether." He glanced from Rhea to the pizza box to the little tray at the side of the chair all set up with the tattooing supplies. "I rather doubt those have anything to do with dinner."

"Leo asked me to touch up the other gauntlet."

"Of course he did. You realize what these marks are, don't you?"

Rhea shrugged. "Protective symbols from Norse mythology."

"Shackles. Stitched into the skin so that they become part of us. Far more effective than any cheap bondage gear."

"If you're trying to convince me you don't need the restraints, you can forget it."

"I wouldn't dream of it." His stomach growled loudly. "But you could give me something to eat."

Rhea opened the pizza box on the counter and took out a slice. "This is a little kinky for my taste, but I don't want you to pass out, so…" She shrugged and took a bite, to Leo's irritation, his brows drawing together and his sky blues clouding. Rhea laughed. "Don't freak out. I'm going to share." She held the slice in front of his mouth.

With a lifted brow, he leaned forward and took a bite. It was unexpectedly intimate to be feeding a man who was tied to a chair.

"I take it Leo didn't appreciate waking up with his pants undone, knowing he didn't get to participate in the fun."

"And letting me fall asleep without remedying the situation had nothing at all to do with trying to goad your own soul."

"Oh, it had everything to do with it." Leo grinned and took the next bite she fed him. "Do you know he strung me up from a curtain rod in the bathroom last night?" He rolled his shoulders. "My trapezius muscles are still killing me. Which means they've been killing *him* all day and damn well serves the miserable bastard right."

Rhea hadn't expected that. Leo was fighting over her...with Leo. "You know, each of you thinks the other is the miserable bastard."

"Well, he's wrong, because *he* is." Leo accepted another bite of the slice she held out for him, and Rhea finished off the crust. "He's the one who locks me up for fifty nights a year because he's afraid of his own free will. And you're just going to let him finish me off. Do his dirty work for him and watch me die at dawn. I hope it haunts you."

"Leo—"

"No, I don't want to argue. Sorry." He licked at a crumb on his upper lip but couldn't quite get it. "I want to enjoy this last night together."

Rhea wiped the crumb off with her thumb. "Do you enjoy it?"

"What, bondage? I think that's more Leo's thing, from what you've told me."

"Spending this time together." Rhea smirked. "I mean, aside from the other night, which it was quite clear you were enjoying."

Leo studied her, his expression serious. "I can't remember ever enjoying any moment more in my entire life than those I've spent with you these past few nights."

Rhea blushed and took another slice of pizza. "By your own admission, what you remember isn't much." She took a bite and offered one to him.

Leo ignored it. "The more cumulative hours of consciousness I have, the more I retain. And the more I recall from past years. But from before my mind was bound by the Norns, I've begun to recall a great deal."

"How much, exactly, are we talking here? I mean, when did Kára…?"

"When was I spared on the battlefield from the death that ought to have been mine?" Leo tilted his head toward the slice she was still holding, and Rhea held it out for him to take another bite. He took his time chewing and swallowing, while Rhea nibbled on the pizza. "What do you know of Viking history?"

Rhea swallowed her mouthful. "Um…yeah…nothing, actually. Wasn't my area of focus at the university."

"The raid on which I received my mortal wound was in the last millennium."

She couldn't help the surprised little laugh.

"What's so funny?"

"The last millennium was seventeen years ago."

"Ah. Leo doesn't make much of an effort to keep me apprised of current events." Leo pondered a moment. "Then it was one thousand and…forty-nine years past."

Rhea nearly choked on her pizza. Not that it should have been a surprise. As soon as she'd made the Valkyrie connection, she'd suspected he wasn't exactly from the modern era. But more than a thousand years old?

"So you're, what…one thousand and…?"

"Seventy-four. I admit the age difference is a bit of a barrier, but I'm a young one thousand and seventy-four." His eyes twinkled, and all Rhea could do was wonder how he didn't have any crow's-feet. No wonder his tattoos looked faded.

"So the marks, as you call them, they're that old, too?"

"The originals, yes. Evidently, Leo has them refreshed every so often, because he's a complete twat."

Rhea glanced at the prepped table. "So I guess I shouldn't…"

"Of course you should. Why not? It's not as if he won't do it tomorrow anyway after I'm gone."

"But I'd have to remove the restraint."

"How could I possibly get away with my other arm still locked down?"

Rhea shook her head. "No can do."

Leo sighed. "You're a cruel mistress, Rhea Carlisle."

"I'm not your mistress." She tried not to think about the implications of the word. "I can do the handle portion, though." Only the top of the hammer was fully covered by the restraint. "I mean, what else are we going to do all night?" Rhea laughed as Leo waggled his eyebrows. "I promised him I wouldn't."

"Gods, that soul of yours. Almost as irritating as his." Leo pouted. "My last night, and I don't even get a kiss goodbye?"

"Well, maybe one. But only if you behave and let me work without being difficult."

"That promise, my dove, will keep me going for hours."

She put the pizza away and held a water bottle for him to wash it down before settling beside him and pulling up the tray. She'd already shaved his arm, so after a quick swab, she started on the black.

As unproductive as her attempts to read Dressler had been, Rhea hadn't even considered the potential for another inadvertent reading from Leo, but given her previous experiences with him, she should have seen it coming. The moment she made even proximal skin contact, it was like the tattoo was buzzing with anticipation, waiting to tell her stories.

Focusing on reinforcing the black lines of the design, she managed to shut out the images threatening to overwhelm her, but they were vibrating in the air, wanting to be read.

Leo watched her biting her lip in concentration. "Why not take a peek?"

Rhea kept her head down over the machine. "I don't think I want to see what you're thinking right at the moment."

"The vision you had before didn't reflect what I was thinking. Why do you assume it would work that way now?"

Rhea laughed. "It might not have been your uppermost conscious thought, but you were definitely thinking it." And judging by the visible bulge in his jeans she was trying to ignore, his current train of thought was similar.

"And what are *you* thinking?"

"I'm thinking this is going to be a long night."

"The longest," Leo agreed.

Rhea paused to switch out the needles and ink. "You know, I usually spend this night with my sisters."

"Sorry. Didn't mean to keep you from them."

"You're not. We didn't have anything planned this year. Theia's still up north—not that I'm talking to her, anyway—and Phoebe and Ione have other things on their minds."

"What sorts of things?"

"They're both in new relationships."

"Ah, so they're busy fornicating."

Rhea laughed. "Sometimes you have quite a way with words, Leo. But yes. They are, I'm quite sure, busy fornicating."

Leo watched as she readied the red ink cap. "He's adding color?"

"It was my idea. The old lines have lost a lot of definition around the edges, so I thought we could fill in some of the spaces between with color to delineate them better. He said to go for it."

"I doubt the Norns would be pleased." The last word was cut off on a sound of surprise in his throat as she put the needles to his flesh. The first stroke of the red ink seemed to have an instantaneous physical effect on him. And Rhea was feeling it, too. It was beyond arousal, beyond desire. It was a sense of *rightness*, as though they were kin. And not in a creepy incestuous way, just an overwhelming sense of belonging together.

"What is that?" Leo stared at his arm where she'd continued tattooing in a kind of trancelike state. "What did you do?"

"I don't know. Do you want me to stop?"

"No. It's...*nice* isn't quite the word. It feels a little like ants crawling through my veins, but I have to admit, it's strangely pleasant. Satisfying."

"Yeah." That was the word that had been eluding her. "I mean, I don't feel the ant-crawling thing, but this feels very satisfying. I don't want to stop."

"Weird," said Leo, but he didn't seem too disturbed by the odd sentiment. "It's like...an itch being scratched."

Rhea nodded, head bent over her work. "It's funny. My tattoo has been itching like crazy lately, but it stopped as soon as I started on yours."

In less than half an hour, she'd finished the knot work on the handle, which was super fast for her. Of course, the rest of the tattoo was still covered by the restraint. Rhea took her foot off the pedal. Leaving the tattoo incomplete was maddening. *That* was an itch that needed scratching.

Rhea pondered the fishing knife she'd tossed into a drawer that first night. He wouldn't be able to escape with one arm still shackled. Not unless he somehow managed to grab the knife from her and stab her so he could do it himself. She didn't think he was capable of that, soul or no soul, but she'd be on her guard.

She set down the machine and got up to get the knife.

Leo's eyebrow ticked upward. "And what are you planning to do with that? Is this some pagan ritual you've been leading up to culminating in a blood sacrifice on the eve of the solstice?"

"Just getting this out of the way." She slid the blade beneath the outside edge of the cuff pointing away from his skin and slashed downward and out. It barely made a dent in the leather. But it did make a dent.

"Careful," said Leo as she started sawing at it. "You don't want to slip with that thing. I've already lost this hand once. If the Norns wanted my mind in exchange for restoring it, I don't even want to think about what they'd want this time."

"Relax. I'm not going to cut your hand off." It took some doing, but at last the far edge of the leather came away, leaving him free to wriggle out.

Leo ran his fingers up her arm and drew her close. Rhea had enough presence of mind to toss the knife onto the counter out of reach before she gave herself over to the pleasure of his mouth. God, this man could kiss. This was master class–level kissing. She wrapped her arms around his neck and hooked her fingers in the hair at his nape, twisting it mindlessly until he made a slight noise of discomfort against her mouth.

Rhea drew back, releasing his hair. "Sorry. I got caught up in the moment. Forgot the hair was attached to anybody." She earned one of those surprised, delighted, deep-throated laughs from him. He was still wearing that damn knit cap. Rhea took it off and tried to smooth the flyaway hair into a tidier semblance, but it was a losing battle.

Leo studied her as she played with it. "That was unexpected. What did I do to earn my partial freedom?"

"It's not freedom. I'm not going to cut the other one. I just wanted to finish this damned tattoo."

"Fair enough." He laid his arm across the armrest, and Rhea sat once more and went to work on the sections she hadn't been able to get to, switching out to do the rest of the black lines first so she'd have more control to fill in the red. Images tugged at her once more, but Rhea tuned them out.

He watched her quietly until she'd finished the rest of the black and started to switch out the ink for the final time. "I suppose Leo has filled your head with cautionary tales of horror about me turning into a giant snake or something if you were ever to set me free." His eyes were teasing, but the question seemed genuine enough.

"Actually, he said he thought it would unleash the destructive energy of Jörmungandr. It hadn't occurred to him that you might change form and make that energy literal until I suggested it."

Leo laughed. "But it's absurd. No one can change form. The physical selves, the *likamr* and *hamr*, are just as distinct as the formless selves. They're governed by the laws of physics."

"What would you say if I told you I'd seen more than one person transform into something similar?"

"I'd say you'd been smoking too much cannabis."

She was sworn to secrecy about Rafe and Dev, but he would remember none of this tomorrow. Which was depressing. She tried not to think about that and started working on the red fill. Both of them relaxed into the peculiar "rightness" from before.

"No weed necessary. I know a man who regularly sprouts wings and can take various animal forms temporarily."

"Do you, now? Who's this magical fellow?"

"He's called a quetzal. He's the human embodiment of the Aztec god Quetzalcoatl. He also happens to be my sister Phoebe's boyfriend."

Leo leaned back against the headrest. "You're serious."

"As a heart attack."

"So this is the new relationship she's in, the one you mentioned before."

"The very same."

"You said there was more than one person you'd seen transform."

"Ione's boyfriend. He shares physical form with a dragon demon. Not simultaneously. Only one of them occupies the skin at the same time. Kind of like you and Leo. I mean you and your *hugr*."

He was regarding her dubiously. "How is it that two of your sisters happen to be involved with these shape-shifters?"

She wasn't sure she wanted to get into the whole Lilith connection. If she mentioned it, he'd use it as an argument for her to free him, that it was fated. And she wasn't ready to accept that fate controlled her.

"I told you, we're a magical family."

"The demon blood."

Damn. She'd forgotten she'd already mentioned the connection. She wiped away some of his blood as she pondered it.

"So you think I might actually shift if you released me."

"Not necessarily."

What she was thinking was that if she had sex with him, there would be no escaping fate. This guy had *literal* Fates messing with his life. She'd have to be crazy to do anything more with him. Not that she was going to. She'd promised Leo she wouldn't. She was going to be the responsible one. Even if she *had* torn up one of Leo's expensive leather restraints. And she sure as hell wasn't setting him loose.

"But you're not taking any chances."

Rhea shrugged. "I also made a promise."

Leo jerked his arm away as she was about to press the needles to it, his eyes dark with anger. "Fuck your promises. Fuck both of you."

"If you want to screw up this tattoo permanently, just keep doing stupid shit like that while I have a bunch of needles full of ink poised over your skin." She set the machine aside. Maybe it was time to wrap it up for tonight. She'd done just about everything she wanted to. Any sharpening she'd missed could be addressed during touch-up. Rhea peeled off the gloves and rose to wash up, but Leo grabbed her hand before she could step away.

"I'm sorry. I think. I mean, I don't have a soul, but

I'm experiencing a general sense of displeasure and discomfort with myself right now thinking about the way I snapped at you, so I'm pretty sure this would be categorized as regret."

Rhea looked down, not wanting him to see her smile, but he had the advantage of being seated.

"So this is you forgiving me, right? Because now I have a pleasant, relieved feeling."

She couldn't keep from laughing. "Yes, dammit. I forgive you. I wasn't all that upset with you in the first place. You have a right to be pissed about the situation you're in, and I know I'm not making it any easier."

"That's not true. You've made it quite a bit easier." He pulled her closer to the chair. "Come make it easier some more and I'll forgive you, too. I mean, if that's a thing I can do—"

"Shut up, Leo." As Rhea straddled him and kissed him to silence him once more, her conscience nagged at her. She'd promised Leo nothing untoward would happen. But it wasn't as if she was going to do anything she hadn't already done.

With his arm free, however, that wasn't entirely up to her. Leo slid his hand up her side, letting his fingers brush lightly against the underside of her breast. It was very middle-school, over-the-bra kind of contact, but it sent a delicious shiver through her.

He moved his fingers higher, stroking her nipple with his thumb as he cupped her breast. The nipple was already hard, but the motion tightened the flesh. Without meaning to, she was rocking into his lap.

Rhea disengaged her mouth, though he leaned forward to pursue her. "We can't get too carried away here."

Leo made a dismissive noise. "Why not? What's he

going to do about it? Nothing. Just like he's been doing. Is that really what you want? Me gone and Leo the Dull being excessively cautious and polite until he bores you into frigidity?"

"Okay, that was a little harsh. And you're forgetting you won't, in fact, be gone at all. You'll be sharing the skin with him."

"How do you know? Are you an expert on Norn curses? If I can't remember ever being him, how is he me? Maybe the real curse is that he has no will except for these stolen hours once a year? No desire at all—that's me, the *munr*, absent entirely. Are you willing to take that chance? What if he's worse than dull by tomorrow morning?"

Rhea frowned. She hadn't thought of that. But he would say anything to be free, which she couldn't even blame him for. Who wouldn't?

"Leo, I—" She paused. She'd become gradually aware of a familiar scent, like someone had set a fire in the fireplace. But the shop didn't have a fireplace. It also apparently didn't have a functioning smoke alarm, because as soon as she'd made the realization, her eyes began to water. "Shit."

Chapter 16

Leo tensed beneath her. "Is that smoke?"

"I think the building's on fire." She swung off his lap, and Leo grabbed her arm.

"You can't leave me in here."

"Leave you? Are you insane?" She pulled away from him and grabbed the fish-scaling knife.

The smoke was getting thick as she sawed frantically at the leather. Rhea coughed into her sleeve, eyes watering.

"Let me do it." Leo took the knife from her hand. "You go. Get out. I'll be right behind you."

"No, I'm not—" A coughing fit swallowed the rest of her protest.

"Get out, goddammit! Get the fuck out!" He'd switched on the rage as suddenly as before, though this time it was designed to anger her into leaving. She started to object once more, but he'd yanked the knife upward and severed the restraint. Leo grabbed her hand and ran with her for the exit.

The fire had started on the stairs. They could feel the heat through the door.

"There's no back way out?"

Rhea shook her head, coughing. "We'll have to go out the window."

Leo grabbed the stool behind the counter and threw it through the window, shattering the pane, before she could tell him it opened easily from the inside. That was going to be expensive. The absurdity of the thought hit her. The whole building was going to be gone, if not the entire shopping center.

Leo kicked out the jagged pieces and took off his shirt, folding it up and placing it over the sharp edges still clinging to the frame, and held out his hand. "Come on, you first."

Rhea peered out dubiously. They were only one flight up, but she was going to break her shins—if she even landed on her feet, which was doubtful.

"What are you waiting for?"

"It's a little far down. I'm trying to gather my nerve." The last word was a strangled cough.

"You don't have time to gather your nerve." Leo moved her aside. "If I go first and promise to catch you, will you jump when I tell you to?"

Rhea nodded, and he climbed through the window and leaped before she could even catch her breath. "Leo?" She hurried to the edge and looked down, expecting to see him digging himself off the sidewalk covered in scrapes and cuts, but he was standing there holding up his arms. Something crashed behind her.

"Jump, Rhea. *Now.*"

She climbed onto the shirt-covered frame and flung herself out, closing her eyes in her panic, and barreled into Leo like a wrecking ball. He broke her fall, catching her firmly in his shirtless arms without even stumbling back.

Sirens were blaring when she looked up at him, fire trucks already coming up the hill.

"You must be freezing," was all she could think of to say.

"Not really." Leo shrugged. "Feeling the cold must be a thought-self kind of thing."

And he didn't have his thought-self—and if they understood the curse correctly, he never would again. Rhea looked up at the flames engulfing her shop, the Demoness Ink sign singed around the edges. She almost wished she were missing her own thought-self so she wouldn't feel this crushing heartache at realizing her dream had gone up in smoke.

After talking to the firefighters and the officers who'd arrived on the scene while the crew put out the blaze, Rhea discovered a note tucked under her windshield wiper. *"Thou shalt not suffer a witch to live,"* it informed her in a cheery font. And to make sure she got the message, they'd added, *"You're all going to burn. Keep Sedona pure."* A couple of swastikas were thrown in for good measure.

"I'm not even a witch," she muttered, sinking against the car door.

Leo stroked her arm. "I'll drive you home."

"You don't have your glasses."

"Those were his. I don't need them." He held out his hand expectantly. "Do you have the keys?"

Rhea started to laugh, and it turned into crying. Of course she didn't have the keys. Had her brain been even partly functional, she might have grabbed her bag and her tablet before jumping out the window. Even her phone was inside.

"I don't even have that damn fifty," she whimpered against him as he gathered her in his arms.

"It's okay. The important thing is that you're safe. Things can be replaced."

Rhea choked in a breath in a strangled laugh against his bare chest. "Is that sympathy? Do *munrs* have that?"

"I don't know. Is sympathy when you want to kick someone to death for hurting your girl?"

"Your *girl*?" Rhea wiped her eyes. "I don't know if I like that. And no, that sounds more like vengeance."

"Okay, well, I've got that, anyway." He reached into his back pocket as she straightened. "I've also got Leo's phone."

At least one of them had been thinking. Which was ironic, since he was missing his thought-self. Rhea accepted the phone, staring at the screen. She couldn't get into her apartment, and it was way too late to be calling the landlord. She didn't even have the landlord's number, for that matter.

Phoebe was her first choice, but Ione's number was the only one she remembered since Ione had only recently gotten her first cell phone. Everyone else had been available at the click of an icon for ages. Rhea hadn't realized how much she depended on one little metal-and-glass box.

Ione came immediately, her dark ombré hair natural

instead of ironed straight, as if she'd just crawled out of bed, and she was in full mother hen mode. "Are you okay?" She looked Rhea over, still standing in the parking lot. "What's this?" She held up Rhea's right palm, caked with dried blood. A piece of glass was embedded in it that Rhea hadn't even noticed. Leo watched them with interest, leaning back against Rhea's MINI with his arms folded, dwarfing the little car.

Rhea introduced him while Ione picked out the glass. "This is Leo Ström."

Ione looked up, her eyes narrowed at the shirtless Viking beside her little sister. "And who is 'Leo Ström'?"

"He's my…" Rhea felt her face go hot. "Goddammit. I don't know." She was too tired for long-winded explanations.

Leo chuckled and stepped forward, holding out his hand. "Rhea was tattooing me when the fire broke out."

"Ione Carlisle." She shook his hand, her expression still dubious, eyes taking in the Norse tattoos and pendant. "Can I drop you somewhere?"

"He's with me," Rhea said before Leo could answer.

Ione's expression was more mistrust than dubiousness at this point, but she nodded. "Let's get you guys warmed up. You'll catch your death."

Maybe Rhea would, but she was beginning to doubt whether Leo even *could* die.

Ione's place was toasty warm despite the giant glass wall along one side, and it smelled like cinnamon. Rhea paused in the entryway to take off her boots before stepping on Ione's carpet, but Leo had taken his off before strapping in for the night.

Dev, looking like he'd stepped off the cover of *GQ*, as usual, greeted them in the kitchen with hot cocoa.

Leo looked dubiously at the mug Dev offered him. "Got anything stronger?"

Dev's golden-brown eyes twinkled. "Give it a taste."

Rhea took a sip and grinned. "Wow. Now that's what I call hot cocoa."

Dev was pleased. "I got the recipe from Rafe. It's Mexican cocoa with tequila. And a dash of cayenne pepper."

Leo drank his experimentally and looked up with a surprised nod. "I wouldn't have thought to put that together, but it's not bad." He turned with another look of surprise when Ione draped one of Dev's shirts over his shoulders.

"Let's get that hand cleaned up." Ione steered Rhea to the bathroom as if she were still in grade school.

Rhea sighed as she submitted. "Yes, Mom."

"Don't 'mom' me, young lady." She took the mug out of Rhea's other hand and set it on the counter before examining her palm. "So are you going to tell me why a half-naked man was there with you? And why you didn't tell me you'd rented a place to hang out your shingle? I could have helped you with that."

"I didn't want anyone to help me. Everyone's always trying to help me, dammit." Rhea grimaced at the sting of the rubbing alcohol and the look from Ione. "Let me rephrase that. It's wonderful having sisters who believe in me and want to help me succeed, and I adore you, but I needed to do this on my own. Of course, now everything is gone, so I guess it's Universe one, Rhea zero."

"You didn't have insurance?"

Rhea tried to set fire to Ione with her eyes, and Ione dropped the subject.

"And the naked guy?"

"He was not naked, for God's sake. He used his shirt to keep me from cutting myself on the broken glass when I jumped out the window."

"You jumped out a *window*?" The adhesive bandage Ione was trying to peel the backing from snapped in half.

"Can I have my cocoa back now?"

Finally managing to get a bandage in place, Ione picked up the cocoa but held it out of Rhea's reach. "First, tell me about Leo."

"I already told you. I was touching up his tattoo. There's nothing more to tell."

Ione shook her head and drank Rhea's cocoa.

"Oh, come *on*." She'd never been able to pull one over on Ione. It was ridiculous to try. "Fine. I hired him to help get the place ready before opening, and I'm paying him in ink. Or I was."

"And?"

"And…we kind of have…a thing…something. I don't really know. He called me his 'girl.'" Rhea stomped her foot in a mock tantrum since Ione was treating her like a child. "Give me my cocoa."

Ione passed it back, half-empty, licking whipped cream off her upper lip. "He has a snake tattoo."

Rhea drank the rest of the cocoa without stopping until it was empty. "Yep. Yes, he does. And he's…" She wasn't sure she was ready to share everything about Leo with anyone yet. Leo was hers. Well, not *hers* hers. But she finally had something all her own to keep secret and she didn't feel like giving it to the entire family just yet. "He's maybe under some kind of curse. We don't know yet." He hadn't turned into a serpent, anyway, and he'd been free for a couple of hours, so there was that.

"Okay. But you're in love with him."

"Oh my God. Stop leaping to conclusions. I just met him a week ago."

"And you are also a Carlisle who has Madeleine Marchant's Lilith blood in her veins, and he's got something serpentine going on. And…he looks like Thor, for crying out loud. If *you* don't want him, maybe I'll see if Dev minds if I get a little something on the side."

Rhea put her hands over her ears. "Please stop. You're creeping me out."

"But if you don't *want* him—"

"I want him!" Rhea's eyes widened and she covered her mouth with her hands. "Oh my God. I hate you, Di. That was so loud."

Ione pushed away from the counter with a smirk and opened the bathroom door.

Dev and Leo were in the kitchen, where Leo had discovered the bottle of tequila.

Leo sniffed the open bottle appreciatively. "As enjoyable as that was, perhaps you have a shot glass or two around here?"

"I think Ione does, yes."

"Top right cabinet," said Ione from the doorway.

Dev got down four shot glasses and started to pour.

"None for me, thanks." Rhea took her mug to the stove. "I think I'll stick with the magic cocoa." She ladled more into her mug and Dev poured two shots into the cup. Rhea laughed. "Okay, I didn't realize how much you'd put in there. But to be fair, Di drank mine." She stuck her tongue out at her sister, trying to act as if they hadn't heard her loud declaration.

"Whipped cream's in the fridge," said Dev. "And you can sprinkle some cinnamon on top if you like."

As Rhea sprayed the canned whipped cream into her mug—clearly Dev's influence, since Ione was all about the real thing when it came to pretty much anything and preferred to make hers from scratch—she noticed the bottle of tequila. "Peligroso" it was called, and the embossed symbol on the glass was a coiled snake with rays fanning out around it that looked like they were meant to be feathers.

"Interesting bottle," she said to Ione.

"Rafe recommended it to Dev apparently. They've developed a bit of a bromance."

Leo tossed back his shot and poured another. "So Rafe, he's the one who channels Quetzalcoatl?" He looked at Dev. "So you must be—"

"Okay," Rhea interrupted loudly. "That wasn't exactly meant for public consumption, Leo."

Eyes flashing, Ione dragged her aside to the living room. "You told him about Rafe and Dev? About us?"

Rhea swallowed a gulp of cocoa and burned her throat. "He wasn't supposed to remember."

"How exactly was he not supposed to remember?"

"I told you about the curse. From dusk to dawn during the period between All Souls and Yule, he separates from his *hugr*—"

"His what?"

"It's like his soul. It goes off somewhere, and when it rejoins him in the morning, it leaves him without memory of the previous night."

"This just gets better and better. So you're telling me he doesn't have a soul right now?"

"Who needs one?" Leo entered the room behind Ione

and smiled when she turned. "Bothersome things." He tucked his hands into his pockets, the crisp white shirt he'd borrowed from Dev still unbuttoned. "I should probably get going. I appreciate you coming to our rescue."

"Going?" Rhea extracted her arm from Ione's grasp. "Where are you going?"

"I have a little money. I can get a room somewhere."

"With the holiday room rates?" Ione shook her head. "Don't be ridiculous. You and Rhea are staying in our guestroom until we can get Rhea back into her place in the morning."

"It seems a bit awkward. I don't want to be any bother."

Dev leaned against the kitchen doorway behind him, his warm-copper skin a striking contrast to Leo's Nordic pallor. "You think this is awkward, mate? You don't know the Carlisle sisters. And you especially do not know Ione. When she says you're staying, you're staying. I've already set up the guestroom." He smiled. "Nice chat. We'll see you in the morning." He stepped forward and took Ione's hand, ignoring her attempt to hang back, and led her up the spiral staircase to her room on the second floor of the split-level house.

Rhea sat on the sofa to finish her cocoa, careful not to spill anything on the cream-colored cushions. "So you're staying, then."

Leo laughed. "I don't seem to have much choice." He sat beside her, manspreading both arms and legs. "Sorry about that. I didn't realize it was a secret."

"It's my fault. I had no business telling you."

"Have you told your sister about me?"

Rhea lowered her voice. "As little as possible."

"Yeah." He nodded thoughtfully. "I imagine she's not

too keen on the idea of her baby sister dating someone so much older." He winked one impossibly vivid blue eye at her.

Rhea regarded him slyly. "So we're dating, then?"

"Well. You were quite insistent that you wanted me." The teasing look in his eyes was merciless.

Rhea set the mug on the coffee table and groaned into her hands.

Chapter 17

The guestroom had a somewhat narrow bed, but it beat being strapped to a chair.

As Leo started to unbutton his jeans, the expression on Rhea's face, staring him down with her hands on her hips, made him pause. "What?"

"What are you doing?"

"Taking off my clothes."

"What exactly do you think is about to happen here?"

Leo shrugged. "*Munr*. Not big on thinking."

Rhea sighed, sitting on the bed. "First of all, that's total crap. I don't know exactly what a thought-self does, but you've done plenty of thinking. You were the one who got us out of a burning building an hour ago. Second, I think we've already established that I made a promise to Leo, and there won't be any hanky-panky."

He couldn't help but smile at her quaint choice of

words, even though her insistence on not crossing some imaginary sexual line was becoming tiresome. "I can sleep in my clothes—can't really recall a time when I had a choice—but I have to point out that you're the one who seems to have trouble keeping your hands off me."

"That's because you didn't have the use of *your* hands." Rhea's gray eyes darkened, a dead giveaway that just thinking about touching him had gotten her blood pumping. "Also, my sister, who was basically my mom growing up, is directly above us right now, and there is no way in hell anything is going to happen, even if I wanted it to happen."

"Which you do."

"Leo."

"I'm merely stating the obvious, not trying to persuade you to acquiesce to your own desires. If you want to sleep side by side in this little bed like chaste siblings, that's your call. I can't remember the last time I slept at all, so it will be a novel experience for me nonetheless." He re-buttoned the jeans and started to remove the shirt. "Can I take this off, at least? It's not really my style."

"No."

"Now you're just being petty."

Rhea threw back the covers and climbed between the sheets. "Nope. Just acknowledging my own limitations. You're the one who pointed out that I couldn't control myself around you, so you have only yourself to thank. And button it," she added before rolling onto her side to face the wall.

With a shrug, Leo complied and climbed into bed beside her. He snuggled up behind her, spooning her, and she didn't resist, her arms curving around his. Her hair smelled like smoke. And violets.

"So what happens at dawn?" she asked quietly, giving voice to the question in the back of both their minds since they'd escaped the fire.

"Honestly, I don't know for certain. But I know what I want to happen. Absolutely nothing. I want to wake up beside you and remember this entire weird, wonderful and terrifying night. And when I do, perhaps you'll stop waiting for him to come back and let yourself feel what you feel without having to analyze it and berate yourself for it."

In truth, he was afraid to fall asleep. Afraid he'd wake to find himself in another town, in another motel room, miles and months away from Rhea Carlisle and the smell of violets.

But it turned out Leo the Dull had been right about how this worked. He'd fallen asleep despite himself and despite the fact that Rhea was in his arms…and had woken up in the morning. And he was still here. Still himself. He didn't feel like he was missing anything. Maybe the curse only served to keep him from remembering his true self. And breaking the bonds had broken the curse. This was who Leo was supposed to be. He was free.

He nibbled at Rhea's earlobe, and she swatted at him in her sleep. The collar of her flannel shirt slipped down to expose her shoulder, and he kissed the warm flesh. He recalled brief flashes of memory of his daytime life over the past however many years, and he knew he'd been intimate with more than a few women, but it was like the memory of a recorded event, not the sensations. Like watching it on television. But Rhea was real.

He moved slowly up the slope of her neck, planting a chaste kiss every half inch.

Rhea shivered and stirred. "Leo?"

"The one and only." He slipped his hand beneath her shirt, teasing his fingers upward along her side.

She rolled over to face him. "One and only. Are you saying…?"

"I haven't gone anywhere. And I remember everything." He meant he'd remembered everything that had passed during his nightly confinements, but it was clear from her response she believed he'd remembered his daytime self as well. That he was whole. And he considered himself whole, so there was no reason to split hairs.

Rhea slid her arms around his neck. "That's wonderful news. No more nightly flights on the Wild Hunt." She kissed him, and he felt like Sleeping Beauty awakened. Not the most masculine of images, perhaps, but the symbolism fit. He tasted her mouth as if for the first time, explored the velvet softness of her lips and tongue, forgetting to breathe until her hand slipped down between their bodies, making him gasp.

He covered by nipping at her ear. "What about your sister-mom?"

Rhea's hand was making it hard for him to concentrate. "Not above us anymore. I hear her banging around in the kitchen. She'll be busy for a while."

Leo laughed nervously, his forehead against hers, feeling like an adolescent losing his virginity. It was absurd. He'd spent four of the last five nights doggedly trying to woo her, and now a single touch from her, knowing he was about to get what he wanted, made him nervous.

Rhea's forehead creased. "What's so funny?"

"Just that I feel this is the first time I've been myself

in hundreds of years and I somehow feel like an amateur. I hope I still remember how to do this properly."

It was Rhea's turn to laugh. "I'm pretty sure you'll figure it out." She pushed him onto his back and climbed over him. "But in case you don't, I'm happy to give you a refresher." Rhea took off her top and tossed it aside before she began working through the buttons on his borrowed shirt.

He wove his fingers together behind his head and watched her with a grin. "So I don't have to keep the shirt on?"

"Only if you want to seem like a creepy businessman having a nooner with a prostitute. But the socks are going to have to go. That's just a rule I have." He pulled off his socks with his toes while she bared his chest and ran her hands over his skin, sending little ripples of anticipation through him connected directly to his groin, before pausing to examine his pendant.

"Yggdrasil," he said. "The World Tree."

"It's lovely." She moved on to the pants. Her fingers were cold, but the slight shock of it against his flesh when she tugged down his briefs and exposed him was part of the pleasure.

Rhea's eyes went a bit wide as she curled her hand around him. "Well, hello there. Aren't you a big boy?"

Leo breathed in, trying to suppress the groan that wanted out. "Not sure I care for being called a boy," he managed to say with what he felt was the right touch of amusement and arousal.

Rhea flicked her gaze up to meet his with an amused arch of her brow. "I wasn't talking to you."

It drew an unexpected laugh from him, earning one of those smiles of hers that said his laugh turned her on, which turned him on more, making his cock twitch eagerly in her hand.

"But maybe you'll remember the feeling next time you're tempted to call someone a girl." She winked, her fingers corkscrewing slightly around his shaft.

Leo closed his eyes to slow his breathing. "I will," he said after a moment, opening them again. "I will indeed remember the feeling."

"Glad to hear it."

She was still wearing her pink lace bra, and Leo nodded at it. "Are you going to keep that on?"

"Why?" She cupped one breast in her free hand. "Did you want me to take it off?"

"I would very much like it if you did, yes." He let out a slight gasp as her hand twisted once more against him. "Please," he added to cover the gasp. It was probably the sort of thing someone with a thought-self would say, anyway.

She seemed to appreciate the gesture. His cock ached when she let go, but it was worth the deprivation to watch her twist the little clasp of the front-closing bra—the best kind—and open it, freeing her petite breasts, dusky peach-colored tips hard in the cold air.

"Oh, gods." He hadn't realized he'd groaned the words aloud until she blushed. "You are utterly fantastic," he added with a grin. He unhooked his hands from behind his head and reached to touch her, but Rhea seized his wrists and pushed them down to the pillow, her breasts now out of his reach yet tantalizingly close.

"No touching. Just looking."

Leo raised an eyebrow. "Is this what we're doing now?"

"For the moment. I need my concentration. Nipple stimulation is my kryptonite."

"I will keep that in mind."

When she let him go, he tucked his hands behind his head once more, watching her shimmy out of her pants. She kept on the matching pink lace panties, rising onto her knees as she straddled him, and Leo's cock bobbed in his lap when she inched them down, slowly, maddeningly, revealing the tip of her dark, trimmed bush.

"This is some kind of torture, isn't it? That's what you're trying to do? Torture me?"

"I don't know. You're the expert. You tell me." Something sparkled between her thighs as the panties went lower, a little gold ring, nestled into her...

"Ohhhh, *fuuuuuck*." The words escaped him slowly, luxuriously, as it dawned on him. The hood of her clitoris was pierced.

She tilted her head, multicolored pastel strands falling forward into her eyes. "Something wrong?"

Leo moved one hand to his cock compulsively, choking it, his thumbnail hard against the tip to keep from having the ultimate adolescent moment. "Something," he groaned, "is exactly one hundred percent the opposite of wrong."

Rhea grinned, one hand moving up to pinch her nipple while the other slid down to tug on the ring. As she opened her mouth, presumably to tease him further, the door behind her swung open.

"Rhea, what do you and—" Her sister's face went white.

"Oh my *God*!" Rhea dove forward, ostensibly to cover herself but effectively throwing herself on top of his erection. "What the fuck, Ione? Get *out*!"

The white of her sister's face went crimson, and she backed out and pulled the door closed with a snap.

Leo put his arms around Rhea, stroking the silk of her skin as the ring decorating her pussy rubbed against his cock.

She moaned against his chest, but it wasn't a moan of pleasure. "I can't believe she did that."

"From the look on her face, I think she feels the same."

Rhea wriggled in his arms, shaking with a sound between crying and laughing. Above the pink lace, her ass cheek was tattooed with a little blue crescent moon.

"*Älskling*, if we're not going to finish, I need you to move a bit. Or *I'm* going to finish."

Rhea choked back the laugh-crying and rolled onto the mattress on her side, burying her face in his shoulder. "Sorry. This was not how I intended this to go. But there's no way I can—"

"Totally understandable. If incredibly uncomfortable." He pulled up his briefs, trying to tuck in his erection.

"I knew I shouldn't have tried to do anything here." Rhea sighed regretfully and propped herself on her elbow. Little tattoos decorated the insides of her arms. There were others between her thighs and her lower belly he'd noticed only peripherally while watching her panties come away.

He stroked one on her arm, a little sprig of pink blossoms. "Did you do this? All these?"

"Most of them. They're not my best work. I was still learning."

"No, it's beautiful. You're like a canvas, a living sketchpad. The portfolio of the artist on her own skin. You shouldn't cover them all the time."

"I figured they wouldn't be good examples to show clients."

"Nonsense. They would be stunned by the evidence of your growing talent. I don't imagine tattooing oneself is the easiest thing to do."

"No, it isn't." Rhea brushed her fingers over the fresh work on Mjölnir, visible beneath the unbuttoned cuff of the borrowed shirt he still wore. "I didn't get a chance to bandage this up at the shop, and I forgot after. But it looks good. You heal fast."

"The benefits of being charmed."

A tentative knock sounded on the door, and Rhea hitched her panties up and pulled the sheet up over them both. *"What?"*

"Sorry. Not coming in. I wasn't going to bother you, but Dev made pancakes. But we can reheat them later."

Rhea made a growling huff of frustration. "We'll be out in a minute." She glanced at Leo. "I mean, we don't have to. She's a pain in the ass. If you need to…uh…"

Leo laughed. "No, I'll be fine. And pancakes sound delicious." Everything sounded delicious. The bastard had rarely left anything within his reach to eat.

While they ate breakfast, Rhea showed Ione the note from her windshield. "I assume this was from whoever keeps vandalizing the parking lot at the shopping center. And Leo tore down a poster the other day with the same words as the graffiti." Rhea swallowed a bite of her pancake. "You're going to hate what it said."

Ione narrowed her eyes as she handed the note to Dev. "What did it say?"

"The impure shall be cast out."

"Goddammit." Ione clenched her fist around her fork.

"He's like a cockroach." She looked at the note again as Dev passed it back. "I'll talk to Phoebe later and see if she can put on her PI hat and find out if anyone else is visiting Carter in prison."

"You don't think it could be Laurel again?"

Ione shook her head. "No, she's learned her lesson. I don't think she ever wants anything to do with Carter Hamilton again, let alone us."

Rhea was fine with that outcome. If only Theia would leave it alone.

It took the better part of the day to chase down the landlord for a spare set of keys and get a replacement set made for the car while also, at Ione's insistence, stopping at the bank to get her cards replaced and at the cellular store to get a new phone. With Ione chauffeuring them about, Rhea felt like she was back in high school, her "date" relegated to the back seat. Which totally didn't make the awkwardness from this morning worse.

Once Rhea had everything sorted, Ione dropped her off at the site of the fire—formerly the site of her business—to assess the damage and see if anything had survived among the ashes. She sent Leo to buy some clothes, insisting he take the car and some cash and get what he needed. Right now, she desperately needed alone time.

Her best tattoo machine was charred rubble, the electrical cord a melted piece of goo. Not to mention the water damage. She had the one she used at home, but it hardly mattered. It wasn't as if she had any clients. The ink bottles were ruined, but the packages of needles and steel tubes inside the drawers and cabinets might be salvageable. Everything else was gone.

Rhea collapsed onto the couch, bizarrely still standing largely intact among the wreckage. She tried to focus on restoring her phone from the cloud backup to avoid thinking about the money she'd sunk into this business and the fact that she was now officially unemployed.

The little bell that had once been on the door made a sad thunking noise as someone stepped on it. Rhea looked up, surprised Leo would be back so quickly. Instead, the most out-of-place person she'd ever seen stood amid the charred doorframe and warped floorboards in a long and absurdly expensive fox fur coat with the hood drawn up.

"We're not open for business," said Rhea in a stunningly stupid statement of the obvious.

The woman drew back her hood, revealing a long fall of red waves, and glared at Rhea with piercing green eyes. "What the hell have you done?"

"I… Huh?" She couldn't seem to form words. She'd seen this woman before. In Leo's vision and with the Hunt. The Valkyrie, Kára, was standing in Rhea's burned-out shop.

"You've let him loose. Your job was to protect him, not free his pettiest self and condemn him to wander as a wraith for all eternity."

"My job?"

"I came to you in good faith because you had the gift of vision. You promised to protect him."

The power of speech was coming back to her, awe giving way to irritation. "Look, lady, I've never met you before in my life, and I sure as hell never promised you anything."

A look of supreme annoyance overtook the flawless features. "I forget how small the human mind is." As the words left her mouth, the fur she wore shimmered and transformed into a living coat, her hair blending with the fur, pointed ears rising from it, and the fur covering a face that ended in a petite black snout.

"Vixen." Rhea shoved back hair in desperate need of product and a cut. She'd been played by the Valkyrie who'd enslaved Leo. God, she was stupid. "So I guess you're not my *fylgja* after all."

"Really, now. Why would *your fylgja* look like this?" Vixen smoothed her hands over her disturbingly curvaceous fox form. "You're so simple."

"Could you please *stop* looking like that? You're kind of creeping me out right now."

The fox shrugged, and with a little shake of her hair, she was a woman once more. At least, she seemed to be. Who knew what she really was.

"So what are you telling me? That Leo's lost his *hugr* permanently? He told me he remembered everything, that he was finally himself."

"He is himself. The self he believes to be central to his being. And he won't give it up without a fight."

"So it can be given up. He can be restored?"

"If he does so voluntarily before the Hunt has scattered on the wind for another year. It ought to have ended on the longest night, but I have managed to assure the Hunt will linger until Yuletide's end. You must persuade the *munr* to take back his other selves before the Hunt has ended or he will be forever broken. You have also left the Chieftain of the Hunt vulnerable to his enemies. They will seek to destroy him."

Neck aching from looking up at her, Rhea stood, though the Valkyrie still loomed over her. "You said other 'selves.' Are you saying he's missing more than one?"

"It is only the will that remains within his skin. His *hugr*, his *fylgja*, even his *hamingja* will be lost on the wind."

"So Leo has a *fylgja*, too?"

"Of course he does. Every man does. And every woman. Except for you, that is."

Rhea breathed in too sharply and nearly choked on her own spit. "Wait, wait." She pounded on her chest, coughing until she caught her breath. "Wait a minute. Why wouldn't I have one if everyone else does? Is there something wrong with me?" She'd always suspected there must be.

The Valkyrie smiled as though Rhea had said something adorable and amusing, stepping close to her. "Because you *are* a *fylgja*." Rhea felt her face go white as the Valkyrie stroked a finger along her jaw. "And your sister is yours."

"My...my sister? You mean Theia?"

"Monozygotic twins are always each the *fylgja* of the other."

"So you're not saying I'm only half a person or something."

"Oh, goodness, no. You have all your other selves. It's only the *fylgja* that splits off in twinning. Every human has a complete set of selves otherwise."

Rhea shook her head to clear it. "Okay, let's forget about me for a moment. What was the other thing you said? The other self Leo's missing?"

"The *hamingja*. It's not so much a separate self as his personal embodiment of luck. Without it, he will be plagued with misfortune."

Becoming chilled in the open room, Rhea tucked her hands into her pockets and began to pace. "And how am

I supposed to help him get them back? Especially if he doesn't want them? Where do I even find them?"

"The *hamingja* will come on its own if it chooses to, once the others have returned. The Chieftain, his *hugr*, you have seen. He leads the Hunt nightly. And his *fylgja* would have shown itself to you. It accompanies his warden spirit, watching from the shadows."

"You mean the black wolf?"

"I cannot say how it will appear to you, but if you have seen this wolf near him, it is most likely the one. You must seek its aid."

Rhea regarded her with mistrust. "And why can't you do any of this? Aren't you the one who did this to him? Shouldn't you have been protecting him? Why can't *you* round up the troops?"

The Valkyrie fluffed the collar of her fur beneath her throat. "Leo left me."

"But I've seen you riding with him in the Hunt."

"My spirit rides with the Chieftain, yes. But he has not recognized me since…"

"Since you gave the Norns his mind."

Her preternaturally green eyes went wide. "How do you know of this?"

Rhea shrugged. "I see things."

"Wyrd could simply have healed him," she said bitterly. "But she refused. And I couldn't let him die. Not after all we had been through. I let her take his mind as she had taken his will. That is when he came to know me as Faye in his waking hours. He didn't remember Kára, who saved him, who gave up everything for him. So I became what he needed me to be, and I helped him when his memory failed him. But eventually, he left. So

I whispered in his *hugr*'s ear to encourage him to choose someone worthy to be his human protector."

"But why would I be worthy?"

"Because of your blood. And because of your strength. I admit I was surprised at first to see whom he'd chosen." She smiled again, almost fondly. "But though thou be but little, thou art fierce."

The reference made Rhea smile despite herself. She'd played Hermia in *A Midsummer Night's Dream* in high school.

Faye sighed and drew up her collar, once again all business. "He cannot know I have spoken to you. You must convince him to do what is necessary on your own. And you must ensure no harm comes to his *hugr* in the meantime. I will ride beside him in the Hunt, as Kára, and try to protect him as I always have. But you must stop the one who has been seeking him before he comes too close." Faye turned toward the door as she spoke, and Rhea took a step after her.

"What one? How do I stop him?"

But when she followed Faye through the door, there was no one on the other side. And Leo was coming around the corner.

Chapter 18

Rhea pondered how to broach the subject of Leo's missing selves without mentioning Faye as they drove to her place. Had he deliberately deceived her this morning, or was it as Faye said, that he believed himself to be the self he was meant to be?

His eyes were on her as she parked the car. "Anything wrong?"

"Why would anything be wrong?"

"You're very quiet. I know it must have been hard seeing the place like that. After everything you put into it."

"Yeah, it sucks," Rhea agreed with a sigh. "But I talked to the owners of the shopping center, and they're going to refund the January rent   eventually. They're assessing the structural damage, and it might even be possible to move back in after they've made repairs in a couple of months. In the meantime, I'm going to have to borrow money from Ione to cover rent for my apartment. I'm royally screwed. Of course, I do have the check from Brock, since I deposited it electronically before it got burned up."

"Brock?"

Rhea studied his face. He didn't have a clue who Brock was. Which meant Faye was right. This wasn't the whole Leo.

"You have no idea who I'm talking about, do you? My first client. The guy you punched in the face."

Leo was obviously trying to hide his surprise. "Of course. I'd forgotten that was his name."

"No, you didn't."

Leo frowned at her. "What do you mean, I didn't? It slipped my mind for a moment. Brock Dressler, the neo-Nazi asshole I punched on the street."

That was unexpected. Maybe Faye was wrong.

He flexed his knuckles, still lightly scabbed over from the encounter, though the cuts on his fingertips had already healed. Rhea wondered if the physical evidence had jogged his memory. He'd said before he had flashes of memory from Leo the Dull's daily life.

"How are your fingers, by the way?"

Leo's expression was guarded. "Fingers?"

"The paper cuts you got when you were putting up those posters for me the other day. Looks like they healed up."

He turned his palms up and nodded as if he knew what she was talking about. "Yeah, it was nothing. I barely remember it happening."

"You don't remember it because that's not what happened, Leo. You tore down some racist propaganda and there were razor blades on the back. You sliced open the tips of your fingers pretty badly. There were bandages and everything. But you don't remember because it happened when your *hugr* was occupying the skin, and since you heal so quickly, there wasn't anything to jog your memory. And your *hugr* isn't in there, is he?"

"Rhea…"

"Why did you lie?"

"I didn't lie."

"You said you remembered everything."

Leo leaned back against the seat. "I meant that I remembered the night. That I was still me."

"But you knew that wasn't how I took it."

"Are we going to argue about his precious soul, now? About your promises to him?"

"It's your soul, too."

"Well, I don't need it. I've never felt the lack of it. I am perfectly whole, *mitt hjärta*. I promise you. We don't need him. *You* don't need him."

"What's that mean? *Meet…?*"

Leo blushed. For a man without a soul, he seemed sensitive enough. "*Mitt hjärta*. 'My heart.' It's a term of—"

"I can tell what it is." Rhea took his hand, and Leo raised her knuckles to his mouth and brushed them with his lips. Maybe he didn't need the *hugr*. But the *hugr* needed him. She couldn't just abandon it. And Faye had said he would be forever broken if the *hugr* was lost.

They got out of the car without further discussion, taking the salvaged supplies and Leo's new duffel bag of clothes up the stairs to her apartment.

When they'd stepped inside, Leo tossed his bag on the floor and took the shopping bag from Rhea's hand to set it down carefully before closing the door.

He pressed her back against it, his lips at her temple.

"Let me make you forget him," he whispered. His amber-resin scent was intoxicating.

Rhea closed her eyes. Maybe just for a night. She could figure out what to do about Leo's broken pieces in the morning. Maybe just for tonight she could let him do this—let him pull her shirt over her head and toss it on the couch. Let him open her bra with one expert snap of his finger and thumb and slide the straps down her arms, making her nipples tighten in the cold air. Let him unzip her pants as he bent to suck one hard nipple into his mouth until she was moaning. Let the pants pool at her ankles while he dropped to his knees and peeled her panties down with his teeth. Maybe just for tonight she could let him open her with his tongue and—

"Oh. *God.*"

Her knees nearly buckled as he took the gold ring between his teeth and tugged while his tongue curled inside her and lapped at the wetness dripping over his cheeks. The orgasm was powerful and immediate, and she couldn't catch her breath. Rhea felt the room going gray.

"Rhea?" She came around to find Leo lightly slapping at her cheek. "You still with me?"

Rhea nodded and managed to make a vague murmur in the affirmative.

Scooping her up into his arms, he carried her to the bedroom like a bride over a threshold, letting her jeans slip to the floor, and laid her gently on the bed. "You scared the hell out of me. Has that happened to you before?"

She rubbed her bare arms in the cold air. "Can't say it has."

Leo placed the fleece throw from the end of the bed around her shoulders. "Where's your thermostat?"

"In the hallway next to the kitchen."

Leo went to switch it on and came back to wrap her in his arms. Pretty attentive for a soulless *munr*. How could Rhea even be sure Faye was telling her the truth, anyway? Maybe she just wanted him back in one piece so he'd remember her and return to her. But keeping Leo fragmented just to keep him from remembering some past love would be a pretty shitty thing to do.

"I know what you're thinking," he said, startling her.

"You do?"

"You're wondering if you can put me back together."

"Would that be so terrible?"

Leo shrugged, tightening his hold on her. "It doesn't matter. It can't be done."

"How do you know?"

"Because I remember the curse. The original one, spoken by the Norn. 'If the bonds be not broken 'ere the dawn, the wandering spirit will come anon. Should the will be loosed before the light, the spirit thought shall swift take flight; an it not return by break of day, the wandering wraith shall hie away.'"

The wandering wraith. Faye had called the *hugr* the same. But Faye had told her the *hugr* could be persuaded to return. Leo either didn't know there was a remedy to the curse or he didn't want Rhea to know. She considered revealing what she'd learned from the Valkyrie, but his reaction the other night when Rhea had mentioned the Kára of his past had been explosive. Keeping it from him felt awkward and made her uncomfortable, but if he knew about Faye, he might be the one to take flight and never return.

The real question was whether Rhea could even find any of Leo's other selves. "Second sight" notwithstanding, the Hunt only appeared to her when it wanted to. She hadn't sought it out. How could she seek out the invisible? Then the obvious hit her. She happened to know two people who possessed the ability to communicate with shades. And what was a shade but a disembodied soul?

Leo nuzzled her ear. "You're awfully quiet. Just sleepy?"

The suggestion made her yawn, and Rhea nodded. "It's been a long day." She looked over her shoulder with a grin. "And you kind of wiped me out, to be honest. Not that I'm complaining."

"So you're not avoiding me."

"Why would I be avoiding you?"

Leo sighed against her shoulder. "You realize you keep rephrasing and repeating my questions instead of answering them. It's making me feel a bit suspicious."

She sucked at keeping secrets. "I'm sorry. You're right. I didn't realize I was doing that." She turned to face him. "But I am *not* avoiding you."

Leo stroked his hand down her arm beneath the throw. "I mean, it's perfectly fine if you want to go to sleep." The Mjölnir tattoo brushed her side, making her shiver. There was something about that ink that was like an aphrodisiac. "*I'm* perfectly fine, is what I'm saying." He drew her closer, and she could feel the hardness through his jeans against her bare thigh.

"Are you? Perfectly?"

Leo gave her a sly half smile. "I suppose I should let you be the judge."

"It's kind of hard to judge with all those clothes on."

"Maybe I should do something about that."

"Maybe you should." Rhea drew the throw around herself as Leo climbed out of the bed and stood to remove the borrowed shirt he was still wearing. He unbuttoned it slowly, teasingly, revealing his well-toned pecs, the Yggdrasil pendant lying between them, and his ungodly abs. She nodded approval. "So far, so good."

"So far, eh?" He tossed the shirt at her, and Rhea dropped the throw to slip it on. He nodded appreciatively. "Looks good on you. You should dress like that all the time."

"I'll consider it. Quit stalling."

Leo laughed. "There's not much else you haven't seen, if you recall what we almost did this morning."

"I do recall, yes. And the initial inspection was very satisfactory. But I haven't seen your ass."

"I didn't realize that was a deal-breaker."

"Oh God, yes. Have you never read a women's magazine?"

"Not that I recall. I'll have to defer to your expertise." He unbuttoned the jeans and stepped out of them, the white cotton of his briefs straining, clearly at capacity. "You'll want to see the ass first, I take it."

Rhea nodded. "Naturally."

Leo turned away, legs planted firmly apart, giving her a glimpse of his well-shaped glutes within the briefs before drawing the garment down.

Rhea put her fist in her mouth to muffle a groan. From the glimpses she'd gotten of his ass in jeans, she'd already known it would be spectacular, but it was completely unfair that any man should have an ass like that, rock hard yet lightly rounded at the top. She wanted to bite it.

Leo looked over his shoulder, the briefs still at his thighs. "Does it meet with your approval?"

"I'm afraid I'm going to have to do a tactile inspection before I can make a final determination." Her voice was amusingly gruff with desire, when she was trying to be nonchalant.

Leo stepped out of the briefs and turned to climb back onto the bed, his expression amused at the involuntary high-pitched humming noise that escaped her at the sight of that glorious cock.

He lay on his stomach and turned his head toward her, resting his cheek on his folded arms. "All yours." She could get used to those words.

Rhea climbed over him and sat on his thighs, smoothing her hands over the tight curves of his ass. "Yes, this will do nicely." She gave one cheek a little slap, and Leo lifted his head with a noise of protest. "That's what you have to do," she explained. "To test the firmness. Like with a mattress."

"I think you'll find the other side much firmer." Leo rolled beneath her, and Rhea came up on all fours over him, their bodies tantalizingly close.

"You are," she murmured, "indeed, perfectly fine."

"Would I lie to you?" He pulled her down, their bodies skin to skin, and wrapped his arms around her as he brought his mouth to hers.

Rhea moaned softly into him, her eyes closing, every inch of her skin where it touched his tingling with arousal. This morning, she'd thought he was fully Leo. Now that she knew only the *munr* was in the skin, she shouldn't be doing this. She'd promised him. But what if the Leo she'd made that promise to was gone forever?

Leo's hand slid down her back to her ass, caressing

it before sliding farther into the cleft, his fingers teasing at the edges of her pussy. She reached back and took hold of his hand, pushing it lower as she opened her legs to encourage him, and Leo drew back from her mouth with a deep laugh.

"Am I going too slowly for you, *älskling*?"

Rhea grinned. "Just a bit."

He pressed two fingers between her thighs and entered her, eyes locked on hers. "Better?" When Rhea nodded, biting her lip, Leo went deeper, stroking slowly inside her. "Do you want me to fuck you?"

"God *yes*." The second word came out in a long moan.

He pumped his fingers into her a few more times until she was squirming. Just as she was ready to beg for it, he moved his fingers away and brought the head of his cock against her.

Rhea grabbed his hand. "What are you doing?"

Leo blinked. "I thought… Didn't you say—?"

"Where's the condom? You have a condom, don't you?"

His winter sky blues looked blank.

Rhea groaned and rolled onto her side. "This is one of those things you have no memory of, isn't it?"

Leo gave her an amused smirk. "A lesson once learned in the body remains in the flesh. I'm quite certain I can find my way without any trouble."

"Oh, I have no doubt of that." After the expert way he'd used his tongue, she was sure it would be fantastic. "But we can't do it without a condom. A prophylactic," she explained. "A rubber." He kept shrugging. Why the hell didn't she keep any herself?

Rhea rolled out of bed and started digging through the dresser for something to throw on.

Leo propped himself up on his elbows, watching her, his impressive cock like an absurd flagpole in his lap. "What are you doing?"

"I'm going to drive to the convenience store and buy some condoms." She pulled on a pair of black paisley leggings without bothering with underwear, hopping as she pulled them up, and dragged an old sweatshirt on over her head before shoving her feet into a pair of furry boots. "I'll only be a few minutes, so…" She glanced at his erection. "Hold that thought."

"You're not serious."

"I mean, you can hold it or not hold it, but we can work on that when I get back."

Rhea came to the bed to give him a kiss, and he nearly succeeded in distracting her once more into throwing caution to the wind, but she managed to tear herself away.

"Ten minutes," she promised and hurried out the door before her body could persuade her to forget the condoms. He was over a thousand years old. He was going to wear a condom whether he remembered what it was or not.

Stepping back out into the cold was brutal after having his body warm her. Rhea dashed to the car and ran the windshield wipers with some wiper fluid, with the heat on full blast until the window defogged enough to drive.

The trip to the store was uneventful. She managed to get the condoms, ignoring the clerk's look at the evidence of her hasty dress. It was obvious why she was out looking like this and making this purchase. Let him snicker.

But as she got back into the car, she saw a dark shape in the rearview mirror. The black wolf-dog sat directly behind her in the path of her vehicle.

Chapter 19

Starting the engine and turning on the lights did nothing to persuade the wolfish dog to move. If she started backing out, maybe it would get the hint. Rhea put the car in Reverse and let it roll back an inch or two, but the dog just sat there panting idly.

"Goddammit, dog. *Move*." She growled in frustration while staring at it in the rearview mirror. "You don't get it, dog. I *really* need to have sex."

The literally mind-numbing orgasm that had resulted in her fainting from the sudden dearth of blood to her brain had marked the beginning of the end of an epic dry spell she'd been denying to herself. Ever since the visions started, in fact. She hadn't even had sexy time with *herself* in weeks. Listening to Phoebe go on and on about Rafe's quetzal stamina for months now—then finding out uptight, reserved Ione had picked up a crazy-hot stranger in a bar and screwed him so hard he'd turned into a dragon—had driven her right to the edge of the cliff she hadn't even known she was perched on.

Rhea laid on the horn, startling a kid walking out of the store with beer he'd obviously bought with a fake ID, but the dog didn't budge.

Fists clenched against the steering wheel, she closed her eyes. "I hate you, wolf-dog." Of course, wolf-dog, if Faye could be trusted—and who wouldn't trust a Valkyrie-turned-sexy dominatrix-turned-talking fox?—was Leo's *fylgja*. Maybe, like Vixen, he was capable of human speech. "All right, dammit. You win."

She shut off the engine and opened the door, cautiously stepping out with one furry boot to peer around the car. It could be a wild animal for all she knew. It might not be a *fylgja* at all. No sense taking chances.

The dog stood beside her bumper, watching her expectantly.

"Okay. You've got my attention. What do you want?" This had to look awesome on the store's security camera.

As soon as she stepped out of the car completely, the dog took off running across the parking lot and out onto the road.

"God*dam*mit!" Rhea jumped back into the car and restarted the engine.

The dog was no longer blocking her way. She could forget about this and go home, climb into that warm bed with Leo, and get her brains screwed out. But Faye's exhortation to help Leo find his way back to himself nagged at her conscience. She was Leo's only hope. Faye had said Rhea would have to seek the *fylgja*'s aid, and the *fylgja* was currently trotting down the highway.

With a sigh, she pulled out of the lot and turned in

the direction the dog had gone. There had still been a little twilight left when she'd gotten in the car, but it was already pitch-black out here away from the city limits, especially on a moonless night. But her headlights illuminated the dog's shadowy form a hundred yards away—in the opposite direction from where Leo and her warm bed were waiting. Rhea followed, slowing when she caught up with the animal. The dog kept to the side of the road but continued trotting along at a good clip.

The box of condoms sat forlornly on the seat beside her. Magnum. Because *goddammit.*

She followed the stupid dog for at least a mile before it turned off onto a path that barely qualified as a road. If she'd thought it was dark before, this was like driving into a cave. Rhea switched on the high beams, illuminating the rocky twists and turns in the road, and after several minutes, the dog abruptly disappeared.

Rhea slowed the car. Fantastic. She could be in bed with Leo finding out if those magnums even fit, and instead she was out driving around in the middle of nowhere. In lazy-bitch pajamas. And it was starting to snow again.

She was about to stop and turn around when the circle of her headlights fell on a wooden paddock a few yards ahead. She'd reached the end of the road.

Rhea sighed and pulled over. She drew up her hood and stuffed her hands into her pockets as she got out. Why hadn't she grabbed a coat? Oh, right—because she was just going to get some damn condoms so she could get laid.

As she approached the paddock, something moved in the darkness beyond the fence. Fear seized her, and she clutched the pepper spray canister on her keys—a stocking stuffer from Theia. Something snorted and pawed at the ground. She was going to be eaten by wolves. Wait, did wolves snort?

As her eyes adjusted to the darkness, the large head of the beast turned toward her, eyes glowing white, and Rhea realized with relief that it was a horse. What was a horse doing in a paddock at night? But it wasn't alone. Shapes began to define from the darkness. There were half a dozen horses here. Maybe more. What kind of asshole would leave horses out in the snow?

She stepped up on the bottom rung of the fence, arms hooked over the top, and reached out to pet one of the muzzles, but her hand stopped halfway. Their eyes weren't just glowing from the reflected light. In fact, there was no reflected light; her car's headlights were pointing the other way. These were the specters of the Hunt, their hides stretched tight over their skeletons as if there were no muscle beneath. Certainly no fat. They were like the horses of the Apocalypse, except they were all Famine.

The closest of the horses had lifted its muzzle as if hoping for a treat, and her hand passed right through it. Rhea snatched her arm back with a shudder. It hadn't felt like passing through air but like putting her hand through gummy spider webs.

The message chime on her phone sounded from her pocket, and Rhea nearly jumped out of her skin and joined the specters. A message from Leo was on the screen.

Having spent many a night staring at the red glowing digits of a hotel alarm clock, I have a very keen sense of time. Also, I am staring at the red glowing digits of the clock by your (now rather cold) bed. It has been more than ten minutes. Where are you? I "Googled" condoms, and I must say I'm rather offended.

Rhea typed back a quick note.

They didn't have any. Taking a quick run into town to find some. Nothing to be offended about. Google "safer sex."

Before she dropped the phone back into her pocket, she noticed it was just after eight. That was about when she'd seen the Hunt the first time. These horses were awaiting their riders.

Her phone chimed once more, unnerving her as much as the first time.

Do you have chlamydia?

"Oh my God." She muted the phone.

Pockets of air shimmered around her in rainbow colors like the membrane of a soap bubble, and when the "bubble" popped, noise burst out of it—raucous, excited voices, as though a window had opened onto a party— seconds before the images of the hunters coalesced from the smoky shadows.

The riders took to their mounts as soon as they materialized. The others didn't notice her, but the Chieftain— Leo's *hugr*—doffed his cowboy hat in her direction as he mounted his horse.

He looked more substantial, less spectral than he had before, more closely resembling the vision she'd first had of the Hunt. His eyes were clear, blue as the Sedona winter sky at high noon. How she could see that, she wasn't sure. They did seem to be glowing a bit.

The other riders were heading out, the horses leaping straight over the fence, but the Chieftain lingered.

Rhea took a step toward him. "Leo?"

"That name did once belong to me, but no more." He held the hat to his chest and bowed over the horse's mane. "You may call me Gunnar."

Rhea's lips parted in disbelief. "Gunnar?"

"I must extend my gratitude to you."

"To me?"

"You have freed me to pursue my sacred calling, fair Rhea of Carlisle. I am no longer bound to the base appetites of the flesh to which the spineless Leo Ström returned me each morning through his foolish and slavish devotion."

"Leo is not spineless. He's a decent, responsible person trying to do the right thing."

"What has he done to earn your admiration? What valiant deeds has this giant of bravery done that you defend him so?"

Rhea folded her arms, half in umbrage and half to keep warm. "He punched a Nazi douchebag in the face the other day."

"Oh, yes. That takes courage. Saving humanity from a sad little braggart by assaulting him with a surprise right hook."

He set his hat on his head and urged the horse forward, leaping from the paddock and over Rhea's head while she ducked.

After she'd spun about, "Gunnar" turned back. "Careful rolling about in the mud with that mindless animal you've trapped in the skin. He knows nothing but his urges." The horse took off after the rest of the hunters at a gallop as the Chieftain let out an exuberant battle cry that echoed off the snow-covered rocks.

Rhea's eyes narrowed as disbelief gave way to aggravation. Leo's *hugr* was a pompous ass.

Teeth chattering, she hurried back to the car and huddled behind the wheel, holding her hands up to the heating vents. Good thing she'd left the engine running.

The condom box judged her silently from the passenger seat. Rhea pulled out her phone to find Leo had left another message. *Jesus*. It was accompanied by the most impressive dick pic she'd ever seen, his hand wrapped around the base.

You told me to hold the thought. The fact that I have no thought-self notwithstanding, I have been holding this for nearly an hour. I am fairly certain it's going to fall off if I hold it any longer. Difficult to Google left-handed, but several articles of dubious authorship seem to support this claim.

Rhea dashed off a quick response. So sorry. Found some. Heading back now. She put the car in Drive but paused and picked up the phone again to add VERY photogenic before tearing up the unmarked dirt road to get back to the highway as fast as she could.

She'd driven farther than she'd thought. The lights were out when she entered the apartment. *Please let him be setting the mood.*

But Leo was sprawled on the bed with his phone still in his hand, naked and sound asleep. Rhea slid the phone from his fingers and set it aside. He didn't stir. With a sigh of regret, she picked up the throw where she'd tossed it on the floor in her haste to get condoms and laid it over him. It barely covered the magnificent physique. The physique she could be riding right now like a Brahma bull if she hadn't followed Leo's *fylgja*.

And speaking of *fylgjas*—or not—she hadn't seen the Valkyrie with the Hunt tonight. What did that mean? And what dictated when she appeared as Vixen? Rhea hated to think of the fox woman appearing in her bedroom if she and Leo ever did manage to close the deal.

While she contemplated the idea, someone pounded on her front door. Would Vixen knock?

But when Rhea opened it, Phoebe stood on her doorstep looking slightly manic, like she'd had too much caffeine after waking up in the middle of the night.

"Rhea Iris Carlisle!" Her sister swept in and closed the door. "Why didn't you tell me you were nearly killed in a fire?" Phoebe hugged her and shook her simultaneously. "And why did I have to hear it from Ione?"

"My phone was torched and she said she'd call you. And I wasn't nearly killed. There was a small fire, but I'm fine—"

"A *small* fire? I saw it on the news, and it was not small. Not to mention they think it was arson. And Ione said you had to jump out a two-story window!"

"Barely one story."

"But your shop. Honey, are you going to be okay? Do the police have any idea who did it?" As Phoebe let go of Rhea, her gaze fixed on the box of condoms still in Rhea's hand.

Cheeks flaming, Rhea tossed the condoms onto the coffee table.

Phoebe's eyebrows lifted with amusement. "Am I... interrupting something? Cowgirl?"

Rhea rolled her eyes and flopped onto the couch. "Not exactly."

"Uh-oh." Phoebe joined her after taking off her coat and tossing it over the armrest. "Did you guys have a fight?"

"No. I just took too long getting condoms. He fell asleep."

"Oh, boy. Amateur. You're supposed to keep those in stock."

"You don't say." Rhea put her fur-clad feet up on the coffee table and crossed one boot over the other.

"Damn, those are cute." Phoebe tugged on one of the pompons dangling from the decorative ties. "When did you get those?"

"Theia gave them to me for our birthday last year." Rhea frowned, remembering their last gift exchange. Theia had bought them so Rhea would have something to wear in the winter when she moved up to Flag with her, which had been the plan at the time.

"She's over at my place, by the way."

Rhea glanced up. "What's she doing there?"

"She had a dream you were in trouble. She knew you wouldn't talk to her, so she came to me." Phoebe nudged Rhea's foot with her own on the coffee table. "And it's officially Christmas Eve as of twenty minutes ago."

Rhea blinked at her. "No, it's not. It was just..." The winter solstice had been on the twenty-second this year. And that had been yesterday. Or, rather, the day before, since it was now after midnight on the twenty-fourth. "When does Yuletide end?"

"Yuletide?"

"The original Germanic Yuletide. How long is it?"

"Why would I know?"

Rhea reached for the bag that held her tablet before remembering she didn't have one anymore. "Dammit." She grabbed her phone instead and looked up Yuletide, but scanning the first few links yielded several answers. "Damn the stupid internet."

"Rhea, *what* are you looking for?"

"I need to know how long it lasts. How long he has left."

"Who?"

Rhea stopped thumbing through links. "Leo. There are some things I didn't tell you the other day. And then I found out some more things."

Phoebe leaned in with interest. "What kinds of things?"

There had never been secrets between the Carlisle sisters. At least not before Theia had started keeping them. But this wasn't her story to tell. She supposed she could tell her as much as she'd told Ione, though.

"Leo's under some kind of spell. His will—his id—is separated from his ego during Yuletide."

"Are you talking about his other selves? Like the *fylgja*?"

"That's exactly what I'm talking about. His are fragmented, and because his ritual confinement was interrupted the other night by the fire, he can't naturally reintegrate. I have to convince him—all of his selves—to come back together before Yuletide ends or his soul and his ego will be lost forever. He'll be nothing but id. Broken. So I need to figure out when Yuletide ends officially, but it doesn't look like there's anything official."

She tossed the phone down, gesturing at the search results. "Could be a couple of days, could be twelve."

Phoebe looked thoughtful. "Does this have anything to do with the serpent energy we were talking about?"

"Maybe. The other Leo—the whole Leo, the one you met the other day—said he thought his *munr*—his id— would unleash the negative energy of the Midgard Serpent if the ritual was interrupted." She was so *not* telling Phoebe about the restraints. She'd never hear the end of it after all her teasing about the sex tape.

Phoebe caught Rhea's little hesitation, and her eyes narrowed, but she didn't press. "Maybe Rafe can figure out the dates for you. He has a Covent Compendium from his father containing a lot of obscure ritual information. Come to think of it, Dev should know if Rafe doesn't. He was a Covent assayer for years before Ione—"

"Boned the dragon out of him and got him fired?"

"She didn't get him fired. He quit voluntarily."

"However she wants to spin it. Anyway, that's promising. I still have to figure out how to get the soul and the id back together, whenever the deadline is. I had a chance to talk to his *hugr* tonight, and this is not going to be easy."

"Wait, how did you talk to a disembodied soul? That's my area."

"Remember that Wild Hunt I kept seeing?"

Phoebe's eyes widened. "You're kidding. He's a Hunt wraith?"

"He's *the* Hunt wraith. The Chieftain. Leader of the Hunt."

Phoebe's phone chimed. After glancing at the message, she got up and put her coat back on.

"That's Rafe. He's all by his lonesome in front of the

fire." She grinned. "I just wanted to make sure you were all right. You brat." She flicked Rhea's arm as she turned to go, and her gaze fell on the box of condoms. "Hope you get a chance to use those before dinner tomorrow. Today. You know what I mean." Phoebe paused on her way out the door. "And your bucking bronco is totally invited, in case that wasn't clear."

"Brahma bull." Rhea groaned as she realized she'd walked right into that one.

Leo didn't stir when she climbed into bed beside him. She folded the bedspread over him from the other side, even if he didn't feel the cold, and got under the covers on her side, snuggling up to him. She left a condom on the nightstand just in case.

Leo opened his eyes and stared at the ceiling once he was sure Rhea was asleep. He should have known something was up when she was gone so long. She'd been with that insufferable *hugr*, conspiring against him with the bastard who'd chained him up nightly over a thousand Yuletides.

He rolled over and observed her, silvery pastel strands of hair sticking to cheeks flushed pink with the heat of sleep. He'd believed she'd fallen for him at last, that she wanted *him* and not that passionless milquetoast who cared about nothing but his uptight morality.

Leo let his hand hover over her, wanting to pluck the sweat-damp strands from her cheek. The other Leo could never have given her so much pleasure that she fainted in his arms. Wouldn't have bothered. But the other Leo was the one she wanted: the one too timid to act on his desires, even if they burned inside him as they must if he, the *munr*, embodied them.

She had called him broken. The word twisted in his heart like a shard of glass as he'd lain listening to their voices, awakened by the sound of their affectionate banter. The way she was with her sisters made him love her more—*desire* her more, he amended. A stupid, brutish *munr* couldn't love. Rhea had the sort of familial bond he'd never experienced. He barely remembered his life before Kára, but he knew there had been nothing like that.

The idea of spending a holiday with Rhea and her family, playing at being an ordinary man for a day, was tempting. But Kára had owned him, the *hugr* had enslaved him for her, and now he was free. There was no way in Hel he was going to be made anyone's captive again. And certainly not by someone who thought of him as broken.

He couldn't stay till morning. If he did, he'd end up making love to her, and then he'd never be able to leave. Just the smell of her skin beside him made him want to give up his freedom just to touch it and taste it again. He still smelled of her himself. She was imprinted on his senses. Leo slid quietly off the other side of the bed and gathered his clothes, taking them to the living room to dress.

On the table in front of the couch was the box of condoms she'd purchased. He'd done enough Googling to know that if he happened to meet someone else to take his mind off Rhea, she'd expect him to have some of these. Leo slid the box into his pocket before slipping quietly out the door.

Chapter 20

Leo had gotten up early, apparently, maybe to take a shower. But he wasn't in the house. Maybe he'd gone out to get breakfast for the two of them. It would be just like him. It was ironic that the *munr* with no thought-self was more thoughtful than anyone she'd ever dated.

Then she discovered the box of condoms missing from the table.

Son of a bitch. He'd really had her fooled, making her think his relentless expression of desire was specific to her, when it was simply that he *was* desire. She'd left him at home for one night with the internet at his disposal, and he'd gone off to find someone else who maybe wasn't so difficult.

It hurt even more that he'd gone off without leaving a note. Not that she had notepaper lying around. But he could have sent her a text. Well, screw him. Now she didn't have to worry about fixing him, convincing his stupid *hugr* to make nice and step back inside the skin.

Rhea stalked to the kitchen and opened the fridge, looking for something to eat. She'd been trying to live on the bare minimum until she got a few clients, and her grocery reserves were dwindling. She had oatmeal, but there wasn't even enough milk for a bowl of cereal. She supposed she could eat it without.

As she closed the refrigerator door, Rhea let out a yelp. "Dammit, Vixen. Have you ever considered knocking?"

The Valkyrie pulled her fur coat tight around her. "It's dreadfully cold in here. And there is no Vixen, darling. I made her up." She sniffed and looked offended. "Now, then. Care to tell me what the hell you've done to Leo?"

"Who says I've done something to him?"

"He was your responsibility. And now he's gone. Do you think I wouldn't be able to tell? I took him from the battlefield. I am attuned to the rhythm of his breathing and his heart. I know where the body is and what he's doing with it at all times."

Rhea rubbed at her neck. "All times?"

Faye smiled knowingly. "He's quite talented, isn't he? Sadly, I have never had the pleasure of experiencing his talents when the *munr* alone embodied the skin, but I did teach the skin itself."

"Okay. Too much information." Rhea leaned back against the fridge with her arms folded. "So what's he doing with it? Shouldn't you know where he is?"

"I know *where* he is. It's why he's there instead of here with you that I wish to know. How do you intend to bring his selves together if you've driven him off? And how on earth did you manage to do so after the pleasure he'd given you?"

"Okay, look. We are *not* doing this. You are way too interested in my sexual intimacy with Leo." And it was weird how Faye wasn't the least bit bothered by it. "I don't know why he left. I woke up and he was gone. He fell asleep last night while I was out getting condoms."

An expression of pure surprise lit Faye's features before her entire being seemed to explode into delighted laughter. "You thought you were going to get a mindless *munr* to wear a condom. No wonder he left. A *munr* does not care to have its pleasure compromised."

"Oh, really? Then why did he take the box of condoms with him while I was sleeping?"

Faye's eyebrows rose comically. "Did he really? How peculiar. He also took your car."

"What?" Rhea ran to the window and looked out. Her spot was empty. Tears of frustration burned behind her eyes. She had four years of car payments left.

"There's a simple remedy," said Faye when Rhea let the curtain fall. "Report the car stolen. When he's apprehended, you can collect him."

"Collect him? He's not a piece of property."

"But he is your responsibility."

"Why the hell is he my responsibility? You're the one who did this to him. Why don't *you* go 'collect' him?"

Faye looked wounded. "That is part of the price I paid to spare his life. I cannot affect his will. I ride with the wraith, though he does not know me. But I cannot be with him when only the *munr* inhabits the skin. Only when he is whole can I interact with him and have him see me for who I am."

"So that's what this is about. You want me to put him back together so you can be with him."

Faye shrugged, though the gesture seemed to belie some deeper emotion. "See it how you will. The fact remains that you are the one who released him—"

"My shop was on fire. Should I have let him burn with it?"

Faye fluffed her collar. "He cannot burn. He would have felt it, but it would not have damaged him."

"Oh, well, that would have been just fine, then. Let him *experience* burning to death."

"The greater issue is that you've left his *hugr* vulnerable to attack."

"So you've said. You know, I spoke to his *hugr* last night. And he was an insufferable bore."

A half smile lifted the corner of her mouth. "He is... single-minded."

"You keep saying his *hugr* is vulnerable to attack. From whom? The Norns?"

"Oh, no. Wyrd and her sisters prefer to stay far above the fray, maintaining their fiction of blamelessness, all the while weaving and cutting capriciously." Faye's eyes flashed with anger. "His enemies are those who seek to undermine the Hunt itself. Many have come through the ages, intent on overthrowing him as Chieftain, but while his body and his *munr* remained bound to him, they could not harm him. Now, thanks to you, he is fair game." Faye gave her a reproachful look. "And now you've lost his body. I suggest you make that report and get back what belongs to both of us."

Rhea opened her mouth to object, but Faye had apparently said all she intended to and was simply gone.

Despite the Valkyrie's insistence, she couldn't bring

herself to get Leo arrested. She'd have to report the car stolen eventually, but it seemed like a betrayal of trust to use the police to track him down. Maybe she was being a fool. He'd betrayed her trust first. But she wasn't going to have Leo thrown in jail—shackled again—on Christmas Eve.

Anyway, how did she know Faye was even telling her the truth? She'd revealed her true motive for reuniting Leo's selves. She wanted him for her own selfish purposes, just as she had when she'd interfered with the course of his life a thousand years ago. These "enemies" she claimed were after him didn't sound all that credible.

When she called Phoebe later to tell her she couldn't make it to Christmas Eve dinner, Phoebe wouldn't have it. Rhea had made up a story about her car being in the shop, and before she knew it, Phoebe was at her door to pick her up.

"Don't think I don't know what this is about," she said when Rhea answered the door. "You're avoiding Theia. But it's Christmas Eve and this has gone far enough. Get Leo and let's go."

Rhea hugged her arms. "He's not here."

"What do you mean, he's not here? Where is he?"

"He left."

"That's all you're going to tell me?"

"I don't want to talk about it."

"Okay, well, you have two choices—tell me and you can stay here and sulk, or get your butt in the car. And tell me later."

"You're really going to let me stay here if I tell you?"

Phoebe rolled her eyes. "Are you high? It's Christmas." She pointed to her Jeep in the parking lot. "March."

After exchanging the sweatshirt for a more festive

chartreuse and fuchsia vintage sweater set from the '80s and running some sculpting cream through her hair, Rhea reluctantly got into the Jeep, rubbing her arms through her coat sleeves. "Who drives a Jeep in the snow?"

"It's not snowing at the moment. And it's not like the top is open."

"It's a lot like the top is open. Your windows are made out of vinyl."

"Stop stalling. What happened to Leo?"

"Oh, so this is 'later,' is it?"

Phoebe grinned as she pulled the Jeep out onto the highway. "Yep. And now you're my captive, so we're driving around until you tell me."

Rhea sighed. "There's nothing to tell. I woke up this morning and he was gone."

"That's it?" Phoebe glanced at her. "You didn't have a fight or anything?"

"Nope. Just gone. I have no idea when he left. Woke up about nine o'clock and there was no Leo, no note and no condoms."

"No." Phoebe nearly pulled the Jeep over. Rhea could only imagine what her sister would have done if she'd mentioned the car. "That is just evil."

Phoebe's house was a winter wonderland. In addition to a plethora of lights and a nine-foot tree, luminarias lit the walkway, and a host of marvelous smells struck Rhea as Phoebe opened the door. Cinnamon and cloves from the mulled cider mixed with the scent of fresh pine and the mesquite wood burning in the fireplace, while scented candles in peppermint and caramel apple and pumpkin pie perched on every surface.

Rhea was the last to arrive. Dev's and Rafe's impressive forms dominated the kitchen, where they were busy adding their family specialties to the feast—in matching Hello Kitty aprons that had to be Phoebe's doing. Ione and Theia sat cross-legged by the fire taking turns petting Puddleglum, stretched on the hearth between them like feline royalty. And Phoebe, true to form, had the classic Christmas carols from their childhood playing on her sound system.

Rhea tried studiously not to look in Theia's direction, but the ranch house was too small to accommodate acting like a child. She sat in the coveted papasan chair, temporarily empty, as Ione got up to help Dev with something in the kitchen.

Theia looked up at her with a hesitant smile. Her eyes looked a little puffy. Maybe it was all the perfumey candles. All four of them were a bit allergic to perfume, and all of them suffered through it, because they loved scented things.

"Hey," said Theia. "I'm glad you came."

"Who would want to miss Rafe and Dev in Hello Kitty aprons?"

Theia grinned, pulling her knees up and wrapping her arms around them as she glanced into the kitchen over the breakfast bar at the pair of khaki-clad muscular behinds topped by the pink bows of the apron strings. "Yeah, the view is pret-ty nice from here."

"Of course, it would be better if they weren't wearing pants."

Theia covered her mouth to stifle a loud burst of laughter. "Dammit, Rhe, now I'll never get that image out of my head."

"It's a good one, isn't it?" Rhea rested one ankle on

her knee, and Puddleglum came unglued as the pompons from the furry boot swung from the end of the tie. Without Rhea having to do a thing to entertain him, he was batting and flipping the furry balls wildly, hanging on with both paws as he twisted around.

"Those are the boots I got you."

"Yeah. They're perfect for this weather. It's kind of crazy, huh?"

Theia leaned back with her arms behind her, palms braced against the stone hearth. "We don't even have this much snow in Flag yet. Guess you're learning to drive in the white stuff, now, huh?"

"A bit, yeah."

"So what happened to your car? It's still under warranty, isn't it?"

Rhea jiggled her foot to swing Puddleglum, now attached by both feet and his jaws. "It's just the alternator or something. I'm sure it's covered."

"Listen, whatever I did—"

"We don't have to talk about it."

Theia's face fell. "We do, though. I want to make it right."

"You can't."

"Rhe—"

To Rhea's relief, Phoebe swept into the room with a tray full of tapas, ending the conversation. "Okay, we've got puris from Dev and empanaditas from Rafe, and of course Yiayia's spanakopita."

Ione followed, setting out little plates decorated with holly, and Rhea got up to load her plate.

Phoebe set the tray on the coffee table amid the candles. "And the vegetarian options are on the left for you weirdos who are tormenting yourselves in that fashion. Luckily, everything's delicious."

Rhea slapped Phoebe's hand as she reached for one of the options she'd pointed out. "If they're all so great, stick to the carnivore side, meat monger."

"*Meat* monger?"

Rhea popped a curry puff into her mouth. "If they're all so delicious, you can leave the vegetarian stuff to Ione and me."

Ione reached for one of the beef empanaditas as the words left Rhea's mouth. "Oh, I'm not doing that anymore. We have to keep meat in the house all the time for Kur, and Dev has to eat a fair amount of it himself because of his metabolism, so I kind of gave up on it."

"Gone to the dark side because of a man. Typical."

After dinner, they all struggled to make room for Phoebe's pumpkin pie accompanied by eggnog spiked with tequila and whiskey—another of Rafe's specialties. Being the heir to the Diamante Construction fortune had its perks, one of which was apparently having a massive wet bar of the finest liquors.

Rhea had just sat down with a second piece of pie when they heard a car on the drive. She tensed and threw an accusatory glance at Theia, thinking she'd gotten Laurel to come after all, but from her spot by the window, she saw the car was a MINI. She paused in midbite. Leo was driving it.

Chapter 21

Sitting across from her on the faux leather chair, Phoebe followed Rhea's glance. "Isn't that your car?"

Rhea nodded dumbly, watching as Leo's large frame somehow managed to exit the vehicle with grace. He stood beside the car, looking around as though he wasn't quite sure how he'd gotten there. Neither was Rhea.

She set down her plate and went outside. "Leo. What…?" She couldn't think of a reasonable question.

He stuck his hands in his pockets and swayed back on his heels. "I was halfway to Tucson when I just… felt wrong and had to turn back. And something led me here."

"Felt wrong? You stole my car."

Leo's eyes were defiant. "I didn't come back because I was sorry."

"So you're a jackass and you decided to come tell me that on Christmas Eve."

"No, I—I don't know why, but I had to come back."

Rhea hugged her bare arms, the cardigan abandoned inside by the warmth of the fire. "Why did you leave?"

"You want me to give up my life. For *him*."

Her stomach knotted. "You heard me talking to Phoebe. Leo, it's not that I want you to give anything up. I'm trying to help you. You need your *hugr*. And it needs you."

"Says who?" He paced away from the car, his expression pained. "I came back because the farther I drove away from you, the more the sense of wrongness overwhelmed me. Not emotionally or physically but in everything around me, as though the fabric of the world was unraveling. I've felt this before." He took a breath. "It's magical."

"Magical?" She smiled quizzically, thinking he was talking about the two of them together, but he didn't return the smile, and hers faded.

"I'm bound to you. I don't know if you did it consciously—"

"Leo, I would never—"

"Then it's her. It's Kára. She's behind this." He stepped close to her finally, and the defiant look was gone. "But if she had to bind me to someone, I'm glad it's you." He stroked Rhea's cheek with the back of his hand, making her shiver. "I won't go back, you understand. I will fight you. I will fight *him*. But I didn't like being away from you, magic or no."

She didn't know how to respond to that. Parts of it made her feet feel floaty beneath her, and parts of it felt like a threat.

But Leo didn't wait for a response. "You're freezing." He rubbed her arms and pulled her into the circle of his own. "Should we go inside? Or do you want to be alone with your family?"

Rhea shook her head, looking up into eyes as bright and blue as tumbled sea glass. She'd felt wrong too with him gone. She couldn't bear the thought of him leaving again.

"Are you guys coming in or what?" Phoebe was at the screen door. "We're about to open presents."

Rhea turned, biting her lip. "I didn't bring mine." She hadn't brought them because she hadn't bought them. Because she was flat broke.

"Sweetie, Rafe has so much money he doesn't know what to do with it. The only present we need from you is you."

After bringing Leo inside, Rhea introduced him to Rafe, who was standing just inside the living room. It was the first time she'd ever seen Rafe look shorter than anyone, which she assumed was an illusion of the sunken floor until Leo stepped down to shake his hand. Somehow, it was irrationally pleasing that Leo was taller.

"Ione and Dev you've already met," said Rhea. "And this is my…" She glanced awkwardly from Leo to Theia, remembering belatedly that they knew each other all too well.

Theia rose and held out her hand. "As you know, I'm her evil twin. Nice to see you again."

Leo studied her quizzically as he shook her hand. "Have we…?" He paused, still holding her hand as she tried to pull it back, looking embarrassed. "Ah! Theia Dawn. The one who 'swiped right.'" He pulled her hand to his lips and kissed it. "Delighted to make your acquaintance in the flesh."

Theia frowned as she withdrew her hand. She probably thought he was messing with her.

"Leo has some short-term memory problems," said Rhea. It was the easiest explanation for now.

Theia still looked suspicious, like maybe Rhea was in on whatever game Leo was playing. "You don't remember meeting me?"

Leo smiled and shrugged. "Not specifically. I am aware of who you are, though. Of how we met."

Theia glanced at Rhea, trying to gauge the situation.

"It's complicated," said Rhea. "He retains certain details, like a narrative, even if he doesn't consciously recall them as having happened to himself."

Theia nodded, clearly not convinced.

Leo put his hands in his pockets. "I'm afraid I've interrupted your gift giving." He looked around for Phoebe.

Phoebe smiled. "You didn't interrupt. We were just about to get started."

Dev offered Leo his seat on the couch as Ione brought an extra slice of pie and a glass of eggnog from the kitchen. Leo examined the glass as he sat. "What's this?"

"It's nog." Rhea grabbed her own and took her seat in the papasan, not wanting to appear like lovestruck teens who needed to sit in each other's laps and couldn't keep their hands off each other. Like certain sisters she could name.

"Nog?" Leo's eyes crinkled. "Is that like glögg?"

Rhea shook her head, taking a sip of hers. "Eggnog. It's cream and eggs with tequila and whiskey."

Leo looked askance at the glass. "Eggs?"

"Just try it. It's good. What's glögg?"

"Mulled wine," said Theia.

Leo tasted the beverage hesitantly. "Interesting." He looked up at Rafe. "This has your Peligroso in it, doesn't it?"

Rafe smiled quizzically. "How did you know?"

Dev grinned. "I made your Mexican chocolate for them the other night."

Phoebe was hauling presents out from under the tree. "Okay, enough about alcohol. Present time. Theia, this one's for you. And one for Rhea."

Rhea's was weighty…and felt like some kind of metal case. "No. No, you *didn't*." She ripped the paper off to find a full professional tattoo kit, complete with more than a dozen bottles of ink, ink cups, needles and the works. "Oh my God. You guys…" She was too choked up to thank them properly. Theia smiled at her, acknowledging the unspoken gratitude. Only Theia would have known exactly what brand Rhea preferred.

"And this one's for Leo."

Leo's expression of surprise was almost comical as Phoebe set the package in his lap. "You got me a gift?"

"Of course we did. It's Christmas. It's from all of us."

He turned the package about as though it were a foreign object. "I don't really do Christmas. I'm not a Christian."

Phoebe snorted. "Neither are we."

"Speak for yourself." Ione's tone was reproachful.

"Right. Sorry," said Phoebe. "With the exception of Ione, the high priestess of her local coven of witches, neither are we."

"Nice," said Ione. "And…not wrong." She admired the candleholder she'd unwrapped.

"So call it a Yule present," Phoebe said to Leo. "Go ahead. Open it."

Leo unwrapped the paper carefully, setting it aside before opening the plain white box. Nestled in tissue paper inside was a leather-bound book with a fancy pen.

"It's a blank book," said Phoebe. "For writing down things you want to remember. They say doing it physically with a pen and paper helps memory."

Leo smoothed his hand over the leather cover. "That's very…thoughtful." He glanced around at the others, seemingly overcome. "I don't remember ever receiving such a nice gift."

One thing Rhea had come to realize since Leo's *munr* had been freed was that he had no use for casual lying to make someone feel good. The *munr* was motivated strictly by his desires. He didn't do flattery.

Pretending to examine one of the bottles of ink, she looked down at her lap to suppress the sudden rush of feeling for him, that he was so moved by such a simple gift. And that he'd never received anything thoughtful before was a testament not to his lack of memory but to what his existence had been since the curse. His memories through Leo's experiences would have yielded that sort of detail. And his personal memories were of nothing but confinement. It made her heart ache.

Dev, standing by the breakfast bar, picked up a small gift bag from the floor. "Ione and I got you a little something else as well."

Bemused, Leo took the bag and folded back the tissue paper, pulling out a knitted scarf and a matching cap in a pale grayish-blue. He put the scarf around his neck and tugged the cap onto his head with an amused smile directed at Rhea. The cap he'd worn before had belonged to Leo the Dull. The color made the blue of his eyes pop like aquamarine gemstones.

"Rhea mentioned you'd lost a few things in the fire," said Ione. "We thought you could use a little something to keep you warm."

"But that's really just the wrapping," said Dev. "Dig deeper."

Eyebrows knitting with curiosity, Leo fished in the tissue in the bottom of the bag and pulled out a bottle of Peligroso with a red bow tied around the neck. His laugh as he held it up was the sort that made Rhea tingly.

"Thank you. Sincerely." He gripped the bottle like he'd won an Oscar. "This will indeed keep me warm."

Rhea's imbibing, meanwhile, had made her more than warm. She got up to use the bathroom, and when she came out, Theia was waiting in the hallway.

Before she could step aside, Theia steered her back in and shut the door, blocking it with her body. "Okay, *who* is that?"

"What are you talking about?"

"That is not Leo Ström. Not the Leo Ström I met. When Phoebe told me you were seeing him, I thought, 'Well, that's nice for Rhea. He's a little indecisive and aimless but very cute, and very sweet. She'll have fun with him.' But that guy…" Theia jerked her thumb over her shoulder toward the door. "He's like something out of a sexy pirate movie. He talks different, and he exudes—" Theia's cheeks colored. "He's like walking man candy."

Rhea blinked at her, stunned. "Are you actually jealous of me?"

"No, I'm not j—" Theia stopped and looked at the ceiling. "Okay, yes, in the pure abstract, I'm seething with jealousy. Not because I wish it had worked out between him and me but because I've never had anybody look at me the way he looks at you—like he worships the ground you walk on."

Rhea laughed. "Yeah, sure you haven't."

"What's that supposed to mean?"

"Oh my God, Thei. *Every* guy looked at you like that in school. You were the one they wanted to ask out. I'm the one they came to when they wanted to know whether you'd say yes if they did."

"That's not true."

"Jesus, what alternate reality were you living in?"

"That doesn't even make sense. We're identical."

"Really? You're trying to play the 'identical' card with me? Look, I'm not upset about it. I mean, sometimes I am, because it sucks being the one guys want to be friends with so they can get close to my sister who looks just like me. But it is what it is. I've never blamed you for it. We're different people. Just…own it, for Christ's sake."

Theia's arms dropped to her sides. "I had no idea you felt this way. Honestly, I never knew that was happening when we were in school. I guess maybe I was a little self-absorbed."

"Well…wake up, Cupcake." Rhea flicked Theia's forehead with her thumb and forefinger, like she would a ripe melon.

"Ow!" Theia rubbed her forehead ruefully. "My apparent superiority aside—" she jumped to the side with a grin to avoid another head flick "—quit avoiding the question. Who is that guy?"

"He's Leo Ström. Mostly."

"What do you mean, mostly?"

"He's…" Rhea lifted her shoulders with a sigh. "He's a

thousand-year-old Viking living under a Norn curse that separates his essential selves every Yuletide while his soul goes off to lead the Wild Hunt. His soul is AWOL at the moment. That's why he can't remember anything. The Norns exacted a price for his life—his mind and his will. Leo—the Leo in Phoebe's living room—is his will, and he's been trapped in a sort of limbo until I helped free him the night of the fire."

Theia leaned back against the door abruptly, her head striking it with a thud. "Wow. I—did not pick up on that on our handful of awkward dates."

"Well, you know…you're self-absorbed." Rhea grinned. "So you really think he worships the ground I walk on?"

Theia laughed. "Yeah, I really do." She shook her head, still looking a little dazed. "What are you going to do about his soul?"

"Honestly, I don't know. Neither of them seem particularly keen on reintegrating. But if he doesn't do it before Yuletide officially ends, he won't be able to do it at all."

"So the soul-Leo—"

"The *hugr*. This one's the *munr*."

"The *hugr*. Is that who I met in Flagstaff?"

"Oh, I doubt it. The *hugr*'s kind of an asshole. I assume you met the same one I did, the fully integrated Leo, except with his mind and will suppressed."

A loud knock sounded on the door. "Other people have to pee, you know." Phoebe rattled the handle.

Theia opened the door. "Don't you have another bathroom?"

"Yeah. That's why I said *people*, as in more than one peeing person. Ione's using it." She moved Theia aside. "You two are welcome to stay in here and watch me do my thing if that's what floats your boat, but I'm not waiting any longer."

Theia grabbed Rhea by the hand and headed out the door. "No, thanks. You can float your own boat…and that metaphor is really gross, Phoebes." She paused in the hallway after Phoebe shut the door. "So we're… Are we good, Rhe? I've really missed you."

Rhea shrugged, pulling her hand out of Theia's and hugging her arms. "I've missed you, too. But you're the one who shut me out."

"What?" Theia looked genuinely confused. "Rhe—"

"We never kept things from each other before. But you knew about Dad, and you knew about our other sisters, and you kept it from me. We shared everything. And now I feel like I don't even know you."

The hurt in Theia's eyes was palpable. "Rhea—"

"You can't make things right by giving me sad eyes, Theia. I'm sorry if that hurts you. But you hurt me, and you're just going to have to live with the way that makes you feel." Rhea started down the hallway but turned back before she reached the living room. "And also? I don't know who you went to for that Lilith tattoo, but they messed up the lines."

Belatedly, Theia covered the inside of her forearm with her palm, and Rhea turned and rejoined the gathering.

Chapter 22

Leo glanced over at Rhea as he drove her home after the gathering wound down. Though she'd argued the point briefly, she'd been in no condition to drive, amply demonstrated by nodding off as soon as they hit the road. He'd wanted to talk to her about the other Leo, but that would have to wait.

He chafed against the idea of being bound once again, but he had to believe her when she swore she hadn't done it herself. He had to believe her, because if she would lie to him—this beautiful contradiction of soft and hard, fierce and vulnerable, sarcastic and sensual presently slumped in the seat beside him with a bit of drool on her cheek—if she could lie to him, there was nothing worth desiring in the universe. Everything was pointless rot and decay, and he was nothing but a revenant reanimated by Kára to no purpose.

And as he'd said to her earlier, if he had to be bound to someone, he would want it to be Rhea. The new ink in Mjölnir on his right arm tingled with that sense of rightness he'd felt as she'd tattooed his skin. Skin that might have been the other Leo's by morning if not for the fire. He couldn't bear the thought of that insufferable version of him being with Rhea in his place, bound to *his* Rhea by the Valkyrie's magic. But *he* had the skin now. And he had Rhea. And even if he was a stupid, besotted fool without a soul, he wanted to be hers. The question was whether he was enough for her, or whether she would always be seeking the other. But he wasn't about to give up the skin now that he had it.

He tried to rouse her when they arrived at her apartment, managing to get her out of the car and briefly onto her feet before she went boneless and floppy and he had to pick her up and carry her inside. Leo set her on the bed, and she murmured something and curled into a ball like a cat. With a little nudging, he was able to tug the sheet from the unmade bed from beneath her. He took off her fluffy boots and covered her before removing his own boots and climbing in beside her.

Something poked his hip at his back pocket, and it wasn't his phone. Leo worked the item out of his pants— the box of condoms. He set it on the bedside table with a sigh. Eventually, he hoped, they'd actually have a chance to use them.

Rhea's sleep was uneasy. A shadowy presence followed her through dark corridors and curtained, labyrinthine places out into the night, where the streets were unlit and empty and led to an endless succession of parking lots on which the ground tilted and swayed. The unpopulated landscape eventually morphed into a macabre carnival that remained in total darkness while the presence pursued her onto carousels and Tilt-A-Whirls, always one seat behind her, no one else on the rides. The shadow seemed to have been always there, always in the background, waiting for its moment.

She woke around three to find herself in bed at home, with Leo asleep beside her. Her phone had buzzed in her pocket. Rhea got up to use the bathroom and opened the message as she sat on the toilet, yawning.

This is important. Don't delete.

What was Theia up to now?

Come to the Chapel of the Holy Cross.

What in the world? She sure as hell wasn't going to drive up to the Chapel of the Holy Cross at three in the morning.

Another message popped up before she could fire off her terse refusal. I have your fylgja.

Rhea stared at the text. What was she talking about? Had Phoebe told Theia Rafe's theory about Vixen being her *fylgja*? And how could Theia "have" Vixen? There was no way Theia could capture a Valkyrie. More to the point, why would she?

Something about the wording, beyond the oddness of the request, was off. A feeling of dread settled in her stomach. Theia? Is this you?

The screen showed a message in progress for several interminable seconds. Perhaps I should have said, "I have your doppelgänger." It's remarkable how genes dictate biological destiny, isn't it? But I suppose you have your own fingerprints. Nature is not fooled.

Rhea's thumbs were shaking as she typed. Who is this?

Let's just call me Skuld for now. A laughing emoji followed. That was an unintentional play on words. But think of me as your destiny: that which is happening. And her destiny. I see you share a tattoo.

Rhea began typing a furious reply, as if words could somehow bridge the physical distance to intimidate whoever this was, but another message interrupted.

No more talk. Do not contact anyone. Do not wake the soulless munr. Come alone.

Rhea sat trembling before getting up to pad carefully into the bedroom and grab her boots from beside the bed. Leo didn't stir. For a few panicked minutes after searching the top of the bureau she thought he must have the car keys in his pocket, but she discovered them in the living room lying on the coffee table. She let herself out quietly and descended the stairs to the parking lot to start the car, sick with anxiety while she waited for the window to defog enough to drive.

As she pulled out of her space, she saw something dark in the shadows, and her heart leaped into her throat. The presence from her dream had somehow emerged from it with her. But in the dim light of the parking lot lamps, she saw it was the wolf-dog.

Rhea hesitated. The person who'd texted her hadn't said anything about not bringing a dog. She opened the passenger door, and the animal trotted over with purpose and jumped in, making itself comfortable on the seat as though it rode with her all the time.

"Okay, dog. I don't know if you're part of Leo or what, but we're going to get my sister Theia, and I need you to be on board with this, got it?"

The dog regarded her with a patient gaze. She supposed that was all the answer she was going to get.

The darkness was almost total as she wound through the hills toward the highway, as if the dream had followed her into reality. At least the snow had stopped, though it left a chilly, damp air and a slick of ice on the road, forcing her to drive more carefully than usual, when she wanted to be reckless and fast.

"So, you're not like Vixen, are you? I mean, you don't talk, do you?" She glanced at the dog. "Then again, you look like an actual, normal wolf-dog, not a creepy, upright, oversexed fox, so I'm guessing you don't."

No response.

"I still don't know what a *fylgja* does, exactly. They say if you see your own, it's a portent of death, but you're not mine, so I'm hoping we're cool. Anyway, mine is apparently my own twin, and I've been seeing her my entire life, so I don't think that necessarily bears out."

The only sound was the soft hum of the heater and the quiet whir of the wheels against the highway.

"Maybe you have some of Leo's consciousness. I don't really get how this whole thing works. But you led me to the *hugr*, so he certainly doesn't share your consciousness while you're separate or he'd know you had. Not that I'm trying to keep it from him. You. I mean, I guess Leo knows now anyway because he heard me talking to Phoebe."

She was possibly losing it a little bit. What if this was

some random stray that happened to be hanging around her car? Rhea gripped the wheel as she turned onto the winding road leading toward the hillside into which the cross-shaped chapel was built. Wherever the dog had come from, she needed to keep talking to stave off the fear of what was happening to Theia. Who cared whether it was really Leo's *fylgja*?

"I hope you can understand that I only want what's best for you. I don't want you to be lost or broken. And Kára…who knows what she wants? I mean, she wants you, obviously. Or him. Whatever."

She'd passed through Sedona proper already and had reached the turnoff onto the twisting drive up to the hill-top where the chapel perched between red buttes that appeared gray and flat in the darkness. A gate blocked the road, apparently intended to discourage visitors after hours. Except whoever had taken Theia had obviously gotten through. Unless he'd walked all the way up the hill. Maybe that's what she should do. There weren't any other cars parked here, but Theia's kidnapper could have parked on a side road.

Rhea stopped on the shoulder and turned to the dog. "I guess this is where I get out." But as she spoke, the gate creaked in the silence and swung open. "Or not." She started through slowly, afraid someone was going to come running out to stop her, afraid something terrible was waiting on the other side. Nothing was, and no one did. Rhea continued up the hill, her high beams illuminating only the two hundred or so feet ahead of her. It was like her dreamscape.

After she'd parked at the top, Rhea sat in the car trying to breathe, trying not to be terrified. She had to be able to face this, whatever it was, for Theia.

The dog growled softly, staring at nothing.

"That's not helping, dog."

Rhea turned off the engine and clutched the pepper spray in her hand, heart battering her chest as she opened the door. The dog leaped over her, nearly giving her a heart attack, and landed on the tarmac, where it paced as if keeping guard, still softly growling. She got out. The dog flanked her. She felt a little braver with the wolf-dog beside her.

Another metal guard on a hinged post was positioned across the walkway before the chapel. The dog went over it, and Rhea went around it. The chapel was dark. What if somebody was just yanking her chain? The place was locked up tight. She turned to ask the dog its opinion, but it was gone. *Great. Abandon me now, weird* fylgja *wolf-dog.*

As she pondered the darkened chapel, one of the glass doors swung slowly open.

Rhea swallowed, her palms sweating. "Hello?"

Flickering candlelight she hadn't noticed through the tinted door illuminated the altar beneath the towering cross that formed the four panes of the far window. Someone with a familiar silhouette was seated on the front row of benches, facing the altar.

"Theia?"

A figure moved in the shadows beside the cross. "Thank you for following instructions." The figure emerged before the altar.

Rhea blinked, confused. "Mr. Dressler?"

"Please. Call me Brock. Come have a seat with your lovely doppelgänger and let's have a chat."

How could he have hidden this intent from her when she'd read him?

"The thing about second sight," said Dressler as if he'd read her mind, "is that it's painfully obvious when it's being used on someone else who also possesses it." He gestured to the pew. "Please sit. This won't take long, and I'm not interested in harming you. I just need something you have."

Rhea walked slowly up the aisle, the pepper spray cap still flipped up.

Dressler nodded toward it. "You won't need that. I promise. But keep it if it makes you more comfortable."

"If it makes *you* uncomfortable, I'm keeping it." She'd reached the front. On the pew, Theia stared ahead with a vacant expression, not bound or gagged, just…empty. "What did you do to her?"

"She's in a trance state. She'll be fine. Once I say so."

Rhea sat beside her and took Theia's hand, to no re-action. She glared daggers at Dressler. "What the hell do you want?"

"First of all, let me say how pleased I am with the tat-too." He folded back his sleeve, showing her the heal-ing ink: *I am. I think. I will.* "You do excellent work. I wouldn't be surprised if the fire turns out to have been only a momentary blip in your budding career."

"Great. You can give me five stars on Yelp."

He smiled, somehow managing to seem genuinely nice despite having abducted her sister to use as bait. Rhea fiddled with the pepper spray lid as Dressler turned to the altar and picked up some kind of short-handled blade. Maybe it was an athame, although this was the wrong kind of altar.

"What I want is very little. Just a drop of your blood."

Rhea laughed, though her skin had gone clammy. "Is that all?"

"The key is to take it with this." He held up the blade in the candlelight. The handle was a broken stick, and the hammered metal tip gleamed like gold. "It took me many years to track this down. This is the Holy Lance that pierced Christ's side on the cross. Adolf Hitler had it during the war, and afterward, it was supposed to have been returned to its reliquary in Vienna's Hofburg Palace. But I went there to acquire it shortly after the war, and I knew immediately it was a fake."

"Shortly after what war?"

"World War II, of course."

"I see. And you're…?"

"Very well preserved." Dressler grinned. "You see, I used the lance myself while it was in the Führer's possession. It was said to bestow immortality. Which may be true, since here I am. Unfortunately, a prick with it also results in an unhealable wound. And more than a prick, well…let's say Adolf wasn't long for this world anyway when he shot himself in the head." He rolled his sleeve higher, revealing a gauze bandage taped above his elbow, and pulled the tape away. The smell that emanated from what looked like a necrotic sore nearly made Rhea vomit. Dressler grimaced. "Not pretty, is it?" He covered it again, somehow masking the smell, to her relief.

"So you gave yourself a little prick and now you're rotting. What does that have to do with me?"

"You have the magic ingredient to heal the wound for good—the blood of the first demon."

"I'm pretty sure it's extremely diluted by now."

"Doesn't matter. As evidenced by the gifts you and your sisters possess, its power is still quite strong." He stepped toward her.

Rhea raised the pepper spray. "I thought you said that thing was a fake."

"This? No." Dressler turned the relic in his hand. "This I recovered several months ago with the help of a friend." He smiled. "A necromancer."

No. Effing. Way. Would that asshole never go away? "Let me guess. His name is Carter Hamilton."

"The very same. He's the one who told me about you and your six lovely sisters full of demon blood. He'd hoped to have two or three of you in his thrall by now, but he's greedy. And a bit uncouth in his magical methods. Frankly, he's nuts." He wasn't going to get any argument from her there. "Like I said, all I need is a drop."

"And you think I'm going to give you one."

"You forget I have second sight myself. I know you are."

"Why did you choose me? I mean, I'd rather you didn't choose any of us, but you already had Theia. Why didn't you take a drop from her?"

"Your twin was my first target. We ruled out the three half siblings. They have a different strain, unpredictable. And Phoebe and Ione, Carter felt, would give me too much of a fight, particularly with their dragon consorts. You two, on the other hand—you're very easy to manipulate. I don't mean that as an insult. You're just more trusting. Perhaps your older sisters have shielded you from the ugly realities of the world. Or perhaps they had it harder losing your parents in their teens. And then there was one more crucial element."

Rhea's hand was getting stiff gripping the spray can. "And what would that be?"

"The Viking."

"So you *were* stalking him."

"I wouldn't call it stalking. I learned of his existence before the war, when I was a leader in the Hitlerjugend. He was a legend. The warrior who couldn't die, cursed to lead Odin's Hunt. I saw it once, you know. Those wild horses whinnying like banshees, the ghostly riders. Their appearance changes with the time and the place. When I saw them, they looked like SS officers. They'd come for the Führer, in fact. They smelled the stench of dark magic on him. The funny thing is, Hitler didn't even believe in the relic. He'd cut himself to show it was nonsense. But as these things often go, before they could get close enough to him, he did the job himself."

Rhea's hand was cramping. "That's a lovely story. I still don't see what Leo has to do with my blood."

"It's not that he has anything to do with your blood, per se. It's that, together, his blood and your blood will give me what I need—the chance at true immortality. And I already have his. But the most important thing you did for me where Leo is concerned was separating him from his *hugr,* which is crucial to my future aims. I have plans for the *hugr.*"

Rhea finally connected the dots. "*You* set that fire."

"It was a little desperate, I admit, but I was out of time. I would have had to wait yet another year for an opportunity, and this damn wound is becoming unbearable." He took another step toward her.

Rhea stood and aimed. "If you think I'm going to let you stab me with that thing and take on an unhealable wound, you're out of your goddamned mind."

"Oh, but that's the beauty of it. Your blood mitigates the effects of the physical corruption. And I'm not going to stab you. I only need a finger prick. Which you *are* going to give me."

Rhea opened her mouth to tell him where he could shove his Holy Lance, but a smell far worse than his rotting wound suddenly filled the air, making her stomach convulse and her head swim. She grabbed for the pew to steady herself, but it was too low, and she dropped onto the seat beside Theia, who seemed unaffected by the stench.

Gagging, Rhea threw her arm over her mouth and nose. Her vision blurred and doubled as something—*shambled* was the only word for it—up the stairs from below. The hair rose on the back of her neck. She wanted to turn around, desperate not to have some hulking thing behind her she couldn't see, but the dizziness was too intense.

"He's a bit unpleasant, I admit," said Dressler. *A bit?* "But he's intensely loyal. Kurt served under me in the war, and he died doing it. But I learned how to use the Old Ways to bring him back."

"Kurt" shambled into view, a bloated, gray obscenity in the shape of a man, with putrescent flesh that looked as though it might slough off at any moment. From the dizziness and the sensation of cold in her bones, she recognized the dark presence from her dream. Rhea's stomach rebelled, and she lurched forward over the pew and vomited up her lovely Christmas Eve dinner. Which somehow managed not to smell anywhere near as awful as Kurt.

As she huddled, dry heaving, with her head between her legs, something sharp pricked her finger. She couldn't remember when the pepper spray canister had fallen out of her hand. Let him have the damn blood. She was going to die of vomiting if that nasty thing came any closer.

Dressler's blurry image wavered before Rhea, wrapping the Holy Lance carefully in a scarlet cloth. "Kurt will stay here and keep you company for a bit."

Rhea gagged out the word *no*, but he ignored her.

"I need to take care of some things, and I don't want to have to worry about where you are while I'm doing them. But once my business is handled, I'll use the spell to send Kurt back to his grave. And your sister should be back to her eternally optimistic self by daybreak. She really is charming, isn't she?" Dressler's blurry face smiled— probably. "Thank you so much for your little gift. It means the world to me." His footsteps sounded on the floor as he headed for the door. "Oh, and keep in mind, Kurt can be rather irritable. Try not to provoke him."

Rhea tried to swear at him, but she only got as far as "fuh." She had to get some distance between this thing and herself. She swayed to her feet, and Theia rose with her automatically. Rhea grabbed her hand and lurched toward the door, but the thing moved faster than it looked like it ought to be able to—hell, it didn't look like it ought to be able to move at all—and stood between them and the doorway.

"Look, Kurgh—" Rhea put her hand over her mouth and swallowed bile, focusing on the floor to try to keep it down. Against the leg of the pew across from her, the keychain with her pepper spray canister lay just two feet away. It must have slid across the aisle when she dropped it. She let go of Theia's hand and took a wavering step toward it. The creature didn't move. Rhea dove for the canister and caught herself against the pew before aiming the pepper spray at Kurt and squeezing the trigger.

The thing let out a bellow of outrage that Rhea could only describe as the sound of decaying flesh trying to swear. It lunged for her, and its clammy, putrid hand went around her throat.

The ground swayed beneath her, the chapel floor tilting like the tarmac in her dreams, and the candles lighting the altar seemed to go out. She was no longer in the chapel but in some nightmare-scape. Blighted, misshapen trees loomed and swayed around her in a foul wind, something scrabbling through their branches. And something was crawling in the creature's mouth. The dead maw opened, and roaches swarmed from it, down Kurt's cheeks and along his arms toward her.

She tried to scream, but no sound came out. And then the hand dropped from her throat, and she was back in the chapel, stumbling backward. The creature had turned toward the doorway. Someone stood in it. She couldn't focus on the figure, but something bright and metallic flashed in the figure's hand as the dead thing charged forward with that same inhuman, pulpy growl. The shiny metal swung and went clean through its neck. Kurt's rotten head tumbled onto the floor and rolled under a pew, one of the eyes sliding out of the socket with a wet sound.

Chapter 23

Rhea's vision cleared. "Leo?"

He stood holding the axe that had decapitated the thing, dressed in leather and furs and homespun flax, his hair long, two plaits braided at his temples, like Leo in Viking cosplay. "I am his *vördr*."

Damn, how many of him were there? "What's a... vorther?"

"The warden of his soul," said Leo. "The guardian. You and the other damsel are not harmed?"

"Damsel?" Rhea gave him a dubious look. "No, we're fine. At least, I think she's fine." Theia still stood motionless in the aisle. Rhea took her hand and sat her on the pew by the door.

The stench had lessened considerably, and Rhea was no longer gagging. Kurt's body was dissolving into some kind of nasty sludge.

"Thanks for stepping in when you did, though. I'm not sure what that thing was doing to me."

"Rotting your brain, I should think." Leo's *vördr* wiped the blade of the axe on his sleeve and set it in the loop on his belt. The long hair and those little braids were kind of sexy. As was the thick kohl lining his eyes. "A *draugr*'s purpose is to drive one mad."

"Well, thanks for not letting it rot my brain." She grimaced at the now gelatinous pile of goo that was left of the *draugr*. "I suppose we'd better clean this up somehow. And I kind of made a mess in front of the altar." She wasn't a practicing Catholic, but she wasn't feeling too good about desecrating a church.

"You must get your sister home. I will see to this."

Rhea was in no mood to argue. "Whatever you say." She prodded Theia up once more and stepped around the *draugr* goo but paused outside the door. "If you're the *hugr*'s guardian, why are you here? Is the Hunt nearby?"

Leo's *vördr* regarded her, a sort of hidden smile behind the crystalline blue gaze, though his expression didn't change. "It was not the *hugr* I said I watched over. I am the warden of his soul. And what is dear to it."

"Oh." The word made her unreasonably warm. She couldn't meet those intense eyes of his any longer. Rhea mumbled her thanks again and hurried Theia out. "I don't know how much of this you're going to remember tomorrow," Rhea murmured as they walked down the drive, "but you can keep that 'dear' comment to yourself, if you know what's good for you."

Once they reached the car, she guzzled a bottle of water she'd left in the pocket behind the seat, gargling and spitting out the last of it onto the roadside to get the nasty taste out of her mouth.

Theia's silence was unnerving as Rhea drove toward home, and Rhea rambled to fill in the awkwardness and keep herself awake. When she pulled into the parking lot, Leo stood on the landing in the open door of her apartment.

He scowled as she got out of the car. "Where did you go?" He paused when he saw Theia in the passenger seat and his accusatory expression turned puzzled. "Is that your sister?"

"She's in a trance," said Rhea. "Help me get her inside."

Leo moved quickly down the stairs to open the car door and scoop Theia up.

Rhea swallowed an irrational twinge of jealousy at the sight of Theia in Leo's arms. "She can walk, actually, but sure, that'll work."

He took Theia inside and set her on the couch. At least he hadn't put her in Rhea's bed. Rhea groaned inwardly, immediately feeling guilty about begrudging Theia anything. There was no telling what that creep had done to her.

"What happened?" Leo lifted one of Theia's eyelids to peer at her. "Who put her in a trance?"

"Well, you're not going to believe this. Or maybe you will. Maybe you'll say 'I told you so.' But Brock Dressler kidnapped her to get me to meet him. It turns out he's a full-on Nazi, as in actual World War II German Nazi— or at least he claims to be—and he wanted my blood. He says the trance is supposed to wear off by daybreak."

Leo looked baffled. "Who the hell is Brock Dressler?"

"Jesus. Are we doing this again? We went through this the other night. The Nazi you punched. Sorry—that Leo the Dull punched."

"Oh. No, I remember him. I remember punching him, anyway. Or I remember *him* punching him." Leo slumped onto the couch next to Theia and brushed his hand through his unkempt hair in a way that seemed to belong wholly to the other Leo. "It's exhausting trying to keep this straight. Thank the gods I won't have to try to figure out if I'm remembering my own life anymore." He didn't seem to notice her frown. "So why would this Nazi want your blood? And how did you manage to get away from him without giving it to him?"

"He said it would make him immortal. Or heal the consequences of the relic he used to try to make himself immortal. I'm not sure whether it was supposed to add to the immortality part. But I didn't get away. He stabbed my finger." The adrenaline that had been keeping her going abruptly deserted her as she held out the insulted finger, and she wobbled on her feet.

Leo leaped up. "*Älskling*, I'm sorry. *You* should be sitting down." He led her to the couch, and Rhea sank onto it gratefully. Leo examined her finger prick. "That's it? He abducted your sister and put her in a trance just to poke your fingertip?"

"Maybe he was testing my blood sugar level." Rhea laughed at the absurdity, and the tiredness made the laugh sound a little hysterical.

Leo frowned. "Why didn't you wake me? Why would you go off on your own to face some lunatic?"

"He said he'd hurt Theia if I didn't come alone." Rhea jumped up again. "Dammit, I forgot. I have to warn your *hugr*. I think Dressler's going to do something to him."

Leo's face was stony. "He's not *my hugr*. Why is it your responsibility what happens to him? Can't he take care of himself?"

"He needs to know what he's up against. It's my fault Dressler has some kind of power over him." Rhea headed for the door, but Leo stepped in front of her with his arms folded. "Get out of my way, Leo."

"You're not going anywhere except back to bed. You can barely keep your eyes open."

"Don't tell me what I'm going to do."

"You would rather be with *him*, is that it?"

Rhea growled in frustration. "When are you going to stop being so damned competitive with your own freaking soul?"

After staring her down for a moment longer, Leo sighed and stepped aside. "Do what you want, then, but you're on your own. Somebody needs to stay here to watch over your sister."

Even though the intent was to be spiteful and sabotage her efforts to save his *hugr*, she couldn't help but be touched by his concern for Theia. "No, you're right. Thank you, Leo. I'll be back as soon as I find him and give him the message."

Leo stared openmouthed as she went out. He obviously hadn't expected her to call his bluff.

Getting back into the car right now was the last thing she wanted to do, but whether he wanted to acknowledge his *hugr* or not, Leo's life hung in the balance. And Rhea was the reason he was vulnerable.

Rhea waited after starting the engine, hoping to see the wolf-dog nearby. No such luck. She figured she'd drive the same stretch of highway where she'd seen the Hunt before, and if she didn't find it there, she'd go back to the paddock.

But after driving for almost an hour, her plan seemed a little less certain. She was bone tired, and there was no sign of the Hunt and no sign of that stupid road she was sure she'd turned down last night—or two nights ago, technically, since it was now Christmas morning. She was about to give up when her phone rang. Thank the goddess for psychic sisters. It was exactly the person she needed.

"Phoebe. I was just about to call you."

"Is Theia with you?" Phoebe's voice was raspy with sleep and worry. "I got up to get some water, and she wasn't in her room, and her car is gone—"

"She's fine, just got into a tiny fender bender. She's asleep at my place."

"Your place? Where are you?"

"I'm on Dry Creek near Boynton Pass, and I could use some magical help from you and Rafe."

"Magical? Right now?"

"The deadline for saving Leo's soul got moved up, and I need to know how to find a wraith."

"What do you mean you need to find Rafe?" Phoebe was still half-asleep.

"Not Rafe, a *wraith*." A shuffling noise followed before Rafe apparently took over the phone.

"Hey, Rhea. What's up?"

"I need to find the Wild Hunt. I thought maybe you'd know how to seek out a wraith since you can command shades."

"I *can* command them, but I don't, generally. I prefer to respect their autonomy. But a wraith is different. They're something between living and dead. Cursed souls. I assume it would require a special ritual to summon one, and I'm afraid it's not one I'm familiar with."

But Rhea had accidentally summoned one before.

"I think I might know how to do that, actually. Do you have any idea where I would find pristine snow?"

"Pristine snow? I guess it would have to be somewhere no one's been since the snow fell. Probably just about any hiking trail, since it's not light out yet and the last snowfall was just a few hours ago."

"Perfect, thanks."

"Do you need any help?"

"No, I think I've got this. Tell Phoebe not to worry about Theia. I'll bring her back in the morning."

Boynton Canyon Trail was just up the road. Rhea parked at the trailhead and grabbed the fish-scaling knife out of the glove compartment—rescued from the wreckage of her shop—and gave it a scrub with her hand sanitizer. It would have to do.

The snow-covered trail was as pristine as she could have hoped for. Rhea chose a spot where the snow was thick enough to qualify as a "bank" and crouched to pull up her legging, steeling herself for the cut. She watched her breath fog in the air. Damn, it was cold out here. And absolutely beautiful. Snow blanketed the surrounding scrub brush and the branches of the cottonwood trees in a lacy rime that made her feel like she was in a fairy realm.

She took a deep breath and put the edge of the blade to the tattoo. Here went nothing. Rhea made a shallow nick, just enough to get the blood dripping.

The first drop struck the snow, and then a second, but nothing happened. She wasn't sure exactly what she was expecting. Maybe she needed to be touching the— Rhea swallowed. Something was watching her.

She clutched her keys, standing slowly. A pair of eyes glowed at her through the snow-laced trees, low to the ground. Maybe it was a coyote. She didn't want to have to pepper spray a coyote. It moved between the low branches, and Rhea held her breath, but as it emerged from the brush onto the trail some yards ahead of her, she saw the curled-over tail. Rhea heaved a sigh of relief and hurried after the *fylgja*.

Snow clouds hung low around the sandstone formations up ahead, wispy forms moving like mist, increasing the otherworldly aura of the place—as well as the chill. Rhea had forgotten to wear gloves. She put her hands in her pockets and hurried on. The wolf-dog had disappeared around a turn of the trail.

"If you've come to persuade me to return to the skin, you have wasted your time."

Rhea nearly jumped out of hers. Not two feet in front of her, "Gunnar" sat mounted on his spectral horse.

She shivered and found her voice. "I came to warn you. That 'sad little braggart' you thought was so inconsequential? He's coming after you with a piece of the Holy Lance."

"No weapon can harm me. I am made of spirit, not flesh."

"Apparently, this one can. It's imbued with your *líka-mr*'s blood—and mine—and he means to use it to steal your immortality."

Gunnar smiled. "I appreciate the warning, but I have things well in hand." Gunnar held his hand down to her as a distant hunting horn sounded. "Would you like to see?"

"Would I like to—?" Rhea let out a squeal of surprise when he clasped her arm and hoisted her in the air to toss her onto the horse behind him.

"Hold fast to me" was the only warning she got before the phantom mare thundered into the frigid air.

Rhea shrieked, throwing her arms around Gunnar and clinging tight as they galloped over nothing but currents, charging into the mist. The clouds shifted and swirled into the roiling, surf-like thunderheads she'd seen the Hunt ride in on before, and the ghostly horde appeared before them, cowboy-Viking wraiths shouting war cries and spectral hounds baying eagerly, on the scent of their prey.

Gunnar spurred his horse onward to take the lead, and in the pale, predawn light, Rhea saw the object of their pursuit. As they thundered onto the desert floor, the hunting party had effectively herded him into the box canyon—a human rider on an ordinary horse. Gunnar's horse touched ground and galloped toward him, and the hunted man turned his mount to face them.

Brock Dressler's pretentious smile greeted them as if he were out for a morning ride.

Rhea grabbed Gunnar's arm. "It's a trap."

He ignored her warning and dismounted, drawing his sword as he advanced. "Pray to your gods, mortal, for today you meet them."

"I'm well prepared." Dressler dismounted and drew his own weapon, the gold gleaming in the soft ruby glow of imminent dawn. "Though I'm not so certain you are."

Rhea leaned forward, clinging to the phantom's mane. "Don't let him touch you with it!"

Dressler glanced in her direction, evidently surprised to see her there. "I suppose I might have saved myself the time and trouble of luring you if I'd factored in the intensity of your devotion. Could have just collected what I needed from you here, eh?"

"You will collect nothing but your just reward." Gunnar raised his sword, powerful arm drawn back, but

Dressler dodged as he swung, darting forward before Gunnar's arm could change course.

"No!" The word burst out of her as the relic made contact with Gunnar's side, the blade cutting deep. Rhea made an awkward, fumbling dismount from the horse, landing on her ass, and picked herself up to run to him.

But he'd caught Dressler by the ear and was lifting him off the ground with one hand, apparently unaffected. "Your crude talisman is useless against me." Slapping Dressler on the side of his head with the flat of his sword, Gunnar dazed him and swung the smaller man like a shot put. Dressler landed with a startled grunt on Gunnar's horse, scrambling for a hold on the mane. With a smooth, running leap, Gunnar swung back into his saddle behind him and raised his sword in the air. "For Odin and Freyja!"

A victory cry rang out from the spectral horde, an unearthly whooping and howling that made the hairs rise on the back of Rhea's neck.

Gunnar tipped his hat to her with a wink of one glowing blue eye. "Many thanks for your help." He raised his sword once more. "To Náströnd!"

"Wait! What about your *munr*? Your *líkamr*? You can't just leave!" But the wraiths were galloping into the air, their ghostly edges gilded by the dawn as the thunderheads closed around them.

Chapter 24

The trance state had rendered Rhea's sister highly suggestible. When Leo asked if she might want to lie down, she'd gotten up and gone into the bedroom, where he'd covered her with a blanket, leaving the door open a wedge so he could see in from the living room in case her condition changed.

A knock on the door woke him sometime later, and he realized he'd dozed on the couch. He jumped up to open it, thinking it was Rhea and not stopping to wonder why Rhea would be knocking on her own front door.

An unremarkable fellow with brown hair buzzed short at the sides smiled at him when he opened the door. "Leo Ström. Just the man I wanted to see."

Leo tilted his head. Had he met this man while Leo the Dull held the reins?

The visitor held out his hand. "We met at the genetics in biotech conference. Brock Dressler."

Leo took the hand automatically before the significance of the name struck him, and something passed from Dressler's palm to his. Something invisible. And magical. Leo stumbled back, staring at his palm, his reflexes slowing along with his thought processes.

"What did you...?"

"It's a simple spell, designed to give you temporary mild euphoria." Dressler stepped inside. "There's something I need from you."

Leo's tongue felt heavy. "You took... Rhea's blood."

"That's right."

"Now you want mine."

"Not precisely. I already took your blood. Remember when we ran into each other the other day? I provoked you on the street." Dressler smiled. "You don't really think I'd have stood there and let you punch me in the face if it wasn't my plan?"

Leo looked down at his knuckles. He remembered that punch. It was very satisfying. And he remembered something else.

"You put up those posters. With the...sharp blades."

"A fail-safe measure in case the first plan didn't pan out." He was full of shit. The punch had been lucky happenstance.

Leo tried to stay focused. "What do you want?"

"Something you don't even want." Dressler took an object wrapped in red silk cloth from inside his coat. "Your soul."

Leo laughed. "The *hugr*? You can have the damn thing. But it's not here."

Dressler slowly unwrapped the cloth. "As it turns out,

it *is* here. It's your *hamr* that currently rides in Odin's Hunt, an astral projection of your physical form. The *hugr* has remained within the skin. The Norns' curse suppresses the mind and the will by default. It's only during the dark hours of Yuletide that they awaken."

Leo shook his head. "How do you know any of... You know the curse?"

"I've been studying you for many years." He unfolded the last corner of the cloth, revealing a jagged piece of ancient wood topped with a gold-plated spear tip. "The Holy Lance would have given me what I needed long ago, but your blood was insufficient. It needed a catalyst. And then a friend of mine turned me on to the Carlisle sisters' stash of original demon blood. Theia's, it turned out, was inert. I put her in your path to see if it would spark something, but you didn't respond to her. There was something special, however, about her twin's magic. Something intimately tied into her art. So I sold her the ink I'd blended, which already had some of your blood in it along with the ash of Eyjafjallajökull from the land where you were meant to die."

"Iceland?" Leo shook his head. "I was wounded in the Battle of Sulcoit on the island of Éire."

"That's all the Valkyrie told you, no doubt. I suppose she failed to mention the second mortal wound you received in the Battle of Haugsnes that sealed your fate. She seems to have left out a great many things for her own convenience." Dressler moved without warning, and Leo's reflexes were too slow to respond. The artifact plunged into his gut, and he stumbled against Dressler with a grunt of surprise. "Such as the fact that the *hugr* remains within your skin."

"You—son of a whore." Leo gripped Dressler's forearm, too late to stop the blade but determined not to let him yank it out. But there was something beyond pain here, some sense of wrongness spreading inside him— like the wrongness that made him turn back when he'd tried to leave Rhea, but far worse. "What are you doing?"

"Relieving you of your burden." Dressler shoved him off the blade, and blood seeped from the open wound. Leo fell to his knees. "Your soul is mine now. And Odin's Hunt will ride to do my bidding."

The icy first light of dawn spilled in through the open doorway as Leo slumped to the floor, illuminating the blood soaking into the carpet. Rhea was going to lose her deposit. *Dammit.* He'd really wanted to stay with Rhea. Now he couldn't even say goodbye.

"Leo?"

She was standing over him, soft gray eyes wide.

"You're here." He smiled, holding his hand up to her. "I thought you'd gone."

"Oh God! Leo, what happened?" She knelt beside him, hands pressed against the hole in his gut, the pain making him abruptly alert. It wasn't Rhea after all but her dark-haired twin.

She had to hike back out of the canyon on her own, leading the abandoned horse as far as she could, and ended up calling Phoebe again to have Rafe come take the animal to his stables. Rhea drove home, exhausted and resigned—and feeling guilty because a part of her was relieved. The thought of losing the *munr*, even though it meant having Leo whole, had begun to make her increasingly unhappy. It wasn't just that she'd miss his unfettered desire, it was the way he said what he was thinking without trying to hide his feelings or his thoughts, the way he experienced things so deeply and purely—the way he laughed. Not having a soul somehow made him more human than anyone she'd ever known.

When she pulled into the parking lot to find Theia waiting on the landing looking fully alert, Rhea jumped out and hurried up the stairs. "Thei! I'm so glad you're okay. And I'm so sorry I've been such a bitch…" Her voice trailed off at the look on Theia's face as she drew closer. There were tearstains on her cheeks. "Theia?"

"Did you find his soul?"

"I talked to him, but he wouldn't… Theia, what's going on?"

Fresh tears streamed down Theia's cheeks. "You'd better go in."

A sick feeling settled over her as she opened the door. The carpet was stained with blood.

"Leo?" Rhea felt her own blood drain from her cheeks as she ran to the bedroom. "Leo, are you here?"

It took her a moment to understand. Faye sat on the side of the bed, lengths of blue silk draping the floor and flowing red locks draping the recumbent figure whom Rhea's mind refused to recognize. He lay with a sheet covering the lower half of his body, his hair dark with sweat and his skin gray and clammy. Bloody bandages were taped over his abdomen, and his hands were at his sides, covered by the sheet. It was only the tattoo of the serpent around his upper arm that demanded she acknowledge his identity.

"Leo?"

Faye raised her head, her cheeks damp and her eyes sorrowful. "With his *hugr* gone, I can finally be with him. And yet still he does not know me."

Rhea stood paralyzed in the doorway. "His *hugr*... I tried to convince him to come back, but—"

"You tried to convince the *hamr*. A projection of the physical self. Like a *fylgja*, but with more agency. I tried to keep him safe from the Norns by hiding the *hugr* within him, even from himself. Even though it meant I must be banished from him whenever he *was* himself. Rejoining his other selves would have returned him to the curse but would have protected him."

"Protected him? From what? What happened?"

"There have been many who have sought his power of immortality over the centuries. Men like that vile little worm, Brock Dressler. But I have no dominion over living men. Only through the Hunt can we rid the world of them and only through the power of the Chieftain. And this man—this *worm*—has stolen his *hugr*. I felt it as soon as it happened. I knew immediately the one we were hunting was like the Chieftain, a projection acting as a decoy while his true self attacked my Leo. I left the Hunt to come to his side, but I was too late. Unless I take him to Valhalla, the wound will fester and corrupt, killing him without killing him. He will eventually become *draugr*."

Rhea's skin went cold. "No. No, we have to do something. What can we do? Can't the Norns heal the wound?"

"And what price would they exact this time? They have taken his will and his mind. In punishing me, they have punished him for more than a thousand years. To save him from death yet again, in defiance of the laws I've broken, they would have nothing less than his heart." Faye began to sob. "And I would give it to them. I would give them anything, but it is not mine to give."

The words delivered a hollow victory: *because it's mine*. Leo's heart belonged to Rhea—and she was losing him. And yet it was obvious the Valkyrie's love for him was genuine. Rhea put her hand on Faye's shoulder, and Faye gripped it, lowering her head. As her weeping grew silent, Leo's labored breathing seemed frighteningly loud.

A soft knock on the doorframe broke the silence. Rhea turned to see Theia beckoning to her.

"What is it?" She slipped her hand out of Faye's and came to the door.

"There's someone outside you need to see."

Rhea followed her, puzzled by the odd phrasing, until she saw who was waiting for her in the parking lot. An extremely healthy version of Leo in traditional Viking attire leaned against her car, dwarfing it. Though she knew it wasn't her Leo, the sight of him, whole and hale, made her heart skip a beat.

"I have made a grave error." He pushed away from the car, and the little MINI rocked under the easing of his weight. "Though it is one I would make again if given the choice between your sanity and my existence."

"I'm not sure what you…" She seemed to lose her train of thought when looking at this Leo.

"I left the soul unguarded to protect you. I walked right into the trap that had been set for me."

"I think we all did."

"There is a recourse, however. If you are willing."

Rhea leaped upon the little ray of hope. "Of course I'm willing. What is it? What do I need to do?"

"You must convince the *hamr* of its true nature. The one known as the Chieftain who leads the Hunt. Once it recognizes itself for what it is, the *hamr* can seek his enemy to retrieve the soul and return with it to rejoin the *líkamr*."

The fleeting ray of hope dimmed. "I couldn't even convince the *hamr* to return when we both believed it was the *hugr*."

"That is why you could not convince it. The *hamr* perceives itself as the essence of the being that is Leo Ström. It believes you have freed it to dwell in its purest form. But the longer it remains apart from the physical body, the weaker it will become, until it simply fades away."

"Wouldn't it be more likely to believe this coming from you?"

"The guardian can only be seen by someone other than the self. All I can do is watch out for the *hugr*. And I have failed at that."

"What about Faye? Kára, I mean. She knows him best. She rides beside him in the Hunt."

"The Valkyrie is the one who convinced the *hamr* of its own authenticity. Her magic prevents him from seeing otherwise." Warden-Leo took her hand. His form, though it appeared physical, turned out to be not quite solid after all. His touch felt like an electrical field buzzing across her flesh. "What I ask of you, dear one, is great, but you are our only hope."

Rhea nodded, not trusting her voice to ask the question she needed to ask, but the *vördr* seemed to know it already.

"You need not seek the *hamr* on your own. I can lend you the *hamingja*, the embodiment of the soul's luck. It will reside within you. The *hamingja* will take you to the *hamr*. And it will tell you what to do when the time is right."

Rhea swallowed. "Okay. So how do we…?"

Still holding her hand, he stepped in close and slid his other not-quite-corporeal palm against her nape and kissed her. As with the vision of the climax she'd had with Leo's *munr* that time in the chair, the *vördr*'s kiss nearly knocked her off her feet. It was like kissing a live wire—not a painful sensation but unbearably wild with energy—her mouth felt as though it were having an orgasm all on its own.

When he let go of her, a sense of relief warred with a longing for it not to have ended. She opened her eyes to discover the *vördr* had disappeared.

Behind her, Theia coughed politely. "So…who was that, exactly?"

Rhea's first attempt to answer resulted in nothing but a raspy, high-pitched squeak. She cleared her throat and tried again. "Leo's warden spirit. He was at the chapel with us. I take it you don't remember any of that."

"Not a bit, no."

"It's probably better that you don't." Inside her head, she sensed a thought that wasn't her own. *Go back to the paddock.* "I have to go."

"Go? Go where? Don't you want to…to be with Leo when…?"

"He's not dying. Or he is, sort of, but his bodily functions won't stop. It's part of the curse. I have to get his soul back."

Chapter 25

A light snow fell on mostly empty streets. The few other drivers, probably on their way to celebrate with family, smiled at Rhea as they passed. Instinctively—though it was the *hamingja*'s instinct and not her own—she knew Gunnar would be keeping close to the paddock. It was only his second day as an independent being, and with the vanishing of the rest of the Hunt at daybreak, he would be on his own without a plan or a place to sleep.

Sure enough, when she arrived at the paddock, he was there. Leaning against the fence in his Western attire, he had his arms crossed over the top rail as though watching invisible livestock. Which maybe he was.

Gunnar turned at the sound of her car door opening and gave her a pleased but quizzical smile as she approached. "Fair Rhea. How did you know I would be here?"

"Just had a feeling."

"Your company is welcome, but you must understand there is nothing you can say to persuade me to return."

"I'm not here to persuade you."

Gunnar looked skeptical. "You are not?"

Rhea stepped up to the fence beside him and hooked her arms over it, gazing at the nonexistent herd. "I was hoping to engage your services."

"My services?" Gunnar returned to his earlier pose, mimicking her stance, and watched her with amusement. "And how can I be of assistance?"

"I need to track down an immortal Nazi."

"If you mean the one who sought my power, he is hardly immortal. He is presently a denizen of the underworld. He cannot escape it."

"I hate to tell you this, but the guy you took this morning was a decoy. The real Dressler is still at large. And now he's immortal."

"Impossible." Gunnar rested one booted foot on the bottom rail of the fence. "He needed my life force to achieve immortality, and he failed in trying to acquire it."

"Did he really seem like he was trying all that hard?"

"He was a weak, ineffectual man."

"That may be true, but he had a plan. He managed to finagle blood out of your *likamr*, kidnap my sister to lure me to him so he could steal my blood, use a *draugr* to keep me there while he went off to steal your *hugr*... and then just let you corner him and box his ears and take him to hell?"

Gunnar's frown said he was troubled by her logic, but he wasn't persuaded yet. "He commanded a *draugr*?"

"A real nasty one. I mean, I suppose they're all

nasty…" She let her words trail off, trying not to think of Leo's body rotting away.

"But I remain free. How can he have become immortal without my life force?"

Rhea turned to look him in the eye. "You don't have any life force. You're a decoy. Just like the man you defeated this morning."

Gunnar shoved away from the railing, his eyes glowing with offense. "Nonsense. I am the Chieftain, leader of the Hunt. Every night during Yuletide for ten centuries I have left the skin of Leo Ström to lead it. I am the *hugr*. I am no decoy."

"So you're made of spirit, not of flesh."

"Of course I am."

"Take off your shirt."

"I beg your pardon?"

"I want to see if you have Leo's tattoos on your spirit skin."

"What difference does that make?"

"Don't be a pussy. Just take off your shirt." It wasn't her favorite insult—as someone who happened to own a pussy, she thought they were pretty great, actually—but it seemed to be effective on thousand-year-old Viking pride.

Eyes flashing with anger instead of the preternatural glow, Gunnar took off his coat and hung it on one of the fence posts before unbuttoning the shirt and tossing it at Rhea.

Jesus. Those abs. She almost forgot why she'd wanted him to take off the shirt.

The ink was replicated as thoroughly as every other delicious part of Leo's skin. Rhea traced her fingers over the lines of the snake, and Gunnar shivered. Not very spirit-like. She pressed her palm to the ink and held the question in her mind: *Is this spirit or is this flesh?*

The snake began to uncoil. It was all she could do not to yank her hand away. Rhea had never experienced a vision like this. As it writhed beneath her hand, the ink became bumpy—*scaly*—a tactile, 3-D tattoo. Suddenly, she understood. The mark Faye had placed on Leo's skin was meant to keep not just the *munr* but the *hugr* bound to the skin. It was how she'd fooled the Norns. But it was also the home of the curse itself, the Jörmungandr energy Leo had so feared. Just as it would have on Leo's flesh, the mark was becoming manifest in the *hamr* through her—her connection to Leo through ink and blood. She was calling it forth, summoning the snake more surely than she had summoned the first vision of the Hunt.

Gunnar stepped back, breaking the connection. "What are you doing?" His eyes had gone from blue to a vivid aquamarine, the irises variegated with dark lines like fissures in marble, pupils elongated into vertical slits. Was it wrong that she was finding a bare-chested, cowboy-hat-wearing version of Leo with snake eyes super hot?

"Shifting your shape, apparently. Because you're *hamr*, not *hugr*. You're a projection of Leo's flesh. You are *not* spirit."

The *hamingja* gave her a mental fist bump.

Gunnar paced away from her, blinking his eyes, blinking away the shift. "If I am not spirit…where in the Allfather's name is the *hugr*?"

"Dressler stabbed Leo with the Holy Lance and took it. Leo's body is dying. Without it, Faye says he'll become *draugr*."

Gunnar's brow furrowed. "Faye?"

"It's the name Kára goes by now. She's at Leo's bed-side."

"Kára. So that is where she went. Yesterday, we spent the day together. I thought we might today, but she never returned."

Rhea tried to shake off the little sting of unexpected jealousy. This wasn't Leo. It was only the physical pro-jection of his form. He could spend his time with whom-ever he pleased.

"Leo's *vördr* said you'd know where to find Dressler—the real one."

He looked at her sharply. "You say he has acquired the blood of Leo Ström. If this man has also stolen the *hugr* of the rightful Chieftain, he will have rejoined his *hamr* in Náströnd, the Shore of Corpses, where the souls of those taken by the Hunt are relegated. He means to trap the *hugr* there to seal his immortality." Gunnar's eyes darkened. "It will also make him the leader of the Hunt."

"Shore of Corpses?" Rhea shuddered. "He can go there?"

"As an immortal, he can."

"And can you follow him?"

"Until the *hugr* is bound and I become nothing but the echo of a dying mortal man, yes." Gunnar took off the cowboy hat, looking defeated, and dropped it in the snow. Rhea watched, puzzled, as he braced one hand against the fence and removed his boots and socks. When he unzipped his pants, she cleared her throat.

"Uh…what exactly are you doing?"

"Preparing to follow the whoreson." Without the slightest bit of self-consciousness, he stepped out of his pants and his briefs and laid them over the rest of his clothes on the fence. "I will need your assistance."

Rhea tried to keep her eyes on his face. "With… what?"

"Releasing the snake."

"Excuse me?"

"To go below, I must take on the form of one who moves among the dead. Your touch upon the mark of the snake seemed to spark the change. If you would…?" He turned his tattooed shoulder toward her.

"Oh. Right." Rhea laid her hand over the ink once more, and the 3-D sensation of movement began immediately.

His eyes were changing, and as he stepped back, a transformation had definitely come over him, but for the moment, he still had the appearance of a man. And his expression was sad.

"I'm sorry."

He tilted his head. "For what?" It was becoming difficult to look at him as the perception shifted, like a lenticular print being tilted in the light.

"That you had to find out you weren't *hugr*."

Gunnar shrugged, resigned. "One cannot fight destiny." In the next instant, he coiled to the ground, no longer a man, but a massive serpentine reptile as thick as the man's waist, with a spiked head and short, lizard-like limbs—the Jörmungandr tattoo come to life, a sea serpent on land with a dragon's legs.

The aquamarine eyes blinked one last time as if to say goodbye before it slithered away into a crevice in the rocks.

Rhea turned to head back to her car with a feeling of vague unease. If Gunnar couldn't get the *hugr* back, what then? How would she even know what had happened in the underworld? An insistent thought reminded her that the *hamingja* was still with her: *Perhaps you know of someone else who moves among the dead.* Of course she did.

Ione answered her call with a cheerful, "Merry Christmas!" Apparently, Phoebe hadn't told her about Theia yet. Or any of this.

"Okay, don't freak out, but—"

"Rhea Iris Carlisle." She'd done an instant switch into mom-voice. "How many times have I told you not to lead with that if you don't want me to freak out?"

"Sorry. But you're going to freak out. And…just don't."

"Rhea—"

She delivered the words in a single, rapid breath before Ione could interrupt her. "Theia was kidnapped and put in a trance by a Nazi dickweed, but she's fine now, and I need to borrow Kur to get my boyfriend's soul back."

"Theia was…? What… Nazi? Rhea!"

"I told you, she's fine now. He just wanted to lure me to his altar so he could swipe some of my blood to help make himself immortal."

"This is Christmas, not April Fool's." Ione's voice said she was about to hang up.

"I'm not joking. Any more than Phoebe was joking that night when she tried to tell you that you were dating a necromancer."

That got her attention. "Where is Theia now?"

"She's at my place with Leo. The Nazi who burned down my shop stabbed him and took his soul, and now Leo's shape-shifting astral projection is seeking him in the Viking underworld, and I need someone who can move among the dead."

A button clicked on Ione's phone. "I'm putting you on speaker. Dev's here. Tell him what you need."

"Hello, Rhea. Happy Christmas."

"You know you're not Christian, right?" She couldn't resist teasing him even in the middle of this. Or maybe teasing made her feel less like freaking out herself.

"Ione likes Christmas, so it's Christmas. What do you need me to do?"

"I need Kur. When he's inside his cage, he's in the underworld, right? And he can go anywhere in it?"

"In essence, yes."

"Can you communicate with him?"

"To some degree, but mostly it's a shared sense of emotion."

"Oh." Maybe this wasn't going to work after all.

"But Rafe can command him. We've discovered Ione can call his shade from the cage without releasing him physically into our world. And once he's shade-walking, he's in Rafe's domain."

Awesome. Might as well make it a family affair.

When they'd gathered at Ione's place, Rafe stripped down to his briefs to conjure the quetzal power, spreading his gorgeous wings that stretched the width of the living room, the tattoo of Quetzalcoatl on his back expanding with them, becoming a second skin. Ione had to coax Kur's shade from Dev before Rafe could see it, and Rhea was afraid he wouldn't come, until Rafe began to talk to the invisible dragon.

"Sorry to disturb you, my friend, but I have a favor to ask of you. I need you to find someone in Mictlan—in the Realm of the Dead."

"Gunnar called it the Shore of Corpses," Rhea put in.

Rafe nodded patiently. "Shore of Corpses or Mictlan from my own tradition, the demon will perceive it as equivalent to his own underworld." He turned his focus back to the dragon's shade. "I need you to seek another dragon. A serpent. One projected by a living man who is of this realm." Silence followed as Rafe listened intently, frowning, before he spoke again, addressing Rhea. "He says he already knows of this man and that there are two dragons."

"Two?"

"'The dragon who gnaws is loose,' he says. I don't know what that means, but it sounds like the two are fighting."

Nidhöggr. The name came to her with certainty. *Malice Striker. The dragon that gnaws at the roots of Yggdrasil and feeds on the bones of the dead. Náströnd is his domain.*

"I need to go to him." This was what she had to do. The *hamingja* was insistent. "I need to go to the Shore of Corpses."

Ione rose from the couch. "We are *not* putting you into a magical coma so you can leave your body to go to the underworld." It was how Dev had gone below to release Phoebe's soul when Carter had sent it there, a risky move that had almost cost them both Phoebe and Dev.

"But I can help him."

Rafe rolled his shoulders, and the wings disappeared. "I'm sorry, Rhea. I can't be a party to that."

Dev inhaled sharply, as if breathing in the shade, and shook his head. "Neither can we."

Beside Dev, Ione took his hand, her expression sympathetic but firm. They were a united front against her.

"I can help you."

The others turned swiftly, startled by the sudden appearance of the redhead inside Ione's foyer, but Rhea was becoming used to her pop-up entrances.

Dev took a step toward her, his golden-brown eyes going a little dragony. "Who the devil are you?"

"She's the Valkyrie." Rhea regarded her with skepticism. "How can you help? Leo's *vördr* says you're the one who kept the *hamr* from understanding his nature."

"Of course I did. How else would I have kept his *hugr* from Wyrd?" Faye smoothed a plait of hair over her shoulder. "Be that as it may, I can escort you into Náströnd. But there is a price." Naturally. There was always a price.

"And what would that be?"

"It must be negotiated there."

Ione folded her arms. "You tell her the price now or she's not going."

Rhea gave her a warning look. "Back off, Di."

Ione's eyes widened with surprise. She was used to being the final authority in the Carlisle family.

"As long as it doesn't mean giving up my soul or staying forever on the Shore of Corpses," said Rhea, "I'm in."

Faye gave her a slight smile, the first since she'd seen her at Leo's bedside. "It will be within your power to give. No souls or lives will be asked of you."

Rhea nodded. "All right. Let's go."

Ione stepped toward her. "Rhea—"

But whatever she was going to say, Rhea never heard. Faye touched her hand and the room winked out.

Chapter 26

They stood on the shore of a dark subterranean lake.

"Watch your step."

Rhea glanced down and leaped backward from the writhing snakes covering the ground, nearly sliding into another coil of them on the rocks behind her.

She steadied herself against Faye, swallowing the urge to scream. "This was not in the brochure."

Faye pulled up her fur hood, glancing up. "And watch your head."

Globs of something black and snotty-looking dangled from the stone ceiling, slowly dripping to the ground like thick molasses. Where it struck the snakes, they hissed and writhed as if the stuff burned.

"Nidhöggr's poison."

Rhea hunched her shoulders. "How am I supposed to avoid that? I don't have a hood."

Faye sighed and removed the coat, giving it to Rhea. In its place, a more Valkyrie-like horned helmet appeared on Faye's head, leather body armor and gauntlets replacing her flowing dress. Girl was looking badass.

Rhea shrugged the coat on quickly, narrowly missing a drop of poison that slid off the fur as though deflected by it. "So how do we find Gunnar?"

"Ask the corpses."

"What cor—?" Rhea swallowed. The waves on the churning lake had grown more defined. That wasn't water. It was, as the name should have warned her, a lake of decomposing bodies.

Those still in one piece rose up from the churn, and some climbed onto the shore, slouching closer. "Whom do you seek?" They spoke as one, and the sound from the decaying mouths reminded her of the *draugr*'s roar. These, at least, were well beyond the bloating stage of decomposition and smelled more of dank, rotting plant matter than rotting flesh.

Rhea glanced at Faye. "Gunnar?"

"Nidhöggr," said the Valkyrie. "We seek the Malice Striker."

The corpses creaked and shuffled as they raised their arms together and pointed into the darkness toward a passage thick with snakes.

Faye pressed a weapon into Rhea's hand—a battle-axe that had appeared at her side, the sharp curve of the blade carved with intricate runes. "You must go alone from here."

"*What?* Wait—"

"I have brought you as far as I can. This is not my realm."

"Well, what am I supposed to do?"

"That you must figure out for yourself."

"What about the price? You said we had to negotiate."

The Valkyrie answered without any of her usual sly smiles and affectations. "Leo is the price."

Angry heat rushed to Rhea's face. "You said no souls and no lives."

"Not his life. Him. The Norns have taken him from me piece by piece—his will, his mind, his soul that I cannot touch though he lives because of me—and now you have taken his heart."

"Look, you're the one who encouraged him to seek me out as his protector. I didn't ask for him to fall in love with me. I was perfectly content on my own." She hadn't been, though. She'd thought she had, but now the idea of being without Leo was crushing.

"If you succeed here, if you bring his selves back together, if he lives…he lives with me."

Before Rhea could object, the Valkyrie was gone.

She gripped the handle of the axe and took a deep breath. There was nothing else to do but go into the tunnel. She wasn't about to stay here and hang out with the corpses, who were looking unsettlingly interested in her life force. She stepped carefully, dodging snakes, hoping none of them were poisonous, which they probably were. There was almost no light in the tunnel, just the glow of something at the other end, and there was no getting through that carpet of snakes by simply walking. Rhea's fingers closed tight around the axe. She hated the idea of killing a defenseless creature just trying to survive, but she had the feeling these weren't exactly living. And it was them or her.

She took a step and swung at anything that came toward her or wouldn't move out of her way, wielding the axe like a machete clearing brush in a jungle or a scythe cutting down wheat. There was more of the drippy goo inside the tunnel, which actually helped, since it got rid of more snakes she wouldn't have to step on or kill. The whole environment seemed fairly impractical, but it was the underworld after all. *Swing. Step. Now dodge. Swing right.* The *hamingja* was guiding her. She'd forgotten it was there. Its presence was comforting, a bit of Leo with her in the darkness.

The gloomy light at the other end grew larger, and the snakes grew fewer until at last she emerged into a sort of smoggy mist.

"Fancy meeting you here."

Rhea jumped, the axe held in both hands in front of her. "Who's there?"

A figure distinguished from the mist, short-cropped hair at the sides visible before the features of his face became clear. "I suppose the Valkyrie let you in," said Dressler. "You're too late, though. I've delivered your Leo's soul to the ruler of this realm and released Nidhöggr from the fetters that keep him here. I've just been waiting around to see the dragon emerge into the living world. Shake things up a bit." So that was his deal. Typical "embrace disruption" chaos-loving-bro bullshit.

"Don't get too excited." Rhea clutched the axe. "You're the one who's going to get shaken up." She said it with more confidence than she felt.

Dressler laughed. "What are you going to do? Swing that at me? I'm immortal, thanks to you."

Rhea swung as he spoke and the blade of the axe sliced across his thigh, cutting his laughter short. "Probably still hurts, though, huh?"

Dressler swore and stepped back, looking ready to

swing his fist, but the ground beneath them rumbled with a heavy impact, and a dark, leathery beast the size of a tank barreled into view within the mist—which turned out to be smoke after all, coming from the thing's nostrils.

"Ah, here he comes now," said Dressler. "Behold— Malice Striker." There was no sign of Gunnar yet.

Rhea had to keep Dressler talking until she figured out where Gunnar was or thought of something to do. "How did you set him free?"

"With the lance, naturally. I offered him Leo's soul as tribute, an immortal warrior kept from Valhalla through a bargain with Destiny. The lance contained the *hugr*, so the dragon consumed it whole. I was a bit surprised, but it had served its purpose. And that's when he broke free."

Consumed? Rhea's heart lurched. Leo's *hugr* was gone. She really was too late.

Look to the ground. Rhea scanned the cavern floor, expecting to see more writhing snakes, but out of the corner of her eye, she saw the movement of something much larger: the Jörmungandr-Gunnar. Or Jörmungunnar. Whatever. It coiled around the larger dragon's legs, striking at the underbelly while Malice Striker thrashed its tail and roared outrage at what amounted to a pest.

She wondered if Gunnar knew the *hugr* was gone. Perhaps he'd been here in the shadows watching as Malice Striker swallowed it. How long would it be before he faded from the world? Leo might be lost, but she still owed Gunnar something.

Step in to the right and aim for the breast.

Without second-guessing the *hamingja*, Rhea followed its instructions and leaped, swinging, into the fight.

"You're wasting your time," Dressler called out. "The creature is invulnerable."

Her axe sank into the flesh between the dragon's front legs, and the dragon reared back with a roar of pain, contradicting Dressler's claim. Unfortunately, the blade stuck, and the dragon's movement yanked the handle from her hands.

Jörmungunnar went for the creature's flank, distracting it long enough for Rhea to dash in and grab hold of the handle again. She hung on tight while the dragon swung about and did the work of twisting out the blade for her. When it came loose, she dropped and rolled, her body instinctively moving at the *hamingja*'s direction. Rhea came up on her feet, the axe still gripped in front of her, to find the dragon charging her, hot smoke billowing out of its snout. Rhea screwed her eyes shut, feeling the heat of its breath, waiting for the teeth to close over her head, but instead the dragon made a yelp of pain.

She opened one eye to see Jörmungunnar at the larger dragon's throat. The serpentine body of the shifter coiled around the dragon's torso, tightening against the rib cage as the jaws clamped down. Malice Striker's wings extended with a jolt as the dragon twisted in the serpent's grasp, and they both took to the air, though the cavern ceiling was less than twenty feet high.

The smaller but more lithe creature spun the larger onto its back, and the dragon fell to the cavern floor with a ground-quaking thud. Malice Striker's claws raked the air as it struggled to breathe, and Rhea realized it was preparing to blast its foe with dragon fire.

Climb the shoulder. Between the eyes. Rhea obeyed the thought without hesitating, practically running up the side of the wheezing dragon, and swung the axe as hard as she could into the fleshy bump between its red, rage-filled eyes. Something cracked beneath the impact, and the blade sank deep. There was no way she was getting it out again. Rhea tumbled off, coming out of the roll standing once more, ready to run. But the dragon's eyes had gone dull, and a gurgling sound came from its throat—the life leaving it.

At some point during the combat, she realized, Dressler had slipped away.

Jörmungunnar hadn't moved, its jaws clamped tight to the dead dragon's throat, the aquamarine eyes blazing and wild.

"Gunnar. Let go." Rhea stroked the scaly, serpentine body. "You won. It's dead."

His eyes blinked as he tracked Rhea's movement, and the horizontal slits flattened into circular pupils, the opposite of the serpent eyes in the man's face. Beneath her hand, the scales rippled, and the serpent uncoiled while the jaws slowly loosened.

Rising onto its hindquarters, like a cobra being charmed, the serpent shuddered and shifted. And then Gunnar was standing naked before her. He'd taken some vicious swipes of the dragon's claws to his torso. He was lucky it hadn't gutted him.

Rhea stepped toward him. "You're bleeding."

Gunnar shivered as Rhea's hand touched the gashes. "It matters not. I am not real."

"Oh, bullshit." Rising on tiptoe, she slid her arms around his neck and kissed him, and Gunnar kissed her back gently, surprised. "Did that feel real?"

"But I am only the *hamr*—"

"*Hamr*, schmamr. Every single one of your selves is infuriating with this 'but I'm not a real boy' crap.

You're Leo Ström. Whether you prefer to call yourself Gunnar or not. Whether you're joined with the *líkamr* or not. Whether you're solid flesh or ghostly spirit or an astral body projected in dragon form. You're Leo. So quit whining."

The surprise on Gunnar's features morphed into amusement.

Rhea glanced at the dragon's corpse. "I just wish we'd been able to save the *hugr*."

"Nidhöggr swallowed it."

"I know."

Gunnar turned toward the dragon, his gaze focused on the axe embedded in its skull. "Where did you come by that?"

"Kára lent it to me. And your *vördr* lent me your *hamingja*, so I was able to wield it."

Gunnar continued to stare at it. "It is Valkyrie-forged?"

"I guess so."

He took hold of the handle of the axe, bracing one foot against the dragon's neck, and yanked back and forth on the weapon until he'd worked it free. Rhea watched as he approached the dragon's massive torso with the axe raised above his head in both hands and swung it in an arc, slicing the belly open.

Rhea covered her mouth and nose at the smell and backed up as Gunnar plunged his fist into the cavity. After wriggling his arm around, he drew it out, the Holy Lance clutched in his bile-covered fist.

Rhea spoke behind her hand, trying not to throw up in her mouth. "Jesus, that's gross."

"But precious." Gunnar smiled. "It still holds the *hugr* within it."

Her hand slipped away from her mouth. "It's still alive?"

"It's immortal," said Dressler behind her.

Rhea whirled. Where the hell had he been hiding?

"And you're not leaving here with it." He stepped out of the smoky haze and murmured something in Old Norse, holding his hand out toward Gunnar. The *hamr* turned pale.

"Gunnar?" Rhea took a step toward him. "What's he saying? What's the matter?"

Gunnar tried to speak, but something was happening to him, fissures forming along his cheekbones and spreading across his face.

Rhea jerked on Dressler's arm. "What are you doing to him?"

He smiled and said nothing, and Rhea watched in horror as the lance and the battle-axe fell from Gunnar's grasp, and the *hamr* crackled into a thousand gossamer filaments that fell apart and blew away.

Dressler scooped up the Holy Lance and headed for the passageway before Rhea could react.

"You son of a bitch!" She grabbed the axe and ran after him, remembering to pull up her hood as she plunged blindly through the darkness, flinging away snakes on the edges of her blade. She broke into the outer cavern upon the Shore of Corpses to find Dressler hauling back his arm with the lance in his hand as if to pitch it into the lake with the dead.

Throw it now. At the *hamingja*'s urging, she hurled the axe toward Dressler. It tumbled through the air and came down on his forearm as he brought it forward for the throw. The blade sliced clean through flesh and bone, and the Holy Lance, still in his hand, dropped with it to the ground among the snakes.

Dressler wheeled to face her, his expression furious, as though he hadn't yet felt the loss of his hand, and grabbed her with the other. "I told you, I'm immortal!"

A thick glop of black poison dropped onto his cheek, and Dressler shrieked, stumbling backward toward the lake. His flesh was sizzling away, revealing muscle and bone.

Rhea scrambled for the lance, taking it from the severed hand. "Guess not without this." She held up the relic, and Dressler made one more lunge toward her, nearly catching her off guard, but she swung her fist with the instinct of the *hamingja* and popped him right in the kisser. As Dressler tumbled back onto the shore, the bodies rose up around him and drew him into the lake.

The dead were not looking friendly. Rhea turned to flee and realized she had no way out without Faye or Gunnar.

Climb. Her eyes went toward the rocks on the far end of the cavern wall. *To the crevice.* Rhea shoved the handle of the lance into the deep inside pocket of the fur coat and scrambled up the wall toward the narrow opening in the rocks like a pro, climbing through it into a cavern of frozen mud bounded by what appeared to be the roots of a massive tree. She remembered Rafe saying the underworld was less a physical place and more of a metaphysical one, its attributes perceived as the soul expected it. So she just had to "perceive" herself once more in the realm of the living. If only it were that simple to craft one's perception.

The Lilith bond. Call upon your blood. Of course. Theia had been the one to propose it, that the power of their blood was strengthened exponentially by combining their energy. And Theia was her *fylgja*, as she was Theia's. She placed her palm over her Black Moon Lilith tattoo and pictured the one on Theia's arm, concentrating on her twin's location while sending out a psychic "broadcast" of her own. *Theia, can you hear me? I need a hand.*

At first, nothing seemed to happen, but when she sent the thought again, the frozen mud in the roots above began to crumble, revealing a fissure of light. Rhea began to dig, trying to ignore the panic of claustrophobia setting in as the crumbling earth tumbled down on her. And then her fingers met someone else's reaching into the earth from above. She clutched the hand and scrambled out into the winter air and sunlight—and tumbled into Theia.

Rhea rolled onto her back, grinning as she caught her breath. "Thanks for the hand. You just had to go literal."

Eyes wide, Theia helped Rhea to her feet, brushing the snow and dirt from her clothes. "And just where the hell have you been?"

Rhea laughed shakily. Where the hell, indeed? "Oh, just slaying dragons and punching Nazis."

They stood beneath the snow-brushed trees surrounding Rhea's apartment complex. Leo had spoken of the World Tree, in whose roots Náströnd was buried. She'd crawled up through the symbolic representation of Leo's conception of the underworld. Of Gunnar's.

Gunnar. He was gone, faded away as surely as he'd feared. She reached inside the coat and clutched the ancient piece of wood in her hand. But she had Leo's soul.

Chapter 27

Leo looked like grim death.

Rhea stood in the doorway of her bedroom, afraid she might be too late somehow, that Gunnar had been wrong and the *hugr* hadn't survived Nidhöggr's stomach. Faye, head bowed over Leo's body, still wore the armor of the Valkyrie.

Rhea closed the door and held up the lance when Faye turned at the sound. "I have it." Faye reached for it, but Rhea held the relic away. "First, we talk about your price."

Faye's eyes darkened. "You would prolong his suffering out of jealousy?"

"No, but you obviously would. You say you're banished from his side when the *hugr* isn't dormant. How do you intend to keep him bound to you with his *hugr* returned to him?"

"His *hugr* will be suppressed as it always has been, except during the hours of the Hunt. I can be with him as I was before—if you are not in his heart."

"And how do you plan to make that happen?"

"The *munr* will remain suppressed as well. When he wakes, he will already have forgotten you."

Rhea's chest felt like lead. "So you win by cheating. You can't make him love you, but you can take his love for me away with magic. That's pretty pathetic."

Faye rose, tall and menacing in her Valkyrie attire. "His 'love' for you is nothing but your own spell cast upon him, the result of your demon blood and the magical ink you used on him."

"Magical ink?"

"The ink made from the ash of Eyjafjallajökull." Faye traced the Mjölnir tattoo on Leo's wrist. "That pathetic little rodent sold it to you so you could bewitch my Leo."

The ink. *Bloodbath.* Dressler had sold it to her?

Rhea looked at Leo, wasting, unnaturally pale. It was when she'd tattooed him with the ink that they'd both felt that tingling sense of rightness. The bond that had made him come back to her when he'd meant to leave. And it had been a lie.

"Can you remove it?" she asked quietly. "The ink... I don't want it in me. Or him."

Faye narrowed her eyes. "You would break the spell that binds him to you?"

Tears blurred her vision. "I don't want him that way. I want him to have his own will, his own mind. His own heart."

Faye's demeanor softened. "I can neutralize the ink, if that is your wish. But I will need your blood."

"Just a drop, I suppose?"

"Slightly more than a drop, I'm afraid, but not enough to do you harm."

Rhea glanced down at the lance. "And not with this. It's done nothing but harm." She opened the door, nearly stumbling over Theia, who'd been standing with her ear pressed to the wood.

Theia started guiltily, hanging back while Rhea went to the kitchen to get a sharp knife.

She squeezed Rhea's hand when Rhea returned with it. "I'm sorry, Rhe. But I think you're doing the right thing."

Rhea nodded, unable to trust her voice, and closed the door again. She handed the knife to Faye. "Do what you need to do."

"I must take the blood from the tattoo."

Rhea set her foot on the end of the bed and pushed up her legging to reveal the Black Moon Lilith. Faye sliced across the tattoo without giving her any warning, which was just as well, because Rhea hadn't expected it to go that deep, and now it was too late to object. She hissed in air through her gritted teeth in a belated reaction.

"Let the blood drip." Faye turned to Leo and made the same slash across Mjölnir. Placing one hand against his wrist and the other against Rhea's calf, she intoned, "Let the blood of influence drain into the Well of Wyrd. Let the bond between these two be broken." The red pigment of the ink began to fade as if the ink itself were bleeding out.

Rhea could feel the magic leaving her. Leo wasn't hers anymore.

As she took the lance from inside the coat, she remembered the coat wasn't hers either and took it off, handing both of them to the Valkyrie. "Give him back his soul."

Faye untaped Leo's bandage, revealing an ugly wound that was already beginning to fester, and held the point of the relic above it.

Rhea couldn't watch. She opened the bedroom door and went out, closing it behind her, and headed for the front door.

"Rhea?" Theia jumped up from the couch. "What happened? Is he okay? Rhea?"

Rhea's hand was on the doorknob when she felt a tremor inside her—the *hamingja* leaving her. She turned and sank to the carpet.

Theia grabbed a towel from the kitchen and came to blot at the blood at Rhea's calf, but Rhea shook her head.

"It has to stop flowing on its own."

Theia stared at the tattoo. "When did you do that?"

"A couple of weeks ago. I didn't know about yours. I guess great minds think alike."

Theia pushed up her sleeve and looked at her forearm. "I got this one because I had a dream. That's why I didn't come to you to have it done. I didn't want you to ask where I'd gotten the idea."

"What dream?"

"The moon was swallowed up by a snake that ate its own tail, and then the snake became a bull that you were riding, and then a wolf…and the wolf devoured you. I saw the tattoo on your skin, and the words *Black Moon Lilith* came to me, so I looked it up when I woke up. I knew it was you in the dream, but it was kind of the generic, mental you and we still looked the same. I thought if I had the tattoo, whatever it was—it would happen to me instead."

Despite her aching heart, Rhea couldn't help a little smile tugging at the corner of her mouth. She looked down to try to hide it.

Theia nudged her with her foot. "What is that look? Why are you smiling?"

"That was really sweet of you, Thei, but...you're not going to be devoured by the wolf." She met Theia's eyes. "That happened the other night, right here up against this door. And it was a-*ma*-zing."

Theia looked puzzled before understanding dawned on her. "Oh geez." She smacked Rhea's arm. "You minx."

"I had my one brief, shining moment with him, anyway. I guess that'll have to be enough."

Theia's grin faded, and she sat beside Rhea and put her arm around her. As it had always been between them, no words were necessary.

He couldn't remember where he'd gone to sleep. Leo stretched his arms, feeling incredibly rested, and opened his eyes.

Kára sat on the edge of the bed beside him. "Hello, beautiful one."

Leo sat up swiftly. There was no fog of missing memory, no sense of fragmentation. His entire long life stretched out behind him in a cohesive narrative.

"What did you do? Where's Rhea?"

"I have returned what belongs to you. That which was yours is yours again."

Leo touched his bare chest as though he could feel the pieces of himself physically inside him. "My will... my soul?"

"All there. I have bargained a final time. That Which Became is past. That Which is Happening shall not happen again. That Which Must Become…will become. Your life is yours once more, your destiny unwritten, your future finite as any mortal man's. You are free to choose with whom you will spend it." Kára's smile was sad. "You will still be the Chieftain, but you will lead the Hunt on your own terms. There will be no curse separating you from yourself."

Leo took her hand and turned it in his, stroking it. Though resentment had turned it to hate, there had been affection between them not so long ago. She had bound him to her for her own selfish reasons, but they'd been through a great deal together. Not all of it had been unpleasant.

"Why? Why now, when you have owned me for so long?"

"It seems I have been beaten at my own game. The one I accepted as your human protector stole your heart. And I see now it was not through magic as I'd thought. You gave it to her willingly. So I must do the same." Tears sparkled in her eyes in a rare display of genuine emotion. "I thought you were dead, my love. It gave me some perspective."

A tear escaped, and Leo wiped it from her cheek with his thumb and kissed the spot to say goodbye.

As swiftly and as life-alteringly as she'd first come to him on the battlefield to take him to Valhalla before choosing to spare him instead—she was gone.

Leo threaded his fingers through his hair and took his first breath of freedom. He realized he was cold— a sensation he hadn't fully experienced in a thousand years. As Leo the Dull, he'd responded to such stimuli as a mortal man should, but he hadn't really felt it.

Leo laughed aloud. *Leo the Dull.* He supposed he

had been a bit. He could blame it on the suppression of his memory, but there were choices he'd made that had been his own foolish doing. Like not taking Rhea right then and there in the tattoo shop when she'd wanted it, jealous of his own unfettered desire. A mistake he intended to remedy right now.

The bedroom door opened, and Rhea lifted her head from Theia's shoulder. Leo was beautiful and whole. And wearing nothing but her lavender faux-fur robe.

"Leo." With a surreptitious swipe at her eyes, she got to her feet as he approached. "Is Faye...?"

"She's gone. For good."

Rhea stared up at him, confused. "But aren't you...? She said..."

"She's dissolved her bargain with the Norns. I'm mortal. Mostly. I'll still lead Odin's Hunt, but not as a wraith and without the associated curse."

"So you'll ride with her."

"With her?" Leo stepped in closer and rested his large hands on her hips. "*Mitt hjärta.* You are my wild, ecstatic goddess. My Freyja. I will ride with *you*, if you will come." He put his mouth below her ear, lips brushing her jaw and making every hair follicle on her skin tingle and stand erect—not to mention other parts. "I will ride with you right here, right now, if you like." The sexy growl made the meaning unmistakable.

Theia was on her feet in a flash. "Okay. So, I'm gonna go." She grabbed Rhea's keys and coat. Rhea was in no position—or condition—to complain. "See you both at Phoebe's later?"

Rhea was sure she'd made some kind of noise of assent, but she couldn't pinpoint exactly when Theia had slipped out the door. Leo's lips were against hers, nipping and sucking at them, his hands roaming over her, in her hair, at her nape, on her waist, under her shirt.

"I thought—" She tried to form sentences between his kisses. "The ink—was responsible—magic—our bond—"

Leo paused with his hands at the small of her back after unhooking her bra. "What's that, *älskling*?"

"She said you didn't really love me."

"She's out of her mind. If I loved you any more, I'd go mad and wander the earth a blithering idiot instead of a wraith. I need this off." He tugged at her shirt, and Rhea let him pull the garment over her head. The bra slipped off when she lowered her arms, and Leo cupped her breasts in his hands, completely covering them. "By the Allfather, these are fantastic. I almost can't look at them. No, I can."

She giggled involuntarily at the feathery touch of his fingers stroking the outline of her breasts as if sizing them up for a drawing. "You're different."

"No, I'm not. You're just not used to me all in one piece. Gang's all here. Though there's one particular piece..." He let out a soft groan as her hand found it. "I have your condoms," he blurted. "We could use many."

Rhea laughed, and he laughed with her, the deep, delighted abandon that made her want to climb him. She did, threading her arms around his neck and wrapping her legs around his hips as he drew her up against him, hands beneath her ass. His cock ground against her.

"You're wearing my robe."

"I know. I'm freezing."

"Maybe we should go to my room so I can warm you up."

"Good idea." Leo spun around and carried her into the bedroom, flopping backward onto the bed with her on top of him. He grinned up at her. "Condoms, yes?" He produced one from the pocket of the robe.

"Condoms, *yes*." Rhea shuffled backward, peeling off her leggings while he opened the condom and rolled it on like a pro. He was still wearing the robe, which was oddly sexy. "You're still cold," she noted as she crawled over him.

Leo smirked. "I understand most heat is lost from the top of one's…head."

"I have just the thing for that."

He reached to pull her into his lap, but Rhea slid backward off the bed and grabbed his knit hat from the top of the dresser, the gift from Phoebe and Rafe. He laughed when she shoved it onto his head.

She straddled him, perched on her knees as she stroked his cock. "Merry Christmas, Leo."

With his hands on her hips, he drew her down until she was positioned just above him. Rhea sank onto the rock-hard heat of his erection with decadent slowness, moaning as he filled her, her arousal heightened by his unabashed groan of pleasure and relief.

Leo wrapped his arms around her and hugged her against his chest, rocking her into his hips. *"God Jul, mitt hjärta,"* he murmured and kissed her hair as he drove himself deliciously deeper. *"God Jul."*

* * * * *

Looking for inspiration in tales
of hope, faith and heartfelt romance?

Check out **Love Inspired**® and
Love Inspired® **Suspense** books!

New books available every month!

CONNECT WITH US AT:

Harlequin.com/Community

Facebook.com/HarlequinBooks

Twitter.com/HarlequinBooks

Instagram.com/HarlequinBooks

Pinterest.com/HarlequinBooks

ReaderService.com

LIGENRE2018

LOVE
Harlequin
romance?

Join our Harlequin community to share your thoughts and connect with other romance readers!

Be the first to find out about promotions, news, and exclusive content!

Sign up for the Harlequin e-newsletter and download a free book from any series at

www.TryHarlequin.com

CONNECT WITH US AT:

Harlequin.com/Community

 Facebook.com/HarlequinBooks

 Twitter.com/HarlequinBooks

 Instagram.com/HarlequinBooks

 Pinterest.com/HarlequinBooks

ReaderService.com

**ROMANCE WHEN
YOU NEED IT**

HSOCIAL2017

Reward the book lover in you!

Earn points from all your Harlequin book purchases from wherever you shop.

Turn your points into *FREE BOOKS* of your choice
OR
EXCLUSIVE GIFTS from your favorite authors or series.

Join for FREE today at
www.HarlequinMyRewards.com.

Harlequin My Rewards is a free program (no fees) without any commitments or obligations.

MYR17